MARY & JANE FINDLATER

Mary Findlater (1865-1963) and Jane Findlater (1866-1946) were two of three daughters of a minister of the Free Church at Lochearnhead in Scotland. On their father's death in 1886 the family moved to Prestonpans near Edinburgh, and a decade later the sisters began their writing career. Mary's first publication was a collection of poems, *Songs & Sonnets* (1895), and Jane's was her acclaimed novel, *The Green Graves of Balgowrie* (1896). Such was their poverty that Jane was forced to write this novel on discarded sheets of paper from the local grocer. Its admirers included Gladstone and Ellen Terry, who wrote to its author, 'The dear Green Graves stands out in my memory ... as one of the best books in the world.'

Between them, Mary and Jane Findlater produced twenty-four books: novels, poetry, short stories and non-fiction. Mary wrote six novels alone, and Jane five, but their greatest works were three novels they produced together: *Crossriggs* (1908), *Penny Moneypenny* (1911) and *Beneath the Visiting Moon* (1923). From poverty-stricken daughters of a remote Scottish manse they became celebrated and self-supporting authors. In 1904, on a visit to America, they were entertained by Amy Lowell, and William and Henry James, and in Britain their circle included May Sinclair, Walter de la Mare, Mary Cholmondeley, Rudyard Kipling and Sir Henry and Margaret Newbolt.

For years the sisters wintered in Devon, due to their mother's ill health, but by the 1920s they had moved to Rye in Sussex. This decade, however, saw a decline in the popularity of their work. In the summer of 1940 they returned to Scotland, moving to Comrie, a few miles from their childhood home at Lochearnhead. Although Mary underwent an operation for cancer in 1923, she in fact outlived her sister by seventeen years. When Jane died in 1946, the sisters had been together for eighty years, during which time they were scarcely ever parted.

CROSSRIGGS

MARY & JANE FINDLATER

With a New Introduction by
PAUL BINDING

PENGUIN BOOKS – VIRAGO PRESS

PENGUIN BOOKS
Viking Penguin Inc., 40 West 23rd Street,
New York, New York 10010, U.S.A.
Penguin Books Ltd, Harmondsworth,
Middlesex, England
Penguin Books Australia Ltd, Ringwood,
Victoria, Australia
Penguin Books Canada Limited, 2801 John Street,
Markham, Ontario, Canada L3R 1B4
Penguin Books (N.Z.) Ltd, 182–190 Wairau Road,
Auckland 10, New Zealand

First published in Great Britain by Smith, Elder & Co. 1908
First published in the United States of America by
E. P. Dutton 1913

This edition first published in Great Britain by
Virago Press Limited 1986
Published in Penguin Books 1986

Copyright Mary and Jane Findlater, 1908
Introduction copyright © Paul Binding, 1986
All rights reserved

Printed in Finland by Werner Söderström Oy

TO

KATE DOUGLAS WIGGIN

AND

NORA ARCHIBALD SMITH

TWO SISTERS,

FROM

TWO SISTERS

MARY AND JANE FINDLATER

INTRODUCTION

Crossriggs was the first of the three novels that the Findlater sisters—Mary (1865-1963) and Jane (1866-1946)—wrote together. Their collaboration must not be seen, however, as one between two inspired amateurs, but as that of two wholly serious, already proven and successful (in both senses of that word) practitioners of the art of fiction.

  Jane Findlater's first novel *The Green Graves of Balgowrie* (1896)—still today imaginatively disturbing—won for her the admiration of Mr Gladstone (''much struck with it indeed'') and of Ellen Terry (''*Green Graves* stands out in my memory still as one of the best books in the world''). When Mary and Jane were staying with William James and his wife in Cambridge, Massachusetts, they were invited to a dinner-party at which the table was covered in roses in celebration of Mary's fourth and strongest novel, *The Rose of Joy* (1903).[1] Other admirers, who were to remain faithful to the sisters—whether they wrote singly or in duo—included Henry James; his sister Alice; Rudyard Kipling; Walter de la Mare—whose work the sisters appreciated intensely—and, later, Virginia Woolf. The last, on receiving a fan letter from Mary, wrote: ''I am particularly glad to think that writers whose work I admire should find anything to please them in mine." These great literary names have been cited to show that the Findlaters' fiction appealed to some of the most sophisticated minds of their time, minds moreover with which they themselves felt in communion. It is all the more ironic, therefore, that when—after their last joint novel, *Beneath the Visiting Moon* (1923)—their reputation began to decline, it was generally thought that this was due to some old-fashioned element in the sisters' art which connected them irretrievably to the late Victorian popular novel (they had enjoyed a sizeable middle-brow readership). The sisters themselves, who lived to good ages, and remained interested to the last in the world around them, seem almost to have acquiesced in this judgement. It is hoped that this reissue of *Crossriggs* (1908), possibly the most praised and widely read of their novels, will show how wrong-headed such a verdict was.

Crossriggs is set in a small village one hour by train from Edinburgh, and like most of the sisters' fiction depicts the interactions and inter-relationships of a handful of members of the Scottish gentry/upper middle class. We are concerned here with the Hope family—widowed father and two grown daughters, the younger of whom, Alexandra (Alex), is the central figure of the novel; with the rich, famous and reclusive scholar, Robert Maitland, and his dull invalid wife; and with the inhabitants of the big house of the neighbourhood, Foxe Hall: blind, bigoted Admiral Cassilis and his handsome, bored young grandson, Van. The other characters, sharply and often humorously drawn though many of them are, act as chorus to the presentation of these intertwined lives—quiet lives, demanding patience; and quietness and patience with detail are dominant attributes of the sisters' art in revealing them to us. We are at once reminded of Jane Austen's remark made when writing *Emma*: "Three or four families in a country village is the very thing to work on."

Emma is indeed remembered at a crucial point in

Crossriggs—and by Alex herself—and lovers of Jane Austen's
novel will find many points in common between the two
works, above all in the affective relations of the three families
chosen. The heroine's aged father, Old Hopeful, valetudi-
narian and much concerned with diets, irresistibly recalls
Mr Woodhouse and his bowl of gruel. The contrast between
clever, energetic, thwarted Alex and her more placid elder
sister is strongly reminiscent of that between Emma
Woodhouse and Isabella. The two men in Alex's emotional
life, Robert Maitland and Van Cassilis, bring to mind,
respectively, Mr Knightley (the detached wisdom, the
unselfish dependability) and Frank Churchill (the impetuous
and sexually rooted charm, the youthful egotism). These
similarities—which could be amplified—were, I believe,
present in the sisters' minds during the writing: hence the
reference to the earlier novel. (And we also know from letters
that the sisters much admired Jane Austen.) However, the
differences between *Emma* and *Crossriggs*—and I am speaking
here of the philosophy of life behind the books, of the
approach to character and the significance of action—
greatly outweigh the likenesses. *Emma* is a comedy—albeit of
the profoundest kind—whereas *Crossriggs*, for all its humour
and gossip and pleasant domesticities, is a tragic work. And
in considering the novel's tragic nature we must remind
ourselves that the Findlater sisters were Scottish and heirs to
a very different culture from that of Jane Austen and her
descendants; it is not London that is an hour's journey away
(as in *Emma*), but the utterly dissimilar Edinburgh.

Robert Louis Stevenson—who was to suggest to the sisters
one of their most vividly realized characters, the doomed
Lorin Weir of *Penny Moneypenny*—made some very helpful
remarks about the difference between the English and
Scottish characters as culturally formed, in his essay "The
Foreigner at Home". The English catechism, he points out,
begins with the prosaic question: "What is your name?",
while the Scottish Shorter Catechism opens challengingly

with: "What is the chief end of man?", the answer being: "To glorify God and to enjoy Him for ever":

> I do not wish to make an idol of the Shorter Catechism, but the fact of such a question being asked opens to us Scotch a great field of speculation; and the fact that it is asked of all of us, from the peer to the ploughboy, binds us more nearly together.

Certainly it must help to account for that strong spiritual element in so many Scottish writers for whom indeed metaphysical matters are frequent determinants of character and event. *Crossriggs* may not exhibit this in the dramatic manner of Hogg's *Confessions of a Justified Sinner* or Stevenson's *Master of Ballantrae*, but it does exhibit it nonetheless. And this is not surprising, because Mary and Jane Findlater were daughters of the Manse, with a minister grandfather from remote Sutherland whose principles had led him to break with the established church in the famous Disruption of 1843. The sisters' father had a living in Lochearnhead; the sisters' mother was a tireless and zealous server of the welfare of that community, and often took her young daughters to visit sick- and death-beds. In later years, however, Eric Findlater and his wife confessed to each other that they did not accept as Christian the idea of Eternal Damnation. Mary and Jane later shed an even greater part of Christian orthodoxy, though they retained respect for the religious tradition in which they had grown up, and remembered too a strange and terrifying intimation of mortality they had received together in childhood while on a mountain walk—to be repeated in old age.

The sisters, who as successful authors lived their maturer years in England, won through to that viewpoint not untypical of the intellectuals of their generation and which permeates *Crossriggs* and indeed all their major work. It is essentially Darwinist-Deterministic, though strongly tinged with neo-Platonism. All human beings possess spiritual awareness and emotional hunger in some measure or other but there is no guarantee whatever of their realization in this life or in any other: in truth, the pointers are to the contrary. Alex in *Crossriggs* is much concerned with the waste of human lives on this earth, and in her despairing moods she is tempted to think that her own existence illustrates such waste. To balance against this, though, is a consciousness of the prolixity and power of Nature—and of its beauty which tempts the sensitive to Platonic thoughts of a universe of absolutes. Throughout *Crossriggs* there are passionate descriptions of the countryside, of the effect upon it of the seasons, of the indomitable putting forth of bud and flower. The confrontations of the reality of pain and suffering do not necessarily detract from this near-numinous sense of creation.

Thinking of the blindness of Admiral Cassilis, Alex says: "There are some trials that are just a little *too* hard for flesh and blood to bear, and that's one of them ... they make the government of the world look altogether wrong." Nevertheless, what she chooses to read to the Admiral is a passage of one of Wordsworth's most Platonist poems, "Laodamia", in which a spirit speaks of the world beyond life:

No fears to beat away, no strifes to heal,
    The past unsighed for and the future sure.
Spake as the witness of a second birth
For all that is most perfect upon earth.
Of all that is most beauteous, imaged there
    In happier beauty—more pellucid streams,
An ampler ether—a diviner air,
    And fields invested with purpureal gleams.

And somehow—while never perhaps accepting this as an intellectual credo—Alex does seem, in the course of the novel, to learn from such apprehensions, such intimations, how to endure and survive; so, at the close of the book, after great sorrows, she does perhaps truly deserve her surname of Hope. A few years later and her creators would probably have described her as sustained by the Life-Force. For Mary

Findlater read Bergson:

> Lately I've been contented with the thought (suggested by
> Bergson) that *there isn't any future*—that is in the sense of there
> being no great sort of map of our future in the hands of the
> Creator—as we used to be taught, but that life being continuous
> Creation—Being—every moment unfolds something new and
> unknown. We make it as we go by right and efficient action, and
> it cannot be foreseen.

Nevertheless awareness of death (*pace* the Shorter
Catechism) is an important aspect of the Findlaters'
presentation of life, and the culmination of *Crossriggs* is a
death as moving and, in an unsensational way, as shocking as
any in British fiction. Yet of this death Alex—in a scene quite
unimaginable in a Jane Austen novel—has had a
premonition, echoing that dreadful moment in the sisters'
girlhood when they felt death upon the mountainside. In
Crossriggs the moment occurs under an ancient yew tree
where Alex and the young man who loves her have sheltered
in a rain storm:

> She rose and stood leaning against the seared trunk of the great
> tree. "*Silence and foresight—Death the skeleton and Time the shadow* . . .
> we're here for such a moment; is it all worth while? Think of all
> that has passed and that will pass here after we're just earth
> again—like that!" She pressed her foot into the dry, soft ground.
> "I do so love the living of life—it's dreadful to think of it."

Another notable legacy of Scottish religion to Scottish
literature is its sense of dualism, its vision of warring and
opposing forces within the human personality. The most
famous fictional account of this is, of course, Stevenson's *Dr
Jekyll and Mr Hyde*. In *Crossriggs* each protagonist has
another, darker side: valiant, generous Alex is also morose,
resentful, bitter and at times cruel, with a cruelty of tongue
that far eclipses Emma's rudeness to Miss Bates. That lovable
high-minded optimist, "Old Hopeful", can also be viewed as
a selfish retreatist, while his genial elder daughter Matilda is,

on a harsh line of vision, guilty of wilful evasions. But the most striking illustration of the Findlater sisters' so Scottish dualism is their portrait of Van Cassilis (the Frank Churchill of the book) and of the woman who becomes his wife, Dolly Orranmore. And here we come to another very remarkable feature of the Findlaters' art: their understanding of the libidinous.

Van's sexual nature, when exercised upon Alex, is sweet, even selfless on occasions; however, frustrated it has a very dark aspect, perverse and relishing, which becomes dominant in his involvement with Dolly, indeed takes him over. Dolly—who, in contrast to Alex, has this to say about Death: ''I'd like to break my neck in the hunting-field and be buried in the next ditch''—is described (by Alex herself) as ''hard and coarse and healthy and handsome—and bad.'' It is a tribute to the Findlater sisters' powers that we feel this badness to be so very real force that we are convinced of its enveloping of Van and of its inextricable relation to sexuality. Here we remember not only the Stevenson of *The Master of Ballantrae* but the Tolstoy of *The Kreutzer Sonata*. Nor is it the only example of the sisters' insight into the nearness of the libido to Evil. *Penny Moneypenny* (1911) provides us with an even more sustained and potent instance.

Thus the ''three or four families in a country village'' are seen very much *sub specie aeternitatis* according to a vision whose light derives from a strong and indigenous Scottish tradition. The delicacy of the art, on the other hand, can be seen as belonging firmly to an English tradition of which *Emma* is both a progenitor and a non-pareil.

It would not be fair to *Crossriggs* to expect in it that extraordinary perfection of form and of moral articulation which we find in *Emma*. It is not entirely structurally satisfactory; in the middle chapters there is a temporary lessening of tension, a slightly frustrating sense of having halted a while. There are times, too, when the authors' partiality for Alex rather gets the better of them (as Jane

Austen's for Emma never does of her); she becomes a little too winningly plucky, nearer to Louisa May Alcott's Jo March (*Little Women*) than to the protagonist of a serious novel. Nor is the tone entirely consistent; the humorous passages are often a little discordant, particularly, I think, those concerning the Reids.

These are but small flaws. The last third of the novel, centring on Van's marriage and destiny, and Alex's response to them, has an unflinching tragic truthfulness, a sombre splendour that elevates the whole book into a very high order of literary achievement. "It was by loving them that he knew them," said Henry James of Balzac and his relationship to his characters. We feel this to be true of the Findlater sisters too; it is the sympathy of their portraiture that makes *Crossriggs* the moving novel it is, that makes it glow in the memory— and, after more than one reading, like some extended act of imaginative charity transfigured through light.

Paul Binding, Anticoli Corrado, Italy, 1985

Notes

1 See Eileen Mackenzie, *The Findlater Sisters* (John Murray, 1964) for this and other biographical details.

CROSSRIGGS.

CHAPTER I.

ROMANCE, I think, is like the rainbow, always a little away from the place where you stand. So the old days at Crossriggs may have been no more interesting than the present—perhaps it is only the distance of years that makes the picture so vivid. Yet surely certain places, certain periods of time are touched with interest independent of the glamour of the past?

O cold north wind from the sea, did you ever then blow through the tree-tops without the twang of a musical note in your sound! Was the winter sunshine not suffused with some magic even on the fallow fields, or when it fell across the broad, irregular street? Did not the first snowdrops that struggled up to the light from under that iron sod sigh out indescribable promise in their faint suggestive breath? Even the enveloping veils of mist, the grey distance, the low hills that stood beyond the village seemed a fitting background for the lively scene of human life that was enacted there.

How well I remember it all!—Alexandra Hope, and young Van Cassilis, and " Old Hopeful," as we called Alexandra's father, with his venerable white head, his beaming. benevolent eye, his hopes for the world, and his hopeless want of common sense.

173

Miss Elizabeth Verity Maitland, too, the terror of us all, and Robert Maitland and his wife. They pass before me now like a troop of ghosts.

To-day, I suppose, other people live at Crossriggs, inhabiting the old houses, treading the very same stones on the roadway that once we trod; but those new-comers could never seem real to me, I think; the former generation is in possession still.

The village of Crossriggs, you know, stands on the top of a long ridge of land. On one side, very far away, lies the sea; on the other, a line of low blue hills. But much prosaic country comes between. There are flat, fat fields, divided by thorn hedges and long straight roads, with now and then a row of cottages. It is a rich, unromantic bit of agricultural country, full of food and prosperity. Lot might have chosen it for his share had he stood on the ridge and cast his eyes over the fertile land.

The village is only a single street ending in an old market-place, in the centre of which still stands an ancient stone-cross. A row of tall lime trees on either side of the street make it almost like an avenue, because the houses stand well back, so that the line stretches on unbroken to the ancient cross in the Square. In winter, those trees show a network of bare branches; green they are in spring, and in summer the scent of their blossom makes the whole air sweet. Then one by one they turn a gracious golden colour that adds a spurious cheerfulness even to the sodden November days.

There are some commodious old houses in Crossriggs, built for people of local importance in the days before the cities had sucked the country dry; for even here people came and went, so that many of the houses had changed owners several times. Some had sunk, and some had risen in the world by putting out a bow-window, or removing the old garden walls to make room for a new iron railing.

But the house that had once been the Manse remained much the same always—no bow-windows or iron railings there. A tall man (and the Maitlands were all tall men) had to stoop his head to enter the low doorway—an open door it had always been to rich and poor alike. The square hall was half-dark and paved with black and white flags; the sitting-rooms, low-roofed and sunny, wore always the same air of happy frugality with their sun-burnt hangings and simple, straight-legged furniture. There was no attempt at decoration for decoration's sake, only an effect which was the outcome of austere refine-ment in the midst of plenty.

While much had changed in the parish, the Maitlands had remained there for many generations, for the church records show that a Maitland was the first minister of Crossriggs after the Reformation. Then follows a break in the succession, and after that the names of two others of the same family; then another break until the John and Gilbert Maitland—grandfather and father of the Robert Maitland whom we knew.

Good, just men though they had mostly been, this long rule—over so small a kingdom—had tended to develop a mild autocracy. The family trait was especi-ally marked in our day in Miss Elizabeth Verity Mait-land—" Aunt E. V." we called her—we shall never look upon her like again. It was a sight to see her walk down the street of Crossriggs, with head erect, her unflinching green eye looking here and there, observant of the life around. The village trembled before her; the drunk-ard when she met him instinctively straightened his gait; the children ceased their bawling as she passed by the door.

Her nephew, Robert Maitland, had not followed the ancestral calling; early in life he had taken another course, but after his father's death he had bought the old manse and settled down at Crossriggs. In the great world he had already some fame as a scholar, and it was no uncommon sight to see a stranger standing at the Manse gates trying to look in. Then Aunt E. V. would step to the window and draw down the blind in a final way. " The house where Robert Maitland was born ? " she would say. " Many a good man before him has been born in this house ! " She would add : " It's a vulgar age ; we live in public "—nothing could have been farther from the truth in her case—" Our very homes invaded ; our gravestones an advertisement ! "

On the other side of the Square, and nearly opposite the old Manse, stood Orchard House, where the Hopes lived. What a family that was ! Some interest or excitement was always simmering in their midst.

Long ago, Alexander Hope had dissipated his share of his father's money in a hundred schemes of unpractical benevolence; but then, as he used to exclaim, " What is money ? Yellow dust ! A simple life, surrounded by my books and my children, with leisure for thought, and time to grow my own fruit and vegetables—what more could any man desire ? " Never was a more consistent man ; he was entirely content with his lot, but what about those who were dependent on his vagaries—those two girls, Alexandra (Alex, we called her) and Matilda, who had to grow up as best they could, wanting sometimes the necessaries of life, and at all times its luxuries ? Poor dears ! I think I see them now in their thin, ill-made gowns, so bright and interesting, that their very poverty seemed an additional charm. They made the best of it ; but we only saw the outside—the seamy side of poverty, I fear me, is neither bright nor interesting to any one.

Matilda, the elder of the two girls, married when she was quite young, and soon went out to Canada. Hers was an easy little courtship, ending in an ordinary little marriage, crowned, in the space of ten years, by a more than sufficient family. Peter Chalmers, her husband, was a delicate young man, with no prospects and no money at all except his salary. But Matilda had been blessed with a good share of her father's temperament, so I suppose neither of the parents worried much about the future of their children. From time to time, Alex would tell us that " life in Canada seemed very hard," or that " Matilda had enough to do to make ends meet "— but when people are so far away, you know, it is diffi- cult to realize things; and I, for my part, was much more interested in Alex herself, and in what was going to become of her.

There was that about Alex which compelled your interest. She was a tall woman, and carried herself well, otherwise she had no claim to beauty except her long, thick hair, which was of a fine, rich brown. Her real charm lay in the passionate interest she took in life— she was alive, every inch of her, all the time. Some people thought she inherited this from her father, and so she did, in a way. She had all his versatility, a great deal more than his cleverness, and, what Old Hopeful never had, a strong sense of humour.

It was well for her that she had this latter gift, for it carried her through many a trial. " When she wanted a ribbon, she adorned herself with a smile," and what a con- tinual jest she made out of their poverty !—poverty that in other hands would have been merely squalid. She was able to laugh, too, at the limitations of her own life, so that instead of becoming bitter as she grew older, she sucked positive pleasure out of them.

" It's a shame," we used sometimes to say, " that Alex should waste all her youth and cleverness moulder- ing in Crossriggs !" But if Alex felt this, she never said so—and I don't believe she did feel it; as a healthy stomach will assimilate almost anything in the nature of food, so her magnificent mental digestion throve upon the unpromising materials that surrounded her. Life was a continual feast to Alex in those days, no one need have pitied her.

We made at Crossriggs a tight little society within a very small circle. True, the village was only an hour by train from a capital city; but our excursions there, and our returns, only made our independence the more marked. Crossriggs was no suburb—owed none of its life or interest to another place. Edinburgh was our shopping centre; some of us had business, and all of us had relatives there; our surgeons and our boot-makers lived there; but socially, Crossriggs hugged itself in a proud isolation from "town." We didn't want it; of course, "town" would never have believed that, but it is true all the same, and although the Scottish capital is at all seasons swept by sufficiently bracing airs, one of our customs was to draw a deep breath on alighting from the train at our own station, and remark with satisfaction, "How good the air tastes after being in town!"

Indeed it was pleasant, on an evening in early spring, to come from the horrid din of the noisy streets into the abundant quiet of the country; to hear the blackbird chuckle from the high trees, and smell the fresh earth of the ploughed fields.

Each family in the neighbourhood was known to us all, and surely even the excitements of dislike are more amusing than life amidst the unknown hordes of a town? Time would fail me to tell of all our neighbours, and some of them have no particular bearing upon this story, yet every one had a distinct value in the little Crossriggs world of those days.

One of the figures most familiar to us all was old Admiral Cassilis of Foxe Hall. He was blind, poor man, and we used to watch him pityingly as he drove through the village, sitting forward in his carriage, looking about from side to side with his sightless eyes, as if he would try to pierce the cloud which had fallen over him. He was very lonely. His wife had died years before, and his only son was, as the saying goes, "unsatisfactory," and lived abroad. Now and then some relation would arrive at the Hall to keep him company for a week, and to drive with him in an apathetic way, making forced conversation; but mostly he lived alone. He was not, as this fact revealed, a very delightful person, and, moreover, had a tremendous idea of his own importance. His wish was to be visited by the great landowners of the county, but these gentlemen would not be troubled with an unattractive, blind old man, so their calls were of the perfunctory annual nature, and the Admiral was forced to content himself with the society of his less important neighbours at Crossriggs.

The Maitlands, from their long residence in the district, were privileged people, and "went everywhere," as the vulgar phrase goes, even before Robert Maitland's fame as a scholar had made every one anxious for his acquaintance. But the Admiral was not quite sure about including old Alexander Hope as one of his visitors. " Hope is, of course, amongst the best names in Scotland," he was reported to have said years ago, when the Hopes first settled at Crossriggs, " but then, there are Hopes and Hopes. The question is, Who is *this* Hope ?"

It was only when he had satisfied himself that Old Hopeful was, as he expressed it, " A Hope " (albeit an unsuccessful and unimportant member of the family) that the Admiral decided to call upon him.

I remember the day when the Cassilis chariot drew up before the sagging gateway of Orchard House, and the Admiral was helped out to pay his first call on Old Hopeful.

That good man was weeding his untidy front plot at the moment, but no thought so petty as shame of his occupation ever crossed his mind. Those, you must remember, were the days before gardening had become a fashion, and it was considered only the occupation of an eccentric or a labourer. Disgust was visible on the face of the footman who supported the Admiral, when

Old Hopeful, flinging down his hoe, came forward with outstretched, soil-stained hands to welcome his visitor.

"It is Admiral Cassilis, I think?" says he. "Will you sit in the porch, Admiral, or come indoors? These late autumn days are full of health in the garden, I maintain."

"Indoors—indoors by preference," said the Admiral, and they disappeared within.

The visit didn't turn out particularly successful. Old Hopeful feared God, but he certainly did not regard man, and in the course of their first conversation, he aired some of his alarmingly radical views to the Admiral, who promptly contradicted them. Only the timely entrance of Robert Maitland saved the situation.

Now, whether from the first difference of opinion, or, as I am inclined to think, for the more sordid reason that the Admiral thought the Hopes' way of life altogether too small for such as he to be much associated with, the acquaintance never ripened into any sort of intimacy. Old Hopeful was incapable of taking in that any one could wish to be cold to him, and he used to call genially once a year at Foxe Hall; but Alex knew, and she would say, "It's just like watching a cat and dog, to see them together—my father, of course, being the nobler animal."

Crossriggs's society was, in fact, divided into those on whom the Admiral did or did not call—subtle distinction!

There were, for instance, our good neighbours, the Reids. No better people existed; but the Admiral did not call on the Reids. Then his social intercourse with Mr. Scott, the new minister, who had succeeded old Mr. Maitland, was strictly limited. The Admiral went to Mr. Scott's church, so was in duty bound to acknowledge his existence, but that was all. "A vulgar fellow— I cannot ask him to dinner," was his summing up of the situation. This social sifting was one of the few joys left to the old man, now deprived of the bolder occupations of his youth. " I have a natural talent for it," he once said proudly—and indeed he had ! " *In the county, but not of it,*" was his saying about the Barlands—good rich people who had rented a house in the neighbourhood. " *Consulted, not received,*" was his verdict upon the doctor from Crosstown, who probably, as he had a family to support, preferred the former position. " *Neighbours, but not friends,*" was one of his most frequent and final distinctions.

No description of Crossriggs would be complete without a picture of the Reids, even although the Admiral did not call on them. They were such permanent features of the place. I seem to see Miss Bessie Reid walking across the Square as I write. " A brave effort," was the phrase that her neighbours always applied to Miss Bessie. Living as she did a monotonous life, spending much time in tending a paralyzed aunt, it was only a brave effort that kept her going at all, and she made it unceasingly. Whatever tragedy lay in her past, it was now hidden beneath an over-sprightly manner. Her thin face was withering, but set into curves of galvanized cheerfulness; her laugh rang out ready, if a trifle tinny in its sound ; her waistbands were trigg and tight ; her unlovely hands covered with inexpensive rings. Buckles and bangles were always jingling about her, and she had a constant succession of showy, ill-made clothes. Miss Bessie's taste was not coherent, and as time went on, this want of sequence increased. It seemed as if she could not adhere to a scheme even in braid and buttons, for her bodice would be trimmed with one kind of lace, and her wrists (those bony wrists with their plaintive jingle of bangles) with cascades of another pattern. In her headgear especially she was addicted to a little of everything—a bow of velvet, a silk ribbon, an ostrich " tip," a buckle, a wing from some other fowl, and always, always a glitter of beads— they winked from every angle of her person, and when

combined with the glance of an elderly eye, no longer
dewy, and the repeated flash of teeth which had already
been several times renewed, gave an impression of constant, unspontaneous vivacity.   " It's wonderful how
she keeps up ! " we always said, and it was true.   There
had been a time when Miss Bessie left the aunt in charge
of a married sister, and went abroad for six months.   She
had spent most of her time in a Pension, "where we had
quite a group of cultured people."   Afterwards one of
the contented matrons of her acquaintance remarked
with a smile, " There was some little romance, I believe ; "
but what the little romance had been, no one ever knew.
It had withered away without fruition, and Miss Bessie
returned to tend her paralyzed relative—a little thinner
in face, and to grow thinner yet, voice perhaps on a harder
note, but facing the world as ever with the continued effort
of her smile.

Miss Bessie had a brother, a banker, who resembled
his sister in face, but not in vivacity.   James Reid could
certainly not, even by the most charitable, have been
called interesting.   Yet every one liked and respected
him, and it was a source of constant annoyance to Alex
to know that many of her neighbours considered he would
have been a most suitable, nay, desirable, match for her.

Some people will tell you that to the student of human
nature there are no human beings unworthy of observation ; but, as Alex used to say, " For the good of your
own soul, at least, it's as well to notice some of them as
little as possible."   Mr. Scott, the minister, and his
wife, were among this number.   Mr. Scott was a very
stout man with a rolling gait, whose chief characteristic
was laziness ; his wife, a sharp-eyed, vulgar woman with
that curious look, when she met you, of appraising,
almost pricing, everything that you had on.   They
were hated by the poor, and avoided by their richer
parishioners, and, in consequence, they felt their life to
be a martyrdom, and said so freely.

These, then, were the principal characters in our little world of Crossriggs—a world that jogged along very quietly as a rule, and where "nothing ever happened," as the children say. Then, quite suddenly, two things happened. Matilda Chalmers' husband died in Canada, and we heard that she was coming home with all her children to live at Orchard House. That was the first event.

The next was that the Admiral's good-for-nothing son died abroad, and young Van Cassilis, his grandson and heir, came to Foxe Hall.

Then and there happenings began.

CHAPTER II.

On the day of Matilda's home-coming, Mr. Hope was on his way to the station, hurrying along full of benevolent sympathy for his bereaved daughter, when he met Miss Elizabeth Maitland and Miss Bessie Reid. He stopped for a moment to speak with them.

" I am just starting for Glasgow to met my poor Matilda and her five children. There is room in the old house for them all, and plenty of room in our hearts! I must meet her when they land—she will be in need of support and comfort, poor girl," he explained.

His grey hair, which he always wore very long, streamed upon the breeze, his usually ruddy face was pale with emotion. Bessie Reid and Miss Maitland exchanged glances when he had hurried on.

" Poor Matilda—what a home-coming! " said Miss Bessie.

" Yes, poor soul ; she will need something more than *his* support if she has five children to provide for," remarked Miss Elizabeth.

" Alex is very practical, though," said Bessie Reid. " She will manage them all. She must have inherited that from her mother."

" She has her father's temperament," said Miss Elizabeth. " Just a dash of the mother—like a drop of wine in water."

" Mrs. Hope was a clever woman, wasn't she ? " asked Bessie Reid.

" Very."

" And fond of Mr. Hope ? "

Aunt E. V. threw up her head with the faint toss that was a habit of hers at times.

" She died of him," she said in her low, sweet voice. " She was a clever woman, capable and good-looking, but she died of him at forty. Born to suck the life out of other people, he plants his theories on their graves ! "

The next morning, Alexandra Hope ran across the Square and went into t' ɔ Manse, while the Maitlands were at breakfast.

" Good morning ! " she called out. " Please don't mind my appearance. I've been dusting out the attics. I just came in to speak to Miss Elizabeth for one moment."

She did look odd enough, for she carried a duster in one hand, and she had twisted an orange handkerchief round her head to keep the dust off her hair ; one lock, dark and glossy, had escaped from the covering, and hung down on her neck. With the duster in one hand, she stood there balancing her tall figure with the sort of energetic grace that she had. Her warm grey eyes lighted up an otherwise rather plain face, which was not improved by the outlandish headgear she had chosen to assume. Her long, clever-looking hands grasped the back of a chair as she talked.

" They—I mean Matilda and all the children—are arriving at six o'clock this evening, and I'm sure I don't know how in the world we're going to dispose of them ! "

" It is a large addition to your household all of a sudden, Alex," said Robert Maitland, who had risen at her entrance and stood by the window. Mrs. Maitland, pretty and languid-looking, smiled faintly ; Miss Elizabeth tossed her head.

" Seven ! " she said.

" Oh, no, only six—Matilda and five children."

" Is there no nurse ? " said Mrs. Maitland, with mild surprise.

" Nurse ? No, I don't suppose they've ever had one. Oh, Miss Elizabeth, do you think there is any country except Canada where people can live for years and years and return poorer than when they went out ? For if there *is* such a place, we'll all get there in time ! "

" Some people, Alex, might spend years in a gold mine, and come out poorer than when they went in ! " replied Miss Maitland.

And Alex laughed. " My father would, I'm sure," she said, " and we're all much the same. I'm just dying to see the children. I seem to know them already, though I've never seen any of them except Sally when she was four years old."

" Have you got room for them all ? " asked Mrs. Maitland.

Alex grinned. " We must squeeze them in somehow. I'll take Sally into my room, and the baby will be with her mother, and the two boys can have the attic, and little Mike must go into the old nursery."

" And will that be comfortable ? " said Mrs. Maitland.

Alex laughed again. " Well, no, I shouldn't think it would ; but it's all we can do, and even then we are short of beds. That was what I came to ask—can you let us have one ? "

" How old is Mike ? I forget," said Maitland.

" Quite a little fellow—he's only four."

Robert, with his hands in his pockets, began to walk up and down the room. He glanced at his wife, who went on placidly eating her breakfast. She was a pretty woman, with, by this time, a slightly faded prettiness. Her large eyes had really no expression, and the pretty, pouting lips were a little peevish in their line. She was like a doll just faintly endowed with a kind of second-hand vitality if you can imagine such a thing.

" Won't you give us some of the children—as many as you like ? " said Robert to Alexandra. He noticed, as she stood there with the strong morning light falling

sideways on her, that there were faint lines already
upon her brow—lines that should not have been there
for ten years yet.

"Oh, yes, we'd like to have them," said Mrs. Maitland,
languidly.

Alex laughed. "But we can't allow you to have
them. It isn't that we want to get rid of them—not
a bit—only we don't know where to put them yet.
Matilda, poor dear, will be very tired when she arrives,
and as they've probably all been sea-sick, I don't want
her to have to arrange anything. So if you can let us
have a little bed that will do for one of the boys, I shall
be much obliged."

"I think we can. I will see about it—the gardener
can take it across at once," said Miss Elizabeth.

She went out of the room, and Robert followed her,
leaving Alex talking to his wife. He laid his hand on his
aunt's arm as she was about to go upstairs.

"Stop a moment, Aunt Elizabeth."

She turned and looked at him in astonishment, for
his face had lost its wonted serenity for a moment. His
friends used to say that Robert was the handsomest
man in the whole county. The purity of his skin would
have been a fortune to an actress, and both in face and
figure he had a masculine beauty that is very rare.
Even as a young man he had a singularly benign expression that blent curiously with a certain aloofness
of manner.

Nothing seemed to depress or to excite him. After
his marriage, when he returned to Crossriggs, every one
said, "He is just the same," but he was not. The change
was there, silent, but, like frost in the night, it had altered
everything. Happy or unhappy—either phrase seemed
equally futile in describing the man, and as years went
on, one could notice more clearly his strangely imper-
sonal attitude to life. There was that about Robert
Maitland at times only to be described by the word

unhuman (not inhuman, mark), and a keen observer
might wonder at times if any feeling went deep enough
with him to pierce the bland calm of his philosophy.
At this moment, though, his face was troubled. Twice
he began to speak, and each time. the words broke
hoarsely in his throat. Then in a very low voice he
said—

"I wish you to send over the little cot—the one that
Maurice had."

"Do you indeed, Robert? What will Laura say?"

"Laura won't mind. She doesn't know it is there,
probably."

"If you wish it——" began Miss Elizabeth.

"Yes," he said, "I do. After all—why not? You
have a fresh crocus this year for the one that was broken
by last year's storm. I should like another child to
sleep there now. The thing hurts me, besides—I saw
it the other day."

"Very well, I will do what you wish, Robert," said
Miss Maitland.

When Alex came out into the hall, Miss Maitland said
to her that they had a little cot in the box-room which
would be sent over at once to Orchard House.

"A little cot!" said Alex. Then, all in a moment, she
understood, and her face flashed with feeling. "No,
no, dear Miss Elizabeth—Mr. Maitland—I couldn't
take it; I think it would be better not."

Maitland looked at her steadily. "If you please,
Alex, you will allow us to send it. I would rather have
it that way. Perhaps the child that sleeps in it will
have blessed dreams of mine!"

Alex nodded at him—there were tears in her eyes;
then waving her duster in farewell, she ran back across
the Square to her own house.

"A good girl," said Miss Maitland. "But that
orange turban is unbecoming; and she might have
laid down her duster for five minutes, I think!"

Mrs. Maitland came out of the dining-room. " I
wish Miss Hope would sit down when she comes in," she
said. " That way of standing about annoys me. And
what had she got on her head ? "

It was characteristic of Mrs. Maitland that she always
spoke of Alex as Miss Hope, although the rest of the
family used her Christian name. Mrs. Maitland never
formed an intimacy. The neighbours used to say that
this must have been what first attracted Robert to
her—that he thought he had found in her an aloofness
of character equal to his own.

But this was unjust to him, for a kinder or more
constant friend than Robert Maitland never was. Only
he seemed to give everything and to demand nothing in
return ; to have some inner spring of solace that made
him independent of others.

" It's not sympathy he gives, it's tolerance," said Alex,
one day when she felt annoyed with him. It is almost
impossible by description to convey the charm that
may exist, and did, in this instance, along with that
peculiar aloofness from human intimacy. But his wife's
case was very different. She seemed to have no interest
in any one outside the immediate circle of her own family.
On the whole, her neighbours knew very little about
her. She appeared at their houses from time to time,
always pretty, and polite in a dull kind of way, and
every one wanted to talk to her husband instead of to
her. She had the impassivity of a very shallow mind,
and was never heard to express the smallest admiration
of Robert's powers. When people spoke of his work,
she would very soon dismiss the subject with a faint
sigh of boredom. Indeed, if Maitland was a distinguished man—and some people thought him so—he
had been preserved from the too common lot of genius
—that of being, in his own household, surrounded by
humbly worshipping females ! for Mrs. Maitland could
not have been passionate enough to worship any one,

and most certainly Aunt E. V. did not—she never lost
an opportunity of impressing on us all that Robert
was merely one of a family, and by no means the best
of them.

The Maitlands' only child had died some years before
they came to settle at Crossriggs. Mrs. Maitland may
have been sorry about that, because she never took the
slightest notice of other children, or made any allusion
to the loss of their own.

" That child must have been imported," Alex would
say. " I don't believe she ever had it ! "

Laura Maitland regarded her husband as a mere attri-
bute of herself, taking a kind of satisfaction in his charm,
his success—much as she did in her clothes or her house.
" What a woman ! " (to quote Alex once more). " It
gave me quite a start to hear her sneeze. It was like
discovering that the policeman you thought a waxwork
was alive after all ! "

Well, out of a whole world of women, Robert had
chosen and married her, so presumably there must have
been something he admired in her ; but it was difficult
to imagine what that something was. Whatever he
felt about his marriage, he preserved the same happy
behaviour, and it was only an old friend who could
notice the change that, like frost in the night, had turned
summer into autumn without a sound.

CHAPTER III

ABOUT six o'clock that evening a laden fly drove up to the door of Orchard House, and the process of disgorging its contents began. Alex, who had heard the sound of wheels, flew to the door to welcome her sister. The fly was positively bulging with children, with bundles and baskets of all kinds.

Old Hopeful got out first, and helped his daughter to alight. His venerable grey head was uncovered. A really valuable asset it was—such a silvery, gentle, noble-looking old head; any family might have been proud of his appearance.

Alex, standing on the threshold, half tearful, half smiling, held out her arms to welcome them all at once.

"This is Sally—I knew you!" she cried. "And Peter and George—and this must be Mike, and, oh dear, the baby! Give her to me!"

The children scrambled out, the baby was placed in her arms, and then Alex had time to look at her sister.

Only a few months had elapsed since Matilda's sudden widowhood, so that it rather surprised Alex to observe that the face under the black bonnet was nearly as round and unlined as it had been ten years before.

Indeed, a sort of pensive cheerfulness seemed to be in her looks as she stood once more on the threshold of her old home and disentangled child after child from the fly.

She glanced at the opposite house, and seeing some

one at the window, smiled and waved her hand in greeting; then, carrying a yellow basket in one hand, and holding a little boy with the other, she disappeared within, followed by her father, who carried a birdcage indifferently tied up in brown paper, and a bundle of wraps.

Alex lifted the fat baby and hoisted it high on her shoulder, from whence it stared fixedly at everything, as if arrivals were nothing new to it, whilst she herded the other children into the house before her.

"Now, dears, go upstairs, all of you, and get off your things," she called out, "and then come down to supper. May I put the baby to bed, Matilda?"

"Yes, of course you may. We're all hungry and sleepy, aren't we, children? Come away upstairs!"

Matilda ascended the old shallow staircase encompassed by her children, and Alex, hoisting the baby again with a fine swing, carried it up after them.

She remembered acutely at the moment how she had seen Matilda come down that staircase in her wedding-dress and veil, holding a bouquet of white roses, whilst she, a thin, brown-faced girl of sixteen, had followed her at a respectful distance, very careful not to step on the white train, trembling with an excitement far deeper than that of the bride. And what a strangely ignoble figure poor Peter Chalmers had then appeared to play the leading part in that awful and gracious ceremony! Alex vividly remembered it all; and here this evening, as she followed Matilda's black figure up the stairs, feeling the weight of Matilda's youngest child on her shoulder, she felt again what, in her childhood, she called "construction" of the heart that seemed unknown to her more placid sister.

In half an hour's time they were all, except the baby, assembled in the dining-room.

Matilda, a little tired of course, but calm and smooth faced, having shed her few easy tears when she first entered, was now able to smile and talk quietly with her father as she sat beside him at the foot of the table, patting from time to time the hand that he laid on hers.

Alex sat at the head of the table, the children at each side—four of them, fine, well-grown creatures all.

Sally, the eldest girl, was big and clumsy at her present age, but her colouring of pink and white and her auburn hair, like her mother's, were lovely.

Peter was, like his sister, a big, hulking thing, with high shoulders and round face, his eyes shining with intelligence. George, the cleverest of them all, was thinner and uglier and not so well grown.

Then came little Mike, whose round perfectly innocent face, with a dimple set deep at each corner of the bud-like mouth, was already irresistible to every woman. He had squeezed himself close to his new aunt, rubbing his head against her from time to time as he sucked up a mug full of milk, staring hard over the brim at his grandfather at the other end of the table.

Mr. Hope had long been a vegetarian (or "fruitarian," as he preferred to be called), and in winter especially, the preparation of his meals was something of a business.

"No need to trouble about me!" he was wont to say blandly. "My wants are few! An occasional egg and the fruits in their season. Ah, if we could all live like-wise! *Limit your desires, my friends*—that is the secret of happiness in a world full of limitations. You re-member our Shakespeare—

> "Seeking the food he eats,
>   Content with what he gets,
>   Come hither, come hither, come hither!
>   Here shall he see
>   No enemy
>   But winter and rough weather!"

This was one of his favourite quotations. Certainly "winter and rough weather" were enemies that every dweller in that district had to face, and to go out, as he did, in the teeth of a north-east wind after dining on cereals, required extraordinary buoyancy.

In summer and autumn the fruitarian diet was easily provided. On the evening of Matilda's arrival, the table was brightened by a huge dish of red apples from Old Hopeful's orchard. Brilliant in colour, the fruit was mushy and tasteless to an ordinary palate, but he feasted upon it with unabated cheerfulness.

"Apples enough for all! Yes, plenty of red apples for you all!" he cried, overjoyed at the children's ex-clamations when they saw the fruit. Alex smiled, but said nothing; she knew the taste of their home-produce only too well.

After a few bites at his apple, George laid it down, and looked across at Peter in silence. Then little Mike pulled at Alex's sleeve.

"Pease, anozer apple—zis one not nice!" His face had clouded—a very little disappointment is enough to make a tired, excited child cry. Matilda looked annoyed.

"You must not make remarks about your food, Mike," she said, vexed that her children should behave badly on this their first evening. Tears welled into Mike's eyes, and Alex hurriedly gave him some bread and jam, trying to divert his attention.

"Another apple, Sally?" said Mr. Hope, to his grand-daughter.

"No, thank you," said Sally, decidedly.

"What! Not another apple?"

"No, thank you. I'd rather have some bread," replied the girl.

"We got awfully good apples in Canada," said George.

"And on the ship coming home," said Peter.

"Zey wasn't *red*, but zey was gooder zan zeese," said Mike.

"Ah, dear me! Times are changed—children are the critics now-a-days!" said Mr. Hope, looking a little downcast. " When I was a child, boys, a fine red apple was all I could want."

Alex rose rather abruptly and, as they left the room, Matilda detained Sally to whisper to her that they must not make remarks on anything at table.

" Remember, grandfather's house is not your own."

" But you said it was going home, mother," said George.

" Yes, so it is—it was once my home—it is still—but it is not quite the same thing, my dear children, as our home in Canada."

" I wish we were going back to Canada ! " said Sally, and at the word somehow a sniffing began amongst the children ; one said something about " father," then tears came into Matilda's eyes, too, and Alex found them rather a doleful little company when she came back into the room.

" Tears already ! " she called. " Some one is sleepy and wants to go to bed. Come away, Mike, your new aunt will carry you upstairs on her back, and we'll make an awful storm in the bath with soap-suds, so that you may think you are at sea again, only you'll be safe in a beautiful little cot to-night, instead of in a berth like a drawer ! "

Even as she spoke, the children cheered up. Matilda and the elder ones joined Mr. Hope, and Alex took sleepy Mike off to his bed in the nursery.

CHAPTER IV

A FIRE had been lighted in the old nursery that night. The room had been disused for many years, but the same old fender guarded the fire; the same worn scraps of carpet lay on the floor of unpainted boards, and in the wooden box by the window there were still some fragments of the toys that Matilda and Alex had played with in their own childhood. It was an attic room with a sloping roof, the walls covered nearly to the ceiling with pictures that had been pasted on when the Hopes were little girls.

A battered tin bath, with scarcely any paint left upon it, stood in front of the fire; the air smelt of soap and water. Alex, on her knees on the rug, with a towel tied like an apron over her dress, was folding up Mike's little garments that were scattered on the floor. That done, she proceeded to wring out the sponge and to rescue a small metal fish which floated in the bath amidst a heavy surf of soap-suds.

A voice at the door startled her, saying, " May I come in ? " She looked up and saw Robert Maitland standing in the half-darkness of the doorway.

" Come in ! Yes, of course, come in—we want you very much," she answered gaily, holding out a soapy hand. " I can't shake hands—I seem never able to shake hands—either it's ink, or earth, or dust; now it's soap, you see ! "

" My fiss, pease ! " said a solemn voice from the corner.

" Oh, oh—who's this ? " said Maitland, stepping forward into the circle of firelight.

At the end of the room stood a large wooden bed, and beside it was a child's cot—a beautiful little cot, very unlike the other battered furnishings of the room.

As Alex rose from her knees and stirred the fire, the logs blazed up, shooting their light into the shadowy corners. There, sitting up in the cot, was Mike, in his flannel nightgown, the hair still damp on his brow, his eyes round, his little hands spread out before him, gazing in astonishment at the intruder. Maitland hesitated for half a second. Alex had come forward and stood beside him. She saw the feeling that flickered across his face, and in a moment she understood.

" Oh," she murmured in a quick low voice, " does it hurt you ? Do you mind ? For we can send it back at once——"

" No, no, Alex. It only makes me remember what, after all, I can never forget."

He stood at the foot of the crib, and Mike turned and looked *into* him rather than at him, with the grave, self-forgetful stare of a very young child.

Maitland rubbed his hand across his eyes for a moment. " Maurice was only six—but why should I say *only* ? "

He bent down as he spoke to look at the child, and Mike suddenly smiled at him, and laid an open palm, softer than velvet, on the man's hand as it rested on the rail of the cot.

" Have you any mouses in your house ? " he asked, lisping out the words one by one, for his speech was slow and gentle.

" I don't know, Mike. Yes—I think there must be some in our kitchen. You must come over to-morrow and see."

" Live mouses ? " said the little boy. " There's none left in zis house. Aunt Alex says zat ze cat has killed them all. She knew a boy zat had a tame one."

" I hope our house is overrun with mice, I'm sure," said Maitland, smiling. " But I don't seem to have heard of them."

" Oh, think of Miss Elizabeth's feelings if she heard you say that, and of the insult to your good cat, which has been there for so many years," said Alex. " Now, Mike, lie down. Here is your fish. He is sleepy, if you are not, after his long journey, and wants to go to bed under the sea." She laid the child gently back on the pillow as she spoke.

" I'm not at all sleepy," began Mike ; but even as he uttered the words his body relaxed, his eyes closed, and with a sigh he sank into his dreams.

Alex stood for a moment looking down at him with shining eyes.

" Strange, is it not ? " she said in a whisper, " that my poor brother-in-law should have been the parent of a lovely flower of childhood like this ? " She looked at Maitland with a smile. " You remember Peter Chalmers, don't you ? "

" Yes—but Matilda—— " he began, laughing.

" Oh, of course, Matilda is sweet—but Mike is not like her. It's just one of the many puzzles of the universe —he may grow up a second Nelson, or Milton, perhaps —but no, there's a limit to the possible—Peter was no genius ! "

" I came in to see Matilda, really," said Maitland, " and to carry the greetings of Aunt Elizabeth and Laura."

" He might have omitted *that* little fib," thought Alex. But she led him out of the nursery and they went downstairs together. " There's a babier baby than Mike," she said. " But you will see her to-morrow. Aren't we rich ? Come in and see Matilda—you won't find her much changed. It's so absurd to see her with all these children. I could sooner believe they were my own ! "

When they came into the sitting-room, Matilda was knitting peacefully, as if she had been at home for a year.

The boys were playing some game together, and Old Hopeful was reading aloud to them all. The arrival of a family that increased his responsibilities by five was nothing to him, and an hour or two had sufficed to restore him to his full flow of benevolent optimism.

" Delighted to see you, Robert ! " he exclaimed. " We were just having an hour of Homer before the boys went to bed. Tales of windy Troy ! Brave days—brave days ! These youngsters are to be envied, hearing of them for the first time. In my youth, of course, we began even sooner, but there is a fever for the practical—for the bread which perisheth—in commercial countries and colonies like Canada, nowadays. The springs of true knowledge are neglected till late in life, when probably they will never be drunk of at all."

During this little harangue, Maitland had sat down by Matilda, regarding her curiously.

" You look very well," he said. " And I have just seen Mike ; so now I have made the acquaintance of the whole family, except the baby."

Matilda smiled and answered in her sweet way, " It seems strange to think of my children having to make acquaintance with you at all, Mr. Maitland, instead of having you for one of the blessings of life as we had when we were little." She looked at him and went on, " You are such a distinguished person now that I don't know how we have the courage to treat you as an old friend at all. You are just the same, too."

" Oh," exclaimed Alex, " you both look just the same as you did when I was sixteen. It's only poor me who feels the effects of time. I remember on Matilda's wedding-day how I wrote in my diary afterwards, in my account of the scene, ' that Mr. Maitland looked beautiful, and like a Greek.' "

They both laughed at this, and Maitland got up, saying he must go.

" What—already ! " exclaimed Old Hopeful. " I had

hoped to have a talk with you about that book of
Walton's——"

" I cannot, sir ; I must go home. I have work to do
to-night."

" Ah ! never work at night. The evening should be
our social hour. But if you must, you must. I will see
you to the door. A lovely evening—Sirius is particularly
bright——"

With the Iliad open in one hand, holding his spectacles
in the other, he accompanied Maitland to the door. Alex,
as she passed along, saw them standing there together.
There was just enough of light falling from the lamp
in the doorway to touch Maitland's clear-skinned, fine
face as it was turned towards Mr. Hope. There was
trouble in his eyes that night. Alex caught her breath as
she noticed it.

" It hurt him," she said to herself. " I know it did,
but he looked down at Mike like a guardian angel. Talk
of women's feelings about children ! Men care far more
than most mothers."

She went into the kitchen then to confer with Katharine, the old servant who in general ruled their small
household pretty much as she liked, for Alex was no great
housekeeper, and Old Hopeful's fruitarian meals had
hitherto been the only difficulty.

" Well, Katharine," said Alex, briskly, as she entered.
" We'll need to have breakfast earlier to-morrow, I suppose." Katharine, who was bending over the fire, turned
round as she spoke. Her appearance was the picture of
health and neatness, but her face wore an expression of
almost tragic woe. Alex was prepared for this, and went
on brightly, " Shall we say a quarter to eight ? "

" When you like, miss—whenever you fancy. It will
be all the same to me. I'll be up at five anyway, if not
half-four." She wiped an eye with a corner of a spotless
apron.

" Dear me, not so early as all that," said Alex. " I will

be down as soon as I can and help you. I can set the breakfast-table to-night."

" No need, Miss Alex—no need, my dear. I'll not be in my bed till past twelve or more. I'll do it whenever I'm done with my floor."

" But surely, Katharine, you are not going to wash that floor to-night. It's spotless."

" It'll not be spotless long "—with a moan of satisfied complaint—" with all thae children crossing it. The dishes made a pile as high as yer head after supper, miss, and the knives that black with peeling apples ! It'll just take me all my time to get them fit for breakfast. Mrs. Scott's girl (sech a like sight ye never saw—I wouldn't wipe a floor, miss, with her) came in with a message, and ' sit ye doon,' says I, ' while ye may. Ye'r lucky that can. I have been on these two feet since half-six this morning.' "

" Well, Katharine," said Alex, " Mrs. Chalmers and I have been talking about you, and she wants a young girl to come in every day and help until we see how we get on. The household is much larger now, you know."

An ominous silence ; then Katharine began in a low recitative—

" Get yer girl, mem—oh, yes, get yer girl—trauchlin' through the house making more work than she's worth, eating her head off, dirtying plates, and carrying gossip, and her in earrings, likely, and sayin' we can't get through with our own work, and me done every blessed thing in this house, miss, forbye Mr. Hope's food—that's a woman's work itself when spinach and all that has to be prepared. Oh, get yer girl ! I know what the end will be ! "

At this juncture Matilda came into the kitchen. " Now, Katharine," she said in her pleasant way, " I must really have a chat with you. My children are all in bed, and I have a little quiet time."

" Oh, dear, dear—come away, Miss Matilda—Mrs. Chalmers, dear, I'm forgettin' ! " exclaimed Katharine, in high good humour. "*My—but she sets the weeds!*" she murmured, with a deep chuckle of appreciation and a glance at Matilda as she seated herself by the fire.

Katharine stood regarding her with the fond delight in widowhood peculiar to her class, and Alex, laughing to herself, went off to set the breakfast-table for next morning.

"How wonderful Mr. Maitland is," said Matilda, when she and Alex were alone that evening. "He doesn't look much older than when I was married. I suppose Mrs. Maitland is just the same?"

"Well, did you expect her to become different? She's just the same as when we first saw her, only a trifle stiffer. We have very little to do with her really. Aunt E. V. and Mr. Maitland are the ones we see most of. I think Mrs. Maitland dislikes the little intimacies of village life very much. Instead of saying, 'We are going to the Lauries' to-morrow,' she would like to say, 'We have another engagement,' and so on."

"He is beautiful; there is really no other word for him," said Matilda. "He always was. It's nice to find people just as charming as they used to be—years afterwards."

That night, after she had gone to her own room—the presence of Sally there had been averted—Alex took out from a drawer her old diaries, and read on until she came to the account of Matilda's marriage. How it brought back the memory of the whole day to her as she read!— "Mother cried a good deal. Father made a very pretty speech, but I don't think any one but Mr. Maitland understood the Greek bits, and old Mrs. Chalmers wasn't pleased. Then Matilda cut the cake, and every one was very happy. Gracie Flemming and Anna looked very nice in their bridesmaids' frocks, but mine didn't fit, and I think I looked particularly bad, for my eyes were red all round. Every one was very kind, and Matilda looked lovely. She went away at three o'clock. *Mr. Maitland*

kissed her : I thought I could even have married Peter Chalmers for that. Mother was very tired in the evening. I had no time to do my journal, so write it up to-day. I don't think I shall ever marry."

She sat looking at the page with a half-whimsical smile, then shut the book, and tossed it back into the drawer.

" That was fourteen years ago," she said to herself, as she brushed out her long, glossy hair. " I don't know that I quite believed it as I wrote it, but I do now. However, Providence seems to be going to give me the children without the husband. The children—dear things that they all are ! "

CHAPTER V

As news of Matilda's home-coming spread through the village, all the neighbours hastened to call upon her. First came Mr. and Mrs. Scott (who had never seen her before), then Miss Bessie Reid and her brother, and last of all, Admiral Cassilis. This crowning felicity, however, was not granted to Matilda until some weeks later—as though the Admiral would not have her imagine that he was in any hurry to wait upon such an insignificant person.

" A daughter of old Mr. Hope's," he said, when he heard of her arrival. "A pretty girl, I remember. Married some one of the name of Chambers—Chalmers —something of that kind, I think."

But at last he did arrive in great state ; the lumbering, low-hung carriage drawing up before the door of Orchard House, with such a noise that all the children ran to the window to see what it was. Matilda suppressed their curiosity, and went out into the hall herself to meet the old man.

" How kind of you to make this exertion and come to see me," she said, and taking him gently by the hand, she led the Admiral into the sitting-room, talking on in her sweet, slightly discursive fashion all the time. " It is so long since we last met—not since my wedding-day. I have only once been home since. We left for Canada im- mediately—yes—five children—all well and happy, I am glad to say, and a great delight to my father. He is undertaking the education of my two eldest boys himself."

By this time Matilda had guided her visitor to a chair, and seated herself beside him. The old man straightened himself, in a funny way he had when he was led into a room, as if to recover his dignity after the involuntary humiliation. Then he pursed up his lips and repeated—

" Five children, Mrs. Chalmers—five children—a great responsibility ! "

Matilda generally agreed with every one about everything, even if she happened to hold another opinion, so she acquiesced in this remark.

" Yes, indeed, a very heavy responsibility," she said, though really the care of those children weighed but lightly on her spirit.

" There are scholarships—foundations to be had in good schools for likely youths," the Admiral went on. " A matter of influence, it is true—largely a matter of influence. But I daresay, my dear Mrs. Chalmers, it might be possible to work something of the kind. One knows of persons—a word in the ear of the right man *from* the right man——"

The Admiral paused and patted his stock, readjusting the huge, pearl-headed scarf-pin that fastened it, with an action as conscious as that of any schoolgirl.

" Thank you, thank you," Matilda said hastily. " It is very kind of you to think about my poor little men. Their future *is* a matter of some anxiety, but when the time comes, I have no doubt—no doubt at all—that something will turn up for them, they will be provided for."

" No doubt—no doubt. You are not without friends— connections—persons able to use their influence."

The Admiral was quite unconscious that Matilda's simple confidence rested on aught save mortal assistance.

" As I told you," she went on, " my father himself is teaching the two eldest boys just now. He is such a thorough classical scholar, that it is a great delight to him to teach them. He has a great belief in an early knowledge of the classics. When my sister and I were little girls, we were well taught. I have forgotten my Latin long ago," she added, with a smile.

"Much better, much better! What does a charming woman want with Latin?" interjected the Admiral, with contempt.

"Father has a method of his own," went on Matilda.

"There was no method like the old method of the cane!" replied the Admiral.

"Ah, well, perhaps it had its advantages, but my father's is a very gentle one," said Matilda. "He already thinks that my little Peter shows signs of promise. But I must not bore you with a mother's stories! How have you been? I fear your sight is no better than it was?"

"Better? No—worse, a great deal!" the old man groaned. "I can hardly distinguish day from night now, and a few years ago I knew, at least, when the sun was shining."

"Oh, it is a terrible trouble!" Matilda cried, her kind blue eyes brimming with tears of sympathy. "Sometimes I am tempted to grumble over my little difficulties and worries, but how they all disappear before such a trial as yours!"

Her sympathy was so genuine, so simple, that it almost made the Admiral forget himself and his own importance. He gave a great sigh and leant back in the armchair with a wearied gesture.

"Yes, yes—a heavy trial it is," he said. At this moment Alex came into the room. She caught his words as she entered.

"What is a heavy trial?" she asked lightly, and the Admiral groaned aloud—

"Blindness—the long night I live in!"

"Oh, I didn't know what you were speaking about," said Alex, gently.

Both she and Matilda belonged to that small and bright band of persons who do not feel it awkward either to feel emotion or to witness it. As a matter of fact, they much preferred people who spoke about what they really felt. So Alex sat down and plunged into the very heart of her subject at once, instead of trying to talk about anything else.

" It's terrible," she said, as Matilda had done. " Oh, I don't know what I should do without my sight ! Don't you sometimes feel inclined to say, ' Curse God and die ' ? —like the Tempter in the book of Job—it seems so bitterly hard ! "

" Oh, Alex—Alex ! " said Matilda, a little shocked.

" Well, it does. There are some trials that are just a little *too* hard for flesh and blood to bear, and that's one of them—things one doesn't dare to think about at night or when one is alone, for they make the government of the world look altogether wrong."

She paused. The poor Admiral was quite beyond his depth in such abstract questionings of the universal plan. He felt grateful for the sympathy accorded him, but bewildered by the way in which this, his special grief, had been harnessed on to the woe of the world. He pulled himself together.

" Well, well—we must all have our trials ! " he said, feeling that he had uttered a weighty truth.

" We must, indeed ! " Matilda assented, in her cooing way.

" One of my great [deprivations is the loss of the thorough, systematic study of the newspaper," the Admiral went on, happily aware that he had, so to speak, floated into shallower waters again. " I used to be a systematic newspaper reader—my *Times* was read from beginning to end in the old days. Now that is impossible."

" Do you not have it read to you ? " Matilda asked.

" Ah, yes—after a fashion. My good William, a most conscientious servant, he was with Lord Colefield for many years before his death—Lord Colefield's death, I should say—William creams the news for me every day, but it is not done in an interesting manner ; I have sometimes wondered if I could employ some intelligent youth from the village to read to me daily. But such a person would be difficult to find—I am particular. Then you have no doubt heard that my grandson, Vanburgh, has come to make his home with me ? "

" So we heard," said Alex.

" Well, I had hoped much from his coming, but I find him of very little use—an atrocious reader. Though he appears to read a great deal to himself, he cannot read aloud."

" Oh, you should *make* him do it ! " Matilda exclaimed. " It is a privilege for a young person to read aloud to one who cannot read to himself. Don't deprive your grandson of the privilege."

" Well, there are other difficulties," the Admiral began. " He holds the most perverse views in politics. He positively objects to the *Times*, and takes in some low Radical rag of his own, to feed upon its poisonous stuff every morning. Where he imbibed such views I cannot think. My poor son, with all his faults, was a Conservative and a gentleman ! "

The speech was a little unfortunate, considering the political and social views of Old Hopeful. The Admiral seemed to realize this after he had spoken, for he rose hurriedly, holding out his hand to Matilda.

" I must not keep the horses standing in the cold," he said. " Indeed, I merely looked in to pay my respects to you, Mrs. Chalmers. We are glad to see you at home again." Then, some pang of conscience striking him, he added, " Remember me to your father. He is not at home to-day ? No ? Gone away on some of his energetic businesses, no doubt. I must be off. Good-bye ! good-bye ! "

He stood up, waiting with the pathetic dependence of the blind, for some one to take him by the hand. Alex gave him her arm and led him back to the carriage. He turned as he was stepping in to say—

"Don't misunderstand me about my grandson. The lad is willing enough to read to me, and to do what he can, but he mumbles—he mumbles, or else he scurries, just those bits that are worth reading."

"Oh, I quite understand!" said Alex. "It requires a trained voice to make reading aloud agreeable, with the best will in the world."

"Exactly so—quite so—Miss Hope." He paused, and added, with the air of one bestowing largess. "You have a delightful voice, if I may say so!"

Alex laughed. "So I have been told. My Father is very particular about that. It's well, when you have very little else, to have *one* thing that is right about you!"

The Admiral made some polite reply, and drove away. Alex came slowly back into the room.

"I do wonder, Matilda, what that grandson of his can be like? Fancy his having advanced Radical views! He won't have an easy time of it, I am afraid. I don't believe Admiral Cassilis knows what Radical views are! He's such a goose, poor old man! Such a pig-headed, hidebound, intolerable, but sadly afflicted goose! It's a queer combination, isn't it?"

"Oh, Alex, you ought not to say such things about an old man!" said Matilda, laughing all the same, as she spoke.

CHAPTER VI

IT was a great joy to Alex to have Matilda at home again.
The two sisters had seen nothing of one another since
Matilda's last visit to England, many years ago, yet
they met now, not as strangers, but as friends. They
had, indeed, years of time to skirmish over in conversation ; Matilda's whole experience in Canada, and the
smaller details, none the less interesting, of Alex's life
at Crossriggs.

"Letters are all very well," Alex said ; "but there's
so much you can't write. I've been sending a letter
once a week to Canada for the last ten years, and yet I
haven't told an eighth part of all that I now find to say."

"You see, dear, you've grown up so since I left home,"
Matilda said. "And letters don't show the process of
growing up. I have come back to find you with a
character of your own—not an amorphous schoolgirl."

"I suppose you have. I've all sorts of burning ambitions and plans anyway—but I'll never be anything ; the
Gods have denied me the divine spark—that's why I do
so adore it in other people. Oh, how I do adore it ! It's
a joy to me to sit in the same room with Robert Maitland, and to see him pass across the Square—as he's doing
at this very moment."

She let the pinafore she was mending drop on her knee
as she spoke, and gazed across the sunny little Square.

"And do you know, Matilda, just because I adore
Mr. Maitland so much, I never can say a word before him

that doesn't sound silly. Do you think I am very stupid? Yet I seem to say such foolish things to him—rash statements leap to my tongue—they seem to say themselves almost—and he listens so gravely; it only takes a minute for him to find out exactly how foolish they were— then he says something that takes the stuffing, so to speak, out of my observation."

"You *are* hasty with your tongue," Matilda admitted.

"I can sometimes get him to laugh if I speak quickly— right out—exactly what I'm thinking, and that is a great temptation," Alex went on. "It makes me ambitious to do it again and I plunge in, no matter what the subject is, so long as I can say something amusing about it; and that is simply courting disaster, for Mrs. Maitland doesn't understand a joke, and Miss Elizabeth very seldom approves of one, and then her eye is turned upon me—oh, how she disapproves of me!"

"Well, you do sometimes say rash things before her," said Matilda.

"She urges me to it. When that green eye is upon me, I'm moved to a wonderful rashness of speech. But the sort of things I say to Mr. Maitland are far worse. I go on speaking about some subject and then discover that he knows all about it, and has been suffering from my ignorance all the time. Oh, it's so humiliating!"

"Do not try to be so ready to speak, then."

"As if I wouldn't go down rashly even into my grave! The leopard cannot change his spots, but in future I'm going to ask Mr. Maitland to stop me halfway before I've floundered very deeply in any subject that happens to be specially his own."

Matilda looked up at her with mild surprise. "Dear me, Alex, you speak as if Mr. Maitland were a stranger instead of a man whom we've known all our lives, who has watched us grow up and knows just how foolish we are—as well as if he were a relative of our own. I don't understand your minding at all."

" Here he is, coming to the door at this very moment," said Alexandra, turning away her face as she spoke, and pulling out her needle with a jerk.

Matilda leant down and spoke out of the window to Maitland who passed below.

" Are you coming in, Mr. Maitland ? "

" Yes, if I may," he answered, looking up. " I want to speak to your father for a little."

" Do come in. We were just speaking about you," said Matilda as he entered. She drew forward Old Hopeful's armchair for him (a venerable relic—its leathern cover all worn at the corners, so that they had been patched with a brighter shade) and busied herself in folding up the children's stockings that she had been darning, while Alex sat as if she were dreaming, still looking out of the window, with her work fallen on her lap.

" Well," said Maitland as he came in, " and what were you saying about me ? "

He sat down in the armchair facing the light, and drew his hand across his eyes with a tired gesture.

Alex turned round quickly. " I was wondering whether you would do me a great kindness," she said, rising from her place in the window niche and seating herself on a foot-stool by his chair. " You know how many and grievous my sins of speech are. Indeed, I've been thinking that my safest course would be to confine my speech solely within the limits of the conversation lozenge—you know it, I suppose ? It is entirely Scottish ; no soul in the whole of benighted England has ever been gladdened by the sight of one. Katharine's niece gets handfuls of them from her young man ; he is an almost dangerously taciturn creature, a fisherman, and they must be the greatest help to him in all the critical moments of life. They are sometimes white, and some of the more ardent sayings are printed on an intense pink lozenge. Perhaps the remarks might not be very useful in general conventional society—*Name the day*, for

instance, or *Will you be mine ?* Katharine's niece showed
me with shy delight one that she was going to give to her
fisherman—in reply, I presume, to one of those I have
mentioned. It was of a peculiarly acrid pink, brighter
than any village cheek even, and had on it just the two
coy words, *Ask mamma !* As the girl has been an orphan
for years it was a little mixed somehow, but even lozenges
aren't made with *Ask my aunt !* "

"Oh, Alex, do remember what we were saying just
before Mr. Maitland came in ! " said Matilda, laughing.

"Well," Alex went on, not heeding the interruption,
"these remarks wouldn't be of much use to me, but there
are some with only a terse monosyllable, *Yes !* or *No !*
and, after all, many people who pass for intelligent
don't say much more, and slowly build up a reputation
for prudence by the use of them ! "

She looked up at Maitland, who laughed and answered,

"Crossriggs will be terribly dull when you begin to
stick to monosyllables. I think for the present we
can't afford to let you try it."

He looked from one to other of the sisters as he spoke,
noting the contrast between them. Matilda, Alex's
senior by several years, was yet, in spite of widowhood
and all the cares of a family, the younger looking, and much
the more placid of the two. Her low white forehead
was unfurrowed, the curve of her cheek firm and comely.
But Alex had already some lines across her brow, and a
certain tragic expression lurked behind the humour in
her eyes.

"It is on her that the burden will lie," Maitland
thought, "and it is beginning to tell already." He
seemed to see a new, hard line about her mouth, and wondered what had brought it there. Alex, however, was
gay enough just then and rattled on.

"Yes; when I begin conversation by lozenge, then you
clever, prudent people will need to make fools of yourselves—some one has to do that in every community.

I've done it in the most disinterested way for the last dozen years. Now it will be your turn, Mr. Maitland. You will have to fill in silences with *banal* remarks, and hurl rash statements into gaps of conversation, until people begin to think me wise and you foolish."

"You forget that I am always exposing my folly in print—a much more fatal thing than showing it in conversation. It's the penalty of having opinions that one must express them."

"Written words *are* perhaps more deadly ; they can be cited against you for ever, of course, though there is a horrid race of people who remember even spoken words in a distressing way."

"If Alex were a little more prudent, a little less rash in speech, she would not need to be afraid of these good people with long memories," said Matilda, smiling.

"And what is the use of being alive (but once !) in an amusing world if one can't speak about it freely ? I'd rather be misunderstood all the time ! " Alex exclaimed.

"But you have never yet told me what I was to do for you ? " said Maitland.

"Just *stop me*—don't let me make a fool of myself to you," Alex said earnestly. "I don't much mind about other people, but when you give me one of your looks of cold surprise at some of my statements, I wish the ground would open and swallow me up ! "

"Alex, when you say things like that you make me hate myself," said Maitland, with sudden energy. "Do you think I am always criticizing other people and thinking I know more than they do ? "

Now what possessed Alex to make the reply she did was a mystery, unless it were that strange instinct which sometimes leads us almost unconsciously to say the wrong thing.

"I think you *are* rather superior," she said. "You wouldn't be human if you were not, living here amongst so many people less clever than yourself, with all your own little world looking up to you." Maitland did not answer, and she went on. " It's not the intellectual superiority alone, but the other kind, which is so much worse. You are superior about life—you know you are; you never despond or despair or become elated, as other ordinary people do."

There was a moment's silence. " Alex, my dear," Maitland then said, " you do talk a great deal of nonsense about things you know nothing of ; this is one of them. Matilda, did you say I could see your father ? "

He turned away as he spoke to Matilda. But as he did so, he took Alex's hand as if to atone for his hard speech.

When he left the room, Matilda said gently, " Really, Alex, you made a mistake just now. No one likes to be called superior, and I think you should show a little more respect for Mr. Maitland than you do."

" Of course I made a mistake—I'm always making them—just as Nature, darling, made a mistake in making you the mother of all these children instead of me. You'd have been so ornamental with nothing to do except curl your hair and look pretty. And I'm just made for mending and ' sorting ' a large family."

In a few minutes Old Hopeful came into the room looking very well pleased.

" I have good news ! " he exclaimed. " Robert Maitland, ever kind and generous, has given me a large contribution towards my poor friend's scheme."

" Which poor friend, Father ? You have so many."

" Grindly," said Old Hopeful, sitting down and taking up a pile of letters from the table. " I have his letter here—a very old friend; we were at college together, and I had just been feeling sad because a few shillings were all that I could spare—all that I felt justified in sending towards his scheme."

" A few shillings ! My purse contains just sevenpence-

halfpenny at this moment ! " Alex exclaimed under her
breath.

" What is the scheme, Father ? " Matilda inquired.

" Colonization—spiritual colonization," he answered.
" Merely a band of earnest, high-minded young men
going out to tea-planting in Ceylon—just to place a little
ethical leaven there—quite quietly, each one upholding
spiritual ideals amongst a society where, I fear, there
is much need for them. The tea they plant is to be dried
by a new process, which completely deprives it of its
harmful tannic acids, and the plantations are to be
cultivated entirely by some of our noble Hebridean
fishermen, who are leaving their barren rocks to try life
on a new soil."

He found the letter he was in search of, and began
to read, a smile of contentment irradiating his face.

" And Mr. Maitland has contributed towards this ? "
said Alex. Her father glanced up at her, something
in her tone struck even his ear.

" Yes, most generously—as he does all things," he
answered. Matilda trod on her sister's toes, with a
warning glance, and Alex got up and went out of the
room without uttering the words that were on the tip
of her tongue.

She knelt by the baby, who was playing on the nursery
floor with a woolly bear.

" Oh, baby, baby, sometimes you're a little bore
when you cry at night, or won't go to sleep, or will
suck your thumb ; but the old babies are dreadfully
trying at times, and one can't scold them, and they understand so little ! "

CHAPTER VII

It was nearly Christmas time now, and the coldest season of the year had come on. Alex sat alone one evening enjoying an hour of silence, for Matilda and the children had gone out to a tea-party at Miss Bessie Reid's. Miss Bessie's parties were always a delight to children; they admired her decorations, and considered her a fair and charming person, while she on her part never showed to such advantage as when entertaining young guests. What did it matter to them that her ornaments were not stones of price, or that her curls had once clung to another forehead? Her foods were toothsome to childish tastes, her ways were kind, and her sitting-rooms filled with a hundred trifles which amused them. So Matilda's children had set off in great spirits, and after they were gone Alex threw herself into an armchair, without even a book on her knee, to enjoy the unusual quiet.

Enjoyment was, perhaps, not quite the right word, for silence and solitude are all very well when one is happy, but not quite so desirable when one is careful and troubled about many things. And this was Alex's plight. She sat by the fire, one long brown hand covered her eyes, the other hung limply across the arm of her chair. Her whole attitude spoke of weariness and discouragement.

A step sounded on the pathway, and then some one came into the house without ringing the bell, as was the friendly custom of Crossriggs in those days. A minute later Maitland came into the room. He paused for a moment on the threshold.

" Why, Alex, are you asleep ? " he asked.

She started up to greet him.   " Asleep?   No!   Only
irrepressibly idle to-night.   Come and sit down.   How
delightful of you to come in on such a wickedly cold
evening ! "

She knelt on the threadbare rug and poked the
smouldering fire into a blaze, then drew up a chair for
him beside it.

" Matilda and the chicks are having tea with Bessie
Reid, and Father is in town to-day, so I'm all alone for
once.   Do you know, I believe it is a very bad thing to
have time to think ! "

She laughed as she said this, but there was a sound
in her voice that was grave enough.

" Why, what has gone wrong with your thinking ? "

Alex hesitated for a moment.   " Well," she began
slowly, " for the last three months I haven't had an hour
to myself, and when night came I was so tired that I fell
asleep at once.   But this afternoon has been dreadful.
I've just come right up against things, and I don't know
what we are going to do."

" About what ? " Maitland asked, though he had a
good idea what the trouble must be.

" Money—to put it quite plainly.   We were badly
enough off before Matilda and the children came, Heaven
knows ; still, I had all I needed, and Father all he wanted
—he's never discontented, you know—but now there's
not enough to feed and clothe them all.   I've spoken
once or twice to Father about the future, and he just
says, ' The Great Provider will provide,' and quotes the
promise about the young ravens—so descriptive of
Matilda's brood, isn't it ? so callow, and with such immense
appetites.   Then, Matilda, dear thing, has so much of
Father's temperament, she *won't worry*.   All the time
in Canada they had just been peacefully using up the
little capital they had, and before Peter died it was almost
exhausted."

" But he——— "

" Oh, he had the same happy disposition ! " Alex laughed a little bitterly.   " Matilda admired it so much— she said he hadn't a care at the end."

" A man who——— " began Maitland, with energy, and stopped himself in time.

" Yes, I know all that, and quite agree ; but he's in his grave now, poor man, and quiet in it we'll suppose, in spite of the five children unprovided for whom it is now our duty and privilege to support ! "

" Has Matilda nothing ? "

" She has about thirty pounds a year steady, and a few small extras, but what are they among so many ?   I can't make the money buy more than a limited amount of bread-and-butter—and the butter is running pretty short now !   That's what I've been thinking about this afternoon."

She sank back into her chair and sighed.

" I have been wondering about this all autumn.   I did not like to ask you," Maitland said.   He sat gazing into the fire, looking quite as grave as if the whole support of Matilda's brood were on his own shoulders.   His fine, smooth hands, that told of strength, ability, and kind-ness, almost seemed to be thinking too.

Alex watched him for a moment, and then, with one of her sudden rushes of merriment, burst into a peal of laughter.

" Oh, dear Mr. Maitland, don't take it so much to heart ! " she cried.   " You well-off people are far too serious about a monetary crisis of this sort.   We'll muddle through it somehow, like the British army. I've never been in quite such a tight place before, but I'll wedge through it in time, like a cat through a chink in the barn door.   There, that laugh has done me good, and telling you about it, too.   Let us change the subject. Have you heard of Father's latest excursion in fruitarian diet ? '"

" No, but, Alex "—Maitland hesitated, his usual composure of manner gone, his words coming slowly—"I want to say "—he stopped short, then went on with a rush—" it is intolerable to me to feel that you are suffering in this way when I have plenty. I can't bear it; it must not go on ; you must let me do something."

" Give us money? " Alex said, with an intonation that it is impossible to describe. She rose and stood before him with her hands clasped together. " Don't ever speak of it again," she said, " or you'll make me sorry that I told you. I trusted you ; I thought I might tell you."

" Does the friendship of a lifetime not privilege one to offer help when it is needed ? "

" It doesn't make it possible for me to accept it. Yet perhaps when I've tried to earn money and failed, it might be different. Paupers, I've always understood, are those who are unable to support themselves, and so have to fall back on the public."

" And how are you going to earn money ? " he asked, wincing slightly from the subject, as certain men, from chivalrous, mistaken instinct, will always do. " Come and sit down and tell me Alex, and remember it's a natural impulse to feel one should help a woman—every woman— and that my speech was not an insult especially invented for you."

" I don't quite know yet. I'm going to find out. You wait and see."

" Has Matilda no relative of her husband's who can help to educate the boys ? "

" Do you think men like Peter Chalmers ever have relatives except widowed mothers in poor circumstances ? You might know they never have ! "

" Well, I scarcely see why the burden should fall on you. The children are not yours—why should you have to slave for them ? "

Alex gave one expressive glance at him that said a

great deal she could not have put into words. Then she answered—

"Just because we *are* our brother's keeper—you know we are—and I believe I love those children every bit as much as Matilda does. I *want* to work for them. They're little and helpless, and perfect darlings, and if I can work for them it will make my life twice as well worth living—that's all!"

She sat up in her chair, all her langour gone, ready, it seemed, to fight anything; hers was a fighting spirit.

"There they are, at this moment," said Maitland, looking out of the window.

In the dim light they could see Matilda shepherding her little flock across the Square and up the garden path. The children were dancing with pleasure. Each of them carried one of those coloured balloons so dear to the heart of childhood, and the sound of their voices floated in shrilly through the window. They had contracted a Canadian intonation that was funny and rather taking, and had a certain alertness and want of shyness uncommon in Scotch children. Matilda came in, bright and composed as usual.

"Ah, Mr. Maitland, here we come to disturb the peace of the house! We have had such a nice afternoon. Miss Bessie is so good to children, and had prepared such an entertainment for them! You and Alex look very solemn. What have you been discussing?"

"Responsibility, I think, Matilda," said Maitland, rising. "But I've been discussing it so long now that I must go and earn my daily bread. Good-night, Alex. Good-night, Matilda. Glad the children enjoyed themselves."

When he had gone, Alex tried to shake off her anxious thoughts as she listened to the children's enthusiastic accounts of their party. They all gathered round her, leaning upon her, rubbing their balloons against her face, clutching at her hands, and talking in a sort of chorus.

"Pink plates, Aunt Alex—such lovely ones! I wish we had pink plates!"

"And each cake had a lovely frill of pink paper round it!"

"And Mr. Reid was there, and he told us a story, and he asked why you hadn't come too."

"I think Mr. Reid is very nice, don't you, Aunt Alex?"

"Yes, Sally."

"He's nice-looking, too, isn't he?"

"Some people think so."

"Don't you?"

Alex laughed, and glanced at her sister. "Opinions differ so much about looks, Sally. Some people, now, think me very ugly."

"Oh, no, no, no!" they all screamed in chorus, hugging her tumultuously.

"Miss Bessie is lovely, *I* think," said Peter, and the others agreed.

"She had such *beautiful* pearls," said Sally. "I wish you and mother wore jewels."

Alex and Matilda both began to laugh at this, and the children went off with their balloons to dream of the splendours of Miss Bessie's party.

"James Reid is so kind and so good," Matilda remarked when they were alone.

"Very, both, and so dull," said Alex.

"Well, if a man is honourable and kind, he doesn't require to be a genius to make a good husband," said Matilda, with as near an approach to tartness as was possible to her.

"No, indeed, dearest, husbands are seldom men of genius, or rather, perhaps, men of genius are very rarely good husbands. James Reid is as good a man as ever lived."

" Alex, if you would only——" Matilda began, but the expression on her sister's face silenced her.

" If people would only not worry me, Matilda ! I'm no Vestal Virgin, I can assure you, but certain things don't attract me about married life, and I'd rather stay as I am."

" A happy marriage——" Matilda began.

" Of course, we all know that, and pray let every one that can make a happy marriage make themselves happy by marriage. Only let others who differ from them be happy in their own way. Doubtless ten years hence will see me filled with a resolute galvanized happiness like Miss Bessie Reid's. Then I'll be sorry I did not choose the other kind in time ! "

She went off singing to herself, and Matilda sighed, saying half aloud—

" Who on earth can it be ? "

CHAPTER VIII

ABOUT this time the exigencies of income made Alex place the whole household upon vegetarian diet. Mr. Hope was delighted.

"We shall find health and happiness in it, dear Alex, I am persuaded; it is gratifying to see that you at last adopt my principles," he said, and the girl smiled rather grimly, for with a searing wind blowing from the east, and bitter frost making hungry children ravenous, it seemed hardly the weather in which to begin a more ethereal diet. Matilda acquiesced in the new order a little reluctantly.

"I'm not quite sure how it will suit the children. *Can* cabbage be as nourishing as beef and mutton, in spite of all that dear Father says?" she hinted. "Don't you think, Alex, that we might, just while the weather is so cold, run an account with the butcher?"

To this suggestion Alex would not pay heed for an instant.

"No—if we can't pay, we don't eat," she said doggedly.

"But, my dear, consider the children," Matilda objected.

"I don't care. We must try them on this sort of food, and if it hurts them I'll see if I can get a situation of some kind, that's all I can do, only, whatever happens, we mustn't get into debt."

Matilda rather doubtfully agreed to this, and the vegetarian dinners were begun. They were not a success. The children, accustomed to lavish Canadian meals, did not approve of this simple diet, and in spite of all their mother's admonitions could not quite hide their feelings. One bitter day in January the family meal was little short of a tragedy. The cereal which formed its main constituent happened to be singed, and singed cereal is not very nice.

Poor little Mike, who was too young to speak anything but the whole truth, laid down his spoon and said plaintively, " I want meat, please," while the other children, after one pleading glance at their mother, gulped down the singed porridge with an expression of disgust. When dessert came they bit into their frozen apples with little squeals of pain, and tears were rapidly coming, when Alex made a timely suggestion that the apples might be roasted on strings before the fire. This saved the situation, though Old Hopeful protested that the " raw juices " were much more beneficial. Alex produced a ball of twine, and made wonderful arrangements with hat-pins stuck into the old wooden mantelpiece, so that soon a row of apples was rotating before the fire, the sap bubbling with a delicious smell, while the children squatted on the hearthrug to watch.

" Oh, dear me ! " Alex sighed, " this isn't at all a successful day's feeding."

She felt anxious and depressed as she watched the now happy children, who had already, with the blessedly short memory of childhood, forgotten all about the singed porridge.

" I'm going out, Matilda," said Alex, rather abruptly, " going alone, so you'll have to look after the chicks by yourself to-day."

Matilda looked at her in surprise. " Why, what mysterious errand are you going on ? " she asked.

Alex did not answer, and left the room a few minutes later.

She went out, and took the solitary road which lies to

the north of Crossriggs. In old coaching days this was one of the highways between England and Scotland, and many a merry coachload had passed along it. Now it is but little used ; one may walk for a mile without meeting anything more interesting than a string of farm carts or a ploughman with his team.

It was a bitter afternoon, yet when Alex had walked for about a mile she sat down on one of the low dykes by the roadside, apparently forgetting the cold. Her thoughts were busy with something else, and suddenly she exclaimed aloud—"I can't! I can't!" as if she were rejecting some suggestion that had come to her.

The sound of her own voice in that solitary place startled her. She looked up and shivered. The wind soughed across the empty fields with the low, gurgling note of winter's breath. She rose and stood wringing her hands together, as if in an agony of uncertainty. The next moment she began to walk swiftly along the road in the direction of Foxe Hall.

At the avenue gate she stopped and fumbled with the lock—turned back, as if uncertain whether to go through the gate, then opened it, and began to walk even more quickly along the dark, tree-bordered road. Once in sight of the house, however, Alex paused, and came up to the door in a more dignified manner.

She was going to call on Admiral Cassilis, though by this time she had almost got the length of praying that he should not be at home.

"Now then, Alexandra Hope, remember Cranmer or Latimer, or whoever it was, who said in the flames, *Play the man !* That's what you have to do!" she admonished herself.

The Admiral was at home. Alex followed the butler through the hall, where a large fire was burning—quite unnecessarily large, she thought bitterly, for there were not five little cold children squatting round it roasting apples on strings. "If we only had fires like that at home!" she sighed.

"Miss Hope, sir," the servant said, ushering her into the Admiral's study. Like the hall, the room was deliciously warm, and there was a pleasant scent of flowers in the air.

The Admiral did not smoke, and he was feverishly particular, so there was an indescribable atmosphere, perceptible only to the housekeeping sense of woman, that meant well-kept rooms where dusting and cleaning go on continually. Alex was keenly sensitive to the beautiful side of life; even as she crossed the floor to greet the old man, she said to herself, "How wonderfully soothing it must be to live in a well-kept house—heigh-ho for the dust and shabbiness and age of everything we possess—nothing fresh and delicious like this! But oh, it's ugly enough as far as taste goes!"

The Admiral rose to meet her, and stood with a hand on the back of his chair, afraid to step forward without guidance.

The dependence of the attitude struck Alex in a moment and smote her conscience.

"Fancy feeling envious of him—I who have such an excellent pair of eyes!" she thought.

The Admiral wore an expression of no small astonishment, though he said genially enough that he was glad to see her. Alex sat down, and without giving herself time to hesitate dashed at her subject.

"Yes, I'm glad you happened to be at home," she said, "for I've come to see you about business. I wondered if you really did want some one to read to you, because I know a person who would be glad to undertake to do so."

"Ah—umph, I'm sure you're very kind to have remembered me," the old man began, stroking down his stock and fingering his pearl pin as usual. "But between ourselves, I fear that any person from the village would annoy me by provincialities of accent, faults of elocution, and so on. The fact is that I am particular about such matters. I like an educated voice—foolish perhaps—but the pleasure of hearing is one of the few still left to me, and it is essential to my enjoyment of reading aloud that I should hear the voice of an educated person. When my good William reads to me it is a continual annoyance to listen to his enunciation. You understand ? "

" Yes, perfectly. This person I speak of *is* educated ; has been very carefully taught to read aloud."

" Then I am afraid the remuneration I am prepared to give would seem insufficient. Men of education, of course, naturally look for a good return for their talents. The fact is that I want a good thing cheap, Miss Hope —a difficult thing to get ! " He laughed a dry old laugh as he spoke.

" I hope you don't mind my having asked you about it ? " said Alex.

" Not at all—not in the least. The only hesitation I feel is about the quality of the reading. Have you heard this young person yourself ? "

" No ; but my Father, who is a great critic of elocution, has, and is quite satisfied."

" Well, perhaps the young man would be willing to come up and let me hear him. But why is he anxious to get such a small unremunerative post ? I trust he has no bad habits necessitating a stay in a quiet neighbourhood like ours ? "

Alex laughed suddenly and merrily at this suggestion, and the laugh helped her.

" Might I ask, supposing the reader suited you, how much you would be prepared to give ? "

" Hum—let me see. I had scarcely gone into the subject so exactly. What would he say to a shilling an hour, two hours a day ? "

" Would you think two and sixpence a day too

much ? " Alex asked. Her voice trembled ; this was dreadful.

The Admiral tried a little mental arithmetic before he answered, and in the meanwhile Alex sat holding on to the arms of her chair in desperate suspense.

" Well, two and sixpence a day—not a very large sum if the right person were to appear," he announced at last. " But who is the young man ? You have not mentioned his name."

Alex clenched her cold hands together and took the plunge.

" I will not keep you in the dark any longer," she said. " I was going to offer my own services ; not that I am a very good thing, perhaps, but I want very much to earn a little money ; " she paused, and tried to steady her trembling voice.

The old man's face had flushed, an expression of complete astonishment swept across it ; he hummed, hawed, and drummed on the arm of his chair in evident embarrassment.

" But, my dear Miss Hope, I could offer you nothing that would make it worth your while ; I really could not think of allowing you to undertake the work for such remuneration as I am prepared to give."

Alex bent forward ; she was painfully flushed too, though of course the Admiral did not see this, her voice shook, but her words were very much to the point.

" If I can read to you in a way that will really give satisfaction, I shall be very glad to take any reasonable payment you offer."

" But—but really, I had no idea," he stammered.

" My Father taught me very carefully himself, and I have had a great deal of practice in reading aloud," said Alex. " But, of course, I have never done it as a matter of business before, so I should consider the sum you named quite sufficient to begin with."

She paused, realizing that in her eagerness to have the

matter settled she had perhaps made it difficult for the Admiral to refuse her offer. The horrible thought almost suffocated her for a moment. She would have liked just to rise and bolt out of the room without saying another word.

But in matters of business even a foolish old man who has been accustomed to command is more efficient than a clever woman. The Admiral had now quite regained his composure. He cleared his throat and proceeded in a brisk, businesslike way.

" Very good. Now, Miss Hope, if you will be kind enough to take up any book that you happen to see on the table and open it at random and read me a few pages, I can judge instantly whether your style of reading suits my ear, for I am a trifle deaf as well as blind, alas ! "

He sat back in his chair and folded his hands, and poor Alex got up and lifted the first book she saw on the table. Then, sitting down beside him, she pushed up her veil with her clammy hands and opened the book at random.

" Oh, it's poetry—Wordsworth—do you like that ? " she exclaimed, seeing what it was.

" Poetry ? Hum, I prefer prose ; but still it is a test of a reader. Go on, Miss Hope ; one of my grandson's books, left on my table, as usual, I suppose. Is there nothing else ? "

" There's Whitaker's Almanack and a pamphlet on geology," said Alex, with a small laugh.

" Well, never mind, go on with the poem, anything, a few verses merely."

Alex opened the book and ran her eyes down the page, then began to read—

> " The gods to us are merciful, and they
> Yet further may relent . . .' "

She had opened at the middle of " Laodamia," a

poem probably as little suited to the comprehension of the Admiral as anything could well have been ; but it was familiar to her from childhood, and the rising beauty of the words arrested her attention even in this moment of embarrassment.

> " ' He spake of love . . .' "

she read, her low, rich voice growing clear again, as the familiar line flowed on—

> " ' Such love as spirits feel
> In worlds whose course is equable and pure.' "

There was a movement behind her, and the light on the page was obstructed for a moment, but she never noticed it and read on with a sound almost like a musical note in her voice which made her reading at times delightful to the ear.

> " ' No fears to beat away, no strifes to heal,
> The past unsighed for and the future sure.
> Spake as the witness of a second birth
> For all that is most perfect upon earth.
> Of all that is most beauteous, imaged there
> In happier beauty—more pellucid streams,
> An ampler ether—a diviner air,
> And fields invested with purpureal gleams.' "

She drew a long breath, exclaiming, " Oh, surely— surely, they are the most beautiful lines ever written ! "

A sudden sharp clapping of hands made her start wildly and look round, whilst the Admiral turned in his chair.

A tall young man stood on the hearthrug ; a young man with a dark head and very bright eyes, who looked now rather shyly at the palms of his hands, as if ashamed of having clapped them so loudly.

" Is that you, Van ? " called the Admiral. " You have interrupted Miss Hope. Miss Hope, this is my grandson, Vanbrough. I beg to apologize for the interruption."

" So do I indeed, Miss Hope ; I couldn't help it," said the lad, coming forward to shake hands, and now smiling broadly, no longer looking shy, for there was something about Alex which invariably put the most self-conscious young man at his ease.

(" Fatally, I do it," she used to say. " As fatally as I repel old ladies or really proper people of any age do I attract boys. I think my soul was a boy for a time in a previous existence, and I've often wished it were one now.")

She smiled frankly at this one and held out the book, saying, " This is yours, isn't it ? I was just reading to the Admiral as an experiment."

" Yes—yes ; Van, may I ask you to leave the room for a few minutes. Miss Hope and I were transacting a little business."

Van looked from one to the other, astonished, but he left the room as he was told to do.

" Ah," said the old man, as the door closed behind him, " your voice is beautiful, Miss Hope, beautiful, and your articulation is perfect. Poetry, of course, is a thing I have no use for, although you read it remarkably well. We've no poets now-a-days—parrots, all mere parrots, these modern men since Byron died. But now be kind enough to try a page of Whitaker, just as a final test."

" Does he think Wordsworth a modern or a parrot— or both ? " thought Alex, smiling to herself as she opened Whitaker and began to read.

" Very good—capital ! I catch every word. Not such bad reading, Whitaker," exclaimed the delighted old man, who evidently found the page she had been reading very much to his taste. " Well, consider the matter settled, then, Miss Hope. You come every day except Saturday, but Sunday included, and read for an hour and a half, and the remuneration is—shall we say a guinea a week ? "

" You mentioned seventeen shillings, I think," said Alex.

" Oh, but that was for a different class of reader."

" But I cannot——" she began.

He waved his hand. " Don't mention the matter again. I consider it a favour to get your services at any price. So let us consider it as settled. I shall hope to see you "—he corrected himself a little sadly—" to hear you, I should say, at three o'clock to-morrow, if that is convenient to you."

Alex assured him that it was, and she got up to go away, trembling now in every limb with an intoxication of relief because her ordeal was over. She scarcely heard the Admiral's last words, and as she went down the long passage to the front door her feet seemed to tread upon air.

Coming out on the broad flight of steps, she found herself again confronted by young Cassilis, who was teaching a dog to jump over a stick.

At another time Alex would have stayed to watch the lesson ; now, conscious of her flushed cheeks and trembling hands she wanted to hurry past him with a word, but he jumped up, saying awkwardly—

" I'm awfully sorry I interrupted you. I did not mean to, really, only you read so well I had to applaud."

" I'm coming to read to the Admiral every day. We've settled that," said Alex.

" Oh, I say—I wish I might be there too ! Might I ? "

" To listen to the newspapers for two hours without stopping ? It won't be poetry, you know ! " said Alex, smiling at him.

He laughed, walking along with his hands in his pockets, the puppy he had been training walloping about the road in front of them, turning round every now and then to fawn upon Alex with mud-bespattered paws.

The avenue was almost dark, for the high old trees shaded the road, even when they were bare. At the far end the light was shining again, like a door of hope; Alex would fain have shaken off her young companion, for the boy annoyed her almost as much as the dog, and she was longing to fly home as fast as she could, tingling with impatience to tell her news to Matilda. But Van insisted on accompanying her right down to the gate, and only then, with visible reluctance, bade her good-night.

" Poor boy—all alone with that dull old man in that big house—no wonder he was glad to have some one to speak to ! " she thought. " But I was almost afraid that, like the puppy, he would flounce round and run back after me again."

She hurried on, no longer feeling the cold, lifting her face to the sky with a happy chuckle.

" How fortunate I have been ! How glad I am I did it ! Oh, what will father and Matilda say, I wonder ? "

In the meantime the young man had slowly returned to the house. Coming into the library it seemed that there was still in it the unwonted sensation of a feminine presence. The chair Alex had been sitting on was still drawn forward beside the Admiral's, the book lay on the table, the Admiral himself was fidgeting about the room.

" I must tell William to move that table; it is in the way of Miss Hope's chair. I like to have the voice directed towards me as she reads. She has a lovely voice. I always thought that Alexander Hope had traces of good family about him, if he had not adopted these views "—this was accompanied by a nod in Van's direction—" which no gentleman can ever hold. It destroys the natural taste as nothing else does—that loathsome Radical talk."

The young man, standing vacantly by the window in

the twilight, opened his lips to make some retort, and then, thinking better of it, took up his book of poetry and went off to his own room, where he could smoke and read what he liked.

It was not a harmonious household, in spite of being such a small one.

CHAPTER IX

How Alex raced home when she had heard the avenue gate clang behind the young man! The hard, frost-bound road rang under her light footsteps, the keen air whistled past her—it was all delicious! Shod with triumph, she could have run all the way back.

As she came near the village, she moderated her pace. The lights shone in the windows with sudden little twinkles like stars; the great cold kept people indoors now that the dusk was falling, and the Square was deserted. She stood irresolute, wondering whether she should rush home and tell Matilda or go in and tell Mr. Maitland of her good fortune. The blinds were still up in Orchard House, and she could see the children crowd-ing round the table, playing some game together. On the other side of the Square, in the more orderly Maitland household, the blinds were drawn down, and only a dull red glow came through them into the darkness.

Alex turned in at the Manse gate, opened the hall door, and entered quietly. Everything was warm and still and exquisitely tidy as usual. Behind a closed door, she could hear a faint hum of voices—Mrs. Maitland and Aunt E. V. were talking together; but Alex did not wish to see either of them. She ran across the hall and tapped at the study door.

"Come in," said Maitland, and she entered the room where he sat writing at a table. "Oh," he began, jumping up when he saw who it was.

But without a word of preamble Alex came towards him and began, in a breathless recitative—

"Shall it be one leg of mutton, one round of beef, one fowl, one pound of Cambridge sausages? Or—four pounds of stewing steak, seven pounds of neck of mutton, one sirloin of beef, and six pounds of tripe? Or—two rabbits, one fowl, six pounds loin of veal, two pounds shin of beef, and three pounds of mince?"

Maitland stood looking at her, astonished by this outburst of curious eloquence.

"My dear Alex," he said, "why do you favour me with your bill of fare?"

"You think me quite crazy, don't you? But I'm not; wait till you hear my news. I've just been to see Admiral Cassilis, and he has engaged me to read to him for two hours every day, and I am to have a guinea a week for it. And do you know the amount that can be purchased for a guinea a week? I've been doing up imaginary butchers' books all the way home. Oh, I'm so glad, I'm so happy!"

She sank with a sigh of weariness into the chair that Maitland had pushed up for her.

"I'm so tired now that it is done. It was dreadful asking him about it," she said.

Maitland stood beside her without uttering one word. Alex had been too much occupied with her own excitement to notice that when she told him about her engagement to read to the Admiral he had frowned for a minute. Now he made an effort to speak lightly.

"Is it possible that such good fortune has befallen you, that you are going to read to a man like the Admiral for such large sums, when you wouldn't let one of your old friends offer you a little help!"

"Oh, don't be horrid!" cried Alex. "Please understand, *don't* have a tone in your voice like that. You will destroy all my pleasure if you do!"

Maitland walked up and down the room once or twice,

then he stopped behind her chair where she could not see his face, and answered ; but the voice was not quite his natural one.

"All right, Alex. I am very glad you have got what you wanted. It is splendid, and I am sure the Admiral is a very lucky old man."

"He is, as far as that goes," Alex acknowledged frankly. "I'm too good to read *his* sort of reading. But do you think that anything is too good to sell, if you want the money ? "

"But will such a small sum as this really make any difference to you ? " he asked.

"That shows how much you know about small sums, as I've told you before ! You don't really understand about being poor at all. My guinea will provide dinners of endless variety and dazzling quality, if one can use such a word about meat ! I don't care a scrap even if the dear children's clothes go to rags, as long as they have enough of good plain food. Manners, after all, cost nothing, and if a boy is well fed and well mannered he should get on in life, even if his clothes are shabby."

Maitland was silent for a minute, then he answered, "It seems to me you take things too lightly. There is all the future of those children to be thought of—their education, and all their possible and impossible illnesses. It isn't only a matter of food and clothing."

"Oh, my dear sir," cried Alex, "it's easy to see that you've been well off all your life, or you wouldn't speak like that ! " Her face grew grave as she went on. "It doesn't do to look too far ahead if you live as we do, like the young ravens. And it doesn't do to think that *any-thing* is necessary, either. Just take the question of boots now—I suppose you would say that boots were necessary ? Well, the boots will either come, or not come, or partially come—boots for Mike, and none for Peter, and perhaps Sally's only to be ' solt and helt,' as Katharine calls it—somehow or other. One is never

left absolutely shoeless—at least, I never have been yet.
Oh, it doesn't do to take boots too seriously, and so
with most things. It would soon wear out one's nerve
tissues." She paused, laughing now.

" That's all very well in joke, but the matter of these
children's future, Alex, is terribly serious. Do you ever
realize that ? "

Alex's face went suddenly white. She leant forward
with one of her dramatic gestures, laying her hand on
the arm of Maitland's chair.

" Don't make me realize it. Don't make me acknowledge that I do. It's really safer if you have to walk on a
tight-rope across Niagara to imagine that the Falls
aren't there ! It would drive me crazy if I allowed
myself to realize things for a moment. It's only by
shutting my eyes and going on day by day that I get
through it at all."

Maitland looked at her with surprise and admiration,
for she had got hold of a sort of working rule of life
which had a certain value of its own, like the unscientific
yet practical methods by which certain workmen can
produce excellent results, though they cannot explain
how it is done.

" Alex," he said, " you have a genius for living !
You just know how to do it, which is what very few
people know. You get the savour out of it. You're
alive, and most of us, with our prudence and foresight
and realization of our duties, are as dead as stones !
Now tell me about this business with the Admiral. Did
he ask you to become his reader ? "

" No," said Alex, bluntly. " I asked him. Do you
think it was very extraordinary of me ? I screwed
myself up and went to ask him. Ugh ! it was horrible."

Maitland let a pencil he had been holding fall suddenly
on the floor, and stooped to pick it up. His face was
flushed with the faint colour it had when he got angry—
a colour that many a woman might have envied.

Alex glanced at him a little curiously, then she went on. " He was quite pleasant. He is a decent old person, after all. If he had chosen, he might have been so disagreeable ; but he wasn't, he was quite nice."

Maitland grunted rather crossly at this speech. " When do you begin ? " he asked.

" To-morrow, right off. Oh, I'm so relieved ! I feel as if a millstone had rolled off me ! "

As she left the room, she turned to say—

" Oh, I saw the boy too—the grandson—he is a great tall fellow, very good-looking, but not at all the sort of young man to get on with his grandfather."

" No—he's not. I've just spoken to him. He seems very ill-pleased with his life there."

" No wonder. It is trying for a young thing like that. I must go home now, and tell my news to Matilda. See how I've interrupted you ! "

She looked at the papers on his desk in a conscience-stricken way.

" You could never interrupt me," he answered, as he went along with her to the door. The hall was empty, but just as they passed the drawing-room, Miss Maitland came out.

" Why, Alexandra, I did not know that you were here ! " she said.

Her eyebrows were raised in an expression of intentional surprise. The green eye was fixed upon Alex.

" Oh, I ran in to give Mr. Maitland a bit of good news ; he'll tell you. I've no time to wait."

" These are Robert's working hours. It is better to come earlier," said Aunt E. V.

" Yes, I know, it was dreadful of me. I am the chief of sinners ! " said Alex, flippantly, as she hurried away.

" Why are you always so hard upon Alex, Aunt Elizabeth ? " Maitland inquired.

" I was not severe enough," replied Miss Maitland, calmly. " She never considers the look of things.

None of the Hopes do." Robert did not ask her what she meant. "I am fond of Alex," she continued, "if she were only curbed. Mr. Hope, with all his whims, is an amiable man; she has his good-nature, and her sex will keep her from working as much harm in the lives of others as he has done. She won't preach—at least, I hope not."

Alex, meanwhile, had hastened home.

"Matilda! Matilda! Where are you?" she cried when she entered the house.

"Here! What is it? Is anything wrong?" Matilda answered, looking round anxiously, as Alex came into the room.

"Wrong? No, fifty times right!" she exclaimed, sinking into a chair. "Do you know that you are speaking to a professional woman, Matilda? I have got a job that will give me a guinea a week—me—just think of it—without the expenditure of anything but breath. It is what many a ploughman has to bring up a family of nine children on. I shall earn it by my voice! There, what do you think of that, madam?"

At first, when she heard the tale, Matilda was very dubious, but she ended by sharing her sister's sense of relief.

"Oh, Alex," she said, when they had finished discussing the subject in all its bearings, "if there was anything *I* could do, I would do it. I cannot bear that you should toil for the children. I have often wondered if I should not have tried to struggle on in Canada instead of coming home to burden Father and you."

"Hoots-toots! as Katharine says, how can you talk such nonsense, woman! Where should you be, but with your own father and sister? You were not meant to face the world alone, Matilda. You ought to remember the early Victorian man, whose wife had been obliged to arrange affairs during his illness. When he recovered he said, 'I found I had gained an adviser, a competent manager and companion, but I *had lost my gentle, helpless Anna !*' So take warning, and remain what you are, and let me do the fighting !"

She ran away then, laughing. Matilda, not altogether pleased—as who would have been ?—to be called a " gentle, helpless Anna," went off to find her father, and to break to him as skilfully as she could the terms of Alex's engagement at Foxe Hall.

Later that evening (Katharine had already been dispatched to the butcher with an order, causing Old Hopeful to say sadly, " Carnivorous, Matilda, carnivorous ! Your little ones would thrive better on a fruitarian diet, could you but bring yourself to try it for a year "), as they sat together when the children were all in bed, Alex said suddenly to her sister—

" By the way, young Van Cassilis came into the room when I was reading, and he walked down to the gate with me."

" What is he like ? "

" Oh, a tall boy, about twenty-one, I should think, with a black head and very nice eyes. He must be fond of reading, for the book I took up to read at first was a Wordsworth, and the Admiral said it belonged to him. How dull he must be ! We should have him down here and try to cheer him up."

" He won't find much to amuse him here," said Matilda. " Two quiet women and all these noisy children ! "

" Now, Matilda, don't pose—even in your own sweet way ! You know perfectly well that ' two quiet women,' as you call us, are very much more amusing company than old Admiral Cassilis, or, I venture to say, than any one the young man is likely to meet in that house ; and as for the children, there are no children like them, I think, and so do you, so there ! "

Matilda laughed, and did not deny it. She was sewing busily, but Alex lay back in her chair, her long arms hanging listlessly at her sides, enjoying an hour of relief and perfect idleness.

"A nice boy with a black head," she went on, looking into the logs that glowed red on the hearth (dried wood from old trees was one of the few results from Mr. Hope's orchard). "He had understanding eyes, too, but I wonder what he made of—

> "' . . . Such love as spirits feel,
> In worlds whose course is equable and pure '—

"Oh dear, Matilda, how beautiful it is—how divine !—

> "' No fears to beat away, no strifes to heal,
> The past unsighed for, and the future sure.'

"Can't you imagine wakening after the weariness of life, from the sleep of death, on your first morning in heaven, feeling what it was to find that true ? "

But the widow of Peter Chalmers couldn't quite follow her here.

"Certainly Father will be pleased that you are getting some use out of all that reading of poetry now," she answered, as she folded up her work.

"Don't suppose I'm going to read poetry to the Admiral ! " said Alex, beginning to laugh. "A page of Whitaker was what really took his fancy. He would disinherit any grandson who ever wrote a line, I'm sure ! "

CHAPTER X

THE first reading went off very successfully, for the *Times*, when "systematically studied," as the Admiral said, gives a fine variety of mental food. Happily for herself, Alex had been always trained by her father to take a lively interest in public affairs, so her rendering of the political articles was very satisfactory. She even found herself involved sometimes in discussions with her employer, which varied the hours of reading to a surprising degree. Of course the Admiral was one of the men who cannot brook a moment's contradiction, and even a difference of opinion quite annoyed him, so Alex had to be very careful in what she said. His ideas were refreshingly narrow; he simply gave no quarter at all to "innovations," as he termed everything in the nature of progress.

Alex, brought up in a more generous school, could not help contrasting his mental attitude with that of her father. "Progress" was Old Hopeful's great watchword. How often he repeated the axiom : "We cannot stand still ; it is always either forward or backward." Now she found herself confronted with the spectacle of a mind which honestly believed all change to be a mistake.

Yet, as she sometimes thought rather bitterly, her father, for all his ideas, had never accomplished anything of a practical nature in his life, while this hide-bound, stupid old man had been, as far as he knew, a good officer and capable commander of others.

"It's practice, not theory, that works," she thought,

" and perhaps practice is better without theories—better than theories that are never practised!" And then some utterance more than usually crass from the Admiral would make her turn with sudden sympathy to her father's nobler, more open views.

Sometimes, just for fun, she would find herself trying to draw the Admiral into a fuller expression of his creed, and it amused her more than she could tell. He, quite unconscious of her amusement, was only too willing to divulge his views, and began to think her a wonderfully intelligent young woman. One afternoon they had been talking with great animation over something in the papers, and when Alex rose to go she was surprised to find how late it was. The Admiral insisted that tea was just coming in.

" You must stay and have tea," he urged, quite roused and pleased by the way in which his afternoon, generally so long and dull, had passed.

" It's getting dark," Alex objected.

But the old man would not listen to her. " Van will see you to the avenue gate," he said.

So she had to consent to stay.

When Van came in he looked round, thinking how different this was from their ordinary afternoons. His grandfather quite roused and in the best of spirits ; the whole room looking more cheerful ; the young woman making tea for them ; the Admiral's great old hound sitting close beside her as if trying to get his share, too, of the happier atmosphere ; the very tea tasted better, and the Admiral forgot to grumble at Van for having been smoking.

It was quite a happy little party. Alex talked away, and kept both men amused and pleased so that they did not rub on one another, as too often happened when they were alone.

" I hope the reading is a success ? " Van asked. He had never intruded on it again.

"Miss Hope's pitch of voice suits my ear to a nicety,' said the Admiral, with a nod of contentment. "She reads to my entire satisfaction, and though we don't agree in all our ideas—why, a little difference is wholesome."

"Is it? That's something quite new!" Van said in a low aside to Alex.

But the old man caught the words. He coughed, and remarked severely—

"There is a great difference between the somewhat fanciful—if I may be permitted the word, Miss Hope— political ideas that a woman may hold if she chooses, and the "—he began to get angry—"rabid, poisonous nonsense, which would ruin our country in a year if allowed to spread, that your horrid Radical papers rant about."

He coughed again, and set down his teacup violently, forgetting to feel for the edge of the table, so that the cup fell off and was broken. Alex saw his old face flush with vexation at his awkwardness, and she gave a warning glance at Van as she picked up the fragments and hurriedly changed the subject.

"Surely you read novels sometimes! I couldn't live without reading novels," she began.

"No—very seldom," said the Admiral. "I do look into one occasionally, or have one read to me, but I seldom finish them. They do not interest me. A sad one I never read." He coughed, and Alex waited for the time-honoured platitude that was sure to follow. "Life," said the Admiral, sententiously, as if uttering something that had never been said before, "is sad enough with-out fiction." He took a gulp of tea, and thought he had settled the question.

"Oh," cried Alex, "indeed it is! But the sadness is so different—so long and hard and spread out, compared to the brief romantic sorrows of fiction, that it does one good to read about them, I think, and then we can imagine that ours are going to be like that!"

" And there is other nonsense," continued the Admiral, with a clearing of his throat that indicated his determination to utter the very last word that could be said on the subject, "all that nonsense about *love*, so-called. Why, the books now are a disgrace ! In my young days "—he coughed with a moment's hesitation, and Van bent down his head in a convulsion of silent laughter—" there was none of this sort of thing. If a man was going to run away with his friend's wife, he *did* it, and said no more about it, like Lord Nelson. But now in some of these books a man will shilly-shally and talk about feelings and so on through two whole volumes, and many pages of pestilent trash about ' love.' "

" Nelson was a great man," said Alex, smiling as she rose to go away, " but I cannot agree with your admiration of that part of his conduct."

" No, no ; don't misunderstand me, pray," began the old man. " I don't defend such an action, but it *was action*, Miss Hope, not that everlasting talk, talk, talk, that the world is full of now."

Alex bid him good-bye, laughing a little. " I really must go home to my family ; they will think I have been lost on the way."

Van followed her into the hall. " Did you leave your wraps here ? " he asked.

Now the truth was Alex possessed nothing that could properly be called a wrap. Her jacket had already seen three winters' wear, and this autumn she had reluctantly been obliged to remove the bit of bald sealskin which had trimmed it hitherto—it was past use.

" And unless I kill the cat, I don't see where I am to get a new fur necklet," Alex had said to Matilda, and they had both laughed gaily at the little joke. But that had been before the frost came. This evening it was not very amusing to have no thick garment to put on, though Alex would not have confessed it to herself for worlds.

" Oh, I didn't bring anything extra with me," she said.
" I don't wrap myself up much."

She turned the collar of her coat round her ears as
some slight protection against the north wind.

" I'm afraid you'll think me terribly soft then," said
Van, as he shuffled himself into a coat with a fur collar.
" You see, I've lived abroad until now, and it feels
desperately cold in Scotland."

" Indeed it does to-night," Alex assented.

" Desperately cold and desperately dull," the young
man pursued, as they walked along. " Poor old Gran
isn't what you'd call an exhilarating companion."

" Are you going to be here always now ? " Alex asked.

" Yes, worse luck ! Gran is the only relation I have
now that my father is gone."

There was a slight hesitation in his voice that made
Alex remember long-forgotten tales of the Admiral's ill-
doing son who had disappeared below the Crossriggs
horizon many years before.

" Ah, you will soon find all sorts of things to interest
you, and get fond of the neighbourhood, as we have all
done," she said.

" I expect you have a good sort of home, which makes
all the difference," he said, with ill-concealed envy in his
voice.

" Oh, mine is ever such a poor sort of home," said Alex,
" with nothing outward to make it desirable. But there's
one thing—we're never dull. My Father is a great
theorist, and, as Browning says, we 'are hurled from change
to change unceasingly,' our 'souls' wings' never get
a chance to furl ! "

Van laughed delightedly. " How ? " he asked.

" Oh, well, he—Father—is always bringing new people
to the house, or trying new experiments in diet. I used
to think it dreadful when I was younger, but now I've
come to see that it makes life more lively. If we had
not these little excitements we should feel our poverty

much more, and keep thinking about ourselves all the time."

" I think the new diets must be trying. Don't you hate them ? "

" Not altogether—they're sometimes amusing. Great excitement prevails over the preparation of the new repast. None of the ordinary joints and chops, you may be sure ; it will be ' nuttose ' or ' glutose,' or something with even a weirder name, and in very strange colours. But he does not insist that we shall all eat his foods ; he only looks grieved when we eat our own."

" And what sort of people does your father bring to the house ? "

" Well, for instance, last year there were the poor, dear Polish Jews. That was a serious excitement. Father was lecturing on vegetarianism one evening down at Leith, and when the lecture was over he started to go back to Edinburgh, and instead somehow found himself down at the docks. He was thinking over some new problem, and he loses all sense of locality when he begins to do that. When he got to the docks an emigrant ship had just come in. So he stopped to look on, and presently saw a family of Polish Jews, father, mother, and children, none of whom could speak a word of English. Father, of course, has a smattering of every language under heaven, so he spoke to them in Yiddish, and then and there they attached themselves to him. Well, the long and the short of it was that he arrived home late at night *with* those Polish Jews, and they lived in the apple-loft for two months."

" Two months ! " Van exclaimed.

" Yes, and we all got so fond of them ! But the children went and caught measles, and then the mother caught it and had to be nursed. It was a lively time, I can assure you ! "

" But was it not a great trouble to have all these people to support ? "

"At first it was an anxiety ; but after the first week all our neighbours were so good. Father has a theory that one is bound to do charitable things because it urges others to do the same, and really there is some truth in that. The first week every one laughed at our adopted family. The next week, when the children fell ill, they one and all became so kind. They sent clothes and food and money till those Jews were in a fair way to be petted to death. But at last Mr. Maitland, who is the person who does everything for every one at Crossriggs, got work for the man on one of the farms, and they were taken off our hands. Only one thing saddened Father— that there was nothing they relished so much as bacon-fat !" Alex stopped at the avenue gate and held out her hand. "Good-night ! You mustn't come any further with me. It's not a bit dark."

"Oh, do let me come !" Van said, so earnestly that she could not refuse his escort. He began suddenly, "I hate life here because I've no one to speak to who understands the sort of things I say, or the kind of life I want to lead." He paused, ashamed of this sudden confidence, and added impulsively, "You're different, somehow !"

"What do you wish to do with your life ?" Alex asked gently.

"I don't know," he answered ; "but oh—I'd like to do something for the world, something to make it better. My father used to know Mazzini. I saw him once when I was very little."

"Ah," said Alex, "isn't it wonderful how long an influence will live ? It's like a stream of water—even when it seems all lost, it goes on making things grow where it has passed by !"

"I—I—one doesn't forget what one has heard about men like that, even when one lives with old people who think everything that has life in it is wrong, and want one to sink into——"

He stopped, and Alex did not encourage the allusion to his grandfather.

They walked on in silence, the young man looking up through the web of bare branches above them at the pale and distant stars. For a moment Alex felt inclined to laugh at his outburst, but the next she rebuked herself for her want of sympathy.

" We're only young once, and that for such a piteously short time," she thought. " And after all, why should I laugh if he has fixed on Mazzini as his model ? It is better to aim at a star than at a kite, even if it's funny to hear such an aspiration from the grandson of Admiral Cassilis. And it's because we lose these beautiful aims of youth that we do so little in life." Aloud, she answered the young man's aspirations, " Yes, wouldn't it be splendid to have the chance of doing some great thing for others ! But I'm afraid not one person in a thousand gets it, and ' others ' are just made up of people like our own families, after all, which we are apt to forget."

" But how could one have a chance of living a life worth living here ? " Van exclaimed. " Here, pottering around, looking after estate business with the agent, and living with poor old Gran, as hide-bound as a rhinoceros in all his ideas."

" Well, you don't suppose that great people who have helped the world found every one able to understand them ? On the contrary, they were just amongst a crowd of stupid, hide-bound people, instead of contending with only two or three, and that would be much more difficult. Why should the Admiral's ideas do you any harm ? Don't you remember the song—' And in my soul am free ' ? "

" He doesn't like me to call my soul my own," the poor boy complained, and Alex found this easy to believe.

" It is—all the same," she said, " and you've got to keep it free at any cost. I don't at all believe in the outward conditions of life making much difference as long as we can keep ' the fires within ' alive. You know what I mean, don't you ? "

" Yes, yes ! " he assented eagerly.

" My Father, now, has a live soul," Alex went on. " Poor Father—his life has been one long series of mistakes and failures, from a practical point of view, and yet his soul is alive all the time. He goes on believing and hoping and enthusing, whatever happens to himself—" she paused, and the bitterness of years made her add—" *or to others.*"

Van was not too much self-absorbed to notice her tone. He said nothing, only when they parted at the door of Orchard House, he remarked—

" I'd like to know your father."

" Oh, you must come and see us. You'd like my sister and the children, I'm sure."

" When may I come ? " he asked eagerly.

" Come when you like—any day," Alex replied, smiling at him as she turned away.

CHAPTER XI

" ANY day," proved the next day but one, when Matilda was out, and Alex sat by the fire, snatching half an hour of reading before the children all came tumbling in again.

Her thoughts were very far away, for she had the happy power of forgetting the outer world altogether when she read anything that interested her. The shabby room was homelike and pleasant that afternoon, with a blazing fire, and sweet with the scent of some narcissi in pots, which Mr. Hope had succeeded in rearing on a new system that had only produced the ordinary variety, much to his disappointment. " The beautiful things have come out all white and gold as usual," said Alex, " instead of being some livid colour from chemicals and strange lights." The air was fragrant with their scent although they had not turned into anything unique ; the fire crackled pleasantly, and Alex read on unconscious of the faint jangle of the door-bell. (The Hopes' door-bell sounded as if it had lost its voice from talking too much.) In another minute Katharine announced, " Mr. Cassilis," and Alex looked up, too far away to remember for the moment that there was such a person as Mr. Cassilis in the world.

Her first blank look was succeeded by a kind smile as she saw the young man's extreme embarrassment. He sat down on a chair that faced the light, and was overcome by a violent fit of shyness. He looked at his boots, blushed painfully, and made a few staccato remarks about the weather in a suffocating voice.

His little fox-terrier had followed him into the room

unobserved, and when Alex said, " Is this your dog ? " Van bounded from his chair with evident relief and began to haul at the dog's collar.

" I don't know how he got here. I thought I'd left him at the door. I'll take him out," he exclaimed.

" No, no—please let him stay. He'll only chase our cat if you leave him outside," said Alex, laughing. " We have a gaunt, determined cat which could cope with a wolf, far less a little dog like that."

So Van sat down again with a finger in the dog's collar, and the talk became less constrained.

Alex soon saw that the young man had arrived at that stage in the journey of life when he was in revolt against everything. She had sympathy for him, for she had passed that way herself, and come out on the other side. She did not even feel inclined to smile as she had done the day that Van first spoke about his ambitions, when he now assured her solemnly that most things in the world were wrong.

" Indeed they are," she assented, without adding that in a few years he would find it was necessary to accept the greater number of them, wrong or not.

Van's face lighted up with pleasure. He had found some one who understood at last.

" That's the terrible thing about living with my grandfather," he went on. " Instead of seeing how wrong most of our institutions are, he thinks them absolutely perfect, and wouldn't touch one of them for anything."

Alex laughed. " And the terrible thing about living with my Father," she said, " is that he thinks everything is wrong, and wants everything to be changed, so that those who live with him get to feel that they must stand up for the old institutions just because they are being so constantly abused."

" Do you feel like that ? " Van asked, astonished.

" Well, yes, I do at times. Then again I contrast him with some other people and am ashamed of myself.

When I was a little girl, I used to think I should like to be exactly like the rest of the world and hear my elders say and do all the ordinary things that other elderly people said and did."

" But you don't feel like that now, do you ? " he asked in dismay.

" No, not quite.   But still, I do think that there are only a few things in which it is wise to follow one's individual judgment."

" Why ?   One should do so in everything, surely ? "

Alex glanced at his well-cut, rather unusually nice clothes, saying—

" In the matter of dress, to take a very small example, is it not better to fall in with the views of most of our countrymen and class ? "   She laughed at his expression and went on, " There was a time in the family history when my Father became convinced that a single light garment was all that was necessary for health.   It was to be of blue woollen stuff, dyed, woven, and made at home. My mother had some difficulty in persuading him that it was better not to insist on us all wearing this.   He is the true stuff of which martyrs are made.   He went into Edinburgh one morning wearing his own "—she rubbed her hand across her eyes.   " Oh, it was no laughing matter to us then, I can assure you ! "

" No, I can believe that.   What put him off it ? "

" Oh, Mr. Maitland did.   He helps every one.   Father has the greatest respect for his judgment.   He keeps assuring him that true reform is not revolution, that, as he says, the sun of righteousness will arise in the east as usual, and not in the west, and so on, and in time Father listens to him and modifies his practice, though not his theory."

The young man had been sobered for a moment by the picture of Old Hopeful in his single wode-stained garment, but he had found in Alex a listener into whose ear he could pour the long, long tale of youth.

" The Ancient Mariner ought to have been a *very* young one," Alex said afterwards. " Only in the early twenties have we the power of talking so to any one."

But she listened to Van's story—his life abroad, his father's misunderstanding with the Admiral, his own anger because the old man would not permit him to allude to his parents, and so on and so forth.

" I think perhaps you forget," said Alex when he paused, " that there are some things just too painful for speech—especially to a rather inarticulate person like your grandfather. He could not bear to hear his son's name. *You* have no sore feeling on the subject, but if *he* has, why conclude it is because he is unforgiving? It is more likely because he feels his heart too tender to bear even a word. Oh, I can understand it so well! I have seen it before."

" You? When? " asked Van, astonished, but Alex changed the subject adroitly, and as he glanced at the clock it occurred even to the imagination of one-and-twenty that it was time for him to go.

" I hope I haven't shocked you," he said as he rose reluctantly. She had too much tact to let him suppose that he had not.

" Oh, perhaps just a little," she answered gravely, with a smile lurking at the corners of her mouth. Van was young, but not obtuse, and he burst out laughing.

" I expect you just think me an awful bore, and that you will never want to see me again! " he said.

Alex shook hands with him then, telling him he might come whenever he liked, and the sincerity in her voice was unmistakable. Just at that moment the children all came tumbling in.

" Oh, Aunt Alex, there's a horse at the gate, and it's champing so, we want to give it sugar, please, quick! " they all cried in a breath, and then stood still in a little huddle, silenced by the sight of a strange man.

" Come and shake hands with Mr. Cassilis," Alex said,

" and then go and get some sugar, and we'll give it to the horse."

" Yes," said Van, " he's very fond of sugar. Come along and we'll give it to him."

He caught up Mike as he spoke, and set him on his shoulder and carried him off to the gate, the other children scrambling after.

They all stood there and fed the impatient horse—he had found his master's call a long one.

" There are some Belgian hares at my grandfather's," said Van to Sally ; " I'll bring you down a pair of them, if you like."

He was scarcely conscious of the bliss conveyed by this suggestion.

" Oh ! " was the response of all the children, accompanied by a gasp of joy.

" You should have said ' Oh, thank you,' children, and not just ' Oh,' " laughed Alex.

" Oh, thank you ! " they replied in obedient chorus.

" All right—I'll bring them down soon," Van said as he mounted.

" Oh, not *soon*—to-morrow, *please !* " cried Sally, forgetting her shyness in a wild desire to possess the hares at once.

" Very well, you shall have 'em to-morrow morning," he called out laughing, as he rode away across the Square.

The hares appeared next morning, and though tact kept Van from coming into the house, he spent some time in the garden settling the agitated creatures in their new quarters. Two days later Peter's soul was made glad by the gift of a young owl, and the third morning saw George the possessor of some little foreign mice, which spun around like dancing Dervishes in a sort of dizzy waltz whenever they were lifted out of their nests of straw.

" Take the creatures away ! " cried Alex, as the delighted children made them exhibit their powers for the hundredth time. " It's so like most human effort," she said to Van, who was looking on. " We're most of us gyrating like that all about nothing and for no reason. Oh, take them away ! "

She was really in earnest, which of course added tenfold to the children's pleasure in the mice, and it became a favourite game to set one spinning its little aimless dance so that her eye should light on it when she came into the room.

By the time that Mike had got an offering of a puppy, the habit of Van's almost daily visits to Orchard House had become fixed, and after that no one questioned his goings and comings there. His poor horse got so accustomed to stopping at the gate, that when it was ridden by a groom on some other errand, the rider had the greatest difficulty in getting it to move on past the house.

Miss Maitland watched all this from the Manse windows. " The Admiral used to be very particular about his horses," she would remark. " He must have changed ; that beast has been standing at the Hopes' gate for an hour ! "

CHAPTER XII

THAT winter was grim and long. It needed all the fuel that Old Hopeful's trees could supply to keep the rambling old house at all warm. Cold it might sometimes be, but, as Alex had said to Van, it was never dull. With five children to be fed and clothed, washed and dressed, walked out and taken in, reproved and amused, cared for, mended for, and hoped about, there was no time to be dull. The house hummed like a hive from morning to night, for Mr. Hope had many friends, and his interests were varied.

It was certainly no wonder that Van Cassilis, having once found his way there, continued to come whenever he could, until at last his presence became so habitual as to excite no remark within the household, and also—for such is the way in small communities—to excite a good deal of conjecture amongst other people.

Alex continued her daily readings at Foxe Hall, but she seldom saw the young man there, for he had quickly discovered that it was much more amusing to go to Orchard House than to talk to her in the library with the Admiral ready to contradict every word.

There is a lovely hour in mid-winter, just as the sun goes down, when the intense cold seems to pause before it descends, and all the low colours of the season are at their best.

Alex was hurrying home from her reading at this hour on a quiet afternoon just before the sky began to be

tinged with red. In one of the fields a man was ploughing, with a wreath of gulls circling in the air above him;
she could hear his cheery whistle and the whickering
cries of the gulls as she passed along the road.

A few yards further on, another ploughman, with his
team unyoked, was standing by the roadside, deep in
conversation with Robert Maitland. Alex knew that the
country people had a great affection for Maitland, mostly
—as Aunt E. V. took care to tell—for his father's sake.
They came to consult him about their affairs very much
as they used to consult the old minister. As Alex came
up, the conversation terminated, and the man trudged
off with his horses.

"If you are on your way home, Alex," said Maitland,
"I'll walk with you, and defer my visit to the Admiral
to another day. I haven't seen him for some time, but I
know that he is always disappointed when I appear
instead of my Aunt Elizabeth. I have the absurd feeling that I shrink from describing to a sightless person
all that we see. Now *she* just does the opposite, and he
listens like a child while she mentions every trifle."

"Poor old man! I'm so sorry for him," said Alex.
"And doubly sorry that any one with such an affliction
should be so petty and ridiculous as he sometimes is."

They walked along the quiet, smooth road, and thin
threads of crimson began to gather in the sky. Alex
walked lightly, as if she could have gone for any distance.
Maitland, looking at her, was struck by the health and
animation in her face.

"Yes," he said, "it is a great affliction, and yet I
sometimes wonder," he went on, looking about him as he
spoke, "if all our keen senses do as much as we suppose.
Aren't we just looking through bars all the time?"

"Oh, surely, surely not that; think how intensely
some people live!"

He turned to her smiling. "Yes, indeed, and happy
they are! I would rather live like that than understand

all mysteries and all knowledge. It's a secret in itself,"
he exclaimed. " I might give my body to be burned and
never learn it. There's always something between me and
my very life. Have you never felt that ? A distance
always preserved somehow that isolates one like the magic
circle nothing could pass through."

" How can you talk like that ? " said Alex, indignantly.
" Do you mean to say that at your age you have never
felt anything intensely ? "

He hesitated before he answered, turning to look at her
with his intent eyes, a faint tinge of colour staining his
fine skin, as it always did when he was much interested
in anything.

" I have," he said slowly, " once or twice—but only for
a short time — half-griefs, half-joys — a restless self-
consciousness, I'm afraid, always expecting and wishing
for deeper experience, and always impalpably resisted—
the penalty, I suppose, of the vain effort to understand
the game we are meant to play blindfolded after all."
He stopped, and added in an odd, humble, simple way
that touched Alex, " I envy with my whole heart the
people who never think ! "

" Ah," said Alex, laughing, " there are so many of them
that you'd envy half the world. What I envy are the
people who *think* they think and who *know* that all they
think is correct—like our poor old Admiral ! "

" One day of his temperament would make me happy
for years ! " said Maitland, smiling.

" Perhaps," Alex went on, " it is only because your
own experiences haven't been deep enough for you.
Water that will drown a child, for instance, wouldn't come
up to your elbow."

He shook his head. " No, I've just had the ordinary
experiences of a commonplace life that come to the
majority of men, and it's my own fault or misfortune if
they haven't been enough for me."

" Well, of course," said Alex, impatiently, " if birth

and death and marriage, hate and love, and health and sickness don't touch you, our poor little world has no more to offer to one so far away from things as all that ! The ordinary experiences of a commonplace life are more than enough for most of us, thank Heaven ! "

They walked on in silence, and Alex was ashamed of having spoken so hotly.

" How can you," she went on, " you who are the friend and counsellor of us all, speak in that way, as if you were a sort of unfeeling image ? You know you take up half your time listening to other people's worries, from Matilda's and mine to those of my father and James Todd, whom you were speaking to just now ! Please— please don't mind what I say ! "

" My dear woman, I like it ! " he answered smiling. They were at the village now, and Alex stopped at their own gate.

" Won't you come in, just to show you have forgiven me ? " she said.

The gate as usual was open, and a little dog that they both knew stood under one of the trees yapping at the branch above him, where the Hopes' cat, a long, lean animal with a predatory gait and hungry eye, crouched spitting at her enemy.

Maitland called to the dog and laughed.

" Van hasn't brought a horse to-day," he said. " I was beginning to think the Admiral would complain, and always meant to suggest that my stable was round the corner."

" He does come pretty often, poor boy," said Alex, having lifted down the cat and chased her indoors. " But can you wonder ? "

" I don't in the least. I'd do just the same in his place," said Maitland, as they entered the house.

There was a noise of many voices from the sitting-room to the left as Alex opened the door. The room was nearly dark now, lighted only by a great fire. At the old piano Sally sat banging away with both pedals down at the same time. Van Cassilis was lying full length on the hearthrug, one of his arms pinioned by each of the bigger boys, whilst Mike sat on his chest and tried to rub a moustache on his upper lip with a piece of burnt cork.

The lid of a tin biscuit-box on the fender, full of half-congealed toffee, and a pungent smell of burnt sugar told what the amusement of the hour had been.

Van shook the children off and struggled to his feet, looking very funny with his fierce, curling black moustache, which suddenly gave him the air of a much older man. He showed his teeth in a delightful boyish smile as he glanced at his own reflection in the old mirror above the chimney-piece.

Sally left off thumping the piano to "slaister," as Katharine would have said, among the toffee with an old knife. Alex threw off her coat, and sitting down at the piano, began to play softly.

Maitland dropped into Old Hopeful's worn armchair, and leant back to listen, and Van sat on the rug at her feet, leaning his head against the side of the chimney-piece.

The children were tired of romping, and there was a lull in their uproar as Alex played softly in the deepening dusk. Matilda had come in with her sewing, but it was too dark to see any longer, so she sat in the corner of the sofa with Mike huddled up beside her. Looking about him, Maitland did not wonder that Van preferred the freedom of Orchard House to the empty rooms at home.

"Play that again, please," he said to Alex. "It's just like running water."

"It's a funny little haunting song," said Alex. "I don't know who wrote the music, and I don't remember half of the words, for I only heard it once, but it goes like this : "

She bent forward, singing in a low, penetrating voice.

Her singing had much of the same quality that made her reading so interesting, though her voice had not been highly trained.

> " ' Down by the salley gardens—'

(" that's willows, you know," she interpolated—)

> " ' My love and I did stand,
>   And on my leaning shoulder
>   She laid her milk-white hand.
>   She bade me take life easy
>   As the leaves grow on the tree—'

here Alex turned, and smiled down at Van sitting on the floor at her side—

> " ' But I was young and foolish
>   And with her did not agree.' "

Then in a lower voice she went on—

> " ' Down by the salley gardens
>   My love and I did go—' "

(" oh, I don't know the words . . .)

> " ' She bade me take love easy
>   As the grass grows on the weirs,
>   But I was young and foolish,
>   And now am full of tears.' "

She broke off laughing and saying, " Why on the weirs? Isn't it all vague and funny ?—but it's so plaintive.   Oh, must you go ? "

For Maitland got up to say good-bye. He left them rather abruptly, and went out into the frosty twilight that seemed curiously dim and cold as he issued from that merry, poverty-stricken house.

He was humming half-aloud the refrain of Alex's little song—

> " ' But I was young and foolish,
>   And now am full of tears.' "

CHAPTER XIII

LONG ago there had been a quarrel—at least a considerable coldness entailing a life-long frost—between Alexander Hope and his only brother. James Hope seemed
to have a nature the very opposite of our old friend's.
He had made much money and wasted none of it—had,
at any rate, spent none of it in that manner which is
said to be the laying up of treasure in heaven, and his
hard prudence condemned, justly enough, most of Old
Hopeful's schemes as " Quixotic idiocy." For many
years the intercourse between the brothers had been very
slight ; an occasional letter, sometimes a short meeting
if they happened to be in London at the same time.
But James Hope never came to Crossriggs, and neither
Alex nor Old Hopeful ever went to Liverpool, though
once before her marriage Matilda had gone there. Now
it seemed that the two families were to meet again.

Alexandra came into the Manse one afternoon when
Maitland and his wife were alone.

" I've come to ask you to dinner, " she began ; " and
please come whether you want to or not, for we must
have some one from the outside to break the awfulness
of a family circle. You see," she went on, turning to
Mrs. Maitland, who did not look much delighted by the
prospect, " such a difficult thing is going to happen ; my
uncle, James Hope, and *his wife*, are coming to-morrow—
the uncle's bad enough without the wife (as the old woman
said, ' the cat's enough without the kittens '—drowning

them) ; but when both come together I don't know how we shall survive it. I've never seen her, and I sincerely hoped I never should. She was a Popham. You ought to hear Uncle James utter these words ! "

Mrs. Maitland had no sense of humour, but even she smiled faintly at the solemnity Alex threw into her tones.

" Do come on Wednesday evening," Alex went on, " both of you—you'll help us so. Uncle James considers Mr. Maitland a person of importance, and Mrs. Hope— *née* Popham—will admire you."

The little compliment pleased Laura, who answered quite pleasantly—

" I am sure we shall be glad to come if we can help you in any way."

" Have you ever seen your uncle ? " Maitland asked. He looked very much pleased by his wife's unwonted geniality to Alex, for in general they got on so badly.

" Oh yes, once or twice ; and Matilda went to stay with them once, long ago, before her marriage." Alex screwed up her face at the remembrance. " I always thought it was a kind of reaction from that visit that made her accept Peter Chalmers on her return ! You know Matilda is nearly always cheerful, but that house was too much for her. She said everything was so *expensive*—you know what I mean, not only rich in itself, but suggestive of its price—that after she went to bed she kept on making up bills in her head half the night. All the time she was there she never said a natural word, nor did any one else in the house, except when Uncle James stumbled on a footstool and said ' Damn.' There was a great drawing-room with miles of magenta carpet, and the blinds always half down, and two fully clothed marble women, as large as life, holding gas-lamps in the front hall, and all sorts of horrors. The Popham goes up to London to buy her clothes because Liverpool shops aren't good enough for her—a fat, *tight* woman—you know the kind—who makes a faint creaking whenever she breathes."

Mrs. Maitland laughed again. She looked as nearly benignant as she ever could look.

"And your uncle; is he at all like Mr. Hope?" she asked.

"Like my father? Oh, dear! wait till you see him! He's a very strict Churchman and a Conservative, and he looks as if he fed exclusively on the juices of meat. Can you imagine what we're going to do with them?"

"Any one who is discontented with the entertainment they receive at your father's house, Alex, must show a great want of taste," said Robert.

"Oh, that's all very well for you to say, because you're fond of us," said the girl, "besides, you care more what you talk about than what you eat. But put it the other way round, and think of people who would rather eat a good dinner in silence and hatred than the dinner of herbs where love or amusement is—and then fancy them at our table!"

"If I can do anything——" began Laura. Alex sprang up laughing.

"You can't—thank you! One of your nice servants would only bewilder Katharine; we must just do our worst. But if you and Mr. Maitland are there it will give a kind of sanction to the evening." She paused for a moment. "And please put on the charming lilac gown!"

"I certainly will," responded Mrs. Maitland, graciously.

She remarked to her husband after Alex had gone, that "Miss Hope was sometimes very amusing," and he assented, wondering why a more universal charity could not reign in our everyday relations when it was so becoming. Alex had left with a pleasant feeling of kindliness at her heart, and Mrs. Maitland had forgotten her stiffness for the moment and looked quite pretty and animated. And all because of a few little kind speeches on both sides!

When Alex went to the station the next day, to meet her relations, she found Maitland there also.

"I only hope I shan't quarrel with them on the way home," she murmured to him, just as the train came up to the platform.

A few minutes later he saw her piloting the aunt and uncle through the crowd. There was always quite a crowd at that train, though where the people came from, or where they went to, none of us could ever say. They melted out into the country, I suppose, driving off in farmers' gigs, walking away to out-lying cottages: some commercial traveller with his boxes filling a fly: some country wife with her bundles trudging her way home after a day in town, along with the children who had come to meet her. Anyhow, in ten minutes they were all dispersed, and we, the funny little handful of people who made society at Crossriggs, were going our several ways, wondering "where all the people came from."

On this occasion there had been more of a crowd than usual owing to some local gathering, and when Alex reached the gate the only vehicle left unoccupied was a peculiarly broken-down, evil-smelling old fly. Maitland watched with some amusement while the driver hurtled the ramshakle old thing close to the gate, and Alex signified to her relations that they were to get in. There was no mistaking Mr. and Mrs. Hope. "Town" was stamped all over them, from the man's hat to the woman's thin, unsuitable shoes. She was a handsome person of middle age, with a face as inexpressive as a piece of veal, a figure a little too fat and a little too stiff, and all her clothing a little too tight, in spite of which her movements were elastic with energy. She laid a plump hand in a primrose glove—too tight for it—on the door of the fly, and placed a fat foot, in a high-heeled shoe—also too tight—upon the mud-encrusted step, and her husband hoisted her in. Ill-concealed disgust was on her face ; Mr. Hope, too, had an absurd air of thinking himself too good for the situation as he instructed the porter to place a dressing-bag, obviously as heavy as lead, inside the vehicle. Alex waved her hand to Maitland as they drove off. They evidently asked her who he was, and the aunt's face melted suddenly as she heard the important name, while Mr. Hope, keeping a wary hand on the dressing-bag, turned his head to have a look at Maitland as they passed.

"They are dining with us to-night," Alex told her uncle, " you will see him again."

Mrs. Maitland's good humour had continued, so that by dinner-time that evening she put on the dress that Alex admired, wrapped herself up, and said to her husband, with unwonted sweetness, that it was very nice to go out on such a lovely night. A pale April moon was shining down on them as they crossed the Square, and Laura's little feet were not damp in her thin slippers, for the old pavements were as dry and white as boards. As they entered the garden of Orchard House, a smell of frying fat, pungent and overpowering, issued from the kitchen premises—the night air was full of it, and it seemed to flood even the garden. At the door Alex came running to greet them. Laura stood unwinding her wraps in the hall, and really looking pretty in her new mood of amiability, as Alex explained her woes.

"I don't know *what* Katharine is doing," she said, " but everything has gone wrong all day, as I knew it would. Matilda, poor dear, has such a sick-headache that she can scarcely speak. Uncle James and father have ' differed ' all the time, the children have behaved badly, and the aunt is more than dreadful."

When the Maitlands entered they found Old Hopeful alone in the shabby room. He stood by the window with a book in his hand, a trifle less buoyant in his manner than usual as he turned to greet them.

CHAPTER XIV

" Ah," exclaimed Old Hopeful, " I am delighted to see you ! I was just having a sip of Homer—nothing refreshes one like it." (The fumes of fry were here wafted into the drawing-room.) " Sometimes one feels stifled, perplexed by the narrow actualities of life," he went on, laying down the book and pacing about the room with his hands clasped behind him.

He seemed—for him—faintly worried, his clear forehead not so untroubled as usual; the white hair which usually fell about his brow had been brushed back, which gave him a more ordinary look. Presently Mr. James Hope came in, and was introduced to the Maitlands. It was difficult to believe that he and Old Hopeful were brothers—had ever been born of the same mother—not only in appearance, but in personality, they differed so strangely. Old Hopeful, who generally had the graceful manner which comes of entire simplicity, seemed ill at ease with this citizen brother. It was evident that he had been told not to air any of his theories, and was trying hard to find some neutral subject upon which it was safe to converse. There had lately been a rumour of war, and this was one of the things about which our old friend felt most keenly.

" This war is the best thing that can happen," said James Hope, complacently looking down at his own shining footgear. Old Hopeful wore a peculiar kind of square-toed, flat shoe, hygienic of course, but far from beautiful, so that as they stood together the contrast was apparent. " The best thing that can happen," James Hope repeated. " Our armies are ready. Our ships are ready—all rusting for want of use ! It's just what the country is needing. If the Empire is to keep her place in the world, we'll have to fight for it, just as individuals have to do. What man has ever made room for himself without a struggle ? It's got to come."

He uttered this dictum in a fat, low voice, and with the pompous enunciation of a man who takes his ideas ready-made from the common stock and utters them solemnly, thinking himself an oracle. Maitland laughed slightly and shrugged his shoulders, as if he did not care to discuss the matter. He had seen Alex shake her head. But his brother's utterance had been more than Old Hopeful could stand.

" Ah ! " he cried, throwing out his hands with a gesture of horror. " What times we live in ! What a country ! Giving with one hand its thousands to found colleges and hospitals, to heal the sick and (by way of) help the poor, and with the other hand directing the engines of war, things that mash men like caterpillars, and might have been made in hell—drenching the earth with blood and rousing every evil passion—in the name of Christianity, too—prating about Empire when they really mean aggression. Of what use is our vulgar wealth, our so-called philanthropy ? The one founded on iniquity, the other given, it seems, in derision of the very name of humanity ! There will be a retribution on this country before we are aware that its hour has come. ' Go to, ye rich men, weep and howl for your miseries that shall come upon you.'"

Just as Old Hopeful uttered the last words, Maitland glanced up and saw the majestic figure of Mrs. James Hope filling the doorway. She stood still in astonishment, her high bosom unlifted on a deep breath, her bright, small eye glittering in its inexpressive expanse of cheek. Then with awful rustlings and creakings she advanced towards the group by the window.

"Were you speaking about the currency, James?" she inquired of her husband.

"We were speaking about war, and perhaps we'd better say no more about it, Clara," he replied, swallowing down his vexation with difficulty.

"*And why should we?*" said the lady, turning upon her brother-in-law. "*We* are accustomed to society where every one is allowed to hold his own opinions without rude contradiction—a mark of well-bred people, I think," she added, with a mirthless, toothy smile, turning upon Alex.

"Oh, no—pardon me!" said Old Hopeful, new a little heated, but looking at her with his usual simplicity. "In society, no one expresses his *own* opinion—else he would not be there; he only voices the general opinion, most likely an entirely erroneous one, and adds his voice to the clamour about nothing. It is by contradiction that the truth is beaten out, and I fear we who care for truth are somewhat over-hasty in our answers."

"I have perfect confidence in our Government and our country," Mrs. Hope replied with stately irrelevance, and moved with a creak and rustle to the other side of the room, where Alex was standing beside Mrs. Maitland, whose pretty gown and tactful conversation impressed Mrs. Hope very favourably. In a few minutes Matilda appeared, to smooth things over between her father and her uncle. Poor Matilda! She had been suffering all day from a violent sick-headache, so that the very whites of her eyes were yellow and every moment sent a throb of pain through her head. But she smiled bravely, and said "Yes" and "No" in the right place when her uncle spoke, and held Sally's hand, as she stood shyly by her side. Maitland glanced at Matilda sympathetically, then looked at Alex, whose tall figure was held unusually upright and whose face expressed ill-concealed abhorrence of these relatives.

A bell rang loud and long.

" Peter is ringing that, I am sure ! " said Matilda, smiling. " Katharine could never produce such a volume of sound ! "

The party now gladly streamed into the other room, and every one began to talk at once. The dinner, however, was not a success. Katharine, always accustomed to the simplest meals, had got flurried in her attempts to cook a slightly more elaborate one.

" I don't care twopence what they think," Alex had said to her sister. " But I do want them to have enough to eat, even if we all have to starve for a week afterwards ! "

Enough there certainly was. When transparent cod had been succeeded by bleeding mutton, and that in turn followed by sodden apple fritters—responsible for the smell of fry—Alex could see Mrs. James Hope eyeing her plate with scarcely veiled disgust.

" What are you eating there, Alexander ? " inquired James Hope, who had now resolved to forgive Old Hopeful's outburst before dinner.

" The best of all food ! " joyously answered his brother. " The staff of life itself, with a little nuttose and a handful of green peas. Try a little of the nuttose, James—you will find it excellent. When I think of the food *you* have just eaten—when I remember the head—— "

" Can't you prevent this during dinner, Matilda ? " interpolated Mrs. Hope, coldly, but Old Hopeful paid no attention to the remark.

" The head," he continued, " of that beautiful marine creature—— "

" Do you mean the cod ? " asked his brother, his grim face lighting for a moment with a smile.

" I do allude to the cod," pursued Mr. Hope, " the

cod's head. When I think of how that creature lived in the water, and how that other innocent beast——"

" The mutton, I suppose you mean ? "

" Yes, yes, the mutton. Think of white sheep feeding in the green English meadows."

" I should think it probably came from Sydney."

" What of that ? It had a right to its own day of life as well as you. When I think of what *killing to eat* means, I shudder. Do, James, try a little of the nuttose ! "

James Hope peered at the jar which was handed to him, helped himself to a small portion, tasted it, and then took a hurried gulp of wine.

" You don't like it, Uncle James ? " asked Matilda, smiling.

" Like it ! " he muttered, turning to Mrs. Maitland. " It tastes like a mixture of whale oil and dead beetles ! "

Happily Matilda rose from table at this point, so that Old Hopeful scarcely heard his brother's remark.

There was a good deal of strained conversation between the four women in the drawing-room after dinner. Poor Matilda's headache made her incapable of more than a murmur of assent. Mrs. Maitland was never talkative, and Alex would not make any effort to be agreeable. Presently Matilda went off to the nursery, and Alex, with a brief apology, sat down to help Sally with her Latin exercise for the following day, leaving Mrs. Hope and Mrs. Maitland to entertain one another.

" It's a thousand pities Matilda ever came home, I consider," began Mrs. Hope, in low tones. " There might have been some chance of the boys getting on out there, and Sally might have married."

" She may marry here," said Mrs. Maitland.

Mrs. Hope glanced across to the end of the room where Sally sat at the table—a clumsy enough, round-shouldered, growing girl. Her aunt did not see how intelligent her face was, and never noticed her look of health and brightness. Sally wore a shabby pink frock, her auburn hair hung down in untidy slips about her forehead and was squeezed into a badly plaited pigtail behind. She was also sucking her pencil as she looked up at Alex, who stood beside her.

" She may, but it's most unlikely. The boys are very rough," said Mrs. Hope.

" Oh, only noisy," said Laura Maitland, who was roused to something like a feeble defence of the children by Mrs. Hope's manner.

" Excepting Mike," continued that lady, now sinking her voice to a more confidential note. " Mike is a dear child," she went on, " not so much spoilt, and with a little training here and there——" (She flicked her handkerchief with her fingers, as if to express a few deft touches.) Mrs. Maitland smiled her non-committal, doll-like smile. " Mr. Hope and I," Mrs. Hope went on, " have no young people about us, and I intend to offer to take Mike back to Liverpool with us. I should be quite glad to have him."

She said this as if it were the greatest condescension imaginable.

" Oh, I wonder what Mrs. Chalmers will say to that ? " said Mrs. Maitland.

She was not imaginative, but, looking at Mrs. Hope, she thought how much better fitted she was to take charge of a pug than of a little boy. Her figure was like nothing but the wooden stands on which blouses are fitted in shops, and it was impossible even to think of little Mike's head rolling sleepily against that unyielding bosom as it so often fell on Alexandra's breast, when she carried him off to bed. Mrs. Maitland looked quite animated as she sat up and repeated—

" I don't think Mrs. Chalmers would part with Mike."

" Well," said Mrs. Hope, " having no children of my own, I am naturally able to bring them up better than mothers like Matilda." She threw a glance at Matilda, who had re-entered the room. " They nearly always fail

—not particular about little things." She quivered and creaked within her bulwark of bodice. "Alex and Matilda ran wild as children."

Here they were interrupted by the entrance of Old Hopeful, Maitland, and Mr. James Hope, and the inharmonious party dragged through another half-hour of difficult conversation. Alex refused to sing; Maitland had taken a fit of silence; Matilda could scarcely speak coherently, her headache was so severe. Mrs. Maitland alone seemed capable of exerting herself, and charmed James Hope by a string of carefully commonplace remarks uttered with unusual vivacity.

"You were an angel—we should never have got through the evening without you!" Alex said to her, as she was helping her on with her wraps. "I'm sure my uncle thinks you the most charming woman he ever met, and wonders how you and your distinguished husband can be bothered with 'the likes of us!' You weren't very agreeable to the aunt, all the same," she added, turning to Maitland.

"No," he answered; then laughed. "I couldn't be. She awed me, and stared so, and creaked."

"Yes, yes!" said Alex, delightedly. "She always reminds me of what Mrs. Ames used to say: 'There's a kind of square, stout, high-busted Englishwoman that would stand up to anything in creation!'"

Alex remained on the doorstep, looking after the Maitlands as they crossed the square. "I just almost liked Laura this evening," she said to Matilda, when they were alone together, and the Liverpool relations had retired for the night. "One step more and I'd have done it! For the first time I saw what made Mr. Maitland marry her—there's no *spite* about her."

"Spite? Oh, no!" said Matilda, horrified.

"Well, why not? Oh, how I hate my aunt and uncle, and what a providence it is that I wasn't their daughter! I don't wonder you're sick, dear—it's just the effect of their society.　Good night.　Dream there's been a flood, and that the world has begun again with new people in it—except ourselves ! "

She went into the nursery, and bent over Mike asleep in his fine little cot.　The child scarcely stirred as she leaned above him, only rolled his head aside on the pillow, and opened his bud-like lips in a sigh of sleep.

" Did she think for a moment we'd let you go, after she had selected you like a fish from a basket—and thank her for ' taking a burden off us ' indeed !　Oh, you darling, darling things, I'd work myself to death to keep you all ! " she said to herself.　Then standing with her hand on the rail of the cot, she thought, " The Maitlands had a creature like that torn away from them, and he was all they had.　Oh, how do people live through trials like that—even people with tight-laced sort of hearts, like Laura's !　*I'd have died !* "　Then suddenly she drew herself up, shook back her head, and giving a final soft arranging touch to Mike's coverlet, went quietly out of the room.　" *The empty heart cannot be robbed,*" she wrote in her diary, as she finished the brief note for the day.

CHAPTER XV

THE Liverpool relations departed early on the following day. Mrs. Hope had a final interview with Matilda, when she formally offered to "take Mike off her hands," as she sympathetically phrased it. Alex was in the room too, and she flushed with anger and would have made some quick retort, but Matilda laid a hand on her arm, and checked the words on her lips.

"You are very kind, Aunt Clara," she said; "but I cannot part with my little boy. I cannot part with any of my children."

"I never expected you to do so, Matilda," said the aggrieved aunt. "As I said to James last night, the more children people have, and the less they have to give them, the less willing they are to part with them. It's the temperament; the thing is invariable."

She quivered and creaked, and Alex grinned behind her sister's chair.

"Yes, you see," she said, "temperament is just the thing that can't be altered in life. Character, people say, can be built up, or down, I suppose, but you've just got the temperament you're born with to the end of the chapter."

"Well, Matilda, I can say no more," said Mrs. Hope, majestically ignoring Alex's remark; "only I hope you're not sacrificing the child's future to a piece of false sentiment. He would have every advantage with us. James would see to it that he went to a public school,

that alone would differentiate him for life from his
brothers, who, I suppose, will just get their schooling in
Edinburgh. He would, if all went well, be sure of a
post in his uncle's office, and his future would be made.
He might become the head of a mercantile house in
Liverpool as his uncle has done, instead of being like
your poor father."

"It's a dazzling prospect, Aunt Clara," Alex began,
in spite of Matilda's warning looks ; "but you see we
care too much for Mike even to surrender him for that.
He's not very strong."

"The child requires nourishment," began Mrs. Hope.

"Yes," said Alex, dryly, looking hard at her. "Children are easily starved. They do *not* live by bread
alone."

"Who would ever think of such a diet ! "—Mrs. Hope
creaked with indignation. "The best of everything—
what do you mean ? Do you think any one in my
house would live upon bread ? "

"*We live by admiration, hope, and love,* you remember," said Alex, and her aunt rose.

"I don't understand that mystical nonsense. The
child would have the best of everything at Laurel Lodge.
But take your own way, Matilda. Keep all your own
children and bring them up respectably, only don't fall
back upon me and your uncle when you find yourselves
in difficulties."

"I can assure you it is the very last thing we'd ever
think of doing," said Alex, fervently, but Matilda kissed
her aunt's inexpressive expanse of cheek, and again
thanked her for her kind offer. The fly came to the door,
and then, with visible relief on both sides, the visit
terminated. Peter had been lurking with a tin trumpet
at the side of the house, and he blew a joyous toot a
little too soon, before the vehicle had disappeared, causing
Mr. James Hope to look out anxiously, just in time to
see Alex executing a dance of triumph upon the doorstep

along with Sally—poor Sally, who had been particularly suppressed.

"It was the way she looked at me, Aunt Alex," she said plaintively ; "I felt as if I had four hands and didn't know what to do with any of them. I'm going out now. Are you coming ? "

"No, indeed, Sally," said Alex. "I'm going up to Foxe Hall, and when I come home I'm just going to sit in an armchair and read the silliest novel I can find for two hours, and not think once whether there is anything for supper or not, and let everything in the house go wrong if it likes ! " She ran in and got ready to go off to Foxe Hall.

On her return, the children had gone out, so she sank into an armchair with a book, determined to worry about nothing for an hour or two. Everything in the Hopes' drawing-room was shabby : the Turkey carpet a marvel of darning, the curtains faded to a nondescript ash-colour, the chintz covers almost beyond repair. Yet in spite of this it was a pleasant room. The sun seemed to be always shining in it, and as everything was old and shabby, no one troubled to pull down the blinds, as thrifty housekeepers with handsome possessions have been known to do. Alex had a wonderful way of arranging furniture to the best advantage.

"I know the weaknesses of my old friends, the tables and chairs," she used to say, "how one of them can afford to face the light, and another must be doomed to decent obscurity—what spot of the carpet demands a footstool to cover its nakedness, and which side of which vase can be turned outwards ! "

It was perfectly true ; in other hands that room would have looked like an old furniture store ; in Alex's it was a sadly shabby, but delightfully home-like place.

The days were stretching out now. It was the beginning of April, and a softness had crept into the chill air. Alex had brought in with her a bunch of yellow catkins. These harbingers of spring she had placed in an old brown jar—there was not such a thing as a whole flower-glass in the Hopes' house !—on the table by the window. The sun shone in, sending long, heatless rays across the faded carpet with its embroidery of darns, and Alex lay back in her chair, a little tired after her walk, enjoying the brightness of the afternoon. She could see the village postman come lounging up the walk, frankly perusing a postcard as he came.

" I wonder what letters there are," she thought, too comfortably lazy to go and see for herself. " There is never anything very interesting by this post."

" Here is a postcard for you, Alex, my dear," said Old Hopeful, coming in a moment later ; " and I have a document which I fancy is the manifesto of the Kent fruit growers. Let us see—a noble work, theirs ! "

The old man sat down on the sofa, and put on his eye-glasses—they were a very bad fit, and always fell off two or three times before he managed to persuade them to stick on. He broke the seal of the large envelope and read the letter it contained. Suddenly his poor old face contracted with a curious look of dismay and incredulity.

" Alex," he gasped, " Alex, my dear, this is impossible, quite—quite impossible ! "

He ran his fingers through his long white locks in a distracted way, and turned appealingly to his daughter.

" What is it, Father ? Anything wrong with the Manifesto ? " Alex asked lightly. She crossed over to where her father sat, and bent down to read the letter. As she did so, her face became suddenly white. " But, Father, you never were surety for any one ? " she said.

" It was to oblige Ronaldson. I never supposed for a moment that any claim would be made. I assure you, Alex, I thought only of obliging Ronaldson, an old acquaintance ; I could not well have refused," the old man cried, turning his face to her much as a child might have done—a child in trouble.

" Then you did become surety for this amount ? " she asked, her voice very quiet and hard.

" Yes, dear, yes — it was impossible to refuse a friend—"

" And we have to pay a hundred pounds at once ? "

" Yes, yes—I fear that is the amount. Yes, Alex— that is certainly the sum," the old man said, referring once more to the letter in his hand. " These business matters are vexatious—vexatious. The root of all evil is this money. We think too much of it—strive too much for it. It leads to endless, endless ills ! ' "

The subject was a congenial one to him, and in his old chanting voice he would have rambled on much longer if Alex had not interrupted him.

" For Heaven's sake, Father, realize what this means ! " she cried, holding out the letter. " We haven't got hundred-pound notes knocking about doing nothing."

" No doubt it is a serious matter, dear Alex, but we must not despair, we must not be faithless. I did what I thought right at the time, so I have no fear for the results, though of course a little natural anxiety over- takes one."

" How could you, Father ; how could you dream of doing such a thing ? " Alex cried.

In the stress of her misery she rose and paced up and down the room, wringing her hands together. The old man looked at her uneasily.

" What else could I do ? " he asked. " My rule has always been to take the actual words of the Gospel and turn them into practice, and did not He say, ' Give to him that asketh of thee, and from him that would borrow of thee turn not thou away '—what can be more explicit than that ? It never occurred to me to question Ronald- son's probity. I have always held that suspicions hurt the man who harbours them fully more than the man who is suspected. We should honour human nature—believe in it to the uttermost."

But Alex broke in upon her father's meditations in a new, harsh voice.

" It's possible to do all that too much," she said coldly. The old man gave her one long, surprised look, and then left the room. A minute later, Alex saw him hurry bareheaded across the Square to the Maitlands' house.

She flung herself down upon the sofa and buried her face in the cushions, as if to shut out the world from her eyes.

" He's gone to tell Mr. Maitland all about it—oh, I can't bear that he should know that poor father is so egregiously foolish ! What will he think ? Oh, I can't bear it ! "

A slow blush burnt up over her face, she seemed to hear all that was passing between her father and Maitland—the old man's wandering account of his act of fatuous generosity, Maitland's pity and surprise at his incredible folly.

" I've heard him say that the world would be a better place if there were more men like Father in it," she thought, trying to comfort herself a little. " And it's true in a sense, but oh . . what are we to do about this ? Shall I go over and bring father back ? " she thought. " Or shall I just let him expose all his folly? Mr. Maitland must know it pretty well by this time ! And yet I thought I did—and this came to me as a surprise ; I didn't think that even Father could have done such a thing. Ah, there he is coming back."

But it seemed another man altogether who returned ; his step was light, his face beamed with innocent joyousness.

" Well—did Mr. Maitland throw any light on the matter ? " Alex asked, raising her face from the pillows.

" I have had a long, a most interesting talk with our friend over the way," he replied ; " and have come back with my mind relieved—entirely relieved." He threw himself into an armchair and leant back. In both his attitude and the tone of his voice a mighty relief was indeed manifest. "We began, of course, with the practical view of the matter. I explained my position carefully to him, and he seemed to grasp it at all points, ethically as well as practically. There is where I find Robert such a true adviser, he is at heart an idealist, though so strangely able to direct money and other affairs. . . . Then we discussed possible methods of meeting the difficulty, and he went into that matter with a clearness that was really very extraordinary. His knowledge of technicalities is amazing." The intonation Old Hopeful gave to this word was a marvel of expression; it conveyed at once contempt, bewilderment, and respect, if such contradictory feelings can exist together. " He seems to have quite mastered the question of investments, a subject I have never given any attention to. Well, Robert's wish was to find out how and in what our little capital is invested. We touched incidentally on the interesting question whether the individual has a right to possess capital at all. I should have gone further into this inquiry, but Robert suggested another day for the pursuance of this, and we kept to affairs. I am *not* very clear as to my investments; but he made *this* perfectly clear to me—that it is out of the question for me to—as he terms it—' lift my investments.' Then he proposes—in fact he has already arranged with me— that he most kindly advances me this hundred pounds out of some money for which he is at present receiving merely nominal interest. I shall, of course, pay him a good interest yearly on the sum; he proposes two and a half per cent., fully more than he is at present receiving. So all is well, he is benefited and I am benefited. The dark cloud has in fact rolled away, dear Alex, as a hundred times before. We have much—much to be thankful for——"

There was an ominous silence for a minute.

" Then you actually agreed to take this money from Mr. Maitland ? " Alex said. There was, to a hearing ear, the sound of a rising storm in her voice.

"Not only that, dear Alex, but I have it here—a cheque, all carefully made out to me. There can be no mistake."

"Let me see it."

Old Hopeful fumbled in his breast-pocket, bringing out strange hoards ; he seemed to carry all his correspondence on his person.

"This is it—no, that is the memorandum of the appeal to the Home Secretary from the Kent fruit growers. Here —this will be it—no, again ! ' The Eastern Atrocities in a Nutshell '—an eloquent bit of pamphlet work—I am a great believer in the power and influence of the pamphlet. Here—I have it—£100, pay to Alexander Hope (signed) Robert Maitland. Could anything be more distinct, more businesslike ? "

He handed the little slip of paper to Alex. She took it and rose from her chair.

"We've been poor all our lives, Father," she said, in a queer, new voice, hoarse with emotion, "but hitherto we've been self-respecting, and I for one am anxious to remain so. I'd rather starve than take Mr. Maitland's money. I'm ashamed that you should ever dream of doing it. You have no proper pride, no independence. I believe you would go round the village with your hat in your hand begging from door to door without mind-ing——"

"Alex—Alex ! " the old man cried, shrinking back into his chair as if she had dealt him a blow.

"I'm going to give it back to Mr. Maitland," Alex continued. "You shan't make us all beggars, if I can help it ! "

CHAPTER XVI

ALEX did not wait to put on a hat or cloak, but ran across the Square just as she was. She stopped only for a moment at the door of the Manse. There was no one visible in the hall. She walked in, and without further hesitation knocked at the door of Maitland's study.

" Come in ! " he called pleasantly.

Alex entered, and laid the cheque upon his blotting-pad.

" I've come to return this," she said, her eyes blazing with anger, her breath coming short and hard.

" Why, Alex ? " Maitland asked. He rose and stood beside her.

" Because," gasped Alex, speaking with difficulty, " though we are poor, we have not been beggars till now —and won't be, if I can help it. There it is ; I don't even thank you for offering it to my father. You should not have done so. You know how weak he is ; he understands no more about money matters than a baby. You purposely confused him with all that talk about investments, and then made him believe he was doing you a favour by taking this. There, take it back ! " She pointed again at the cheque.

" I won't ; you shall take it from me," Maitland said. " And now that you have said all this to me, you shall listen to what I have to say. But tell me in the first place what you said to your father just now."

" The truth. What I have said to you."

" In the same unmitigated way ? Were you unkind to the old man ? Did you hurt him ? "

" Yes—I meant to. He had hurt me."

" For shame, Alex ! I never thought I should hear you say anything so cruel. Sit down there, and listen to me now." He pointed to a chair, and Alex took it in silence. " Your father's is the right view of this matter ; yours is quite wrong. The word ' friendship ' has no meaning if a friend can't help one in a difficulty. You know how I admire and respect your father. I'm honoured to help him in any way I can. He is old and utterly without knowledge of practical things. I know all about them ; he was right to come to me."

Alex did not respond, and Maitland went on : " You don't yet begin to understand his simple, noble nature. You have got all the common, everyday ideas that the world works with, and the sooner you unlearn them the better. Take that cheque back to your father, and ask his pardon for the way you spoke to him about it. Do you hear ? "

" I cannot take it," she said.

" I am not offering it to you, Alex. Perhaps we are scarcely good enough friends for that—it seems not. I offer it to your father, and I know that he and I understand one another enough to allow of this. But I do ask you to take it back to him, and to apologize to him for all the cruel things you said about it—cruel and foolish. ' What is that betwixt him and me ? ' "

Alex looked up at him like a child that is being scolded. " You don't understand how I feel about it," she said, struggling to speak quietly.

" Yes, quite well. It's only pride, Alex, and for pride you would worry your poor old father almost into his grave. Is that right ? "

" But are our feelings not to be considered at all ? " she asked.

" Not compared with his. You are going to take that

cheque back to him *now*, and make it right with him again. Do you hear ? " There was another silence ; then Maitland spoke again. " And when you have promised to do that, Alex, you have something more to do—you must ask my pardon also."

" I ? Oh, was I rude to you, Mr. Maitland ? " cried poor Alex.

" Yes, you said some very disagreeable things to me," he returned. " Well, what about the cheque ? "

Alex rose and took it from the desk mutely. Maitland came and stood beside her.

" Here, shake hands, and forget our quarrel ! And I may as well tell you that I am coming to see Matilda to-morrow about something. Those boys of hers must go to school—*and I am going to pay*."

Alex winced as if he had struck her. " Oh ! " she cried out in a pained voice.

" Alex, my dear, there are many things you have to learn, and one of them is this—that you have a right to suffer yourself as much as you please for the sake of pride, but that you have no right to make other people suffer for it. I am going to do this for the boys whether you like it or not—however much your pride suffers. I can manage Matilda and—yes, I think I can manage you, too ! "

His face melted into an irrepressible smile as he uttered the last words.

Alex turned away, the cheque held tightly in her hand, and silently retraced her steps across the Square.

Old Hopeful still sat listlessly where she had left him. She fell on her knees by his side.

" Forgive me, Father ! Won't you forget all the horrid things I said ? " she cried. " It's all right about that wretched money ! Here it is ! "

" You have brought it back again ? " he said, sitting up and looking at her in astonishment.

His face was pale and withered, and the white hair, all rumpled about his brow, gave him a pitiful look. Behind him on the table stood the jar full of willow catkins, breathing of hope and the coming of spring. The contrast struck Alex with a pang.

"Yes, Father," she said, holding his hand and smoothing it with her own. "Mr. Maitland explained things to me, and I saw the matter in a different light. I think you are right to trust to your friend and to let him help you, as I'm sure you would help him were he in your place."

"Indeed I should, heartily, gladly, to my last penny. But you seemed so much annoyed—you spoke so sharply, my dear——"

"I know I did. I am very sorry. Do forgive me, Father, and forget about it. Why, you look quite ill!"

"No, no, I am not ill—only vexed. At my age what hurts the feelings hurts the action of the heart, too. I shall be all right presently, my dear. I am just going into the garden for half an hour. Those potatoes must be attended to. That is a little thing I can do, at least, one small but useful contribution to the household, I do think, for what should we do if we had to buy potatoes!"

He went away then, and Alex sat down by the window, her mood of relief all gone, a gnawing bitterness at her heart.

"How I hate and despise myself!" she thought. "I am for ever acting on impulse, and will, I suppose, to the end of the chapter. And how it *hurts* to take that money! Oh, I wonder if Mr. Maitland ever felt angry and abject as I do now? I'm feeling so spiteful and horrid that I'd like to know he did sometimes. What would it feel like to be a beauty—one of those women who can make men grovel at their feet—I wonder? How can I think of anything so hateful—but just for an hour! Oh, what a sickening idea! I am a brute—no fit companion for a woman like Matilda!"

She was roused by Matilda's entrance, and sprang up, saying—

"Oh, have you come in? Father and I have had such

a painful scene. I'm the very worst kind of beast that ever lived, Molly ! "

" Alex, *do* be more moderate ! What have you been doing now ? " said Matilda, unfastening her jacket and sitting down in the armchair.

Alex noted the effect of the long sprays of willow, covered with their fluffy catkins, behind her sister's head, but this time the background suited Matilda's still pretty, gentle face well enough. She sat and heard in silence Alex's account of the whole affair. She treated the incident calmly, as she treated everything.

" I went to Mr. Maitland," said Alex, " and gave him the cheque. I was so angry I could scarcely speak, but he made me take it back."

" How ? " inquired Matilda.

Alex flushed. " Oh, moral suasion, I suppose. Anyhow, I took it, and I hate to, and I hate him at this moment for doing it." She turned quickly away that Matilda might not see her face. " By the way," she called from the doorway, " Mr. Maitland is coming over to see you to-morrow. He is going to talk to you about the boys going to school."

" Oh, dear ! " sighed Matilda, " how I wish he could throw any light upon that, Alex ! I don't know what to do."

" Wait and see," said Alex, grimly. " He's done more difficult things than that."

Matilda was mystified, and would have asked her what she meant, but Alex had disappeared. Her father was in the orchard, the children were scuttling all over the garden. She must be alone and quiet, she felt. She put on her hat, and then she started off at an astonishing pace up the road beyond the village, and at the first corner she almost ran into Van Cassilis, who was coming in the other direction.

" Hello ! " he called. " Where are you off to at this pace ? I was just coming to see you to ask——"

" Don't ask anything," Alex interrupted him, " at least, not of me. I'm too cross to speak a single word. Go and see Matilda, and ask her."

" I won't go on if you're out. May I walk along with you ? "

" No," she snapped, " you mayn't. At least, of course, the high road is free to every one. You can walk where you like. But I want to walk as fast as ever I can for *miles*, without speaking a word."

" All right—here goes ! " said Van. He swung into a pace that was even faster than hers. Alex had to quicken her steps to keep up with him. So they went on—in dead silence—not a word was spoken between them for some time. They passed the plantation beyond the village, turned down the broad road between clipped hedges, where the land sloped in the distance to the sea. Here a part of the side-walk had been laid with shell-gravel, and for a little there was no sound except the slight crunching of Alex's footsteps on the splintered shells. She walked on the pathway, Van in the middle of the road. Then Alex came off the path and they walked together, going nearly at the same pace. Still Van had not uttered a word. He looked round at Alex, and saw that a clear colour had risen in her cheeks and that she was getting out of breath. At last they came within sight of the sea, gleaming grey in the distance, as if light struck on steel. The tender chill spring wind blew towards them, and from the elm trees in the field a bird sang like a soul in bliss.

All of a sudden Alex stopped, stood still, breathing very fast, and then looked up at Van, who had stopped too, and stood with his hands in his pockets and an air of supreme indifference gazing at the sea.

" A good friend ! " she said, laughing. " You're as silent as a dog ! "

" Shall we turn now ? " Van asked. She nodded, and turned to walk beside him more slowly as they went up the hill. But they did not speak till, when Van paused at the road leading to Foxe Hall, Alex held out her hand with a smile and bid him good-bye.

"You're very late, Aunt Alex!" called the gleeful children, as she came into the dining-room, where they were at supper. "Where have you been?"

"I've been out for a long walk with a black dog, as Katharine would say, but I've got rid of him at last," said Alex, cheerfully, helping herself to some of her father's vegetable mess—than which no greater compliment could be paid to Old Hopeful.

"A little of the nuttose improves it very much, my dear," he said, pushing towards her the jar containing his favourite preparation, and Alex was in such a mood of happy reaction, that she did eat a little of it, and gave the rest surreptitiously to the cat—an animal which very seldom rejected anything of an oleaginous nature, even when spread upon Plasmon biscuit.

"I wonder what Mr. Maitland will advise about the boys?" said Matilda, later in the evening.

"That they should be sent to school, I suppose," said Alex, with a hard note in her voice as she spoke.

CHAPTER XVII

So to school Matilda's boys went, and an infinite relief their going was to every one at Orchard House. It was a matter for speculation among the neighbours how Mrs. Chalmers could afford to send her boys to such a good school, but their curiosity on this point was never satisfied. Not even his wife knew that Robert Maitland paid for the education of Matilda's boys. Alex would have liked to tell Mrs. Maitland about it, but she was sternly forbidden to do so. It made her feel quite guilty when Aunt E. V. said to her one day—

" I'm glad Matilda is sensible enough to educate those boys of hers so well."

They were walking back from church together, Robert Maitland and the children a little ahead, when Aunt E. V. made this remark. Alex replied evasively, and turned the conversation by an adroit reference to Mr. Scott's sermon. Alex had an inimitable talent for mimicry, which she very often turned upon the luckless minister of Crossriggs. Her power lay not so much in reproducing the tones of his voice as in inventing the sort of things he would be likely to say on any given subject. She had a *repertoire* of " Scott's sermons," all absolute nonsense, yet each hitting off to a nicety the character of the poor man's unfortunate discourses. Even Aunt E. V., who did not approve of Alex and her ways, was forced to laugh when the girl burst into one of those mock sermons. So to divert the old lady from her talk about the education of

Matilda's boys, Alex began to make mincemeat of what they had just heard.

"I'll construct one on the same lines and preach it to you to-morrow, Miss Elizabeth," she told her.

They paused at the gate of Orchard House as she spoke, and joined Matilda and Maitland.

"What are you going to do to-morrow?" he asked.

"Invent a delicious new Scott sermon," said Alex, "taking, I think, *Lemons* as my subject. Lemons: one, their sourness; two, their scarceness; three, their value." She paused for a moment, waiting for the laugh that generally followed on her efforts, then, with one of her inimitable gestures, "Laugh, Mr. Maitland!" she commanded; "don't make me feel like a fool, even if I am one!"

And Robert threw back his head and laughed ungrudgingly, before the very face of Aunt E. V.

"You know you are really the most savage critic that poor Mr. Scott has," Alex went on. "I *say* what I think of him and of his sermons; you don't say, but your silence is infinitely damning."

"It's perfectly true, Alex, you feel much more kindly towards Scott than I do, in reality. You think that he has some good about him somewhere, while I——"

"The eloquent ellipse!" laughed Alex. Just at that moment, the Admiral's carriage drove past. Van was sitting beside the old man, looking very sorry for himself. Evidently Mr. Scott's discourse and his grandfather's company were proving too much for him altogether. At sight of the little group by the Orchard House gate he seemed to be seized with a wish to join it, for a yard or two further down the Square the carriage stopped and Van got out. He called to the man to drive on.

"I'll walk," he said, and forthwith joined the party at the Hopes' door. "I've sent my grandfather back alone," he said. "It's beyond me to stand any more of it just now."

" It ? " Alex inquired with a whimsical expression.

" Oh—Sundays, and sermons, and Gran ! " he cried.

" Then will you cast in your lot with us ? " Alex asked. " I can tell you exactly what there is to eat—cold mutton, jam roly-poly and—Matilda, I don't believe there is any ' and,' is there ? "

" Good company ! " Van interpolated. " Yes, thanks, I'll stay. I'm awfully fond of cold mutton and jam roly-poly."

" All right—come in ! The children are jumping with hungriness," said Alex, preceding him up the path. Old Hopeful met them at the door. He was the only one of the small Crossriggs community who never went to church, for he held views against conventional church-going. He greeted young Cassilis warmly.

" Come in—come in, to be sure ! We are delighted to see you, or to have you drop in for any meal. We are very simple in our ways, you know, but the simpler the meal, the warmer the welcome. And what have you been about ? Have you found time to read ' The Enquiry into the Causes of Poverty ' ?—a brave attempt to cope with a wide subject. Come in—come this way ! "

He was talking all the time as he ushered his young guest along the dark little hall with its shabby, matted floor towards the dining-room (by courtesy so-called)— that bleak but sunny apartment where the Hopes fed.

" Thank Heaven, Sunday is clean-tablecloth day in poor households ! " sighed Alex, in an aside to Matilda.

But she need not have troubled herself about such matters. Van had not a thought for any little discrepancies that might have annoyed some people. He was perfectly happy and oblivious of other things— already deep in a discusssion on poverty with Mr. Hope, who, had he chosen to look at the question less in the abstract and more in the personal light, might really have been able to contribute some valuable knowledge

to his young friend. Katharine brought in a bald,
ungarnished joint of cold mutton (for parsley was scarce
that spring, and Alex could not afford it), also a dish
of potatoes, and a mess of curious-looking food-stuff
for Old Hopeful, who scorned the carnivorous tastes
of his family.

"This is one of my favourite dishes," he said. "Let
me give you some of it to begin with, Cassilis. Carrots,
sliced, peppered, and stewed so nicely in vegetable oil
by our good Katharine, then surrounded with rice—
rice, the staff of life in wiser lands than ours ! Let me
give you a helping of this."

"Don't—I pray you, don't !" Alex whispered. "It's
an awful preparation ! "

But Van decided to try the curious food, and much
to Mr. Hope's satisfaction was supplied with a liberal
helping.

"Carrots are a generous diet," the old man went on,
"and one well suited to this part of the country. I am
writing a pamphlet just now for distribution through the
country-side on 'The virtues of the Carrot as a food-
stuff.' "

Alex watched Van as he tasted his first mouthful
of the carrot-stew, and now she carved a slice of cold
mutton and laid it on a plate which she pushed imper-
ceptibly towards the young man.

"Change the plates in a minute, when father isn't
looking ! " she directed him, *sotto voce*.

The mute gratitude in his eyes almost moved her to
laughter as he quickly effected the exchange she proposed. Old Hopeful had a great deal to say, meantime,
on the subject of carrots.

"A valuable article of diet that is a good deal despised
among us here in Scotland. We'll give one or two to our
horses as a treat, yet hesitate to feast upon them ourselves." He paused to draw breath, and an awful little
piping voice exclaimed—

" Mr. Cassilis isn't eating his carrots ! " It was Mike, who sat on the opposite side of the table, his round eyes fixed upon the unusual guest.

"And Mike isn't munching his mutton ! " Van retorted, while Alex gave a dexterous turn to the conversation by asking her father to tell Van about his new scheme for evening classes for field-labourers. Old Hopeful was launched on this topic immediately, and the carrots were forgotten.

When the meal, such as it was, had ended, they strolled out into the little orchard behind, from which the house got its name. It was one of those rare days, early in May—rare in Scotland, at least—with delicate blue sky and sunshine which is brilliant and yet lacks the glare of the summer sun. The little orchard was a sheet of bloom ; the old, neglected trees, low-spreading and gnarled, had put on all their bravery. Alex cast herself down on the turf with an exclamation of delight.

" Did you ever smell anything so delicious as this ? " she said. " Shut your eyes and you can fancy that it is blowing straight out of the gates of Paradise from some inner celestial garden ; it almost makes me cry. There's nothing *real* as perfect as that, I'm sure—no happiness like it——"

She stopped, and gathered up a handful of the fallen petals and smelt them rapturously.

" I wonder if there isn't ? " Van asked. He lay on the grass with his hands clasped under his head, gazing up into the mass of blossom above him. Then he sat up suddenly and turned to Alex : " You've had a pretty rough time of it till now," he said. " All your good times have still to come, and they *will*, right enough— they *must*—it's only justice ! "

" I don't believe very much in that argument," she said. " In the first place, I've never done anything to deserve good fortune ; and in the second, there are terrible injustices done under the sun every day. I've seen them."

"Well, they are not going to happen to you—not if I can help it. You are going to have ease and wealth and "—he paused and looked straight at her, and added softly—" and *love !* "

Alex met his eyes for a moment, and then rose hastily, saying with a laugh—

"Ease and wealth I'll never have, my young friend, and as for love, thank Heaven, I've enough of that commodity, for what would life be without it ? I think—yes, I do think—all the children love me, and if the neighbours care half as much for me as I care for them, I'm well off in that quarter too."

She sauntered off among the blossoming apple-trees, talking and laughing as she went, and Van had to follow her, stooping to avoid the low-spreading boughs. His young face was clouded and he was silent.

"I say, Miss Hope," he began presently, "I must go home now." Adding, "I wish I could call you something *kinder* than ' Miss Hope.' Every one is so stiff here. I don't know any one well enough to drop titles with them."

Alex laughed. "You needn't call me ' Miss Hope,' I'm sure, if you don't like it. Call me anything you like. Alexandra Magdalen is my name—Alex is a short-cut ; Magdalen must be taken as a whole. Matilda used to call me Sandy as a child. I was such a little tomboy."

"Sandy ? That's capital ! May I call you that ? " asked Van, eagerly.

"Oh dear, yes ; of course you may ! " said Alex.

She thought no more about it, not being given to " keeping up her dignity " with any one. Only, some weeks later on, when Matilda had heard Van employ the little nickname and looked rather astonished, Alex said to her afterwards—

"He didn't do it without asking leave. I told him he might call me ' Sandy ' if he liked."

" Oh, Alex, it's scarcely suitable, is it ? " said her sister.

" Suitable ? I should hope not ! Who wants to be suitable, except people like James Reid ? " retorted Alex, gaily.

But Matilda shook her head, though she made no further remark.

CHAPTER XVIII

" This is for you, Miss Alex," said Katharine, bringing in a note to Alex one morning some weeks later.

" It's a note from the Admiral, telling me not to come, I suppose," said Alex, as she tore open the envelope.

The note was written by Van to his grandfather's dictation, and expressed a hope that Alex would come rather earlier than usual that afternoon, and that she would stay and help the Admiral to entertain some ladies of his acquaintance who were coming from a distance—"old cats!" Van had commented in expressive parenthesis. This was not at all the sort of thing in which Alex shone, but she did not like to disappoint the old man, and so she put on her best frock and set out earlier than usual.

It was a very hot day in the middle of July, when there seemed to be a suggestion of thunder in the air.

" Just enough to turn the cream, and sour the temper of the old ladies!" as Alex said. " I know they'll be disagreeable to me, and I hate that—it's so difficult not to be rude in self-defence. But I won't, if I can help if, for the Admiral thinks them of great importance, and the poor dear old man may be allowed his own peculiarly petty joys, as he has not got eyes like the rest of us."

" Do take an umbrella, I'm sure it will rain, and your dress will cockle up with a drop," said Matilda.

" Oh, bother my dress, it *must* just cockle then!"

"You really should never have good clothes, Alex," sighed Matilda, "for you are incapable of taking care of them!"

"Quite. I'd like always to be clad in a neat bathing-suit—the most suitable wear for the Scotch climate—and be done with it all at once! Oh, I hope those boresome people won't stay long!"

"Now, Alex, do try to be pleasant to them, even if they are disagreeable. What good does it ever do to be rude?"

"Rude, dear? I never even thought of being rude. Only, of course, if people are frigid, I can play at being frigid, too—quite well; it's one of the easiest things to act, though it's not quite in my character."

She laughed, and tucked the book she was going to read to the Admiral under her arm, then lifted her light skirt from the dust and set out on her walk to Foxe Hall. The day was very hot, and by the time she reached the Hall she was glad enough to get into the shady library, where the old man was waiting for her. Van was somewhere about the house, for she could hear him whistling to himself, though he did not come into the room.

"It is most kind of you to have come early to-day," said the Admiral, settling himself with a sigh of satisfaction to listen to Alex's charming low voice. "The ladies who are coming in presently are, as I think I mentioned, the Misses Brinley, sisters of Lord Lonelands—old family friends."

"Yes," said Alex, "I have met them sometimes at Mrs. Laurence's."

"You have? The late Lord Lonelands was an old friend of mine. They are bringing a niece with them, too—a Miss Pym. Her father was one of the Pyms of Pymsfield, a family very well known in Staffordshire, and her uncle, Ponsonby Pym, was Master of the Hounds in Blankshire in my day. Well, go on, go on. I am interrupting you, and we have not too much time."

The reading went on until the grinding of carriage wheels below the window warned them that the guests had arrived. The Admiral was quite in a flurry, Alex could not understand why. He got up, then sat down again, then got up once more; rang the bell to order tea, fussed over the position of the tea-table, and where Alex was to sit, and so on.

Presently the two Misses Brinley and their niece were shown in, and after a minute the old man began to say—

"Where is Van, I wonder? Miss Hope, did you happen to see him when you came in?"

"I did not *see* him, but I heard him whistling in the background," said Alex.

Both the Misses Brinley turned and looked at her. The niece also, who wore a very large hat pulled far over her eyes, glanced up from under the brim of it. Alex was looking very well: the heat of the room had given her a little extra colour, and her dim lavender dress suited her, showing off the splendid coils of hair which were her only claim to beauty. She sat pouring out tea, and evidently the Misses Brinley could not place her to their own satisfaction. They totally ignored having met her before, although in reality they had done so several times. One talked loudly and volubly to the Admiral. The other sat in grim silence, only now and then assenting vaguely to any remark that Alex made, and looking towards the door.

They were plain women of about fifty and fifty-six, dressed with no regard to taste, but each wore precious ear-rings dangling from very ugly, shrivelled ears; this alone gave any distinction to their appearance. One had a twisted forefinger, of which she seemed rather proud as she spread her hand out on her knee and examined it from time to time. Their boots were large and flat, their voices unsympathetic, and their eyes as cold as grey pebbles. The niece, on the contrary, was rather a pretty girl, with a great deal of very much diffused colour that ran into her neck and ears ; large eyes, a wide hat trimmed with roses, and a cotton gown. She just sat in absolute silence, eating, but not even attempting to join in the very lop-sided conversation that Alex was endeavouring to carry on with her aunt.

" Enough ! " said Alex, to herself. " I, too, will become monosyllabic." A long silence fell.

" Has your garden suffered from the rain last night ? " said Miss Brinley.

" Very little," said Alex.

Another silence. Then the door opened ; Van came in, followed by his dogs, and in a moment Alex saw with amusement the whole explanation of the little comedy.

Both the Misses Brinley welcomed him warmly and almost coquettishly, giving him messages from a nephew, wondering why he had not come to see them for such a long time, inquiring about his plans for the autumn, to which amenities Van replied as civilly as he could, looking, Alex thought, just a little amused. One Miss Brinley immediately plunged into conversation with Alex, while the Admiral was talking to the other—so obviously there was nothing for Van to do but make himself agreeable to the niece. She woke up wonderfully. From under the brim of her big hat she looked up at him and smiled, and, like the dumb man's, " the string of her tongue was loosed." Alex was too much amused to be indignant at the remarks Miss Brinley was now making to her about Crossriggs and the people there. It filled her with humorous delight to watch the whole scene. That any one could take Van and his prospects seriously had never occurred to her before, but now she saw that worldly wisdom is long-sighted. She could have laughed aloud as the Misses Brinley and Miss Pym rose to go, altogether ignoring her in their eagerness to make some appointment with Van for the following week.

"Most agreeable women!" the Admiral remarked, when they had left the room along with Van. "I gather that Miss Pym is pretty, too."

"Does he mean 'as well as the aunts,' or that she only is pretty and agreeable?" thought Alex. She answered gaily, "Oh, quite pretty—a lovely colour."

"Ah, she is an only child—the whole of the Pymsfield estates will come to her," said the artless old man. "Did Van have any conversation with her?"

"A great deal. I think Miss Pym seemed to find *him* most agreeable," said Alex.

"Ah, young people! The boy sees too few of his own age here. There is very little society for a young man in this neighbourhood."

Alex assented, and just as she said good-bye to the Admiral, Van returned—rather heated, a little conscious-looking, perhaps, but gay with the gaiety of indubitable relief.

"Come through the garden," he said to Alex, following her to the door, "I'll let you out by the other gate."

"Isn't it going to rain?" she said, glancing anxiously up at the sky.

"Oh, no—or only a few drops—nothing," Van assured her. But by the time they got into the garden it was a heavy thunder shower.

CHAPTER XIX

THE quick drops, as large as peas, fell heavily from the suddenly darkened sky.

" It's going to be a downpour—what about your frock ? " said Van.

Alex looked hopelessly down at her dress. " I always *knew* it would rain if I put it on. I said so to Matilda. I am the kind of woman who should never put on a good gown—it's doomed to destruction the moment I get into it."

" Make a run for the house," Van suggested. Alex hesitated.

" One drop does it," she said tragically. " It crinkles up with every one. Oh, woe is me ! I must go into the tool-shed and wait there."

" Come under the yew tree. You'll be as dry as lime —it's much better," said Van. They ran along the narrow path, and went through the door that led into the other garden.

There stood the ancient tree which made the only claim of Foxe Hall to distinction. The house, after all, was only two hundred years old, but for ages before house or garden had been thought of that great thing had been growing in the field. Generation after generation had passed away ; houses had been built and had fallen to ruin ; many, many times the land on which it stood had changed owners ; the history of the piece of ground, or the reason of the tree's first planting, had long been forgotten. Still it grew and flourished, drawing into its black branches all the goodness of the surrounding soil, stretching silently up and up and out and out, throwing long, dark arms farther; a thicket of saplings laying hold of the earth, in their turn, from the ends of its farthest shoots.

Underneath the higher branches there was a tent-like space, big enough to have been an ambush for twenty men. Blind night hung there always—always, too, the same dryness where no rain or dew ever fell, the same scent of earth, and the same spicy smell of foliage. A little sort of passage had been made in one place through the branches, and when you lifted the flap of green that covered the opening, you seemed to be entering a twilight room. Van held the branch high to allow Alex to pass; it gave an angry creak, as if at an indignity, and swung back into place again. Under the branches everything was very quiet; the noise of the rain, now pouring in torrents outside, was only a far-away drumming overhead, and a hissing as it fell on the branches far beyond. Not a drop reached the dry, reddish floor of fallen needles.

Alex gathered her thin lilac skirts about her, and sat down on the low bench beside the trunk of the tree. Van threw himself on the ground at her feet, his hands clasping his knees, his head thrown back—in the dim light it looked very fine, like some modern bust, touched with the spirit of the antique. Alex watched him with pleasure: as he held his face at that angle, the curve of lips and throat, the small head, the one straight line made by the brow and nose in profile, always won her admiration.

" A penny, this minute, Alex, if you'll tell me what you're thinking about ! " he said suddenly, turning to her.

Alex laughed. " I was thinking how good you were to look at, and how I'd like to have been handsome myself!" Van said nothing, only smiled. "I don't mind a bit in general," she went on ; " in fact, I've sense enough to see that it only adds a great deal of trouble to a woman's life when she's a beauty. Thank heaven, I've got all the looks that are necessary for everyday, humdrum, human life. Only just now and then, when I see any one beautiful, I wonder what it would have been like to attract in that kind of way."

"You're so *un*-attractive, of course ! "

"Yes, I am—in that way—quite. But I've had all the love I want,"—she paused and added—" or nearly all, without it, so I do very well."

"Better than some of us, if you've got that," Van muttered in a low voice.

He was picking up the scarlet, waxen berries that had fallen on the ground, and now began to shy them at a robin—a dismal, moulting summer robin—which was flittering about amongst the lower branches.

"Do leave that poor bird alone ! " said Alex. "I so respect the shamefaced feeling that makes it lurk in the undergrowth when it is all shabby like that. I've often felt just the same, on the days when I look particularly ugly. I'd like to hop about under a hedge, and never issue into light or company at all."

"I can't imagine you lurking in a hedge at any time, Sandy."

Alex sat looking up into the dense shadow above them and made no reply. In the silence that ensued, they could hear the pattering of the far-off rain, but no other sound.

"What a weird place this is ! " she said at last. "I wonder what things have happened here long ago. Do ycu remember the yew at Borrodale—

"'. . . Beneath whose sable roof . . .
Ghostly shapes might meet at noontide,
Fear and trembling Hope, Silence, and Foresight,
Death the skeleton and Time the shadow ' ? "

She threw out her thin brown hands with a sudden gesture. "Oh, let us come out! It's oppressing me in here. I'll begin to see the ghostly shapes in another minute!" She rose and stood leaning against the seared trunk of the great tree. "'*Silence and Foresight— Death the skeleton and Time the shadow.*' Oh, Van, we're here for such a moment; is it at all worth while? Think of all that has passed and that will pass here after we're just earth again—like that!" She pressed her foot into the dry, soft ground. "I do so love the living of life— it's dreadful to think of it."

"Alex," said Van. He had risen and stood beside her. "You said a moment ago that you had got all the love you wanted."

"So I have, and far more than I deserve!" she said lightly, bending forward to look through a chink in the branches.

"Well, I haven't, I can assure you. No one in the whole world, except Gran, cares two straws about me— and he only a little."

"Well, it's your own fault if that is the case," said Alex, severely. She smiled, adding, "There will be plenty of charming young women ready to care for you some day, Van; don't you begin to see that, even now?"

A remembrance of the little scene with the Misses Brinley half an hour before, amused her greatly. All the same, she looked at Van with a sudden new interest. Was it possible that he was really of importance socially in the eyes of such women—matrimonially even? She laughed again at the mere idea of it.

"Oh—hang the charming young women! I hate them all."

"No, you don't! Or if you do, you're very foolish. Don't begin to pose, Van, it's such a temptation. I did it myself at your age."

"You do it still," said Van, suddenly savage.

"You try to pose as a grandmother. It's so affected, Sandy."

He moved a little nearer to her, and, for an instant, Alex looked into his eager face. Then she turned away sharply, saying—

"Oh, there's the sun coming out. I must fly home now. I have to help the boys with their lessons."

Without looking at him again, she stooped down and ran out of the green doorway, lifting the heavy branch and shaking the raindrops from her dress as she reached the open air, and turned with a sigh that was, perhaps, mingled with a little pain, into the shining outer world once more.

The shower had passed completely now, and the sun, intolerably hot, beat down upon the walks and the drenched garden beds. By the side of the path that led into the garden there was a hedge of flowering lavender. Its sharp scent, drawn out by the rain and sun, filled the air. Alex pulled some of it, stooping on purpose to hide her hot face, and then, twirling the scented sprays against her cheek, she hurried along the garden paths. A hundred flowers, beaten down by the rain for an hour, were beginning to revive, red and blue, roses and jasmine, rows and rows of lilies and carnations—the moisture and the heat brought out all their scent.

"Don't keep that stuff, I'll get you a rose," said Van, looking at the lavender.

"This is so sweet, and it matches my dress."

"An old maid's flower, Sandy—throw it away! See, I've got a rose that hasn't been spoilt."

He brought it to her, shaking off the rain-drops that had fallen on his arm from the bush.

It was a rose very nearly full-blown; a new variety, that glowed almost scarlet at the heart. All passion and unspoken desire seemed to find expression in it as he laid the perfect blossom in her hand.

Alex took it without a smile. "It is lovely," she said. "But I feel as if I had seen a ghost in there."

She glanced back at the great tree, black against the brilliant garden beds.

" What sort of ghost ? " Van asked, walking beside her listlessly now.

" Oh, it was only your face in that greenish light, I suppose. It looked as if you were under water, or something ever so far away."

They had reached the garden door by this time, and Alex refused to let Van walk with her any further.

" Go back and amuse your grandfather," she said. " I'm going to take this rose to old Miss Reid."

Van said nothing. He watched her walk off, noticing her long, free step and the fine carriage of her head, then turned back to the house. He looked at his watch, and for a moment his hand trembled like that of an old man. There was a very deep furrow between his black eyebrows, and, slowly mounting the steps to the door, he breathed like a man who has been running too fast.

Alex walked quickly home. " Scarcely a drop ! " she said, when Matilda called out to know if the rain had ruined her gown, " I was under shelter the whole time. What a lovely evening ! Come, Matty—I want to go along and see old Miss Reid."

Matilda laid aside her eternal sewing, as Alex called it, and they started off together.

The close sitting-room at the Reids did seem very dingy as they came in out of the brave summer world out-of-doors, for Miss Bessie Reid—good woman !— was skilled in all the little arts that make home hideous. There was a specimen of her handiwork at every turn— a painted tambourine here, a stark water-colour there, whilst miniature animals in crockery seemed to crawl on every ledge. Framed photographs, of all kinds, were everywhere, and a vase in one corner (Alex blushed, as she noticed it, for the obtuseness of the kind heart that had put it there) held a quantity of artificial almond blossom, made out of pink tissue paper and stuck upon thorn branches. Taste, I suppose, is only a constant delicate expression of opinion, and Miss Bessie Reid's opinions—poor dear !—must have been singularly confused.

She welcomed her visitors with what Alex used to call " the cold glitter of her toothsome smile," and much tinkling and twinkling of ornaments. Had it been earlier in the day, they knew that very soon the door would have opened and the little maid-servant appeared, clutching a tray containing tea-cups that tasted of dead air (having been turned up for perhaps a week on a shelf), each holding about a thimbleful of pale yet bitter tea. There would also be a plate of broken meats in the shape of bits of cake and stale cakelets, spread by Miss Bessie's own untiring fingers, with sour-tasted, rainbow-hued sugar-icing, and garnished with chips of coloured peel. The collation was inevitable ; no one, at any hour after two p.m., had ever escaped it ; the chink of preparation became audible as soon as the guest was seated. To-day, however, Alex and Matilda had timed themselves to escape—it really was too late, and Miss Bessie did not insist. Her welcome was sincere, and she kissed Alex affectionately. It always made Alex feel a little guilty—this kindness of Miss Bessie's.

" She *is* good and kind, when my life is spent in the effort to keep at bay the attentions of a brother whom she considers the most perfect man on earth," thought Alex. Leaving Matilda to speak to her, she crossed the room and bent over the sofa where old Miss Reid was sitting, bunched up by stiff pillows that supported her in a curiously upright position. Alex was a great favourite of hers, so she brightened and stammered out a few painful sentences.

" I have brought you a rose, Miss Reid," said Alex. " It is a new kind and very beautiful."

The old woman stretched out her trembling hand, and slowly lifted the red, red rose. She bent her flabby face with its poor dim eyes and twisted mouth down to it, and gazed at it long and in silence. Its aroma, its passionate beauty, its perfection, seemed to awe her. She did not speak a word. Just then the maid appeared, and Miss Bessie came up, saying, " it's time for you to say good-night, Auntie." The old woman mumbled out a word or two to Alex and Matilda, and then, still holding the rose in her hand, was led from the room. They could hear her slow, trailing footsteps as she limped off to her unregarded bed—to-morrow another of her eventless days would begin. Alex looked down, and her eyes filled with sudden tears.

" I *wish* I hadn't brought it ! " she whispered to Matilda. Miss Bessie returned in a few minutes, bright as ever.

" How wonderful," she said, seating herself with a clink and a gleam of teeth ; " how wonderful dear auntie always is—so bright ! She seems able to enjoy so much. I was playing her some selections from ' Pinafore ' when James was here on Thursday, and I declare she quite entered into the spirit of the thing ! I try to keep her up as much as possible. I brought her that card on the mantelpiece—the one with the three kittens in men's collars and ties—and she was quite delighted with it ! "

Matilda made some tactful remark that covered Alex's silence, and Miss Bessie went on—

" I was at Mrs. Laurie's in the afternoon, and the two Misses Brinley were there. They didn't know *me*, of course," archly, shaking her head, " but I knew them ; and they were on their way to Foxe Hall. You would see them there, Alex ? "

" Oh, yes ! " laughed Alex. " Don't suppose they would know me either ! They are a study in negatives, those women—not handsome, not well-dressed, not clever, not even rich, I suppose and certainly not agree-able. All they are is just that they *are* the Misses Brin-ley ! " She pressed Miss Bessie's knobby hand in a sudden

access of liking. " Now, Matilda, *don't* say anything
charitable about them, for we understand one another!"

" They are not talkative people, certainly," said Matilda, " but I saw nothing disagreeable about them."

" Silent through pride ; if that's what you call agreeable. I can do it too ; though with an effort. And I
did it for about ten minutes, until I felt that I *must*
talk again."

" Alex, Alex ! James always says you are such a
versatile creature ! " exclaimed Miss Bessie. This was
more than the versatile creature could stand. She glanced
at her sister so meaningly that Matilda was constrained
to rise and say good-bye.

Miss Bessie, chinking, accompanied them to the door,
and they walked slowly away in the delicious summer
twilight.

" Poor old Miss Reid looked very feeble, I thought,"
said Matilda.

Alex replied with a sudden quiver in her voice. " The
living ! ' *The living shall praise Thee !* ' Oh, Matty, don't
you think that so long as we are alive, and move freely,
and feel—if it's even sorrow—we should be giving
praise for that ? " She walked on with her long, free
step and that air of interest in the scene about her that
always made her face so attractive. " I wish I hadn't
given her that rose—it hurt me."

" Did you get it from the Admiral ? "

" No ; from Van," Alex answered rather brusquely,
and Matilda said no more.

CHAPTER XX

THE ordinary limitations of poverty were nothing to a man of Old Hopeful's temperament.

"A handful with quietness! A dinner of herbs where love is! Who would want more?"

He was sitting by the window, a Greek book in somewhat ragged covers in his hand, his face glowing with contentment. Alex had been doing up the household books—not a cheerful occupation for an August evening, but not quite so depressing as in winter. Still, she had sighed once or twice, and when her father asked the reason, she answered rather sharply—

"There's always reason enough when one has to make sixpence do the work of six shillings!"

"Well! well!" said Mr. Hope, placidly. "I cannot say I have often felt the want of money, though I have very little."

"No, I don't suppose you have; but a great deal of money was spent on your education, you know, father."

"And what good has it done me from your point of view," replied Old Hopeful. "Have I ever been able to 'make money,' as men say? No, no; I have rather spent what I had. Remember the fine old saying, Alex: *'What I spent I had; what I saved I lost; what I gave I have.'* How true! Yellow dust! Just yellow dust, when all is said and done. Why, children, I will give any of you a penny for naming one of what I may call the *blessings* of life that can be bought for money. I'm not speaking, remember, of food, fire, and raiment—we've enough of these to meet our wants. There's a puzzle for you ! "

There was an immediate chorus from the children.

" *Nice* clothes," said Sally, wistfully.

" A pony," said one boy.

" A cricket-bat," said another.

" Paint-box," Mike said, in his little, low voice.

" Clothes, Sally ? Fie ! You have clothes enough. Health and modesty in a young girl are far more than any fine clothes," said Old Hopeful. " And why should you wish for a pony, George ? Exercise on your own legs is far better for you."

" *I* said a cricket-bat," Peter remarked.

Old Hopeful sighed. " Well, well ; at your age I should have wanted a cricket-bat, too. Come, we must have pennies all round, I see ! " and they were dispensed, while Alex looked on with a smile, half bitter, half amused. But she said to Matilda afterwards—

" I *must* make some more money, Matilda. Winter is coming on again, with fires and lights, and everything dearer, and the children are growing like mushrooms. I must do something, even if I have to break stones, or offer myself as precentor to the church ! "

Matilda's blue eyes filled with tears, and she pressed her sister's hand for a moment.

" Oh, Alex—I cannot bear to think of all the worry I have brought upon you ! "

" Worry, darling ? Why, the children are the joy of my heart. I could never live without them now. Do you know that I am getting old, Matilda—I shall be thirty next month, and thirty is the half of sixty ! " She burst out laughing. " Only think what Mike said to me yesterday. He stood looking up at me for some time, and then asked in his funny little voice, ' Was zoo ever a servant, Aunt Alex ? ' I wondered what had put such a thing into the child's head, and asked him why he thought so, and he answered, ' Because I heard Mrs. Scott say wat if zoo didn't take care zoo would be an *old maid* in no time.' Mrs. Scott was right, you see."

" Oh, Alex, if you could only marry——"

" Please, dear Matilda, say *would*, not *could*, if it's all the same to you," said Alex, and Matilda, silenced, turned away.

" Look here, Matty," called Alex, cheerfully, " to change the subject, Sally must go to the dentist."

" I don't see how she can, at present."

" Well, it's now a case of ' between the Dentist and the Deep Sea,' " said Alex. " We either *must* pay or she lose the tooth. She has such pretty teeth, too. I'd rather extract all my own with my finger-nails, like the Chinese, than let her lose them. We'll manage somehow. Take her to Winan's. He fills with metal that turns black, and tortures horribly, but he's reliable and cheap. We'll sell those two old brooches of yours, and the old set of teeth with some gold about it that was amongst Aunt Lizzie's possessions—I know it's somewhere in the house—and perhaps we can manage on that."

The small transaction was accomplished in the course of a week, and Alex took the now reluctant Sally into town one Saturday—a cheap ticket day, so, even though it looked threatening, they were obliged to go. The rain did come down in the afternoon, and by six o'clock it was pouring torrents.

Two drenched figures appeared a little later. Sally holding a shawl over her aching mouth, squeezing the water out of her wet skirts when she got in, but bursting into a high peal of triumphant giggles now that the ordeal was over. Alex looked very pale, and her eyes were brighter than usual. She replied indifferently to Matilda, who was standing in the lobby, exclaiming over their drenched condition.

" I'll just go up and change now," she said. " It won't do me any harm."

" Van is here," said Matilda.

" Oh, bother ! " said Alex, almost crossly, as she turned to go upstairs. " Come and speak to me, Matty, while I change ; when you've seen to Sally," she called out.

Matilda came into the room a few minutes later. Alex stood at the glass twisting up her damp hair. She was smiling now.

" What do you think I have to tell you," she said. " It's such a relief, Matilda, you can't think. Do you know that I've got some work in town."

" Alex ! How ? What do you mean ? "

" Well, I mean that I answered an advertisement last week for an elocution teacher in a girls' school, and I left Sally at the chamber of horrors to-day and went out and saw the people, and they're going to take me—three times a week—isn't it grand ? "

" Oh, it is, Alex—if you can do it. But your reading to the admiral ? "

" I'll manage that too. The school is in the morning, and I can be back to luncheon a little late, and go up in the afternoon. The Admiral will shove on his time half an hour, I dare say."

Matilda had to hear the whole story, of course, and when it was finished Alex asked rather impatiently—

" Do you suppose Van is still here ? "

" Oh, yes, I've never heard him go."

" Very well, I must go down, I suppose," said Alex. Matilda had to put the baby to bed, so she went down alone.

Tact and preoccupation with a special subject seldom go together ; so she found Van there, still rooted, as it were, in the drawing-room.

" He just wants a little earth aboot the feet o' him to be growing there, Miss Alex," Katharine had whispered indignantly, when Alex asked her if Mr. Cassilis was still in the house.

There he was, glowering out at the sheets of steady rain, and replying somewhat vaguely to the remarks of Peter and George, who were making a boat by the window. He brightened up instantly when Alex came in.

"Are you cold, Sandy? Are you tired? You look cold. Come and sit here."

He pulled a chair to the hearth where, although it was August, a wood fire was burning. Alex was thankful to sit down. Cold and tired, she would much rather have sat with her feet on the fender and read a novel than talked to Van, but the boyish depression, and very boyish elation at her appearance, touched her. So she thanked him and, leaning back in her chair, waited to hear what he had to tell.

"What have you been doing all day?" she asked.

"Quarrelling with Gran," he answered, coming and standing by the fireplace. He frowned and fidgeted and seemed to wait for her to speak again.

"Badly?"

"Yes, rather. That's why I came out."

"Dear me! What a quarrelsome disposition you have! Can't you keep your temper with an old, blind man like your grandfather?"

"I would—I do—except when he provokes me too much. But there's a limit to one's forbearance, even with old people."

"And what has he been saying now?" Van remained silent. "Well, whatever it is, you ought to say nothing, because he *is* your grandfather. You haven't got enough to do, Van. If you had to work hard for your living, like me, you'd find you had more to think about than what an old man said to you, probably in a moment of irritation or because he was feeling ill."

"That's exactly it, I *haven't* got enough to do," Van burst out passionately. "If I'd been allowed to go into the army, or work at anything that interests me, I'd slave like a nigger. But to be brought back and expected

to spend all my time pottering about the estate—and
I don't approve of landed property at all; all that will
be swept away within the next fifty years, I hope—
talking about cattle or fencing or drainage with an agent
who thinks he knows everything, and wouldn't listen to
a word from me, even if I did know or care about it, and
to dodder about with Gran to the houses of dull people,
instead of being allowed to choose my own friends——"
He paused, and threw up his head with a snort.

Alex laughed a little. She noticed the pause, and
wondered what had really passed between the Admiral
and his grandson.

"I'll tell you what it is," the young man went on,
"have you ever seen a pet collie, Sandy? Well, you
know what a shepherd's dog is like—lean and swift and
able to do everything but speak. Take that beast and
stop all his work, feed him fat and let him sleep on the
rug and tootle around the garden, or walk half a mile
along with you, and, in a year or so, his coat will be all
rusty and his teeth rotten, and the creature good for
nothing at all. That's what happens to a man who has
nothing to do but fool about as I'm doing now." He
sank into a chair, and glowered into the fire with a bitter
look upon his face.

"Well, I don't deny I'm sorry for you, but you ought
to try to be interested in something."

"Oh, I know all that! Gran's always preaching about
the duties of one's order, and the responsibilities of ownership, and so on. There oughtn't to be ownership; and
I might as well speak to a post as to Waycot—he's been
with Gran for thirty years. Much good I can do in that
way!" Alex was silent, and he went on. "You can't
understand what it is to be dependent as I am, not
allowed to be anything else. And he wants to dictate to me about everything; why—why "—he stammered as he spoke—"he'd like even to choose a wife
for me!"

Alex, in spite of herself, burst out laughing, and Van's fury increased.

" Oh, laugh away! Of course you think it a great joke; I'm glad I amuse you so much. Good-night, I'm going."

" No, no, Van dear," called Alex, checking her unseemly mirth, " don't go away yet. I didn't mean to be unsympathetic, I was only a little amused. Is that because you've been to Brinfield?"

The recollection of the Misses Brinley and Miss Pym of Pymsfield made her smile again.

Van nodded gloomily. " I'd never have gone if they hadn't asked me so often, and Gran made such a point of it. I only stayed a week, and I'd much rather never have gone near them at all. And now he's angry with me."

" It will blow over; don't think too much about it. It's natural enough, Van, for old people to think they can judge for the young. We all think we could choose just the right person for every one else."

She soothed him as well as she could, and when Matilda came into the room he took a reluctant leave.

" It's like trying *politely* to get rid of a snail to get Van out of the house sometimes," said Alex, when at last he had gone.

" Poor boy! it's so dull at home," said Matilda. " You look very tired, Alex, are you all right?"

She glanced at her sister anxiously.

" Oh, yes," said Alex. She drew Matilda down on a footstool beside her chair, and they sat in the firelight in silence for a few minutes. Then Alex began all of a sudden. " Matilda, do you know, such an annoying thing has happened. James Reid has asked me to marry him!"

" Oh!" said Matilda, turning round on the footstool and uttering the word with a depth of interest that can be drawn out between women by one subject only.

" Yes," Alex went on, " I have always thought I

could stave it off, but to-night the Fates were against me. We were a little late for the train coming home, because Sally couldn't walk fast, and I had so many parcels to carry, and at the station in Edinburgh we met Miss Bessie and Mr. Reid. It was pouring torrents, and I had given Sally my umbrella. When we met them, Sally and Miss Bessie hurried on ahead, and Mr. Reid insisted on taking all my parcels and holding his umbrella over me.   " Oh, dear, it was all so uncomfortable ! He *would* hold up that umbrella, but whenever he got particularly agitated it swerved, you know, and all the drippings fell into my ear or down my neck, and all the time I knew that my hat was getting drenched. I did not want to be unkind. I needn't pretend I didn't know he liked me, but I hoped it would never have come just to that."

    " Alex, couldn't you—James Reid is——— "

    " A good, excellent man—now *don't !* " cried Alex. " You hurt my feelings so—you make me feel so *poor*. What am I ?   What is life, or one's heart, or one's hopes of—Heaven ?—if any one can remember James Reid, and then pause and begin, ' Couldn't you '——— "

    " I don't agree with you about James Reid," said Matilda, with sudden coldness.   " He is a person I have a great respect for, and he would make a very suitable husband."

    " For some people, perhaps ; but the last thing I want in the world is a suitable husband. All the same, I should like even the refusing of something more romantic than James Reid."

    " I think you are very flighty about things of that sort, Alex," said Matilda.

    She rose and left the room, and Alex sighed to herself. " Dear creature !   Remembering Peter Chalmers, what else can she say ?   Perhaps I am.   After all, I'm just as angry as Van that any one should think they can choose for me !   Poor Van—poor boy ! "

CHAPTER XXI

DURING the following autumn the Hopes were submerged
by one of those billows of misfortune which sweep over
families of their type, until it seems as if the buffeting of
their troubles could only cease when all were overwhelmed.

It began by Katharine, the old servant, turning ill
and having to go home for a time. Her place was very
indifferently filled by a succession of " generals," each one
of whom developed some new and ingenious deficiency.

" They're so surprising," Alex complained to Miss
Maitland one day. " The first we got had a good character, but she couldn't even boil an egg. The day after
she arrived, as we noticed that she had been going about
all morning in plum-coloured velveteen with a deep lace
collar, Matilda took courage to suggest that she should
change her dress before admitting visitors in the afternoon. This she very affably consented to do, and soon
afterwards she was hurrying to open the front door
wearing a scarlet satin blouse, and a rope of pearls.
The next candidate came in for the first time to remove
the crumbs from the dinner table with a carpet shovel
and brush. The one we've got now—she came yesterday—has just escaped imbecility, and is as ugly as a
Kaffir idol, but she already tells me that your gardener
and the postman have both tried to kiss her ! "

Alex was laughing as she spoke, but there was not much
mirth in the laugh, which was only a sort of " whistling
to keep her courage up." A few days after Katharine
left, Mr. Hope fell ill with influenza, then Mike caught
it, and now Matilda was ill, too. Alex had been all

morning in town, and on her return found Matilda too ill to do anything but groan ; so instead of resting, she had been obliged to arrange everything about the house, and attend to her father, who seemed to be very much worse than when she had left in the morning.

" You look tired, Alex," said Aunt E. V., who had come in to ask for Mr. Hope.

" Yes, of course I'm tired," said Alex. " I was up four times last night getting poultices for father, and tnen went into town. The new work is very tiring, you know—I have to stand all the time ; and since I came home I've done nothing but run up and downstairs until you came in just now."

" You must have a nurse, Alex."

" I know. I've been trying to face that all morning. The doctor advised it last night, but I thought I could manage if Mike was allowed to get up to-morrow."

The idea of all the little hoard that she had saved with such difficulty during the last six months being swallowed up in this way was bitter indeed.

" It's bad to be ill, but it's hard to be ill and expensive at the same time," she said pitifully.

Aunt E. V. was silent, being too practical to suggest untrue consolations ; but she went home to consult Robert, with the result that the next day, when the nurse had been sent for, Matilda's two boys and the baby were taken across to stay for a fortnight at the Manse.

" A baby has no terrors for *me*," Miss Maitland remarked, when Laura expressed some doubts about having it.

The boys were awed at first, but soon became very happy, and Baby, after a few tears, settled down with great composure to being the pet of the whole household. Sally was able to help Alex to nurse Matilda, and the nurse attended to Old Hopeful, whose illness had now become very serious. Mike, when he began to get up again, felt himself rather in the shade, as the other boys and Baby were all so fine paying a visit at the Manse. Many were the glowing tales they told him of everything there; from the cakes that the Maitland's cook provided to the qualities of the Manse cat, a great sleek animal, heavy as a lamb and, of course, a hereditary enemy of their own gaunt friend.

But Alex, meanwhile, was going through a very dark time. Poverty, sickness and cold combined, make a depressing atmosphere in which the bravest spirit is tried. The weather was now bitter, the first frosts of winter coming on, and no amount of fire seemed to make the house warm enough for the sick people.

Alex was forced to give up her reading to the Admiral for the time being, but she continued to go into town to her new work three mornings in the week. When she came home—night and day, early and late—she went pounding up and downstairs, making beds, filling hot-water bottles, cooking, setting, or carrying away the myriad little meals required by three sick people; all the time with a dull throbbing in her head, a pain in her back, and at her heart the dread of what would happen if she fell ill too.

Then one day, as Mr. Hope got better, and when Matilda was able to go about again, Alex collapsed entirely.

After a week in bed she reappeared, with a bleached face and sunken eyes, but declaring that she was going to begin her work again as soon as she was allowed to go out.

Van, who had been many times to inquire for her, came in the first day that Alex was downstairs. He exclaimed at her appearance as she entered the room.

"Oh, Sandy, you've been much worse than I knew!"

"Yes, it's been pretty bad," Alex confessed. To Matilda she made light of her illness, but Van's sympathy was very soothing. "It leaves one—this thing—confronting the simple problem of returning to the duties

of life apparently without any spine, if you can imagine
what that feels like ! "

She sank rather hopelessly into a chair, as she spoke.
Van stood by the fireplace gloomily regarding her.

" You want to go away to the South of France, or somewhere, and do nothing but rest and lie out in the sun.
Why don't you get some one to take you ? " he said.

There was a moment's pause. Van was going to say
something else when Alex interrupted him.

" Who—who, pray ? And what would become of my
family in my absence ?—that was a truly practical suggestion ! " she laughed, and shook off her air of lassitude.
" You must tell the Admiral that I will come up on
Monday as usual, unless the day is very wet."

" You're not able to walk across the room—far less
to our house ! " Van retorted. " I won't give your
message at all."

But Alex was so much in earnest that he had to give
way, only, when Monday came, just as she was about to
start on her walk, Van appeared to drive her—and he
drove her home, too, in spite of all her assurances that
she was quite able to walk.

" Van is so considerate," Matilda remarked, when he
had gone.

" I don't think he is, at all," Alex replied. " Or at
any rate, it's only by fits and starts, and for one person
at a time—he'd have considered me to-day and forgotten
all about his blind old grandfather, for instance. He
just ' means well,' as most of us do."

Matilda sighed, thinking that her sister was strangely
difficult to please.

All the same Alex had felt it very pleasant to have Van
taking care of her, and as she sat beside him on their
way home, warmly wrapped up behind the swift-going
horses, she thought to herself that some young woman
would some day have a very comfortable life with Van
to take care of her. As they neared Crossriggs the red

sunset was just fading out behind the low hills ; small pillars of smoke rose into the windless air from the cottage chimneys : in one or two windows the lamps were already lighted. An air of winter peace, of calm and intimate village life, seemed over the whole little picture, and an unacknowledged current of happiness ran through all that Van and Alex said to one another, influencing the very aspect of the outer world to them, making them remember the hour for long as a very pleasant one. On Alex's side it was a delicate, evanescent feeling— merely the pleasure of being cared for and the sub-consciousness of the young man's unspoken admiration, which she would never really acknowledge to herself.

Several weeks had passed, and it was after Christmas before Alex could resume her work in town. Even then she looked hardly able for it, and Matilda tried hard to dissuade her.

" Do wait till the weather is a little better, Alex," she said. " You don't look fit to go ! "

" Oh, I'm all right ! It's much better for me than staying at home to worry. There is that chemist's bill ! And Father still needs so much ! Now that the children are all back again I don't mind leaving you."

" If we are all well again, nothing matters," said Matilda. " You mustn't begin to overwork yourself too soon ! "

" It does me good—what I can't do, is to sit still and worry. Why, the other night, when I thought that Mike was going to be ill, I couldn't sleep until I got up and began to knit Peter's socks. I decided to turn the heel before I lay down again, and I worked so hard that by the time it was done the worries had all vanished, and I slept like a top."

Alex would listen to none of Matilda's entreaties, and, after that, went into town regularly three days a week. She was thankful to have the employment, but often when she came back collapsed altogether and would have to go to bed half blind with headache.

Old Hopeful was never so robust after that illness. He still made an effort to work in his garden, to attend the meetings of the Fruitarian Brotherhood and to spread their propaganda. But he had lost his bright colour : his cheeks were thin, and his poor old hands trembled so that they could scarcely direct his gardening tools, and Matilda had to invent all sorts of excuses in order to keep him from finding that she sent the boys to help him. There was some anxiety about him amongst his neighbours.

One afternoon Maitland came in to inquire for the old man. It was Alex's day in town, and she had not yet returned. Old Hopeful was sitting by the hearth, with a book on his knee, and his spectacles in his hand, looking listlessly into the fire.

" Come in, come in, Robert, you are always welcome," he said, looking up with a start at Maitland's entrance. " I have been out in the garden, but somehow, I scarcely feel able to go on with my work : there is a weakness about my limbs ever since my illness. I have been sadly useless for a long time past ; indeed, I have almost suspected of late that, instead of being the support of my daughters, I am something of an anxiety—an expense— to both of them." He paused and tremblingly rubbed his spectacles.

" An anxiety, I dare say you may have been, sir. What is precious to us is always an anxiety," said Maitland.

" Ah, you are kind, you are all very kind," said Mr. Hope ; " but there are many mouths to feed in our household, and my daughter Matilda does not see eye to eye with me in the matter of diet. Some of my garden produce has, I confess, been a failure. I have often tried experiments that have not always been successful, and have cost some money, but potatoes—

potatoes I have always, hitherto, been able to provide (many of the Irish, a chaste and healthy race, live on little else)—but this winter my crop has somehow entirely failed. I took the first of them to-day out of the pits, with a little help from my grandsons, and lo! they were all black!" He lifted a potato from a gardening basket that stood near him, and held it out piteously to Robert. "It seemed but a small contribution to make to the household economy, but it was steady; and I heard poor Alex exclaim, ' Dear me, even father's potatoes turn out badly—orchids I can understand, but I did hope we might have had some potatoes.' So, you see, Robert, I have had rather a disappointing day. A strange weariness takes me in the afternoons, and I thought I would just sit down with Homer for a few minutes by the fire." He sat in silence for a little; then, glancing up at Robert, who looked particularly well that afternoon, he said, with a smile: "' Rejoice, O young man, in thy youth, and let thy heart cheer thee in the days of thy youth.'"

Maitland smiled too. "Ah, the days of my youth are far away now, sir!"

He had been thinking deeply before Old Hopeful interrupted him, and now he rose to go away, having scarcely spoken a word the whole time, yet the old man had been curiously comforted by his presence.

Matilda came in just as he was going. She had the baby trotting beside her, and it insisted on being lifted up; so Maitland, who had made a great pet of it when the children were at the Manse during Mr. Hope's illness, sat down again, holding the child on his knee, talking to Matilda whilst it quietly counted the buttons on his waistcoat and listened to his watch.

"Father has gone and tired himself out by trying to work in that stupid garden!" said Matilda. "I'm sure, my dear father, that all the potatoes in the world are not worth your making yourself ill about!"

" Ah, but the foiled endeavour, Matilda ! It is not merely the blackened tuber—who could foresee that ?— but that the one who ought by rights to be the head and support of the family has become merely a burden "— his voice quavered—" an expense to you all." He lifted a trembling hand, trying to hide the tears that were trickling from his eyes.

Matilda knelt down by his side and patted his hand cheerfully.

" We are not very well to-day. I think we are all upset by this east wind. My baby was quite cross on the way home," she said, trying to soothe her father.

" No criss," retorted Baby, indignantly, kicking her gaitered legs against Maitland's knee.

Just at this moment Alex came in fresh from her work in town. She had had an harassing morning, an insufficient lunch, and a long walk in the cold. Her face was drawn with fatigue, and there was a deep line between her eyebrows. She walked without her usual lightness of movement.

" Dear me ! The whole family and the family comforter grouped together," she began, as she entered, then, seeing that something was wrong, looked from one to another as if asking an explanation. Mr. Hope had not moved ; he sat silent, covering his face with one hand. Matilda, her face flushed, knelt beside him, holding his other hand.

" What on earth is the matter ? " Alex began to ask. Then her eyes fell on the garden basket. " Oh, it's these potatoes, I do declare ! " she cried. " Haven't we heard enough of them ? If we have got to eat those black potatoes all winter, can't it be done in private at least—and without too much mourning ? " Her voice was harsh and strained.

" You are quite right, Alex. I am a foolish old man," said her father, rising slowly from her chair. " I have been too much in the house—I'm missing my usual exercise."

" Come, Father, let me take you to lie down on the study sofa till tea-time," said Matilda, drawing his hand through her arm. " Come, Baby, we will help grandfather," she called sweetly, and the child ran chuckling beside them.

Alex meanwhile had dropped into a chair. Her mouth was twitching, and she began to warm her cold hands nervously at the fire. When the door had closed behind her father and Matilda, she glanced at the basket of potatoes.

" They were new plants," she said ; " got from some man who had a ' method,' as usual, and they were to be treated with some wonderful chemical preparation that cost a good deal, but we may be thankful that it didn't cost more, for in spring ten pounds worth of seeds and things were destroyed by a different treatment." Maitland did not speak, and Alex went on, " Do you know, I'm a perfect beast, but sometimes I do *want* Father to be miserable over his mistakes—I *want* him to suffer, to realize, for once, all that his foolishness means to other people. I'm glad if he's miserable ! "

" Alex," said Maitland, gently, " you are working too hard. You are tired and anxious, or you would not speak like that."

Alex flung out her hands with a desperate gesture. " Tired ! " she cried ; " God knows I'm tired enough—I work all day and worry all night, and no doubt you think me a perfect horror. What a sweet womanly creature Matilda is ! " she went on, rubbing her hand across her wet eyelids, and speaking in a low hard voice. " How she comforted Father just now ; and yet Matilda sits at home, and I go out and work for them all, and make them miserable when I come back ! " She glanced up at Maitland, who had risen and was standing looking down at her.

" What can I say to you, Alex ? " he said at last. " That you know you are talking nonsense, or that I believe it and detest you ? " He smiled, and added,

" You know that none of us, far less those of your own family, would get on very well without you."

" None of you? What do you mean ? " said Alex, forgetting her bitterness, and sitting upright in her astonishment.

" Just what I say—that your friendship, your presence, your charm, have become necessities to your friends as well as to your own people, and I think we would find life very dull if "—he paused for a moment, and then said— " if you married, for instance." Alex flushed deeply, and Maitland went on, " James Reid, poor fellow, has been asking my advice as to whether it was of any use for him to try again."

" And what did you say ? "

" I said ' *certainly not*,' " replied Maitland, with decision. A flush rose on his face too for an instant, but he looked straight at Alex, as he held out his hand to her. " Good-bye, I'm going. Go and rest, and forget your worries. Your father will never think about your words again."

" I know that he will forgive them, as he has so often done before, but that is a different matter," said Alex.

She lay listlessly back in her chair, after Maitland had gone, until Matilda came in and sat down beside her in silence. Then Alex put out her hand and touched her sister's knee.

" Wasn't I horrid, Matilda ! I'm becoming older and more hateful every week, but I was so tired ! And I had something nice to tell you after all—if I hadn't gone and spoilt my good news by being so cross at first."

" What was it ? Have you heard anything interesting ? " asked Matilda.

Alex leant forward, suddenly changing her tone, and began—

> " ' What is thy name ? '
> ' Opportunity.'
> ' Why hangs thy hair all down in front ? '
> ' So that he that meets me may seize me,'

" I've seized it Matilda—and pulled hard—and what do you think it is ? A woman—a Mrs. Rigby, whose child is at Miss Kerr's school, and who heard me read there, came up to me this morning after the lesson and asked me if I would give a reading at her house, to a large party—about three hundred people—and she hummed and hawed so about the matter, that at last I said boldly that I would charge five pounds and all my expenses. Then I saw from her face that she would have given me more if I had asked for it—but it's splendid—it will pay that awful chemist's bill ! "

She sat up smiling now, her pale face bright again.

" Oh, Alex, it's very fortunate, of course," began Matilda. " But what will Father say—it's almost public ! "

" Almost public ! You dear goose ! Would it were quite so ! I'll be horribly nervous at first, of course, but I'll pull through all right, no doubt, and the millstone of that chemist's bill will be off my neck to-night—I'll sleep as I haven't done for weeks, I'm sure."

In spite of which she heard, that night, all the hours chimed till nearly three o'clock, when, getting up to look out on the chill winter dawn, she saw the empty street, the faint forewarning of day beginning to whiten the east, and noticed that the light was still burning in Maitland's study window.

The wind shrilled through the sere branches of the tall trees like a sigh, she thought, as she turned away from the window and went back to bed.

CHAPTER XXII

THE day fixed for the Reading dawned windy and wet. Now, those who have had to go about much in all weathers thinly clad perhaps, and over fatigued, know that east wind, though some robustious singers have glorified it, is of all things the most trying.

"If it hadn't been blowing so hard I shouldn't have minded the wet," said Alex, as she stood in the doorway just before she started for town, while Matilda fastened her veil.

"Yes, it's a pity—you look very nice, Alex, if only you can keep your hair tidy—and do hold up your skirt well."

"I think I shall go and take off this gown and put on one with a short skirt, Matilda—a working woman shouldn't care how she looks."

"Oh, don't; so much depends on your looking nice!"

"Very well, then; good-bye. I'll be home by seven-thirty if it all goes well, and if it doesn't, I feel as if I would be dead, but no doubt I won't."

"Call out ' *Well, Matilda,*' if it has gone off all right, when you open the front door. If you say nothing I'll understand."

"All right, I will. Good-bye." Alex grasped her long skirt and stepped out into the swirling wind. It was not actually raining, so she did not need to struggle with an umbrella. About half-way to the station she thought that she had forgotten her notes; however, that only startled her, for she found them in her coat pocket

after all. " If the wind would *only* stop for half an hour,"
she said to herself. " I can't think in wind. I couldn't
die in it, I'm sure." Her hat was twisted to one side,
and dragged her hair with its weight. She felt that she
did not wish to speak to the Scotts, whom she saw in
the distance, so went into the little shelter at the station
and sat in a corner, clasping her hands tightly together in
an effort at self-control. Her heart was beating so fast
that she could scarcely breathe : at last the hour had
come. For two nights she had slept only in short,
troubled snatches. Yet, only that morning, Matilda had
wondered how she could be so calm. If she had only
known what Alex really felt ! The depression was partly
due to her recent illness, for she had by no means quite
recovered, and was ill able to stand any strain. But she
would have died rather than allow Matilda to suspect
her fears.

When the train came up she bolted into the first empty
carriage. A minute later, Van Cassilis came walking up
the platform, accompanied by a girl whom Alex had never
seen before. They got into a carriage farther down the
train. Alex had time to notice that the wind had apparently not ruffled *that* young woman's composure. She
wore a dress of a strange deep orange colour, made of very
rough material. " Just the kind of suitable clothing that
poor people can never have ! " Alex remarked to herself
when she saw the short skirt, the long boots of russet
leather, and the cloth cap, worn a little audaciously, but
defying the wind and wet. The girl sauntered up after
Van, and although the guard was ready to blow his
whistle, she stood and pointed out something while the
train waited. There is a limit, however, even to the
complaisance of local officials, and a minute afterwards
she had to get in. Van jumped in also, and Alex sat
back in the empty carriage, her heart beginning to beat
sickeningly again. " Shall I ever, ever, ever be done of
this," she thought ; " be out on the other side ? Oh,

why am I not able to be calm and self-complacent like other people ? "—she clasped her hands across her eyes for a moment—" O Lord! give me courage, I pray, I pray! It's for the children I'm doing it—I must keep things going." She looked up with a start as the train stopped at the next little station, and several people came crowding into the carriage. To her excited nerves, the small journey seemed as if it had never been so long. At last she was in Edinburgh, and black and wet it was! Matilda and she had agreed that Alex must drive from the station to the house. "Even if you walk back," said Matilda, " you will *arrive* dry and tidy." So Alex struggled through the crowd to get a cab.

Van and his companions were nowhere to be seen. " They can't have been coming into town," she thought, not observing that Van was close behind her, and watched her getting into the cab. He stood talking to his companion, but he noticed the very moment when Alex drove off, and he saw, too, how pale she was.

Alex alighted at her destination with hands trembling so that she dropped the coins on the pavement when she was paying the cabman. An awning had been put up over the door, carpet laid on the steps, and even when she arrived, a great crowd of people was already pressing up the staircase.

" I have come to read," Alex explained to one of the servants.

She was afraid of being shown into the drawing-room and getting wedged in the crowd. The man took her into a library, where she stood for three or four terrible minutes pretending to examine the books, in reality seeing nothing, hearing only the beating of her heart, and feeling certain that she was about to fail most miserably, and that her voice had gone so that she would not be able to utter a word.

At last the lady of the house entered, rather in a hurry. " Oh, I'm so glad you've come in time, Miss Hope," she

said. " Will you come upstairs in about ten minutes—I'll
send a message. And wouldn't you like to take off your
coat ? What have you chosen to read ? "

Alex told her.

" It will be charming—but don't you think they are all
a little bit gloomy ? "

" I'm sorry—you said I might choose whatever I
liked," said Alex, dismayed afresh by this idea.

" Certainly—do exactly what you like. No doubt we
shall all enjoy it," said Mrs. Rigby, kindly enough.
" Will you come up when I send for you, then ? I shall
have the lights lowered when you have begun, as you say
you don't really read. Are you sure you don't want to
see your notes ? "

" One lamp on the desk will be quite enough," Alex
assured her, and she hurried away, leaving her to ten
minutes more of misery.

Presently a servant came in, carrying a bunch of mal-
maison carnations.

" A gentleman sent this, and told me to bring them to
you now, miss," he said.

" Are you quite sure they were for me ? " Alex asked.

" Yes, miss, quite sure. He said Miss Hope who had
come to read."

Alex wore a black dress and black hat. She fastened
the carnations at her waistband, and suddenly, seeing the
charming effect, felt her courage revive. She had only
time to adjust them when a message came for her, and
she had to go upstairs. Then the beating of her heart
grew more sickening than ever, and for one moment, as
she entered and saw the great rooms packed with people
all gazing at her, she felt as if she would die. But
stepping on to the little platform she opened her note-
book. The lights were put out, all except one lamp by
the desk. Alex rallied her courage, and made an effort
to begin. Then, to her own amazement, she heard her
voice, clear and smooth as usual, and began to grasp the

sense of the words that at first had only been repeated mechanically.

The first selection was a little ballad poem. During the five minutes' interval, Alex sat down behind the screen, and listened to the buzz that was going on through the rooms, without recognizing its import. Then she read Hans Andersen's " Little Match Seller." There was a dead silence after that. Alex now was trembling so that she could scarcely stand. The lights sprang up, and Mr. Rigby came into the ante-room after her, saying— she thought very coldly—" That was most touching ! " He was blowing his nose so violently, that Alex wondered if he had a cold in his head. He offered her some refreshment, which she refused, then hurried away. Discouraged to the point of shame, Alex returned to the platform and began her third little selection.

" This," she said, looking up for a moment into the half-dark room, where she could just see a weird glimmer of many eyes fixed upon her, " is only a fragment from the most beautiful piece of English prose ever written " (" how often I've heard Father say that," she thought as she spoke)—" ' The Passage of the River of Death.' "

The room was suddenly very quiet. Alex heard some one say something about " Sunday," and then thought she heard titters, and that made her feel desperate.

But as the well-known words flowed on they gave her, as since her childhood they had never failed to do, a shiver of joy. There was, indeed, a note of triumph in them, for was not the end of her own struggle approaching at the moment when she read the last words ?

" ' Thus they got over, and all the trumpets blew for them upon the other side.' "

A dead silence followed ; then some one—one person only—clapped his hands.

" I've failed miserably, as I knew I should ; but it's done, done, done ! " thought Alex. She made a curtsey to her audience, and walked gracefully enough off the

little stage into the ante-room.   There was no one there.
A great noise was beginning to spring up in the drawing
rooms now, so she fled down the empty staircase, and
caught up her coat from the hall, nearly colliding with
a servant carrying up a tray of ices.   Some one—she
hardly saw who it was—followed her, pressing her to wait
and have some refreshment, but she hurriedly refused.
Her one thought was to get out of the house as quickly as
possible, and hide her shame as well as she could.   She
made some excuse about running to catch the train, then
pushed her way to the front door, hearing vaguely a great
noise of voices behind her.

   " Shall I call a cab, miss ? " asked the man at the door.
   Alex answered without looking round again that she was
going to walk, and dashed into the street.   Her blazing
cheeks were stung by the cold wind, but the drumming in
her ears grew less as she hurried along.

   " I've failed, failed miserably, but, thank Heaven ! it's
over ! " she exclaimed almost aloud, as she turned the
corner of the street.

CHAPTER XXIII

A STRONG north-east wind came howling down the empty streets. The lamps were just lit, sending wavering reflections into the pools of water left by the recent rain. Every now and then came a gust of wind that blew Alex's dress against her ankles, and nearly buffeted her hat off.

Coming straight out of the overheated room, the cold was at first almost refreshing, but before she had gone more than a very little way, she was conscious of an overpowering weariness.

She stood for a moment on the wet pavement, whilst the wind drove her petticoats in flapping wreaths about her ankles; it beat her umbrella until she had to put it down, and as she came to the bridge she stopped for a little to readjust her hat and breathe, before beginning to struggle across the unprotected bit of roadway.

Her excitement had all died down now. She felt more than ever sure that she had failed, that the whole thing had fallen quite flat, and that she had only made an exhibition of herself—all for five pounds! Why could she not have just stayed at home and scrimped upon something else, instead of supposing that her pitiful scrap of talent could astonish the public and make money? Were there not actors by the score—people of real genius, and thoroughly trained in their art—who could barely make a living, and she—she!

In her pitiful self-depreciation her heart sank to her very boots. Oh, she was tired! It was a dismal evening, and a dismal world at times, but what was the use of grumbling ? She had got to sludge back to the station in the rain, and then go home and give a cheerful account of her day, that would make the others feel it had been quite a success. Alex was halfway across the bridge by this time, and a moment's lull in the wind made her stop again, to gather up her skirts better out of the mud.

"I'll never wear a long skirt out of vanity again," she thought. "It hasn't really made much difference to my appearance, and it only makes me look silly in the street, and doubles the bother of walking."

She stood looking down for a moment across the parapet of the bridge, held, as always, by the beauty of a scene that even the remorseless climate could not destroy. On either side of the blue gulf, high houses shone with lighted windows ; in the yellow and stormy sky, great masses of vapour rolled above the town, and parted to a clearer space in the east. A darker point pricked out here and there from the mists, and far down below between its gardened banks, the water ran like a ravelled white thread.

"Oh, I'm so cold !" thought Alex, turning again with a shiver—remembering with a woman's envy, the only face amongst her audience that she had readily noticed : a woman rather older than herself, with the smooth flesh spread perhaps too thickly on cheeks that glowed with health and self-delight. Alex had noticed the poise of her shoulders and the fur cloak lined with white satin that hung across her chair. "Dress like that would make any one look handsome !" she thought, with another bitter shiver. "Oh, there is the rain on again, and, my good hat !—I must put up my umbrella ! Never, never again, as long as I live, shall I wear a hat that spoils with rain !"

Now, you must understand that when Alex put up her umbrella she had to let go of her long skirt that went slopping down on one side, and she could no longer hold on her hat, which was immediately nearly blown off by the wind.

"Never mind about the umbrella!" said a familiar voice at her side. "It's not going to rain. Come, Sandy, why are you standing here as if you were going to fling yourself over the bridge?"

"Oh, Van! Oh, Van dear, I didn't see you coming!" She gathered up her skirt, and Van took her free hand and drew it through his arm.

"No—please—I can't let you do that!"

"Nonsense!—it's blowing a hurricane—just until we get to the end of the bridge."

"There are people coming!"

"And who are we that we should mind them? Don't we live in the country? And mayn't we do as we choose in spite of every citizen in Edinburgh?" He had hurried her along as he spoke and for a minute or two she held tightly to his arm, as they struggled against the wind and reached the corner of the street, where it was comparatively quiet again. Her cold hand was warm: life seemed to have returned to her; the rain had ceased, the wind subsided. "Why, you're as white as chalk, Sandy. You're trembling with the effort of your success, I declare!"

"Success! Oh, Van; if you only knew!" Alex cried. Her cheeks flamed with humiliation as she spoke. "I only made a fool of myself—no one applauded; no one listened, I think. There was a great deal of rustling while I spoke, it seemed, and when I had finished, such a silence; not even a rustle—it was too awful! I could not even wait for the lights to be turned up. I knew how people would speak about it, and how they would try to find something comforting to say. So I just said that I would lose my train, and ran away and got out of the house somehow, before any of them had moved from their seats. Oh—oh, I have made such a fool of myself"—her voice sank—"but I did it for the children, you know!"

" I wondered how you ever got out of the house in such a hurry," said Van, calmly. " You were on the platform one moment, and the next you were out of the room, before I had time to look round."

" Van! You don't mean to say that you were there! "

" Where else would I be?—as some one said of the sinner in the church—of course I was there, and I was wedged in between two or three women crying so hard, and so deeply affected, that they wouldn't hear me when I asked them to let me get past."

Alex glanced at his face. They were just passing under one of the street lamps, which threw a strong light upon his handsome profile, with the smooth, youthful cheek and strong neck, and the faint suggestion of a classic line about the shape of nose and brow that Alex always admired. He was smiling a little as he spoke.

" Are you—you must be joking ? " she gasped.

" I ? Of course not. I very nearly—I won't say quite —gave myself away, too, Sandy. It was the sound in your voice when you began the last thing. You have the nicest voice !—do you remember what some one said once ?—' Her voice to my ears is the most delightsome sound in the world : ever was, and ever will be.' There are people as susceptible as snakes to certain sounds, and I'm one of them. If you spoke as you do sometimes, Sandy, you could make me answer from the grave, I think."

But this was a vein of talk that Alex would not encourage.

" So you *were* a little touched ? " she asked.

Van laughed. " I didn't weep—if that's what you mean. You see I was accustomed to it. But you should have seen the handkerchiefs at my end of the room ! "

" People were crying then ! " Alex stopped short and looked at him.

" Yes, of course ; nearly every woman in the room was crying, and half the men were coughing. Didn't you know ? "

" I knew nothing ; except that it was all a most miserable failure, and for a moment or two I wished I were dead ! "

" Well, you'll be jolly glad you're alive to-morrow, my dear girl, when you hear what every one thought of it— why, it was a sensation ! It was wonderful—wonderful, Sandy ! Do you hear ? "

" I hear. I'm hungry, Van, and most awfully tired now. I can't go home till I've had tea."

He looked at her anxiously. " Come in here then— we can have tea together, can't we ?

Alex caught a look in his eye as he asked this question that upset her gravity.

" Yes, yes, of course we can ; they'll think I'm your aunt if any one we know comes in ! "

But Van looked as black as thunder at that, and leant his head on his hand, and stared at the table until tea was brought, without speaking a word to her.

" Come now, that's better," said Alex, when she had drunk her tea. She pushed up her veil, and sat looking at Van in an amused way. Her colour had come back, and her eyes were brighter than usual. She lifted the bunch of carnations, and fixed them better in her dress : Van looking on without saying a word. " These lovely things have got battered by the wind," said Alex ; " some good angel sent them to me just at the moment when I felt most afraid. Was it you, Van ? "

" Yes, it was. Your dress looked so black."

" How did you see that I had on a black dress—you weren't at the house when I came up ? "

" I arrived just behind you, and I saw you at the station."

" I didn't know that you had seen me ! " said Alex ; " it was sweet of you to think of sending me the flowers."

" You can give them to old Miss Reid when you get home," said Van, in an indifferent tone, and then Alex burst out laughing, which had not a soothing effect on him at all.

"Don't be cross, please!" she said gaily, as they rose to leave the shop. "I'm so happy now that I could fly to the moon, and I never want to think of anything distressing again—I feel ten years younger than I did this morning."

"Oh, *my Aunt!*" murmured Van, in a low voice at her side, but Alex pretended not to hear him.

"Who was the girl who came up to Crossriggs station along with you?" she asked.

"That was Dolly Orranmore—hadn't you seen her before?" said Van. "They came over to luncheon; they're staying at Crosstown just now, and Dolly was going into town."

"She looked——" Alex began, and then stopped. "Oh, I'm too tired to find an adjective. She's not exactly pretty, but——"

"Yes, but—I know quite what you mean," said Van, laughing. "They're all 'but'! Gran hates them, still he can't keep them off. They're going to be in the neighbourhood for a long time now. Old Orranmore's rather in difficulties, I believe—he generally is, and Dolly's extravagant, like her mother," he added, "They're coming to stay with us later on. Mrs. Orranmore intimated plainly to Gran that it would be convenient."

Alex, remembering some remarks one of the Misses Brinleys had made about the Orranmores that day when she had met them at Foxe Hall, came to the conclusion that Mrs. Orranmore might have her own ends in view in coming to the neighbourhood. The next minute she reproached herself for the unworthy thought.

"Why, I'm as bad as Mrs. Scott," she said to herself, "that idea was so like one of hers. Perhaps they are perfectly harmless people, and surely the best thing that could happen to Van would be that he should fall in love with some nice girl of his own age as soon as possible."

Alex sat so long silent after this that Van asked her what she was thinking about so intently. " Of how tired I am, and how nice it will be to get home," she answered, as the train drew up at their own station.

She had a cheerful walk down (for the wind had ceased) in the black darkness, with a nephew on each side of her, and the thought of her success warm at her heart.

When she got home, Alex ran up the pathway to the front door, calling out, " Well, Matilda ! Well ! Well ! "

Her sister came running out. " Oh, Alex ! it's all right then ? "

" More than right, Matty," said Alex, and Matilda threw her arms about her and hugged her as if she had been sixteen.

It was a happy evening ; everything seemed so good ; the firelight leaping through the familiar room, the pile of books by Old Hopeful's chair, the tiny items of home intelligence that Matilda had to give in her turn, when she had sucked the very dregs of Alex's news. " I've measured it all, Alex, and the carpet will turn quite well, so that the worn bit can go under the dining-room table. . . . Sally has learnt that duet so nicely—I do think she will play quite well in time ! " and so on. Everything seemed to have been fortunate in Alex's absence. The boys had received such high marks for conduct at school.

" Well," said Alex, when the children had all gone to bed, leaning back in her chair with a sense of luxurious satisfaction and looking across at Matilda, " we do take care of them, as far as we can. Manners cost *nothing*— that's one comfort, Matilda ! You don't spend one penny more because your boys eat and speak nicely—and it's no dearer to be polite than to be rude. I do think we'll be proud of them some day, even though I'm not their mother ! "

CHAPTER XXIV

" SPRING came slowly up that way," as if grudging every
step in advance, and every flower that she threw from
her " green lap " under the bare hedgerows or on the
slopes where the sun first shone. The little hard buds on
the trees were all tight still by the beginning of April, and
looking away in the distance from the highest point at
Crossriggs, you could see patches of snow in the hollow
of the hills. Hints, only hints, of the great awakening
could be gathered from the exultation in the cry of a bird
from the yet barren thickets ; from a strong new leaf
thrusting itself up every here and there amongst the dead
rubbish beneath the hedges ; from the wayside pools
stirred by the plunge of a frog, and from the film of green
upon some of the ploughed fields.

Nature being thus reticent, it seemed to Alex, one day
when she and Matilda were out together and met Miss
Bessie Reid, that their good friend was less than ever
in harmony to the eye.

For reluctant though the season was—and it not yet
the middle of April—Miss Bessie's headgear was a crown
of slightly crushed purple and green grapes, lusciously
festooned amongst black beads. She was walking with
a tall young man, who wore eyeglasses and stooped a
good deal, and they were apparently so much absorbed
in conversation that not until Matilda and Alex were
quite close to them did Miss Bessie look up. Then,

with an arch exclamation, she came forward to introduce her companion, every bead twink ing, her thin
face, under its Pomona-like headgear, rath r flushed.

"I don't think you know Mr. Massie, Matilda. This
is my friend Mrs. Chalmers," she said, and Matilda greeted
the young man with her usual placid kindness, wondering
what he was doing at Crossriggs.

He had no chin, or next to none, and as he spoke a
knob went working convulsively up and down his thin
throat, which was girt about with a dull green necktie.

They all stood in a little group, exchanging remarks for
a few minutes, but Miss Bessie was not as sprightly as
usual. Once only, when Alex had alluded to the snow
still to be seen like a white handkerchief in the hollow
of the blue hills, she looked at Mr. Massie, and exclaimed
archly—

"Doesn't it remind you of the Jura?"

Alex at this point turned rather abruptly away, and
Matida hurried after her, murmuring—

"Don't, Alex, don't laugh till they are out of hearing!"

"The Jura! Oh, Matilda, I saw it all at once," said
Alex, as her sister came up. "He's one f the cultured
circle in the Pension! I know he is!"

"But what is he doing here?" said Matilda. "And
Bessie Reid looked quite excited."

"Don't, please, Matilda—it's too cruel!"

"What? Why, Alex, I don't know what you mean,"
said Matilda, astonished at her vehemence.

"Well, don't then!"

"He's a mere boy compared to Miss Bessie."

"'Boy' isn't the word for him at all," said Alex.
"He must have been a cultured person in spectacles, and
probably bo anical from the cradle, one can see that;
but he s about a hundred years younger than she is,
anyway."

"Alex, you do exaggerate so dreadfully, said Matilda, who did not quite approve of Alex's view of the

Reids. Matilda saw nothing comic about Miss Bessie, and was particularly fond of James.

"Why *grapes*?" Alex went on musingly. "And in combination with a plover's wing and black beads. Matilda, do you think she invents those hats alone? For if so she certainly has wonderful powers of imagination!"

"Really, Alex, I don't think you are very kind in the way that you sometimes speak about the Reids, though Bessie does put rather too much into her millinery."

"Much! Eshcol—and plover's wings!"

"Well, rather a mixture, then; but that milliner she goes to *was* in Paris. I wonder if that young man is staying with the Reids?"

"*I* wonder if she's under the fond impression that he has any chin? She thinks James is handsome, though!"

"Alex, I really wish you wouldn't speak like that!" said Matilda, quite sharply for her.

They were like two pigeons just ruffled for a moment, and giving a peck at one another, when, as they turned a sharp corner of the road, they met Robert Maitland, who was coming towards them.

"We're quarrelling so hard that we can scarcely compose ourselves to speak to you,'" said Alex.

Matilda, slightly pink from her little irritation, was looking very pretty and Maitland, as he glanced from one to the other, thought that Mrs. Chalmers looked by far the younger of the two.

"What have you been quarrelling about?" he asked.

"Oh, my incautious way of speaking, as usual," said Alex. "Matilda is too charitable to see certain things in this world as they really are. 'Blessed are the unobservant, for they shall never be called malicious!'"

Maitland laughed, and seeing that Matilda was still vexed, he tried to change the subject. He had been, he told them, away all morning walking among the hills. He was wearing a suit of rough grey clothes that became him curiously well.   He carried a little sprig of flowering gorse in one hand, and Alex, as she looked at his serene face, felt an access of totally unreasoning irritation.

" You look as if you had been having such a peaceful day ! " she exclaimed.   " I suppose you've been for hours amongst the hills, listening to running brooks, and filled with an infinite calm, and you are now returning to look upon the petty troubles of other people much as we would regard the affairs of ants, if we knew what they were ! "

" Alex, how can you speak like that ! " said Matilda, who was quite shocked by this outburst.

" Pray, what have I done to deserve this ? " said Maitland, smiling.

" Oh, nothing, I suppose, only looking as if you had been on some mount of transfiguration, whilst we have had such a petty and disgusting woman's day, though perhaps some of us would have liked quite as well as you to lie by the side of a burn, and look at beautiful things, and come home to write history—and instead ! "

" We have had rather a trying morning," Matilda explained, " though not one to be treated quite from Alex's tragic standpoint.   Our old Katharine has left us for a time, you know, and since then we have had some very inefficient servants."

" Singed soup, sodden potatoes, burnt apples, house dense with smoke, an unexpected guest to luncheon, one child ill with earache—so much worse than toothache even !—all the others naughty, a new dress come home quite wrong, every one, except Matilda, out of temper— so there, do you think that you could have had beautiful thoughts in that case ? "

" But how do you know that I had them ? " Maitland asked.

" Oh, I know it quite well.   Do you remember about the face of the Danish boy ?   ' *And never was a cloudless sky so steady and so fair.*'   But it's very simple when one has nothing to worry about ! "

Maitland gave a little, hard, sudden sigh, then, as they came to the corner where their ways divided, he handed the sprig of gorse to Alex.

" It prickles, but it's sweet ! " he said, with one of his quick, delightful smiles, and looking at Matilda's amused face, he turned quickly away.

" Dear me ! How cross I was, to be sure ! " said Alex. " But somehow it irritated me wildly for a moment to think what a nice day he had been having when ours had been so horrid."

" Oh, Mr. Maitland is always good tempered," said Matilda.   " He has often seen us cross before."

" Me, you mean—yes, often."

" You are not well yet, Alex," said Matilda.   " You ought to go away somewhere for a change, I think."

Of late Matilda had been a little anxious—as much so as it was in her nature to be—about her sister. She noticed how cross Alex was sometimes, how dry and yellow her skin looked, and how sunken her eyes were, on the days when she had been working in town, and came home very tired. Matilda had no imagination, and fatigue of the spirit, as well as of the body, was a cause that would never have struck her for Alex's failure in health.

" Where would you have me to go ? " Alex inquired. " To lodgings at three guineas a week ? To Liverpool to sit amongst the fully clothed statuary in Aunt Clara's drawing-room ? Don't talk nonsense ! "

Matilda said no more, and they turned in at their own gate.

Alex went up to her room. She stood looking out at the square for a moment, then she took the little sprig of gorse, with its green spines and wine-like odour, and shut it away in a drawer.

CHAPTER XXV

A WEEK later, Crossriggs was thrilled by the announcement that Miss Bessie Reid was going to marry her
cultured friend, Mr. Massie.

The various forms in which the Hopes heard this
interesting news, resembled a game which is played
by several people, each in succession telling the same
story—or rather a very different story, as they remember it.

Alex and Matilda were busy one morning, when Mrs.
Scott, who seldom came to see them, was shown into the
room.

" I'm an early caller, she began, seating herself with
a rustle (fully dressed in curry coloured cashmere
trimmed with plush at eleven o'clock in the morning).
" But I just wanted to ask you, Mrs. Chalmers, if you'd
look in at our girls' sewing-class this afternoon. And oh ! "
she hurried on, wiping her heated face with a folded pocket
handkerchief, " the heat's awful this morning when
you're walking—so sudden too ! Have you heard the
latest ? Miss Bessie Reid's going to be married !—to a
young man, too, young enough to be her son, and con-
sumptive, but he's rich, they say, and half Spanish, and
she's so set up with it there's no holding her ! "

" Who want to ' hold ' her ? And why ? " asked
Alex, who had an unfortunate way of getting angry with
Mrs. Scott.

Matilda hastily interposed, " I suppose it is a Mr.

Massie, if that is the case," she said. "But he is a man whom she has known for several years, and not much younger than she is."

"Younger! I don't suppose he's thirty—and Bessie Reid must be a good bit older than you."

"Even if she is—that is not a great age," said Matilda, smiling. "We must hope she will be happy."

"Happy? It's triumph!" said Mrs. Scott, rising and giving an appraising glance about the room. "As for the age, I don't suppose it matters so long as she is pleased. Mr. Scott's a year and half *my* junior," she added, with a simper; "though you'd never suppose it to see us together. Some people like it—a younger man helps to keep them cheerful." She glanced at Alex expressively, "Mr. Cassilis has come home, I hear." (Van had been away for a month.) "Papa saw him yesterday."

Her hints on this subject were here cut short by the entrance of Miss Maitland.

Now, if there was one person more terrifying than another to Mrs. Scott, it was Miss Maitland, for that lady still continued to rule things in the parish with a high hand.

"Of course, I leave all these things to you now, Mrs. Scott," she would say, before beginning in a few calm sentences to dictate her orders to the new minister's wife.

Once, shortly after his arrival at Crossriggs, Mr. Scott had gone up to consult Maitland about some parish business, and as they were crossing the hall together on his way out of the Manse, he began in a jaunty tone, "Well, and how's Miss Elizabeth?" Even as he uttered the words, the lady appeared in a doorway. Mr. Scott had not noticed that she was there, and went on to address Robert as "Maitland," accompanying the familiarity by a slap on the back. Maitland looked perfectly benign under it, but Mr. Scott glancing up saw that Miss Maitland was standing looking at him.

Her eye was on him. The words died upon his lips, and he took a hurried leave. He slept badly that night.

"Something must have disagreed with you, dear— perhaps it's the cauliflower?" Mrs. Scott remarked.

"No, no, dear, it was that woman!" he blurted out.

"Which woman?" There were so many women who could be disagreeable in Mrs. Scott's eyes.

"Miss Eliza——" he began. Correcting himself, "Miss Maitland—she's enough to make a man run—she looked at me as if I were the dirt beneath her feet."

"At you! Oh, Andrew, I wish you were the Pope and could excommunicate her!" cried his wife. "She's a viper!"

"No, no, Ethel, not that; but she makes a man feel powerless—powerless!" he added, breathing puffily.

"Set her up!" said Mrs. Scott; "she's no lady, Andrew,—just a pretentious viper standing on its tail."

This, as I said, had been a long time ago, but the Scotts and Miss Maitland were still in the same relation to each other. Therefore, when Miss Maitland entered, Mrs. Scott at once went away—greatly to Matilda's relief, for she saw that Alex had been nursing her wrath.

"And what is the use of being angry with a person like Mrs. Scott!" Matilda remarked, when that lady had left the room.

"None at all! I should never think of being annoyed by her, Matilda," said Aunt E. V., tranquilly. Seating herself, as she always did, with a dip like a curtsey, she spread the folds of her grey alpaca skirt carefully around her, and began a few judicious remarks upon the heat.

She had brought some fruit for Mr. Hope. She inquired for him, for the children almost individually, remarked upon Matilda's work, told them that Mrs. Maitland had not been feeling well, made a few statements upon local affairs, and then, folding her hands and giving her head a faint toss, she asked—

" Have you heard a rumour about Bessie Reid's engagement to a young man ? I presume the youth with the long neck, who has been staying with them ? "

Matilda told her that Mrs. Scott had just given them the information.

" I'm sure I hope she will be happy," she said. " But it sounds a little of a risk, doesn't it, Miss Elizabeth ? "

" Marriage always is, Matilda ; in this case I understand the ages are reversed, which increases the risk." She darted a penetrating glance at Alex.

" Well," said Alex, rising, " I'm going to the Reid's now to see for myself, and to offer our congratulations. After all, you know, we've only one life in this world, and if I were Bessie Reid, I'd rather spend the rest of mine with a chinless young man, even if he *were* ten years younger than myself, than with a paralyzed aunt."

She left the room then, allowing Matilda to smooth down the effect of her words to Miss Maitland, and set out along the village street to pay her call at the Reid's.

After the cold, reluctant months of early spring had come a sudden wave of heat, so that already everything was beginning to bud and blossom as if now in a tremendous hurry. The garden at the Reids' house was full of fresh green, and a bush of ' flowering currant ' trained against the wall, was covered with crimson flowers. Agitated sparrows were hauling at long straws and chirruping madly about the rones above the door.

" *They* are excited enough anyway, although it's an annual affair to them," thought Alex, with a smile, looking up at the agitated little birds, after she had rung the door bell.

The Reids' little housemaid, in a new cap, with an air of excited mystery about her, looking not all unlike a sparrow herself, opened the door and ushered Alex into the small dining-room, where Miss Bessie was wont to spend the morning. An art serge tablecloth covered the table, on which were set two little pink glasses filled with primroses ; the room was hot with a fire and sunshine, and its windows were tightly closed. Alex noticed a pair of socks, which Miss Bessie had evidently just finished knitting, lying on the table. " They're not for *James !* " thought Alex, as she observed that they were a pale lemon yellow in colour. Just then she heard the familiar rustling and tinkling that accompanied Miss Bessie's movements, and the door opened.

" Oh, Alex ! Is this you ? Have you come already ? " began Miss Bessie, coming in with outstretched hands. She wore that morning, a green blouse profusely trimmed with coffee-coloured lace, mingled with tatted trimming. Her laces were clasped by a coral brooch, and she had a string of iridescent beads about her throat, and also a jet waist-buckle.

" At least that was all I could count at the moment," Alex said afterwards.

Miss Bessie received her visitor's congratulations very graciously, then as she sat down opposite the light, Alex saw that the galvanized cheerfulness had all disappeared from her face ; instead were deep lines—suddenly sincere, that must have been concealed under her smiles for many a day.

" It has all been very sudden—I am astonished at myself," she began, in answer to Alex's first remarks. " Of course, when we met five years ago at the Pension we saw much of one another, but Ferdie wasn't then in a position to speak, he couldn't say anything definite—and though we looked at many a sunset together " —here for a moment she became arch again—" there was no engagement—now it has all come on so suddenly." She stopped, her thin face worked : " Oh, Alex dear ! " she cried, and covering her face with one knobby hand

—all her rings had been removed to make way for one small circlet, set with supposititious diamonds—she burst into a flood of happy tears.

In a moment Alex had knelt down beside the chair, and was hugging her in a quick access of sympathetic affection. The little scene was cut short by the entrance of Mr. Massie himself.

Miss Bessie sprang up at the sound of his footsteps in the hall, dried her eyes, patted her hair, jingled her bracelets, and by the time that he entered, had nearly reassumed her wonted glittering smile.

The young man came in looking very conscious, and Alex shook hands with him and tendered her good wishes. He thanked her politely, the Adam's apple in his throat meanwhile working up and down so convulsively that she longed to say, "Oh, do make an effort and swallow it for once!"

After a few minutes Miss Bessie suggested that Alex should come with her "To have a peep at Auntie, who," she said, "has been quite revived by all this."

They found the old lady propped up on the sofa, her frail head surmounted by a new cap, stiff with rosettes of violet blue ribbon. She was really able to mumble out something about "Bessie and a young man called Massie. *But who is he?*" she whispered to Alex when her niece had left the room for a moment. Alex made some vague reply and diverted the conversation to Matilda's children. As she rose to come away, she noticed on the table before the invalid, a little book bound in limp leather covers, and entitled "Gems from Mines of Modern Thought." It contained, as a glance assured her, extracts from many modern writers, calculated to confuse a stronger head than poor old Miss Reid's. "Just a tiny token from Ferdie, for dear Auntie's eightieth birthday. He thinks we shouldn't confine all our reading to the Bible, even at eighty—doesn't he, Auntie dear?" exclaimed Miss Bessie. Auntie mumbled, and Alex, bidding her good-bye, was escorted by Miss Bessie to the door.

Outside, the spring sunshine poured down upon the earth, the sparrows chattered, the scent of green growing things filled the sweet air. For a moment Alex felt dizzy as she walked quickly away from the house. " Oh, what a world! Happy! Happy! Satisfied with that? How blind we are! How hard and narrow and blind— that we cannot even get a glimpse into other people's hearts! *But she cried with happiness*, poor dear, over *that !*—it's easy to see that *I* shall never marry."

Blue like the eyes of an angel was the sky above her ; sweet as Heaven the scents and sounds of earth that morning ; but her heart was filled with a sudden shrivelling bitterness, as if it had been scorched by fire.

CHAPTER XXVI

VAN CASSILIS kept a sailing-boat in the harbour of one of the little red villages down on the shore, and he would go in it sometimes for whole days at a time, returning very sunburnt and cheerful. It had been an old promise that Matilda's boys were to be allowed to sail to the island with him, so they were greatly delighted when he appeared one morning asking if they might go the next day. Matilda could not bear to disappoint the children and gave her consent. " You'll come too, won't you, Sandy ? " Van inquired, looking at Alex.

" Oh, I will come if you like. I don't read on Saturdays, you know."

" Then perhaps I had better stay at home," said Matilda, but Alex turned to her eagerly—

" No, no, you must come—please, Matilda—if it's a day like this, the worst sailor in the world would enjoy it —you must come ! "

Matilda agreed, although the prospect of a whole day's sailing was by no means such a pleasure to her as it was to Alex, who loved the sea and all that belonged to it. Old Hopeful and Alex were at one in this, and in former days, they had more than once gone to London by sea, for even the smallest voyage in the grubbiest vessel was a pleasure to both of them.

Van's face brightened in an almost ludicrous way when he heard that Alex was coming. The children were in great delight. Sally was going elsewhere, and

Baby was too young, so only the two older boys and Mike were allowed to go.

The warmth had now come very suddenly. After a cold and dreary month of April came a week of heavenly weather; the sleeping orchards bloomed, the grass took on a livelier hue, the fresh wind came bounding across the fields with a gust of joy, and all the vexations of the changeful season were forgotten.

Alex awoke this Saturday morning with the sense that the day was too radiant, too perfect, for any ordinary occupation. Then she remembered their excursion with Van, and smiled to herself as she did so. It was pleasant to come downstairs and find breakfast laid in the sunny room, with open windows that looked into the orchard. Matilda, too, seemed fresh and cheerful that morning, and the boys were already discussing where they should sit in the boat.

Van came early to say he was going to walk down to the harbour, but would send a carriage for Matilda and the children. Alex had gone to speak to him at the door. She watched him go off along the Square, and then stood in the doorway looking out. A sort of inertia possessed her that beautiful morning. Her father was already busy in the garden, the boys were racing through the orchard, Matilda bustling about indoors, and Alex had a score of trifling duties which ought to have been done; yet she stood idle in the sunlight, her head bare, her hands clasped behind her back, gazing down the street. Presently Matilda came and asked her to do some little errand in the village.

"I suppose it must be done," said Alex, turning to her with a smile and a sigh. "But I don't want to go near a grocer's shop this morning, and I wonder at you for suggesting it, Matilda. Do you remember the expression in the Bible?—'And man did eat angels' food.' Well, that's what I feel this morning—it's an insult to the day to think about earthly things at all."

Matilda, used to what she considered the vagaries of her father and Alex, merely smiled and repeated her message. Alex got ready to go, and was just stepping out at the gate when Van passed by again.

" Hello, Sandy ! Going out ? Why don't you walk down with me ? Would you rather drive ? "

" No, indeed, I'd far rather walk—it's only four miles after all, and down hill all the way. Wait a second whilst I tell Matilda, and then I'll come with you."

She ran back to the house, reappearing in a minute or two.

" It's all right, only I have to stop and give a message at the grocer's as we pass. I told Matilda it was too perfect a day to do anything of the sort, but she won't let me off ! "

She gave her message as she passed the shop, and then they left the village behind, and took the broad road that ran down the long ridge of land to the sea.

Alex threw back her head and snuffed the air. " Isn't it divine ? Did you ever see such a day ? A day to be married on, or to die on, but nothing more ordinary. Now, don't let us even speak about anything disagreeable, but believe that we're in the better world whose atmosphere we're breathing for an hour or two ! "

She went on talking and laughing : Van was very silent. Once or twice he turned and looked at her, but in general he gave only the briefest replies. At last his curious humour dawned upon Alex.

" What's the matter with you this morning ? " she began. " But no ! I won't ask, for if it's anything wrong, I refuse to hear it—only, please, please, shake it away from you, and be happy to-day."

" Nothing wrong, Sandy—only too right ! "

" I don't understand," said Alex, and the next minute was sorry she had spoken.

" Only too near to happiness—to be here, alone with you."

He saw her thin brown cheek flush a little, but she did not look at him, only ignored the remark, as she always did when Van spoke like that, and went on—

"How can you talk of being 'alone' on a day like this, with larks, and bees, and butterflies, and flying things all through the air, and birds in the hedges, and horses ploughing, and dogs barking, and everything expressing its happiness around us—that's what I like—the feeling of sharing it all on such a morning with every other thing that lives!"

They walked on, always going easily down hill, along the broad, smooth road, with hedges on either side, until at last the sea became visible, and the line of cottages by the shore.

The little boat was rocking by the pier. Van sprang into it, and Alex turned to wait for her sister.

In a few minutes Matilda and the boys arrived, and they all embarked—the children in great excitement. Matilda and Alex sat in the stern of the boat, and the boys huddled together behind the sail, their exclamations shrilling out every now and then—

"Oh, Aunt Alex, I see a monster jelly-fish—some of them sting, you know!" "Stop, Peter! I'll put down my arm and see if I can touch him. Whew! How cold!" "Ugh! He's all slimy! I think he stung!" "No, he didn't; it's only the cold!" and so on.

The two women were silent, each absorbed in her own thoughts. Matilda's usually calm brow had a wrinkle on it that morning, and she did not seem to listen to what the children were saying.

Van sat with the ropes in his hand, gazing out at the bright sea. His head was bare, and the light wind ruffled the locks about his sunburnt forehead; in the strong sunshine, his eyes, always pale, had the queer effect of being too light in colour for his face. Some young faces there are, wearing an expression which must be a shadow from the past, or a foreshadowing

of the future, which is unconnected with the emotions
of youth. Van's drop of foreign blood had given the
classic line that ran in his profile, and might also account
for the tragic shadow in his expression.

The faint wind was favourable, so that the boat ran
like a greyhound through the tiny broken waves. Leaving the harbour behind they sailed past the low red
houses, that clung like barnacles to the edge of the
rocks. Overhead sounded the light whistling noise
of the breeze in the cordage; around them the water
shimmered in the sun, but there was just enough of
haze to make the farther shore dreamlike and in-
distinct.

Alex was looking very well that day—as nearly pretty
as she could ever look. She wore a dark blue dress,
and sat leaning forward, with her elbows resting on her
knees, and her chin in her hand—an attitude that would
have shocked Aunt E. V. could she have seen her.

"Look at Edinburgh," said Alex, "how near it looks,
with all those spires and chimneys, and how utterly
away from our little world at Crossriggs!"

"A good thing, too! I wouldn't live there to save my
life!" said Van.

"Now," said Matilda, "you and Alex are really so
unreasonable! You know it would be a very good place
to live in."

"If you were happy, yes—if any one ever was happy
there—but any place is good in that case," said Alex,
smiling.

"Where would you live if you could choose, Sandy?"
Van asked.

Alex did not look up. She rocked herself back and
forwards, still leaning her chin on her hand, and answered—

"I don't know, I'm sure. I know several places I
wouldn't live in, but few places are chosen—most are
preordained!"

"Well, sometimes——" began Van, eagerly. He leant forward, gazing at Alex, holding the ropes in his hand, and Matilda, glancing up at him, surprised upon his face a look that she had never seen there before. It made her start. The idea of his admiration for her sister being anything more than the frank liking of a rather lonely young man for a woman older than himself, who had been kind to him, had never entered her mind for an instant. Now she could not fail to see.

For as Van leant forward, looking at Alex, there was in his face a suggestion of Fate, of passion, that surged into her mind like the suggestion of the deeps below, when she looked, for an instant, under the shining surface of the water at the edge of the boat.

"Goodness! What would the Admiral say?" was Matilda's first instinctive thought—then, with a rally, she assured herself that it must be nonsense, and resolved to think no more about it.

Cluck, cluck, cluck, went the water bubbling at the prow as the boat swept round, and Van sprang up to right the sail.

They were quite close to the Island, and the boys were clamouring to be allowed to land, and eat their luncheon on the shore. Once on land they were as glad to run about again as they had been to clamber into the boat.

They sat down to eat in a sunny corner with a rock behind them, and Matilda served out sandwiches to her hungry brood—those hard-boiled-egg sandwiches which only the digestion of youth and happiness can cope with for a moment.

The meal was soon at an end, and then the boys began to clamour to be allowed to see over the lighthouse, but little Mike was sleepy, so Alex laid him down on a rug with his head on her knee, and told the others to go off without her. She had seen all that there was to see before. Van would much have preferred to stay at her feet; however, he got up with a very good grace to accompany Matilda and the boys.

When they were all gone out of sight, Alex leant back against the rock, and closed her eyes for a few minutes. She could hear the lisping water far down below, and near at hand the sound of some little goats nibbling at the salted turf, and even the quiet breathing of the child asleep at her knees. Clusters of sea pinks grew about the edges of the rocks. The sea shone in the distance, where the ships, like great white-winged birds, were passing up and down the Firth. A dazzling day it was, with blinding light falling on the brisk moving sea, and all the fresh impulse of spring still in the air.

Alex had been very happy that morning—too feminine, perhaps, to be quite unaware of Van's admiration for her—the seriousness of it was unacknowledged even in her own heart. She only had the flattering consciousness that as yet she was perfect in his eyes, and this, to the least vain among women, is always a pleasant thought.

"Some day soon, of course, he will fall in love with a pretty girl of his own age," she thought, "and then my feet of clay will become visible, but meantime I am a goddess in his eyes, and can do no wrong, and if one is plain and poor as I am, it's nice to play at being a goddess even for a little time."

As she sat there with closed eyelids, feeling the sun shining on her face, her thoughts wandered away from the present, from Van, and from the children. A thousand questions, never to be answered on this side Time, swept into her mind, for she inherited Old Hopeful's speculative disposition, along with a clearer head than his had ever been, and many an abstract problem had interested her from her very childhood.

Matilda, whose practical mind dimly realized the undoubted fact that domestic happiness of the common sort, and an interest in the riddles of life seldom go hand in hand, never ceased to lament this in her secret heart.

" In a way Alex is just like Father," she would say. " For when you think she's settled down to something, some new or vague idea will shake it all off again." " It," in Matilda's speech, indicated the solid form and manly virtues of James Reid. " If it were not for those notions——" she would say, and then pause and sigh.

Of late Matilda had seen a good deal of the Reids. Miss Bessie was so kind to the children, and James Reid was often there, and he, too, was kind to the boys, and gave her the feeling that he " respected her grief "—a sensation that was soothing to the widow of Peter Chalmers.

Could she have known her sister's thoughts that afternoon Matilda would have been more vexed than ever, for Alex, sitting there in the sun, was thinking of things very different from her own future.

Opening her eyes at last, she looked lazily about her— at the faint tints of the salt-encrusted grass, at the dim pink of the unsucculent flowers, at the flat, white tone of the lighthouse against the misty distance. The frugality of colour was delicious in the spring light.

" Oh, what an enchanting world it is at times ! " she thought. " But can we be the right inhabitants for it ? What a world to be happy in ! I wonder if any one ever is ? " Then she began to think about Bessie Reid, and then her thoughts came back to Van. " Eight years, nearly nine years, younger than I am—surely I can safely be as friendly as I like with him ! It's all right, I'm sure ! "

Suddenly the sound of footsteps on the rocks below made her glance downwards. She saw that two people, a man and a woman, were scrambling about on the rocky ledge, from which a narrow track wound upwards until the slope of the cliff became more gradual. Alex could hear their voices quite distinctly, though she could not make out the words. She watched them idly, admiring the strength and lightness of the girl's figure. Balancing on slippery stones, springing from point to point of the rocks, she made her way along, followed at some distance by the man, who stumbled heavily once or twice, and appeared to find their course much more difficult.

At last the girl reached the pathway, and with an agile movement scrambled up on to the slope of slippery grass, and there stood upright, bending her lithe body from the waist, her hands on her hips, her head thrown back in a gay little attitude that bespoke no fatigue. She wore a dress of a curious shade of bright brown that was nearly orange, with a very short and scanty skirt, and a small cloth hat of the same colour. Suddenly Alex remembered that she had seen those clothes before.

" It must be Miss Orranmore whom I saw at the station that day with Van," she thought.

The girl stood looking rather mockingly—Alex could not distinguish her face, but the attitude was suggestive—and watched her companion slowly and painfully making his way up to her. He was a big, heavily built man—even at that distance his red sunburnt face was visible. He reached the spot where the girl was standing. She stood still looking up at him, and apparently made some jest as he approached. Their laughter rang out clear for a minute. The man came up, and stood panting, looking down at her, then all of a sudden took her in his arms, pressing her head back till it lay on his shoulder, and kissed her again and again, and yet again. A minute after she sprang away, stooping for a moment to readjust her cap, which had fallen off; then Alex heard her laugh once more, and, turning round, she swiftly mounted the little steep pathway, followed by her companion, and both were presently out of sight.

Alex sat upright, forgetful about the sleeping child, feeling suddenly hot all over. There are kisses and kisses, and even the most innocent woman could hardly have watched the embrace which she had just been the involuntary witness of without a sensation of astonishment. Her movement had wakened Mike, who sat up, yawning and rubbing his eyes, to ask when the others were coming back.

"Come, Mike, we'll go and meet them," said Alex. She jumped up and shook her crumpled skirt, and took the little boy by the hand.   "They must be coming from the lighthouse now," she said.

They started off together, walking quickly across the dry, close turf, and soon in the distance saw Matilda and the boys, Van loitering a little way behind.

"You've been a very long time away!" Alex exclaimed as they approached.

"We met some people Van knew," Matilda explained.

Van added rather hurriedly, "Yes, Dolly Orranmore. Don't you know her?   Her mother's some sort of twentieth cousin to Gran, I believe."

"Oh, a girl in an orange dress?" said Alex.

"Yes, I think she had on something queer in colour—mighty short in the skirt, too.   Her dresses always are," said Van.   "Did you see her?"

"She was walking down below on the rocks with a big man who was not nearly as surefooted as she was," Alex replied.

"That was Wharton—he's married to a cousin of hers.   Dolly is often with them."

Alex felt herself flush suddenly.   She would have liked to hear more about Miss Orranmore, but Van did not seem inclined to pursue the subject.

They all went down to the boat then, and sailed home in an hour and a half.   Even George and Peter were less exuberant, and Matilda looked tired.   Van managed the boat, and spoke very little.

The sun was still bright when they reached the harbour, and Van dexterously guided his boat between the breakwaters.

An old fisherman in a blue jacket who stood propped up against the harbour wall leaning heavily on a stick, watched them as they disembarked. Van stopped to speak to him for a minute, and when he rejoined them he said—

" Poor old fellow ! He's incurably ill—they sent him back from the hospital saying there was nothing more that could be done. Now he crawls out of his house every morning, and just stands about the harbour for the rest of the day."

Alex looked round, quickly noting the cruel contrast between the sunken old face already twisted by incurable pains, and the bright figure of youth that passed him by. The dancing water glittered in the sunshine behind the old man : the boats that he had lived on came and went : he meant to stay there till the end, tasting the very last of life. How faint his visions of another world probably were, compared to the sights and sounds he knew ; to the low, red houses, the unsavoury smells of the little harbour, the cries of his mates, and the noise of oars and rattling cordage. It seemed as if the young man, with his future all before him, would have passed more easily out of life than he—carried away at last from the scenes and actions become so intimately known to him in long years of uneventful living.

Alex had noted the kind inflection of Van's voice as he addressed the old man, his free and generous manner —a manner that had already endeared him to all his grandfather's dependants.

" He will be a fine man some day, if he always takes what Cable calls ' the upper fork of the road,' " she thought, as she watched him packing the children into the carriage.

It was six o'clock by the time they reached Cross-riggs, and the sky was flushing in its cloudless depths. Alex seemed abstracted all the way home.

" Is that Miss Orranmore a friend of yours, Van ? '

she asked ; " I remember seeing you with her once at the station."

" No, no ! No friend of mine—I've seen her often, of course—Gran will have to ask them to stay with us later on."

Alex remembered that he had told her this before, and she made no further remark, but, when they got in, she related the incident she had witnessed to her sister.

" He must have been a widower, and she is probably engaged to him," said Matilda.

" As much as I am ! " replied Alex.

" You do take such views of people," said Matilda. " Isn't it better always to believe the best ? "

" Better, perhaps, but not always possible."

" But, Alex, what do you know—— ? " began Mrs. Chalmers.

" About being kissed ? " said Alex, beginning to laugh. " Probably very little, but I know what shouldn't be done when I see it, and that young woman was no Diana ! "

CHAPTER XXVII

AFTER their day on the island, Alex more than once, when she saw Van, tried to turn the conversation to Miss Orranmore ; nor was this merely from feminine curiosity—the thought of that little scene on the rocks haunted her whenever she thought of Van's future. Yet it was impossible for her to hint to him anything about what she had seen.

" He will not talk about her, anyway," she concluded. " Either she attracts him more than he knows, or else he dislikes her—let us hope it is the last ! " She could not make out which it was, only one thing was certain, that Van would not speak about the girl.

In the meanwhile Alex was not going to Foxe Hall, because the Admiral was away from home. Her school work, too. was stopped for a time towards the end of July so that she was feeling almost idle.

Miss Bessie Reid had decided to be married about the end of the month.

" And now you must call me Elizabeth," she said playfully, " for Bessie Massie would never do ! " The touch of colour, which a suggestion of Mr. Massie's Spanish origin had at first given to the betrothal, had been traced merely to the imagination of Mrs. Scott. " His name *is* Ferdinand, but I think it was only because they thought it balanced well with Massie," Miss Bessie acknowledged, rather to the disappointment of her neighbours, who would have preferred the more romantic version of the story.

Spaniard or no, Mr. Massie was all that Miss Bessie's fondest fancy could desire. She was now occupied constantly in writing voluminous letters, her poker work and plush needlework laid aside for the time—the very way she put the stamps on the envelope was caressing, and to see her slide one of those missives into the pillar-box, was to know that she thought the carrier of her Majesty's mail the very messenger of Cupid.

Matilda, as I have said, by no means approved of Alex's attitude to the Reids, and Alex had to repress some of her remarks upon Miss Bessie's trousseau, for Matilda simply refused to listen to them. Alex had been very seldom at the Reids' of late, and she had managed successfully to evade meeting with James Reid ever since her painful walk with him in the rain. She knew, however, that she must meet him sooner or later, at any rate at his sister's wedding, and resolved to put as brave a face on it as possible. Every one felt glad, on Miss Bessie's account, that the wedding-day dawned with unclouded brilliance.

Matilda had been over at the Reids' until quite late on the previous evening, helping Bessie with her arrangements, and James Reid had walked back with her. But he would not come in, so Alex did not see him then.

There was a tide of universal good-feeling about Miss Bessie's marriage. Every one respected her, most people liked her, and no one had ever envied her, so on all sides the feeling was kindly.

She, good soul, was quite overwhelmed by the kindness of her neighbours, and when even Mrs. Maitland sent her a very handsome gift, along with a moderately warm note, she said to Alex—

" It's just wonderful how kind the world is, Alex ! There is Mrs. Maitland, whom I always considered so cold and stand-offish, sending me those beautiful spoons, and writing so pleasantly. Only Mrs. Scott seems to me to have been not quite so nice as other people."

"How could you wish her to be!" Alex exclaimed. "Any act that could win Mrs. Scott's approval would be degraded in my eyes!"

"James always says that you have such a high standard, Alex," said Miss Bessie, whose frequent allusions to her brother were trying to Alex's gravity.

On the day of the wedding, the whole of Crossriggs put on its best clothes, and went in high good-humour to the church. Matilda had modified her deep mourning for the first time, and Alex thought she looked exceedingly sweet in her grey dress. The children were all in great excitement. Alex had been so busy getting them ready that she had left very little time for her own toilet. She dressed hurriedly, and followed the others, tying the ribbons of her hat as she went.

"Oh, Aunt Alex, you look lovely!" said Peter, as she came up to them. Sally, flushed to the eyes, absorbed in the thought of her own new dress—a very simple white frock made at home, but of infinite moment to her—could scarcely even look at her aunt. Matilda nodded approval, glancing back at Alex as she shepherded the children into church.

Every one was there, even Mrs. Maitland, very gracious for her, and Aunt E.V., severely interested, ready to condemn the folly of a bride of Bessie Reid's age wearing white. Van, who did not know the Reids, had begged Alex to get him an invitation, and Miss Bessie had spoken to him one day when she saw him at the Hopes', asking him to come.

"He is always so pleasant when we meet, Alex," she said, "that even though his grandfather would never acknowledge James socially, I can't help liking him."

Van gleefully accepted the informal invitation, and sent a present at the last moment, which confirmed Miss Bessie in her opinion of the kindness of the world.

The Massie relatives were in a seat by themselves.

The mother of the cultured bridegroom, handsomely dressed in grey; two long-nosed, chinless sisters, who seemed to be falling out of their loose garments; and a nondescript friend or two completed the group—straight from small houses in the environs of Cambridge.

The mother wore spectacles, both sisters pince-nez, a cousin used a lorgnette; the bridegroom, too, was spectacled, and the best man wore almost goggles. It all flashed upon Alex in a moment, and upset her so completely that she coughed hard for a minute or two after entering the church. Matilda, who knew that fit of coughing well, glanced at her warningly as the bride came in, leaning on the arm of her brother.

Miss Bessie had been obliged to adhere to white, but she had contrived to insert a considerable number of materials into her wedding-dress, which had a skirt of one, a flounce of another, and a train of a third kind of silk; and was ruched, gauged, puffed, tucked, and trimmed with all that the bad taste of a second-rate dressmaker could suggest.

She wore around her neck one lovely ornament—Maitland's gift—two fancy combs and a Parisian diamond star secured her veil : her bouquet was rich with ribbon and paper frills : but nothing could obscure the happiness on her face.

Mr. Scott, who was gifted with an unerring tactlessness, contrived, even in the course of a very short address, to say several unfortunate things—praying at the last moment for Miss Bessie's " afflicted relative, so soon to be deprived of her kind care." Here the bride gave an audible sob, for the future of the poor old aunt had been the only stumbling-block to her marriage.

They sang " Oh, Perfect Love ! " (" not Presbyterian, but *so* appropriate ! " Miss Bessie had said when suggesting it to Mr. Scott), and then Mrs. Massie, leaning heavily on the arm of the spectacled bridegroom, came walking down the church, smiling all over her face, and winking the tears from her eyes.

The guests trooped out along the sunny village street to the Reids' house, which was not far from the church. The carriage in which the bride was to drive to the station stood at the door—the horses champing, with white favours at their ears ; the coachman exchanging jests with the Reids' maidservants before the wedding party came up.

Of course the house was filled to overflowing. Alex found herself by Maitland's side amongst the last to enter.

" Let the other people go on in front," she said to him, and they hung back a little, pacing slowly together in the warm light under the great lime trees that bordered the street.

Alex wished the room to be full of people before she encountered James Reid. She had seen him looking round the church as if in search of some one.

" He won't have time to notice me at all, if I come in late," she thought. Maitland sauntered along by her side with his hands behind him, looking rather grave for the occasion. " Oh," she began, " it's all so pitiful and ridiculous, and yet so happy, really."

" Why pitiful or ridiculous, then ? "

" Well, if you don't think it pitiful that any one should find their soul's desire in that man, I can't explain, and if you don't see anything ridiculous anywhere, of course I'm very glad," said Alex, adding, " Don't you think Matilda is looking very nice to-day ? "

" I never looked at Matilda," he answered simply, and Alex glanced at him quickly in surprise.

But his face expressed nothing, and she couldn't make out why he had taken no interest in her sister's appearance. As they came up to the house, Mrs. Maitland was standing in the doorway.

" Do hurry, Robert," she said, a little fretfully.

"They want you to say 'a few words,' or something dreadful of that kind.   Mr. Reid is looking for you everywhere."

As she spoke James Reid came hurrying out into the garden, hatless, white-waistcoated, flushed and nervous. He almost knocked Alex down as he cannonaded up to Maitland; then, catching sight of her, he got suddenly pale, and Alex grew very red.   He apologized for his haste, shook hands with her, and hurriedly turned to speak with Maitland, leaving Alex to enter the house along with Laura.

A few minutes later Alex slipped out of the crowd, and made her way to another room, where old Miss Reid was sitting propped up with pillows, a wedding favour truculently pinned upon her shawl, a cube of wedding-cake placed amongst the objects on her little table, tears streaming down her poor old face, whilst a grim new companion bustled about her, assuring her that all was well in this best of all possible worlds.

She grasped at Alex with her trembling hand, and began to mumble about " Bessie leaving," when the bride came fluttering in to say good-bye.

Her dress was ivy green, heavily trimmed with coffee-coloured lace, and deftly interwoven with beads.   Her headgear had in it " everything except a fox's brush— and I wasn't very sure about that ! " as Alex said afterwards.

" Well, dear Auntie, good-bye—for the present," Mrs. Massie began, trying to speak in her usual cheerful tone, but failing dismally.   Alex turned away that she might not see their parting.   " You'll not forget her rubbing and her cup of tea at six, Miss Tims ? " whispered Mrs. Massie to the new companion.   Then she clasped Alex in her arms.   " Good-bye, dear Alex.   How I hope that some day you may be as happy as I am—if only James——"

But Alex pushed her way, exclaiming that she would

be late for her train if she delayed any longer. So, amidst the congratulations of her neighbours, she hurried out to the hall, where the cultured bridegroom, in an even greener tie than usual, and a very low collar exposing his long throat, was awaiting her.

" Haven't you seen a swan trying to swallow a bit of bread ? " Alex said to Maitland, as they stood together by the hall door, waiting for the bridal couple to pass out. " You know how the bread works up and down the long throat. Well, isn't he just like that ? "

Even as she spoke there was a stampede of guests towards the door as the bride and bridegroom came out.

The hall was narrow. Some one stepped on Miss Maitland's skirt, and then nearly tumbled backwards in the effort to get off it again, and Alex was pressed back until she leant for a moment against Maitland's shoulder as he stood in the doorway.

" Take care, there is a step here," he said, just saving her from slipping down.

Alex quickly recovered her balance, and as she glanced up, caught sight of Van, who was looking at her steadily, as he stood on tiptoe behind Miss Maitland.

The expression in his eyes startled Alex almost as if he had said something rude. She coloured in spite of herself, and as the bride and bridegroom passed quickly out, she stepped into the garden.

" Come, Mike, we'll run home now ! " she said to the child who was at the door ; " and see if we can get in first ! ' Oh, Perfect Love ! ' " she murmured as they went along the street.

Mike was too much absorbed in his bit of cake to pay any attention to what she said. Van came hurrying after them, and Alex had to turn and speak to him. He had been most agreeable and useful to every one, enjoying himself much, and his coat was covered with wedding favours that the children had pinned upon it.

Alex thought he still looked at her a trifle curiously as he came up.

"Why, Sandy," he began, "I've scarcely spoken to you at all, and after getting me that invitation, I think you might have looked after me a bit. How were you to know what would become of me in a strange house?"

"Didn't every one look nice?" said Alex. "I thought that I had never seen Crossriggs appear to such advantage."

"Yes, excepting Maitland," said Van. "He looked such an "—he paused suddenly—" so solemn and out of place somehow. He'd have been so much more suitable at an Olympian banquet or something of that sort."

Alex laughed. "We can't all be suitable to every occasion. I thought he was looking very nice."

"Of course—he always does!" retorted Van, just as they were joined by Matilda and the others.

CHAPTER XXVIII

OLD HOPEFUL had long taken a profound interest in the bee. The conduct of life in the hive was one of his favourite topics, and although, to the outward eye, his were very ordinary bees, and the quantity and quality of honey which they produced was neither great nor particularly good, it was certainly not because of any want of attention from him. He held that change was good for every living thing; therefore, acting on this theory—though with results precisely similar to those obtained by his neighbours without it—once every year he conveyed his hives up to the hills, so that the " singing masons," as he delighted to call the bees, might enjoy the heather season there.

That summer he proposed to take Robert Maitland with him on the little excursion, which was very picturesque, as the party set off during the night, so as to arrive amongst the heather in the early morning.

Sally and the two older boys wanted to be allowed to go, and Matilda gave her permission on condition that Alex went too.

" I've done it twice before," said Alex to Maitland. " It means two hours of shaking in a farm cart in the darkness, getting bruised and stiff at the last, then one hour of ecstasy in the early morning—if the day proves fine—then home again with a splitting headache. All the same, I thoroughly sympathize with the children, and I'll go for their sakes."

" We won't go to bed at all, Aunt Alex," said the boys.
" We'd much rather sit up all night ! "

Alex laughed, and by half-past nine that evening they
were both in bed and sound asleep. She went to waken
them about two o'clock in the morning. The boys,
when well shaken, were alert in a short time, but
Sally's dreams were deep. Each time that Alex spoke
to her, she raised her heavy head from the pillow, murmuring—

" Yes, Aunt Alex, I want to come," and in two minutes was sound asleep more once.

Just at the last moment, when the cart was at the
gate and her brothers exulting in their own superiority,
she did appear, fastening her waistband as she came
downstairs, and yawning widely, but undoubtedly up
and dressed, after a fashion.

The night was fine, dry and soft, without a breath
of wind. Maitland was going to ride, and he waited
with his horse at the gate. The farm cart stood a few
yards further on. Alex came out into the dim summer
night.

" You here already ? " she said to Maitland. " We've
all got to be packed in still, and father is helping James
Todd to carry out the hives."

As she spoke Mr. Hope and the ploughman came down
the garden path, and lifted the sleeping hives one by one
into the cart. A faint smell of honey, and a distant—oh,
so far distant—creepy, creepy murmur came from under
the sacking that covered them.

The children climbed into their places in the cart.
There was a delicious excitement to them in being so
close to a dreaming hive, for though they were assured
that the bees couldn't get out, they preferred to think
it was dangerous.

Alex rolled them · all up in rugs and shawls, and
seated herself between the hives, with the boys curled
up at her feet, and Sally leaning heavily on her shoulder.

Old Hopeful took his seat beside the driver, and with a jingle of harness the horse stepped out.

Maitland mounted and rode at a walking pace alongside. Mr. Hope was the liveliest of the party, for the dour ploughman never uttered a word; the boys were soon half asleep again, and Alex sat in silence, leaning back her head, and gazing up at the dark sky.

"The Bee, James Todd," began Old Hopeful, addressing the huge figure at his side; "is a lesson to every citizen."

"Maybe, sir," responded the ploughman, unconscious of any pun.

Old Hopeful proceeded to relate anecdotes of its "instinct for the common good." His voice flowed on, interrupted only by an occasional grunt from the ploughman, or a "gee up" addressed to the horse. The cart rumbled along the dry roads, the children sank down further amongst their rugs, and Alex sat still, feeling the weight of Peter curled half across her feet, and Sally's head heavy on her shoulder. She was not cold, and did not mind the jolting for the first hour or so.

Maitland rode beside the cart in silence, once or twice he leant down in his saddle and asked if she was tired. It was still so dark that his face was only a pale blur as he bent towards her.

"No, not yet," she answered, speaking up into the darkness.

The cart went more softly as they left Crossriggs behind. There were no lights in any of the buildings. Passing a farm steading the odour of the farmyard came across the road, mingling with the scent of clover from the fields, and a dog began to bark in one of the outhouses. Then some time afterwards, deep in the country, they passed a little lonely cottage by the roadside, with a light burning in the window. No sound came from within and no shadow appeared as the cart rumbled past.

"Did you see that?" Alex asked. "Wasn't it significant somehow? I'd like to stop and knock at the door, and see inside. What do you suppose you would find?"

"Sickness—death, perhaps," Maitland answered.

She thought his voice had not its usual tone, but she could not yet see his face. The soil of the road became very sandy then, and the cart went more slowly. Old Hopeful, too, was silent at last, after having given James Todd a history of the Fruitarian movement, which had been but coldly received. Alex closed her eyes again and listened to the slow clap, cloop of the horse's feet, and the monotonous jingle of the brasses on the harness. Now and then, as the cart bumped upon the rough road, came a grunt from the sleeping boys, and a faint dreamy hiss from the covered hives.

Then suddenly a cock crew shrilly from a cottage yard, and James Todd turned his huge shoulder and grunted out that it was "near morn the noo." Alex looked round and saw a pale brightness dawning in the east. The scents of things had begun to change as they came nearer to the hills—fresher air, perfumes of a different country, scents of bog and thicket, and then, as the sun rose and they reached the foot of the hills, the smell of heather.

"Oh, it's morning!" cried Peter, sitting up and stretching himself; "we've been asleep, Aunt Alex!"

"I should think you had, Peter. Sally's sound asleep now," she answered, gently trying to rouse the sleeping girl.

By this time they had come to the shepherd's cottage where they were to have some breakfast whilst the bees were placed in their new lodgment. They were all very stiff when they got out of the cart, but the sun had risen fully now, and the shepherd's wife stood smiling a welcome at the door.

When the children had had some food, and rested for half an hour, Alex left them and walked away by herself towards the little stream that ran below the bank on which the cottage stood. Old Hopeful and the plough-man had gone off with the shepherd to settle the bees. The morning sun was just coming above the shoulder of the hill and beginning to pierce into the glen that lay behind the cottage. Alex slid down the steep green bank, and sat leaning her head on her hand, and listened to the trilling noise made by the little burn.

One shoulder of the hill rose in front of her, covered with blooming heather, still grey from the heavy dews, but the knolls and the high banks that sloped down to the little stream were bare, except for the short grass where a few sheep were feeding. Already Alex was dreadfully tired. Her strength was not what it used to be, though she struggled hard against the feeling of lassitude that overcame her after any exertion.

" Dear me ! " she thought, " I am getting old. I'm as tired now as if it were night instead of morning, yet I went to bed at nine and slept till two, and surely that is enough ! "

It had not been enough, for as she sat there, she was oppressed with an overwhelming fatigue, and as often happens, bodily weakness affecting the mind and making it sensitive to strange impressions, it seemed that the simple little scene before her there, in the limpid morn-ing light, touched her so that she could have sat and wept.

Just the running water, the few sheep feeding on the bare green hillocks, and a line of stepping-stones where the burn ran wide and shallow.

She sat and looked, her eyes filled with unreasoning tears. Then she heard a step behind her, and looking round, saw Maitland coming down the bank. His presence seemed an intrusion to her just then, she would so much rather have been left alone.

" What have you done with your family ? " he asked.

"Mrs. Sinclair took them with her to feed the hens," said Alex. "So I came away by myself."

Maitland sat down beside her. "Why, you are tired already!" he said.

Alex turned her face away. "I'm often tired now —it's nothing, please don't mind. Isn't this a sincere, peaceful little scene?"

But he was studying her face. "Alex," he said, "you are not well—all this work that you have been doing is too much for you; or else you are worrying about something new. Won't you tell me what it is?"

"Oh, who hasn't worries—piles of them—trifles, mine are just now. When they're all taken together they weigh and suffocate like a feather bed, yet taken singly they're as light as that!" There was a single feather, dropped from the wing of some wild bird, lying on the grass beside her, and she lifted it as she spoke, then suddenly began to laugh. "It's so like the last straw added to one of Miss Bessie Reid's hats. I mustn't call her 'Bessie Reid' any more, I suppose. I wonder how she's getting on? We've had two postcards from Switzerland—they've gone to the historic Pension. To think that wedding was only three weeks ago. It seems such a long time!"

"But you haven't told me what is wrong?" Maitland persisted.

"There isn't anything wrong—at least, nothing that can ever be put right," she answered, turning her face away from him.

She leant her chin on her hand and played with the curlew's feather, then said, with an effort to change the subject and speak as usual—

"How romantic Miss Bessie considered her own history to be—things are so different when looked at from the outside!"

"Of course they are, that is why we make most of our mistakes in life."

" It is one of the weak points of novels, of course,"
Alex went on, " that they prefer to pretend that the
outside circumstances look like the inside—the outside
of the stained glass window like the window seen from
within.　It hardly ever does ! "

" Never," said Maitland, smiling.

" Do think," Alex went on, " what Miss Bessie's
romance with her swan-throated young man appeared
to us ! "

" To me it appeared a remarkably happy arrangement,
Alex."

" Oh yes, of course it was—but not like a novelist's
fancy."　She paused, and added, " Then there is what
the Admiral calls ' All that nonsense about Love '—
that's overdone, too ! "

" Yes, frequently, I think," Maitland assented. " After
all," he said as if to himself, " the instinct of civilized
people is to conceal, instead of expressing passion."

" Oh now, that sounds so dry and grim ! " Alex protested.　" But I suppose it's true.　It's not a romantic
world nowadays, and no one can express anything, so
they needn't strive to conceal it—for the difficulty is to
find words if we try !　We're mostly entirely inarticulate
—except a few of the poets."

' " They can say things," Maitland assented.　He
paused, looking down, and plucking at the blades of
grass.　" ' *Oh, that 'twere possible, after long grief and
pain,*' for instance."　He glanced up at Alex as he spoke,
and then they both, as if by the same impulse, looked
away.　" Or that line from Lovelace," he went on, and
his voice suddenly grew low and hoarse : " ' *I could not
love thee, dear, so well, loved I not honour more.*' "

" I know—I know," said Alex.　There was silence for
a moment, broken only by the voice of the running
stream.　Then she got up very quietly, but the little
feather trembled in her hand.　" The children will be
running wild by this time.　Shall we go back to the

house ? " she said. " Father must have surely colonized the bees and be ready to start."

Maitland rose and stood looking up the little glen. His grave eyes, which were really a very dark blue, looked almost black at that moment, his face was rather pale, but he spoke in his ordinary tone of voice again.

" It was here that I came," he said, " one day in early spring. I met you and Matilda on my way home, and you were very cross with me because you thought that I had been enjoying such peace, whilst you were worried about trifles. I remember the day quite well. The peace was not as great as you supposed."

Alex had got very pale. She looked perfectly withered with fatigue.

" Come," he said, " let me help you up here."

But she shook her head, and scrambled up the bank without touching his extended hand.

Maitland stooped and picked up the little feather which she had thrown away.

" I may keep this, mayn't I—it weighs nothing ? " he said.

Alex smiled, saying, " Miss Bessie's feather ? Oh, yes," and went on to the cottage, where the children were skirmishing about at the door.

Old Hopeful had finished his business with the bees, and even had time for some talk and advice to the shepherd regarding the management of sheep. The cart was brought round again, and the children were packed in somehow.

" I think I shall ride ahead, sir, for I have some work to do when I get home," said Maitland, and he struck off at a pace that left the cart far behind.

By this time the sun was very hot, and the children soon became all more or less cross. The drive seemed long on the way back. When they got home Matilda exclaimed at Alex's white face.

" I'll go upstairs and lie down for a little," said Alex.

"My bones ache, and my head aches, too, with the jolting."

She went to her own room, locked the door, and threw herself down upon the bed. When four o'clock struck she got up, saying to herself, "'Wash thy face, and anoint thine head, that thou appear not unto men to fast,'" and when she came downstairs at the children's tea hour, Matilda thought she looked quite herself again.

"I've been across to the Maitlands," Matilda said. "Mr. Maitland wasn't visible, but Aunt E. V. said that he looked very tired, too, when he came home. I'm afraid early hours don't agree with any one."

"When I was young I could rise with the lark, and feel all the better for it," remarked Old Hopeful, the only one of the party who seemed to have suffered nothing from their early start. "The hours just after sunrise are the most precious of the day."

Van came in then, as he often did, to join the children's tea. He was in high spirits, and the tired children were soon chattering and feeding as gaily as usual under his cheering influence.

"We've all been cross," they told him. "At least, we've been cross and Aunt Alex tired."

"And cross, too, Sandy?"

"Oh yes, very," she said, laughing.

"Well, at least—a little," Peter corrected. "And grandfather was sleepy, too, on the way home. The hives were all right, the bees never slept. They were just beginning to work at once, and we're all very glad we're not bees."

They ran away out to the orchard then, and Van followed Alex into the other room. After a little she left him alone for a few minutes whilst she went to find some book that her father wanted. When she came back Mike was in the room, and he and Van seemed to be having some important conversation.

" All right, then, bring it to me when I go out," Van
was saying.

Mike, on his part, pocketed something that chinked
like coin.

" Now, what is this bargain ? " Alex asked, laughing,
and Van shook his head at Mike, who ran out of the room
in high glee. " You shouldn't give money to the child,
Van—it's not good for him," said Alex.

" We had made a bargain," said Van. " I didn't give
him anything."

In a few minutes Mike came in again, and with an air
of great mystery handed something to Van, and ran away
once more.

" That looks like something of mine," said Alex,
glancing at it.

" It's mine now—paid for, too, Sandy," Van said
triumphantly.

He held it out for her inspection, keeping his hand
closed round it lest she should take it away—a small photograph of herself which she had sent to Matilda before they
all came back from Canada. Alex remembered it well. It
had been done by an amateur, and had some of the fortunate ease that such pictures, when successful, often have.
It was really very like her. She remembered that when
they came home, Matilda had given it to one of the
boys one day. It was enclosed in a little case of green
leather.

Alex felt uncertain whether to be angry or to laugh at
the whole affair, and she chose the latter course, as she did
about most things.

" Well, of course if you think it right to encourage the
children to sell their dear aunt's picture you may have it,
but it's a very bad example to them, just teaching them
scorn of sentiment and greed of gain, as my father would
say."

Van put the little case in his breast pocket with a
smile, and got up to go away.

Something restrained Alex from saying anything about the incident to Matilda, but she said to Mike—

" I don't think it was kind of you to sell my picture, even to Van."

" Oh, did he tell you ? " said Peter, who overheard. " You see, Aunt Alex, he said that we had you to look at whenever we liked, so we didn't want your photograph, and I've heard you say yourself that it was so queer of Mrs. Scott to have four photographs of herself and two of Mr. Scott, and two of the children with her, and one of them alone, all in her own house.

" So I did, Peter. Out of the mouths of babes I'm condemned, but I won't give you any more to sell."

They set upon her and hugged her then, protesting that she was horrid to scold them, and consulting as to what they could buy with their dishonest gains.

CHAPTER XXIX

MAITLAND and his wife both went away for several months soon after the little excursion to the hills with the bees. Laura had not been well for some time, and wanted to try a German heart cure. Crossriggs always seemed a little like a flock without a shepherd when the Maitlands were not there, and on this occasion Aunt E. V. went away also, and the house was left quite empty.

This had not happened for many years, and the Hopes thought it very strange, as night came on, to look across the square, and see no lights in the windows opposite.

Alex had holidays from her school work, and even the Admiral went off in August to Homburg. Van left too, protesting that he would much rather have stayed at home, and so a sort of summer stillness descended upon Crossriggs. There were no tourists there—the place did not interest them. A stray man with a road map, anxious to find his way to some other place, was the only sign that they had swarmed like locusts over the whole coast.

During the long hot days Matilda and Alex sat out in the orchard a great deal, where the green leaves were beginning to turn a rusty colour in the sun, and the fruit showed touches of crimson.

The children's holidays gave both of them more to do, for the boys were skirmishing about all the time, and required some looking after.

" I feel as if this hot weather were going to last for ever now," Alex remarked one day, leaning back in her chair, gazing at the glowing red brick walls where some of Old Hopeful's pears were hanging, looking very beautiful, though she knew their taste to resemble a combination of cotton wool and potatoes.

" With Van and the Admiral away, and all the Mait-lands gone, everything seems different," said Matilda. She added, " I wonder if Van will marry that pretty Miss Pym—she's with her aunts just now, Mrs. Lawrence told me."

" She was a pretty girl," said Alex, too lazy to go on with her sewing, leaning back with her hat tilted over her eyes, " but why should every one be so anxious that Van should marry ? "

" Oh, well, of course, that's natural," began Matilda.

" I don't think it is yet—his character is quite un-formed, and the longer he waits the better, I should say. I'm sure marriage isn't always so happy," she added, irrelevantly.

" Dear me, Alex, surely there has been something annoying you of late," Matilda answered, looking at her sister, " you seem to say such bitter things."

" Do I ?—I'm sorry.   Put it down to the heat and fatigue, or perhaps I'm already becoming ' an old servant,' as Mike translated ' an old maid.' "   She laughed, and then went on, suddenly sober again, " Oh, Matilda, how Mike and Baby are growing up !   And what are we going to do about their education ? "

" Father can teach Mike for a year or two still, though I'm sometimes afraid that it tires him too much now," said Matilda, " and Baby is a girl, of course——"

" And therefore doesn't need to be educated !   Matilda, are you Father's daughter ?   Sometimes you astonish me ! I believe you'll have the sort of luck that does attend views of the kind you so nearly expressed just now, and that Sally at seventeen will marry a rich young man, with a much younger brother, who will do for the uneducated Baby when she ' comes up,' as Katharine says."

" Oh, Alex, what a blessing it would be !   But there is no rich young man ! " said the artless mother.

Alex laughed. " No, nor ' like to be '—you really are too delightful, Matilda. Often I can scarcely believe that we are sisters ! "

Here Sally, all unconscious of her projected fate, came trailing out of the house, and sank with a gasp on the grass beside them.

" I've been playing with the boys until it got too hot to run any longer," she panted, leaning up against her mother's knee.

Her pink cotton gown was faded and badly ironed, her pretty skin heavily freckled by careless exposure to the sun, her auburn hair was all frowsy; but she looked perfectly healthy and contented, and was going to be a very pretty woman some day.

As they sat there in the hot sunshine the door between the garden and the orchard opened, and Old Hopeful made his appearance, looking a little rumpled, holding a Greek book as usual in one hand. Since his illness he had lost much of his bright colour, and looked a very frail old man indeed.

" Alex," he began, lowering his voice, " I was just having half an hour of quiet, when a visitor was shown in —a young man who has a note of introduction from your Uncle James. He is a dark youth, far from prepossessing, but as he is a friend of my brother's, I suppose we must be hospitable.

" Don't ask him to supper ! " Alex cried, sitting up suddenly and pushing her hat off her forehead.

" I have already done so ; he is a little difficult in con- versation," said Mr. Hope, " and as I have been doing my best for a quarter of an hour now, I propose to bring him out here."

Matilda and Alex exchanged glances of despair as he turned back towards the house.

" Well, anyway, if he's a friend of Uncle James's he's not a vegetarian ! " said Alex.

" He might be a Mormon ! " Matilda had just time to exclaim, when Old Hopeful reappeared, ushering his guest into the garden.

Both women were rather disinclined for the company of any stranger that afternoon, and they knew only too well what curious people their father at times presented to them, so when a very ordinary looking young man made his appearance Alex gave a sigh of relief.

" No Cult !—just common," she murmured, as Matilda rose to greet the stranger.

" This is Mr. Charles Morse, Matilda, a friend of your uncle's," said Old Hopeful, introducing him, and then gladly abandoning him to be entertained by his daughters.

A second glance showed Alex that Mr. Morse was dressed with care, and that everything he wore, from his necktie to his shoes, was of the most unimpeachable fashion.   Yet, in spite of this, the dark skin, the rather almond-shaped black eye, and the careful manner strongly suggested something Oriental.   He sat on the edge of a canvas chair, his hands folded on his walking-stick, which, though a plain one (Alex thought), somehow suggested that the ideal of its owner was ivory and gold. One hand displayed a ring which was not, as Alex observed with surprise, either too large or too gay : his hair did not glitter—but you wondered why it didn't— he spoke very little and quite nicely, and explained to Matilda that he was staying with people in the neighbourhood.   When he mentioned the name of the house, they remembered that it was tenanted by some rich manufacturing people, whom they knew a little, and who had taken it for some years.

Sally had run away when the guest appeared, but now came up to ask her mother if she might go and play rounders with the boys. Peter accompanied her, and after shaking hands with Mr. Morse, he suddenly asked him—

" Will you play, too ? "

To Alex's great amusement the young man jumped up with evident relief.

" Yes, I will. Where are you playing? " he said, and Peter triumphantly led him away to the field.

Matilda and Alex sank back in their chairs with sighs of thankfulness.

" He was going to be so difficult, I know," said Alex. " He is the kind of product who only speaks by rule. What a mercy he is gone ! We should have had to talk at him for an hour—and he really wanted to go, too— I saw that. He won't heat becomingly, one can see, but that's his own look out."

" He did seem rather dull," said Matilda ; " but he may have been shy—and wasn't there something——"

" Very vulgar about him ? No, dear, not very—just ever, ever so little, and so carefully concealed too—it's cruel to notice it ! "

" Really, Alex, you are so unkind. I was not going to say that at all," said Matilda, " I only meant there was something—— "

" Semitic ? Probably—why not ? That dear old German Jew whom Father brought here last summer—the one who was going to rebuild the Temple—was such an impressive person. It's nothing racial, Matilda— it's retail trade."

" He looked quite a nice young man."

" Strictly respectable I'm sure—and so rich evidently —he might have stepped out into the garden, like the Prince in the fairy tale, just as we were speaking about Sally's future. It's a pity the dear thing is so untidy and so occupied with childish games. Another year,

and we can begin to think about young men coming to
see her."

The game lasted a long time, and the air was cooling at
sunset before the children trooped back into the garden
again. Mr. Morse, hatless, coatless, and very red in the
face, certainly did not " heat well "—his black hair clung
damp to his low forehead, but his almond eye was bright
with enjoyment, and the children seemed to have found
him delightful.

Sally, with her auburn locks now in wild disorder, and
her frock all stained with green, swinging her hat in her
hand, was walking beside him, talking eagerly. As soon
as they came up to Alex and Matilda, the young man's
stiffness returned. He pulled his moustache, and said,
" Oh, yes," and " Oh, no," and seemed as ill at ease as
ever. Old Hopeful came out once more to press him to
stay to supper, but he politely refused, and after a little,
rather convulsively took his leave.

" We all liked him," said the children ; " he was most
kind, mother, and his boots had such a lovely smell of
Russia leather ! "

" Children, I think you make too many remarks about
people—it's not polite," said Matilda, and Alex laughed.

" Was there a glimpse of something pink visible about
him ? Or was it only that I painted him in gayer
colours than mere brown and grey in my mind's eye ? "

Matilda frowned at her, but a boy interjected, " Oh,
Aunt Alex—pink silk—I saw when he turned up his
sleeves ! "

" Well, we must all go and get ready for supper, and
not stand here discussing Mr. Morse any longer," said
Matilda, who thought, and rightly, that Alex often spoke
rashly before the children.

So they all went into the house as the summer twilight
settled down upon the weary land. The great moon of
harvest was rising like a solemn joy, low down in the
warm sky.

The clutch of Poverty was much lighter in hot weather than in cold; her grim fingers relaxed a little—days were long and nights short, fires and lights not much required, and to sup on bread and milk and gooseberries seemed very good eating to the children in that heat.

After supper, Alex stood at the garden door looking out at the solemn, golden moon; at the fruit-laden trees; the bland peace of heaven and earth.

" What a world to be very happy in !—there must be some secret that would make us so if we could find it— for the stage is here. How seldom we fit it ! " Then the next minute she thought shame. " I must go and see old Miss Reid to-morrow," she said ; " she always makes me so thankful, that I never grumble at anything in my own lot for a week afterwards."

She remembered her resolution, and went to see the old lady the following afternoon. Miss Reid never went out, even in the hottest weather, and she sat propped up as usual in the corner, her little table spread with post-cards sent by her niece from every station of her foreign journey.

Miss Bessie's mock apple blossoms were still blooming in the vases ; all the hundred trifles in the room were unchanged, the grim companion moving heavily about, fulfilling the duties for which she was paid; the autumn sunshine making the hideous room unbearably hot. Alex's heart was filled with shame, and thanksgiving for her own life, before she had crossed the threshold.

She sat with the old lady for a long while, and read aloud to her, for the second time, every word of Mrs. Massie's two long letters. These were always lying on the little table, kept from blowing off when the window was open, by a cast-iron canary coloured a bright yellow, which Miss Bessie had used as a paper-weight.

The companion was knitting woollen slippers—a peculiarly stuffy bit of work for hot weather—in a cosy shade of red too, but Alex noticed she had imagination

8

enough to be reading a book about Greenland. "Though the sudden shock given by pictures of icebergs in this heat must have been bad for the old lady, I'm sure," she said afterwards. Alex talked and laughed, and cheered the invalid wonderfully, and promised to return very soon. Coming out into the hall, she remembered how she had stood there with Robert Maitland on the day of Miss Bessie's wedding.

Once again she encountered James Reid at the door. This time she was going out and he coming in. He had just come from Crosstown, and was less embarrassed than he had been on the former occasion. They exchanged a few words about Mrs. Massie. He inquired for Matilda and the children, and gave Alex quite the impression of a family friend, desirous not to favour any one individually.

She, conscious that the companion was watching their interview from the parlour window, hurried away down the street, rather red in the face and a little out of breath ; and James Reid, much pleased with his own composure, hummed an air to himself, and stood on the doorstep fastening up a bit of the creeper that had fallen away from the wall, without giving so much as a glance after her retreating figure.

"O ye makers of tales and romances," said Alex to herself, "behold all that Fate has given to me for a lover—and am I a particularly unromantic woman ? " She laughed, and then she sighed, and Van's face and another face that had seemed a brightness to her from her very childhood rose up before her mind. "Perhaps," she thought, "'in worlds whose course is equable and pure' things may be adjusted so differently that we shall recognize it was not what we had, but what we never had, that showed us the way to love."

CHAPTER XXX.

The Admiral came home again alone, Van being still away. Then Miss Maitland returned from the north, where she had spent the summer. Her relations on her mother's side lived there: in describing them she would go into labyrinths of genealogy that would have confounded any one else, but from which she could always emerge with triumphant assurance.

Crossriggs seemed more like itself when she and the Admiral returned, in spite of Van's absence, though Maitland and his wife were not coming home until November.

Foxe Hall was very silent without the young man. The Admiral used to try to detain Alex by all sorts of transparent little excuses, which she had not the heart to withstand, so she often stayed with him far beyond her appointed hour.

Her school work began again in September, and she had already received several other offers for reading in public. Neither Mr. Hope nor Matilda approved of this, but Alex would not listen to them.

" You can't make an omelette without breaking eggs," she used to say, " and you can't work for money without work—work that breaks your back in some way or other. I'm only lucky to get it."

So she made her arrangements for readings—one in Edinburgh, and two or three in other places, during the winter months.

On the day that Van returned, Alex had been in town all morning, had eaten a hurried meal when she came home, and then started off to Foxe Hall. After she had been reading for a little the Admiral noticed her flagging voice.

"You are tired, Miss Hope," he said. "Better stop reading. Pray do not go on until you have had some tea. Van will be coming in immediately."

When Van did appear Alex thought that she had never seen him look so well. He was very much sunburnt, but looked altogether more manly and less of a boy than before he went away.

"Well, Sandy, you don't look as if you had had much of a time," he remarked, as he escorted her to the door.

"Don't I? Perhaps the summer has been too hot or something," she answered.

Van walked along beside her with his hands in his pockets.

"Do you know," he said, " the Orranmores are coming here next month—asked themselves. Gran couldn't refuse. You see we can never say the house is full."

"Who are they? Mrs. Orranmore and her daughter?"

"And Orranmore himself—the whole family. In low water, I suppose."

"I remember the girl quite well—we saw her that day on the island," said Alex.

"Oh yes, we did meet her there—I'd forgotten that."

"I had not," said Alex, smiling to think how indelible her first impression of Miss Orranmore was likely to remain. "Did you see your pretty Miss Pym?" she asked pleasantly.

"Why 'your'?—she's nothing to me. But I did see her of course—she was staying with her aunts."

Alex thought the colour deepened a shade on his brown cheek as he spoke. After a minute he broke out—

"The girl's nice enough—I'd like her quite well if it weren't for Gran and those cackling old aunts of hers.

But I —but—but—— Hang it! One can't say anything so conceited. Don't you know what I mean?"

" Yes, of course I do. Only Van, don't allow yourself to be prejudiced against a nice and such a pretty girl just because old people choose to be tactless and foolish about things."

" Me prejudiced! I'm not at all. If we were all alone in the moon, I'd never fall in love with that girl!"

" Very well, we needn't discuss it then," said Alex, closing the conversation with a snap, for somehow she felt it was dangerous ground.

She walked slowly home, too absorbed in her thoughts to notice the loveliness of the golden lime trees against the winter greyness that was now beginning to steal over the land.

Miss Maitland was sitting with Matilda when Alex came in. They had scarcely met since her return.

" You're a little pale, Alex," she remarked. " I think this going into town is too much for you."

" Perhaps it is; but my kind friends seem to forget that it must be done," said Alex, coldly.

Aunt E. V. regarded he with her penetrating glance for a moment and said nothing.

" How is Mrs. Maitland? I hope she is really better?" said Alex.

Better, but not at all well. Robert writes that she has had another slight attack since they came to London. No doubt Scotch air will do her good."

" Then they are coming home soon?" Alex asked. She turned away as she spoke, to put coal on the fire.

" Yes in a fortnight. Robert's intention was to have remained in town, but he does not like Laura to take the journey by herself. She likes attention," said Miss Maitland.

" Oh, we shall all be so glad to have them back," exclaimed Matilda. " Nothing seems right at Crossriggs when Mr. Maitland is away!"

"My father was much missed," said Miss Maitland severely. "And when my grandfather died I have heard people say that the affairs of the parish stood still. Robert does his best," she added as a concession.

"W hear that Miss Bessie, as we still call her, came back yesterday," said Matilda. "Old Miss Reid was quite shaken by the excitement. She is going to stay for a week. Have you seen her?"

"I called this morning," said Aunt E. V. "Poor Bessie!—a thin harvest, but a thankful heart. Women are less critical than they were in my youth. Still, I am told that he has principle—'Culture,' she says; I doubt if she knows the meaning of the word. He appears to please her; no doubt he has good points; Bessie Reid did her duty by her aunt."

"She did indeed; she was an example to us all!" said Matilda warmly.

"And she was perhaps sensible to take the offer made to her by a respectable man," went on Aunt E. V., lowering the eye upon Alex. "Some people err in the other direction, and think no one good enough for themselves."

"Do you mean me?" said Alex, making a sudden attack upon Miss Maitland, and looking fearlessly at her as she spoke.

"I do, Alex."

"Oh!" Alex tried to be grave, and ended by laughing ignominiously. "How I wish I did! It would be so nice to have such a good opinion of one's self."

Miss Maitland rose. "A cousin of mine on my mother's side—one of the Frasers of Beale—refused ten good men before she was twenty-eight; she died single at ninety-nine."

"Oh, tell us more—those stories are so interesting," cried Alex. "Did you see her at ninety-nine?"

"At ninety-seven; they used to say that she changed her waiting-maid every six weeks, her temper had soured so.   Her only sister, as a girl, was plain but pleasant—no one ever supposed she would marry."

" Well ? " Alex inquired.

" At her first ball she met Mr. Sinclair—a good plain man he was—they were married immediately.   She had eleven daughters, and she lived to marry every one of them to gentlemen of fortune and position ! "

Miss Maitland sailed off, leaving Alex to digest the moral of this history.

Maitland and his wife did not return till nearly the end of November.   One day, soon after their arrival, Alex got a note from the Admiral, requesting that she and her father would dine at Foxe Hall on the following week.

" I expect to have the Orranmores with us then," he said, and Van, who as usual had written the note for his grandfather, had added "awful bore" in pencil at the edge.

Alex felt that the party was going to be an odd one, for the Maitlands too had been invited, she knew; but having no good excuse to offer, she accepted the invitation.

CHAPTER XXXI

MAITLAND was in town on the day of the Admiral's dinner-party, and had sent a message that he could not be back in time, so Mrs. Maitland offered to drive Alex and Mr. Hope as there would be room in their carriage. They called at the door to pick up the Hopes. As the carriage stopped at the gate, Alex came out, wrapping herself in a shawl. Matilda was helping her father into his great-coat, and Alex waved her hand to her, calling out—

"Don't sit up for us, unless you feel inclined, Matty." She ran down the path, and greeted Laura and Aunt E. V.

"Whew! How cold it is! How invigoratingly cold! I feel as if I should like to run all the way to Foxe Hall like the horses. How are you, Mrs. Maitland? You look better to-night."

She got into the carriage, and looked admiringly at Laura, who was dimly visible, wrapped in white furs.

"Scotch air, as I said, has done her good," said Aunt E. V., who had a strong belief in the enervating effects of any more southern climate upon the constitution.

"As for myself," she used to say, "I never feel really braced till I get beyond Inverness. There is a want of quality in lowland air."

The evening was almost cold enough to have contented her. The carriage went swiftly, for the horses were fresh and the roads smooth. The pale fields and hedge-rows shone in the light from the spangled heavens, and in the distance the hills were visible, like milky-white shadows.

" There's a strange kind of gaiety about a night like this, isn't there ? " said Alex. " Like the pleasures of the Elysian fields. Couldn't you fancy the shades of the dead meeting for bodiless enjoyment by the light of the moon on such a frosty night as this ? All of us, a troop of ghosts, just meeting in these well-known fields. Oh, I can imagine it perfectly—the queer, shimmering light and the frosty air—all the talk a little thin, none of us palpable, and everything in greys and whites—and the way our eyes would glimmer ! "

" Oh, I don't like your imagination at all ! " said Mrs. Maitland.

" The dead," remarked Aunt E. V., " will be better employed, we hope, in the next life, than wandering about regretting this one, Alex."

" Did I say regretting ? " said Alex.

But here old Hopeful went off into a very learned disquisition on the nether world as imagined by the ancients.

" And have we any right to dispute it ? " he inquired. " Who takes our own detailed accounts of gates of pearl and seas of glass to be literal ? "

" Many a good Scottish divine has done so, Mr. Hope," said Miss Maitland ; but he brushed the remark aside with a wave of the hand.

" Banks of Asphodel are more probable than that ; and Charon and his boat—are they more clumsy than many of our Biblical allusions ? "

" Oh, that had always such an attraction for me ! " said Alex, anxious to prevent her father and Miss Maitland from disagreeing too much. " I began to write something about it once ; but it got no further than the first sentence. When some of the newly arrived—in the other world—ask of a woman, ' *Who are you ? And why do you wait always by the ferry ?* ' "

" Few would wait long—for any one," said Aunt E. V., who seemed to be in a trenchant humour that evening.

As the carriage swung round before the door of Foxe Hall, Mrs. Maitland shivered again.

" We seem to have had such a ghostly conversation," she said ; " I hope dinner will be more cheerful."

As they mounted the flight of broad steps that led up to the door, Alex stood for a moment looking at the pale sky. Then she gathered up her long skirt, and followed Aunt E. V. and Laura into the house.

Very warm and bright it seemed indoors. They were taking off their wraps when some one ran past the open door with a great rustling of silken skirts.

" That must be Miss Orranmore," said Alex. ' Doesn't it sound funny to hear a woman in this house ? " Then, glancing at her own reflection in the glass, she exclaimed, " Oh, how ordinary I do look—how literal this black and red is ! " She wore a bunch of scarlet flowers in her old black gown.

" You look very nice, I think," said Laura Maitland.

She was beginning to say these little, flat, kind things quite often now, and they always gave Alex a twinge at the heart.

" Ah, you are a flatterer. If you could only see your own dress you'd know what mine was like," laughed Alex.

But she did look well, too, as she walked across the long hall, holding her head high, and moving in her graceful, energetic way.

As they neared the drawing-room door there came a sudden waft of perfume upon the air like the scent of carnations. Alex turned to see if the flowers were anywhere at hand, but she saw none, and at that moment the butler threw open the door, and they entered the drawing-room.

The Admiral liked a glare of light, for then he felt it on his eyes, though he could see nothing. So the whole of the long room, which was painted a pale green colour, was flooded with light from the unshaded lamps, thus giving every person and object an unusual detachment.

By the fireplace, where a great fire burned, stood the blind old man, holding out his hand, with his face turned towards the door. There was a tall dog sitting up beside him, and when the Admiral shook hands with Alex the dog, which knew her well, gravely tendered her a paw.

It was always a sight to see Miss Maitland enter a room. She came across like a ship in full sail, holding herself as upright as a mast : yards and yards of crinkly silk upon the floor behind her : her head, crowned by a tiny lace cap, held very high ; a dignity in her port that suggested the day of Hannah More. Mrs. Maitland, pretty though she was, seemed nowhere in comparison. She made apologies for her husband's absence, and hoped that the Admiral wouldn't wait for him. " He said in his telegram that he could not be here till half-past eight," she said—and the Admiral assured her that they would only wait for a few minutes on the chance of his having caught an earlier train.

Alex meanwhile was looking about the room, where, against the pale green background, under the unbecoming glare of light, several other people were standing.

Mr. Orranmore, an insignificant, jaded-looking man ; old Mr. Stewart. the Episcopalian clergyman from a neighbouring village. Alex's heart sank as she recognized him. He exactly resembled an old white cock, and she knew that he would probably fall to her share during dinner. There was Van, standing behind his grandfather, ready to prompt him when necessary. There was an elderly woman whom Alex recognized as Miss Brinley— one of the aunts of the pretty Miss Pym. The two other women Alex instantly knew must be Mrs. Orranmore and her daughter, and as she came nearer to them she began to perceive that the scent of carnations grew stronger.

Mrs. Orranmore wore such an evident wig that it

made one blink to look at it. It was arranged above a white face, seamed with deep lines. She was thickly powdered, and her dress displayed her flabby, dingy shoulders very freely—a woman who had made a great effort to keep youth and beauty, then, finding both were gone, had just recklessly dabbed on her powder, assumed her wig, and given up the struggle.

Behind her, outlined against the pale wall, triumphantly exposing her bare shoulders to the fullest light, a young girl was sitting—Alex recognized her in a moment —with her small, round head turned in Van's direction as she answered some remark of his.

Her skirts fluted out about her like the ruffled petals of a flower. She kept tapping the floor with one restless foot as she spoke. When Van came forward to introduce her to Alex she started up, and again Alex observed the spring and finish of her every movement, suggestive of superabundant vitality.

The hair on her small head was brushed perfectly smooth, only some art of the toilette had imparted to it just one deep ripple above each ear. At first sight she seemed half naked—her dress was cut so low. She wore no ornaments, and her thick throat, smooth plump shoulders, and polished arms were all as bare as circumstances permitted. She was dressed in a gown made after a fashion of former times, which happened to be an affectation of the moment—in colour a deep, unpleasing shade of green.

The girl's face was really not at all pretty, with common little features, but her complexion was fine, and there was a kind of freshness about her like a full-blown flower. Her large, shallow-set eyes moved wantonly from side to side as she stood up and gazed at Mrs. Maitland and Alex, with an insolent stare, remarkable in one so young. Her little, thick, strong hands were white, and manicured to the last degree.

Alex began to speak to Mrs. Orranmore, and the girl

talked to Van, glancing from time to time at the other women with her insolent stare. After a few minutes she moved across the room, the scent of carnations diffusing itself from her skirts as she walked. Alex saw the Admiral turn as if aware of it.

Miss Orranmore addressed herself to the old clergyman, looking across at Van all the time, and drumming with her fingers on the edge of her chair.

"We won't wait any longer for Robert," said the Admiral to Mrs. Maitland at last. "He must have missed the early train."

Van rang the bell, and in a few minutes dinner was announced.

"I hear that Mr. Maitland is dreadfully clever," remarked Mrs. Orranmore to Alex. "You seem to have so many clever people here."

"Have we? I wish we had—not many, I fear; but Mr. Maitland cannot be called 'clever,' certainly."

"Oh well, you know what I mean. And the old man over there—talking to Admiral Cassilis?"

"My father—Mr. Hope, you mean?"

"Oh, is he your father? I thought he was somebody very learned too?"

"He is learned, I think; but he isn't 'somebody' at all—we have only one lion at Crossriggs, and that is Mr. Maitland, who will never play up to the part at all."

Maitland not having appeared in time, there was a man too few—as was generally the case at dinner-parties in Crossriggs.

Miss Orranmore, being the youngest of the party, sauntered in by herself, swinging her arms at her sides as if she had been in the hockey-field. Alex and she were seated side by side, and certainly the position in one way was unfavourable to Alex.

Dolly's dress was hideous; yet beside it, Alex's old black garment, with the bunch of red geraniums, looked

sadly commonplace. You saw, too, that her first youth
was past as she sat there.

For Dolly Orranmore was consciously young; and,
young as she was, the daughter of that mother knew the
commercial value of her own youth; it gleamed from her,
breathed from the freshness of her skin, from the untamed
vitality of her look and bearing.

She laughed and talked with Van, who sat on her other
side, as if he and she were the only people in the room,
shrugging her shoulders, grimacing sometimes, crumbling
the bread beside her into piles of crumbs with her little,
thick, restless hands.

Mrs. Maitland and Mr. Orranmore seemed soon to have
exhausted their subjects. She looked bored enough, and
he had sunk into melancholy silence, eating little, but
drinking a good deal. From time to time Miss Brinley
would put up her eyeglasses and take a good look at Miss
Orranmore, and then let them drop with a click, and
resume her conversation with the old clergyman. Aunt
E. V., too, twice directed her green eye towards the
young woman. There was something in the glance that
would have made a sensitive person wrap her shoulders in a
table napkin, failing other covering, but Miss Orranmore
met the glance without a quiver.

Dinner was half done before Maitland at last appeared.
He could never seem in a hurry, and came in quietly,
without any suggestion of haste. Having explained his
late arrival, he took his place opposite to Alex and Miss
Orranmore.

He and Alex had only met once, and that merely for a
moment in the street, since that day in July when they
had sat together in the little glen in the early morning.

Alex was curiously cold and still for a minute.

She did not know that Van had just addressed a remark
to her. She heard nothing of the talk going on around;
was scarcely conscious of the sound of voices; but seemed
to hear instead a little burn running past with a tender

singing noise. She felt again the overwhelming stab at her heart—then she raised her head and gazed across at Maitland, their eyes meeting full for the first time since he had come home.

She had always admired him, but that evening he was looking strangely well—his eyes seemed nearly black, his shaven face showed its almost faultless line in the brilliant light.

It was curious to see him talking to Mrs. Orranmore. Alex watched him fix his benignant, steady eyes upon her passion-riddled face. Then he looked across at her daughter, once, twice, and, with an almost imperceptible movement, slight, but final—as an animal turns away its head from the hand of a stranger—he turned away to address himself to Miss Brinley.

Miss Orranmore, who had disposed herself to be looked at—and she generally was—was acutely aware that he never glanced at her again.

" You seem a trifle deaf to-night, Sandy ! " said Van, whose voice suddenly became audible to Alex. " I've asked you the same question three times running."

" Have you ? Oh, how stupid of me ! I didn't know you were talking to me," she answered, turning to him quickly, her face flushing.

She was conscious of the sudden oppression of a vast reasonless dreariness ; in her eyes was the look of one who had gazed out across a winter sea. Van looked at her hard as he spoke, a slow red mounting into his face, too. Miss Orranmore, sitting between them, with her elbows on the table, glanced from one to the other, and began to laugh.

" Miss Hope was thinking about mathematics, or something equally clever, I suppose," she said.

Alex tried to shake off her depression. " With all my sins, I've never been accused of mathematics," she said. " Van knows more of them than I do."

" Oh, I thought you spoke Greek and all that ! "

returned Miss Orranmore, with the shrug and stare, which
was now beginning to amuse Alex.

She gave a twist of her bare shoulder that threatened
to break the slender string of green beads, apparently all
that held what bodice she had in its place, said " Oh,
Lord ! " when it gave a slight crack, and with her elbows
on the table and her chin resting on her hands, so as to
shut Alex completely off from Van's sight, she began to
talk to him again.

There was a lull in the voices at the other end of the
table when some of Miss Maitland's conversation with the
Admiral became audible.   The old man almost forgot to
eat his dinner, he was so anxious to hear what she was
saying.

" It's dreadful ! " said Laura Maitland, *sotto voce*, across
the table to Alex.   " You would talk about ghosts all the
way coming, and now hear them on graveyards ! "

The theme, indeed, was gloomy enough—the enlarge-
ment of the old churchyard at Crossriggs.

" Disgracefully crowded by this time," cried the
Admiral.   " Why, ten years ago, when my cousin Philip
Cassilis was buried there, three old coffins had to be
removed."

" The railing has been taken down," went on Aunt
E. V., " and the stone with the cherubs' heads upon
it——"

" Yes, yes, I remember."

" Where it used to stand," pursued Miss Maitland, unconscious of the gloom of her subject, " is the stone put
up in memory of Wright.   You knew John Wright ?—
good man ; he was the son of our old beadle, and made a
fortune as a grocer in Glasgow.   A large red granite stone
about four feet high, with an urn, Admiral, on the top of
it, and on the top of the urn a garment of some kind,
draped—it looks like a top coat—and a great deal of gilt
lettering."

" Oh dear, they spoil everything nowadays ! "

Miss Maitland assented, and went on with emphasis, " There were no less than four artificial wreaths there last Sunday."

" There is no proper supervision," said the Admiral.

" None. It is that end wall they propose to break down ; on the other side of it, you remember, there is a field belonging to Grainger, planted last year with wheat ; there is a little knoll about the middle, with three pine trees, you remember, and an old hawthorn growing on it."

" That is all to be taken in, too ? "

" Yes, nearly to the end of the field."

Old Hopeful remarked cheerfully, " I have bespoken part of that mound already—new soil."

He had some theories of his own upon burial, and Alex was afraid that he was going to begin on them now, but Maitland remarked, smiling—

" Yes, Mr. Hope and I have both encouraged this inno-vation. When I sleep with my fathers we shall be a little separated, for the old corner is overcrowded."

" There will be room in it for me, I hope," said Miss Maitland, tranquilly. " If not, I have directed that I shall be laid beside my mother's people in Ross-shire. I like no innovations."

Dolly Orranmore burst out laughing. "It makes me feel quite creepy to hear you all talking about graves as if they were houses," she said, turning to Van, as the women rose from the table. " I'd like to break my neck in the hunting-field, and be buried in the next ditch ! "

CHAPTER XXXII

As Van stood by the dining-room door when they passed
out Dolly Orranmore beckoned him to come into the hall
while she asked some question about a letter that she
wished to have sent off at once. Alex and Miss Brinley,
who were walking side by side, stopped for an instant as
they passed, to look out, for the front door stood open, and
the inner one being of clear glass the moonlight came
streaming into the hall.

"Oh!" exclaimed Dolly. "What a heavenly night!
It's as bright as day. I'm going out."

She seized a scarf that lay on a table beside her, and
twisted it about her neck.

"Don't, Dolly, it's very cold," said Van, following her
to the door. "Put on a coat at least."

He held out a coat to her, and Dolly put her arms into
it laughing, but it trailed about her feet. She began feeling in the pockets, and pulled out a scrap of paper.

"Poetry," she exclaimed, glancing at it. "Who writes
poetry here? Is it the old Parson?" She looked at it
again. "Why, it's your writing, Van. I must read it.
Take that thing away; it stifles me!" She wriggled out
of the coat as she spoke, and stepped under the light,
spreading out the bit of paper, and beginning to read,
"Your voice——"

"Oh, Dolly, give it to me, please; it's nothing."

Van put out his hand as if to take the paper from her,
but she hopped away from him, calling out—

" No, indeed, I want to read it now ! "

" Please, Dolly—— " he began.

His face had flushed, and Alex could see that he was in earnest; but the girl only laughed. Again he tried to catch the paper from her, but she held it tightly.

" I'll race you for it then," she cried, springing out on to the broad stone steps.

The young man followed her, and Alex and Miss Brinley stood at the door looking after them.

" Do give it to me. I'm in earnest," he began again.

But she turned from him swift as lightning, and then and there flew off across the moonlit gravel, Van following her. She ran like the wind, and in a minute was yards ahead of him. Alex and her companion watched the two figures flying along the straight bit of road, the ends of Dolly's scarf fluttering behind her as she ran. Then as Van gained upon her she doubled with the swiftness of a hare, her light silken skirts ballooning out as she turned and began to dart in and out and round about the flower-beds on the lawn, sometimes holding out the bit of paper towards him as she ran. Van jumped across a border, and seemed about to grasp her arm when, with a scream of delight, she bent forwards, running still more swiftly, and disappeared round the corner of the house. Miss Brinley let her eyeglass fall with a click.

" It is cold standing here. Shall we go back to the drawing-room ? I think we have seen enough," she said, in a voice so awful that Alex nearly burst out laughing. Alex assented, and they turned away. For a moment Miss Brinley was silent, then indignation got the better of her, and she said, " I am thankful my niece was not here to-night. A message girl would have been ashamed of such conduct."

" It was certainly uncommon," said Alex.

In another minute, before they had reached the door of the drawing-room, Dolly re-appeared in the hall, panting now a good deal, her hair all disordered, the scarf she wore twisted in a rope about her throat, her bare shoulders heaving, her thin slippers soaked with the hoar frost.

" My hair's all full of twigs and things," she explained nonchalantly, twisting up the ends of hair as she spoke. " I ducked under the branches of the yew-tree, and it all tangled up."

" Who got the paper ? " Alex asked.

Miss Orranmore stared.   " Van's got it," she said, with a nod at Van, who had entered behind her.

He was rather pale, and the corners of his mouth were set hard.

" I must go and get my hair put up again," Miss Orranmore exclaimed, sauntering off upstairs, after giving another stare at Alex and Miss Brinley—two provincial women whose opinion was nothing to her here or there.

Van went back into the dining-room, and Alex and Miss Brinley returned to the drawing-room again.

When they came in Mrs. Orranmore, Mrs. Maitland, and Aunt E. V. were grouped around the fireplace, and evidently conversation had languished.

" What have you all been doing ? " Mrs. Orranmore exclaimed. " Did I hear Dolly say something about going out ? "

" She has been out—running round the garden," said Miss Brinley, setting her lips.   She walked up to the fire-place, and ostentatiously warmed her hands.

" She's an absurd child," said Mrs. Orranmore.

Miss Brinley folded her lips, and turning away from her began to speak to Mrs. Maitland.   It was evident that she considered the party ill-chosen, and Alex noted with amusement that she had looked about the room, considering which, of the three women, it would do her the least harm to converse with.

In a few minutes Miss Orranmore came in again, her hair all arranged and a very fine colour in her cheeks.

When the men returned to the drawing-room she never

looked at Van, but went up to the Admiral and stood talking to him, trying to make the old hound beg for bits of sugar from her coffee-cup.

Mrs. Orranmore glanced at the clock with the eye of one who counts all time wasted that is not spent at the card-table. Presently the Admiral held out his groping hand.

"Miss Hope, where are you? Will you sing? There is nothing I enjoy more than hearing you sing," he said.

Alex did not want to sing at all, but she could not disappoint him when the rest of his guests all seemed to lack lustre, and she sang so well that even Mrs. Orranmore ceased to glance at the clock. Dolly stopped playing with the dog, and came up and stood by the piano, entranced like a child by the music. Alex had sung what the old man wanted, when Van came up and said something to her in a low voice.

"Oh, he wouldn't care about that," said Alex. "And I hardly know the words."

But Van repeated his request, and she began again to sing that little song which Maitland had heard once before.

> " ' Down by the salley gardens,
>   My love and I did stand,
>   And on my leaning shoulder,
>   She laid her milk-white hand.' "

The air rippled on like a brook. Alex smiled to herself as she bent her head between the verses.

> " ' She bade me take life easy,
>   As the leaves grow on the tree,
>   But I was young and foolish,
>   And with her did not agree.
>
> *   *   *
>
> " ' She bade me take love easy,
>   As the grass grows on the weirs,
>   But I was young and foolish,
>   And now am full of tears ! ' "

There was silence for a minute when she had finished, for her low voice was wonderfully expressive. Then old Mr. Stewart said, "Ha!" Mr. Orranmore coughed. The Admiral said—

"Ah, Miss Hope, we were all young and foolish once."

"And I'm young and foolish still," exclaimed Dolly Orranmore, with a laugh.

It seemed to break the spell that the little song had cast. Miss Brinley rustled in her chair, Mrs. Orranmore stifled a yawn, Mrs. Maitland looked at Aunt E. V., and they rose to go. Alex collected her father from the far end of the room, where he was engaged in trying to prove the narrowing influences of Creeds to the old clergyman. As she passed out of the room she heard Dolly Orranmore saying something to Van about the garden and "shocked."

Van was in the hall with Maitland and Old Hopeful when Alex and Laura and Aunt E. V. came out again after putting on their wraps. Maitland was arguing with Mr. Hope about walking home, insisting that he liked to walk, and that Mr. Hope was to drive.

"I'll come with you as far as the gate," said Van. "That room is too hot. If you wait for a minute—Miss Brinley is just going away."

When Miss Brinley had departed, and her equipage had been followed by the humble fly containing the old clergyman, Van strolled off down the avenue with Maitland. Alex looked out and waved her hand to them as the carriage passed.

Then she sank back in her seat and listened to her father and Miss Maitland discussing the feeding of bees

When they reached their own door she got out, and bid Laura and Aunt E. V. good night rather hastily.

"I'm sorry that Mr. Maitland had to walk on our account," she said.

"Ah, well, a lovely night! At Robert's age, I would have enjoyed it myself," said her father.

Alex ran up the pathway to the door, but before she could open it Matilda appeared.

" Well, had you a nice evening ? " she asked, as Alex stepped into the hall. " There is still a good fire—I thought you would be cold—and like some hot water."

" I'll have some hot water, please. I don't think it was a nice evening," said Alex, unrolling her shawl, and sitting down on the fender.

" Who was there ? Any one interesting ? " Matilda asked, pouring the hot water cautiously into the tumbler as she spoke.

It was a little hard on Matilda that her widowhood kept her from joining in these small Crossriggs gaieties, for she had a naturally sociable disposition, and was really not at all sad.

Even though she had " gone into grey," as the Crossriggs dressmaker phrased it, no one thought of asking her to go out to dinner yet. She went to tea parties, such as they were ; but Miss Maitland had observed that some grand-aunt of hers in Ross-shire had been " widowed for five years before she broke bread in another house," and Matilda had repeated the remark to Alex with tears of vexation.

Alex sat and sipped her hot water, giving brief replies to her sister's questions.

" Oh, there was old Mr. Stewart of course, who should crow instead of speaking, and the Maitlands—Aunt E. V. and Mrs. Maitland—Mr. Maitland came in about half-way through dinner—he had been delayed in town—and there was Mrs. Orranmore and her husband and her daughter."

" What are they like ? " Matilda asked.

" Like ? Oh, the man is like the rind of something squeezed—no use at all to any one, I should think, and the woman is like a Harpy in a wig—and the girl——"

Alex paused.

" Well ? " said Matilda.

Alex looked at her affectionately as she sat on the

fender holding up one hand to screen her face from the fire.

"Oh, Matilda," she exclaimed, "with all your faults you're a nice creature, so good, so chaste."

"Alex, you do say such things! Don't!" said Matilda.

"Why not, pray? A good English word, and a very good thing to be—you're a nice person to return to, Matilda."

"But Miss Orranmore," Matilda persisted.

"Oh, Miss Orranmore! She's—she's—a fine, healthy young woman. I'm glad she's not my sister!"

"Is she pretty? Was she well dressed?"

"No—yes—no, she's certainly not pretty; and I thought her dress, what there was of it—it was mostly skirt and her own shoulders—was hideous."

"Dear me! How horrid. I hope Van won't marry her!"

"I hope not—most likely he will," said Alex, lightly, jumping to her feet. "There's Father coming in. I'm going to bed, I'm very tired. Good night, Matilda."

"But you've hardly told me anything," said Matilda. "Did you look nice? Did you sing? Who took you in to dinner?"

"Oh, Van did, and I looked just as ugly as I could have wished, and I sang one or two songs, and it was all very dull, and they talked about graves at dinner."

"Graves? Father, did you speak about graves at dinner?" said Matilda, laughing.

"We did, we did, Matilda," said Old Hopeful, as he came cheerfully into the room. "Discussed the new extension to the churchyard. Maitland has taken one lot there, and I've bespoken another—Mother earth! Yes, my dear, a little hot water, if you please. Oh, I had plenty to eat, several vegetables, and some plain pudding and fruit—better far than the blood and bones of our harmless animal friends. Good night, Alex.

Leave the lamps in.   Matilda, I shall have a few pages
of Homer before I go to bed."

He settled himself in his armchair, and Matilda followed Alex upstairs.

"I just looked in to see Mike for a moment," said
Alex, coming out of the nursery.   "He's fast asleep
like an infant angel."

Matilda stood holding her candle, looking perplexed.
"You're too tired, Alex," she said.   "I should not have
allowed you to go into town this morning when you were
going out to-night."

"Oh, I'll be all right to-morrow; don't worry your
dear head about me, you've enough to think of with the
children," said Alex.   She began to pull the hairpins
out from her thick hair, and said to Matilda suddenly,
"Were you ever mean, Matilda?   No, I don't believe
you ever were.   Did you ever dislike to think of another
person getting what you yourself didn't want to have?"

"No, of course not—if I didn't want it," said Matilda.
"But I don't know what you're talking about—is it
because you didn't feel you looked nice?"

"No, no; I hope I'm not quite as silly as that! Never
mind, I'm really too tired, and just talking nonsense.
Good night."

Alex was tired, but not sleepy.   She sat down and
wrote in her journal; at the end of the page she added—

"Heard that Mr. Maitland has bought a grave on the
new hillside.   Father says he has got one too, so I suppose some day we'll all lie there.   Mr. Maitland our
neighbour again—I think it would make even death
desirable!"

CHAPTER XXXIII

It was perhaps the effect of her unusual gaiety the night before, or it may have been that she slept badly—anyway, Alex came down to breakfast the next morning in a most uncomfortable humour.

"It's east wind in my mind, Matilda," she said, when her sister, after receiving several sharp replies to her gentle questions, had asked in a bewildered way, what was the matter. "Not anything, everything," said Alex, with a sigh. She stood by the table and looked about her.

"What do you mean, Alex? The weather?"

"Well, would you like to know what I mean? I'll just run over a few things to give you an idea of my lines of thought this morning. Our life has been all wrong from the very beginning, indeed, before that, for it began wrong before we were born, with our parents' dispositions—but we won't go into that just now—anyway, we're all wrong. I've wasted life, and youth is nearly over, and my health isn't what it used to be, and we are too poor to be dignified even in the simplest way, and our house, which ought to be the expression of the soul, is hideous, and our life is limited, and our ideas are provincial, and our neighbours are dull, and the world is full of bores, and your children are just so many responsibilities to squeeze us down, and Father is an unpractical optimist, and Katharine is a nuisance —she can't even boil an egg—the weather is horrid, and going to be horrider—it is a dense wet mist that won't lift all day ; the roads are slime, my boots are leaking, I've got to go out at eleven, and go into town, and I'd rather be hung than teach elocution this morning—and I wish I was dead ! "

She was half laughing, but her lips trembled as she spoke.

Matilda looked at her in silence. " You'd better not go into town this morning, if you're not feeling well, Alex. I'll send off a telegram at once, if you like, to say you're not coming," she said.

" That's not the way people earn their living ! " Alex retorted, turning away. She even muttered, " Nor other people's," when she was climbing upstairs. She began crossly to get ready to go to the station.

A sudden frost fog had fallen upon the land, smothering everything in billows of white, cold mist, that had drifted up from the sea. The roads, which had been so hard the night before, were now all wet and dark.

Alex shivered as she stepped out and took the road to the station. Of course she found the day even worse in town. The lesson hour dragged terribly. Her throat was hoarse, the schoolroom both cold and stuffy, the pupils inattentive and provoking.

She had a fit of disgust at life as keen as toothache as she hurried back along Princes Street on her way home. Men (all ugly) in bulging greatcoats, carrying umbrellas, nearly cannonaded into her every now and then. Draggled looking women in mackintosh cloaks, with peaked, mean faces under shapeless hats, slopped along by her side. Under the black skies, a hideous clangour went on from the traffic in the mud-covered roadway.

The station was a degree worse—darker, more noisy and more noisome. After all, she missed the first train home, and had to wait half an hour for the next one. She was almost moved to bitter mirth by the sight of the row of women sitting in the evilly ugly waiting-room

—their sordidness, their damp, tasteless clothing, their weariful, unattractive faces. Alex looked at one and then at another. " How many of them are married ? " she thought, and began to count. " That one with the hair dragged up behind—and the one, as the dress-maker said, ' Concave, not convex ' in front, in that artless circular cloak—oh yes, and that most repellant, red-faced one with the mountainous bosom—and, of course, the little yellow-haired one in the grey hat. She's only been married for a short time, and is going back to a bridal bower decorated with plated sugar-bowls. Yes, every one of those women has worn a wedding-gown, and had—or pretended to have—an hour of triumph and of happiness. Yet see them now ! How refreshing to look at the nun, although her face is as blank as an empty slate ! How terrible, thrice terrible too, is that grim spinster in the black dog fur—and the other one, in the cinnamon hat, who looks as if she were entreating the world not to laugh at her. I just need to give one glance at my own appearance in that mirror to assure myself that the woman who keeps the waiting-room is a beauty compared to me too—but I won't—I'd rather not know what I'm looking like ! "

She rose, half laughing now, as her train came up, and nodded to the woman who sat sewing by the window —an old acquaintance of hers, but Alex had not the heart to speak to her that evening. " I am prepared now to travel home with Mr. Scott, and that will just finish my afternoon suitably," she thought, picking her way along the sloppy platform without looking at any one. Just as she was getting into a crowded carriage the door of the next one opened, and Maitland jumped out, saying—

" Come in here, Alex, there is more room."

He helped her in almost before she had time to speak, and Alex threw herself back in the corner with a sigh.

" Oh, I was looking about for Mr. Scott," she said.

" Why ? Do you want to see him ? "

" No, I particularly don't—of course, that is the very reason why I was expecting to do so. I've got such a fit of depression on me this afternoon that everything seems absolutely black, and everything in the past and future horrible, and so, naturally, I expected to have the company I most disliked on the way home."

" Well, it's too late now," said Maitland, as the train moved off ; " you must put up with me instead."

They were alone together for the first time for many months. A sudden dumbness overcame Alex, who was already fatigued and depressed. Maitland spoke a little about the dinner-party the evening before, but she could see that he was thinking about something else all the time. At last he said sharply—

" Do you know, Alex, that I have decided to leave Crossriggs ? "

" Oh, I didn't know," said Alex. Her lips were dry.

He turned his face away, and looked out at the window where the rifts in the deep fog showed that they were passing through a wood. The trunks of the trees seemed all wrapped about with the white wreaths.

" Laura's health," he began, then looked straight at Alex, and went on in his charming voice, " It's better, I think, for many reasons. I am going abroad for a year or two. Laura likes Florence. We may possibly settle there."

" Then it means that you leave Crossriggs altogether ?"

" Yes, I suppose it does."

" Oh," cried Alex, looking up at him, and flinging out her hands in her impulsive way, " don't go—don't you go." She stopped and stammered, " I—I—am going away. I mean, I can't stand life here any longer. Oh, let me go. Don't break up your life and everything ! "

She paused, trembling, her face suddenly withered, her great eyes wild and tearful. Maitland made a quick movement towards her, then checked himself, and covered his face with both hands. They were silent for a moment, and the shrill whistle of an approaching train sounded piercingly; it crashed and thundered past; then Maitland lifted his face. Alex did not dare to look at him. He said simply—

"You must let me do what is best for both of us, Alex. All the hard things need not fall on *you*. You have enough to worry about without leaving home."

"Perhaps I should worry less if I did: things are so difficult," said Alex, pitifully.

She knew that her voice trembled, and that this was making an appeal for sympathy which she would be ashamed of afterwards, but just for a moment she let herself go.

Maitland stood up and put his head out of the carriage window.

"We're just coming into the station," he remarked.

And Alex, blushing now with anger at herself, got up hurriedly and began to put on her cloak. Maitland helped her to alight without a word. The touch of his hand was cool and inexpressive as usual. He came behind her in the little crowd that filled the platform, and was just saying, "You will allow me to drive you home?" when Alex saw, to her surprise, that Matilda was coming towards them—Matilda looking strange and agitated. She gave an exclamation when she saw Maitland behind Alex, and pushed past her sister, laying her hand on his arm.

"Oh, Mr. Maitland! I'm so thankful you have come. Miss Elizabeth sent me up to see if you were here. Laura is so ill. We sent you a telegram in case you were staying in town."

In a moment Maitland had hurried on to the carriage, Matilda beside him giving further particulars as they went. It appeared that Laura had been seized with a sudden attack of faintness when she was out walking, and had been taken into a neighbour's house, where she remained for some time. Miss Elizabeth, coming to drive her home, found her apparently much better, but by the time she reached the Manse she had another attack so alarming that the doctor who was summoned told them to telegraph for Maitland immediately.

For one moment Maitland and Alex looked at one another—a glance, on her side, of sudden dread and entreaty ; on his, of unconcealed pain. He drove away from the station by himself, Alex and Matilda refusing to drive along with him.

" How Mr. Maitland's face changed ! " said Matilda. " He must feel much more deeply about Laura than we think."

" Oh, Matilda ! You do say such hopeless things at times," said Alex. " But is she really so dangerously ill ? "

Matilda, who never understood Alex when she was in an intense mood, passed over the criticism in silence.

" Yes, I'm afraid she is," she answered. " The doctor said to Miss Elizabeth that she might rally, but she might not even live through the night."

" Oh, Matilda, how dreadful—how dreadful. Just because——"

Alex stopped and turned her face away. Matilda was almost surprised at her sister's emotion.

" I'm so sorry," she said. " I always liked her better than you did, Alex."

" Don't you understand ? " cried Alex. " That's just why I mind so much. Oh, how I wish I had always liked her better in my heart ! Much better than I did —with something more than just a tepid liking. And he——" Her voice faltered.

" Mr. Maitland is always calm about everything," Matilda remarked. " Whatever he endures he will save other people being pained by the sight of his suffering."

Alex assented vaguely. She scarcely heard what Matilda was saying.

As soon as they reached home she ran upstairs to her own room and flung herself down on her knees by the bed. If fervent prayers could have saved Laura Maitland's life, Alex saved it then—never had she pleaded so hard for any personal blessing as she prayed for Mrs. Maitland's recovery.

The deep mist settled down over the village, choking all the sounds of life. The church clock striking the hours sounded faintly through the fog. As the evening wore on Old Hopeful went to inquire again, and returned to say that Mrs. Maitland's condition was unchanged. After the children had gone to bed the room always became strangely quiet. Then sometimes Matilda and Alex would sit on the fender-stool together and chat over the little events of the day, whilst their father slept in his chair—Homer always open on his knee.

That evening neither of them seemed inclined to speak. Old Hopeful occasionally murmured a sonorous line to himself, and then, waxing drowsy, let the open book slip on to his knee, and nodded gently, one hand covering his eyes.

Alex, too, had been reading, at least she too held a book, but had not turned a page. Her heart beat almost painfully at every sound. She leant back her head at last, and closed her eyes. Behind the little curtains of her eyelids what thoughts and memories were passing that her father and sister knew nothing of! Always she saw Robert Maitland's face as he had looked up at her that morning when they sat together in the glen.

It is one of the curious effects of a too passionate imaginative nature that its forebodings outrun time. So that often when the dreaded circumstance really arrives, it seems as nothing compared to the hours of imaginative misery that went before, as a line that has been already burnt will stop a prairie fire.

The clock struck at last, and Alex got up, saying, " I'm very tired ; I'll go to bed now, Matty."

At that moment the door bell jangled through the silent house, and they looked at one another.

" They wouldn't ring the bell," said Alex ; but she got very pale.

" The door was shut, you know," said Matilda.

Old Hopeful started from his doze and caught at his book.

Alex ran into the passage, and opened the hall door before Katharine had time to appear.

" Is it ? " she began, and then stopped, for she saw that Van Cassilis was standing on the doorstep. He looked almost gigantic in the thick fog. Alex gave a gasp of relief. " Oh, Van, it's only you ! What an hour to come ! We were just going to bed."

" Yes, I know it's late. I have been down to inquire for Mrs. Maitland. She's no better."

He had stepped into the hall, cap in hand, all damp as he was from the wet fog outside, and he stood looking at Alex with a curious new expression on his face—it frightened her. Another man, not the Van she knew, seemed to look out from his eyes. Matilda, hearing what he said, had turned back into the drawing-room to tell her father.

" Don't shut the door, Sandy," said Van. " You look pale to-night."

" I'm tired," said Alex, " and anxious about Mrs. Maitland."

" Yes—yes," he said, looking down at the floor, and squeezing his cap in his hands hard, almost as if he could have wrung water out of it, " of course you are. Well, I only came in to give you the last report. Good night." He put out his hand, and when Alex gave him hers, he took it, held it for a moment, and let it fall quickly. " Cold hands and a warm heart ! " he said, with a kind of choking laugh, and turned hurriedly away, before Alex had time to speak again.

She wondered, hearing his horse stamp at the gate, how he was going to get home in such a fog. For a minute or two she stood listening till the sound of hoofs died away, then she went back, and told Matilda she was going to bed.

" It was kind of Van to look in and save Father going out again on such a night," said Matilda. " I thought he didn't seem quite himself though, didn't you, Alex ? "

" I thought he looked very queer indeed," Alex answered. " But he's a moody creature, you know—probably something has put him out of temper. Good night, Matilda."

After Alex had put out the light in her own room she went to the window and looked out across the Square. She could see nothing, not even a glimmer of light from the Maitlands' windows. Dense billows of fog drifted past, sometimes disclosing the branch of a tree in the reflected light from the window below, but she could not see a yard ahead.

Then a sudden comfort came over her. " Who knows what may happen ? I may be dead, not she, to-morrow. 'The world may end to-night'; we can't see a foot ahead. I won't try, I will sleep, and will not question more.'" And she did sleep—dreamlessly; wrapped, it seemed, in as dense an ignorance of the future as the world about her was wrapped in the fog.

CHAPTER XXXIV

THE news of Mrs. Maitland next morning was much the same. She was no worse, but still in great danger. Alex went to the door and spoke with Miss Elizabeth for a minute before she started for her walk to Foxe Hall.

It was Sunday, and Aunt E. V. wore the dress in which she usually went to church. Though she had been sitting up the whole of the night before, she held herself upright as ever. Her green eye seemed to search Alex through and through as they stood facing one another.

Alex's face was drawn and pale, and her eyes were tragic.

" Is there nothing—nothing at all that we can do ? " she asked. " It's dreadful to be able to do nothing for one's friends when one longs to help—and you have helped us so often," she added.

Miss Maitland laid a thin hand on Alex's arm. " There is only one Helper in a case like this for any of us—let us rest on His wisdom."

It was not her habit to use language of this sort, and Alex was rather surprised. She left the house and went slowly on her way to Foxe Hall, feeling as if it would be impossible for her to read as usual.

The Admiral varied his programme a little on Sundays. They read history instead of the newspaper, and sometimes he selected a letter from the *Country Gentleman* on some subject such as the restoration of churches or old church fonts, or something of the kind, which he supposed to be connected with religion. That afternoon, however, he was far too much excited by the thought of Mrs. Maitland's illness to allow Alex to begin at once.

" I have a letter here," he announced, " ' Moles in Churchyards,' which will be good reading, but first I wish to hear the latest news of Mrs. Maitland. Van was much shocked when he heard of her illness yesterday on coming home. He had gone to Bouton for some pheasant shooting with my old friend Lord Haye "— the Admiral rolled the title like a sugar-plum in his mouth, paused for a moment, then continued—" with Lord Haye. . . . He was so much concerned that he set off at once, late as it was, to inquire himself—such a night of fog, too ! The Maitlands, though not perhaps amongst our most *intimate* friends, are old neighbours. My father knew and respected Maitland's father and grandfather, in spite of some differences in local politics. Mrs. Maitland was a pretty woman, too, in the days when I had the use of my eyes, Miss Hope, I remember that," he sighed. " She was connected, too, with the Aylesford family—a younger branch, I think."

" I really don't know," said Alex. " But she is pretty still."

" Ah, very possibly. I remember her as a bride. She and her husband dined here soon after the marriage. I never saw a handsomer couple in their own way."

" Yes," said Alex, absently. " Shall I begin to read now ? "

" Well, time is passing ; but Sunday afternoon has "— he coughed—" a tendency to be long somehow, Miss Hope."

" It has, indeed—I've often felt it so in some houses," Alex assented, smiling. " At home we do not feel it, because my father's ideas are very lax."

" Hem ! " said the Admiral, who had no sympathy with Old Hopeful. " I like a difference. Sunday is Sunday, just as Monday is Monday."

He uttered the aphorism with some show of satisfaction, and, crossing one leg over the other, leant back in his chair to listen to the article on " Moles in Churchyards." Alex read for nearly half an hour beyond her usual time, but she did not once hear Van's voice or step in the passage, nor did he appear at all before she left. She bid the Admiral good night, and let herself out of the house unobserved, and went quickly down the avenue. The dusk was falling and the air was very still. In the distance the bell of Crossriggs church began to ring for evening service.

How many times, Alex thought, she had walked down that avenue in all weathers! She knew it now under every possible aspect, from the frosts of winter to the green delight of spring and the sleepy warmth of summer —here she was round again to another winter! How quickly the last year had gone: would every year of life glide past at this astonishing pace now? She remembered when the years were long, when a child's joy in April was unshadowed by the thought that spring would be over in a few weeks, when a child's wonder at winter was untouched by any hope of spring.

" Now one sees another season coming on before the first is well begun. Perhaps the child's is the true way of living—it makes a sort of eternity while it lasts. I wonder if Laura Maitland knows or thinks now that her days are going to stop. I wonder if I could *ever* feel that ? "

She raised her head suddenly, and saw Van coming across one of the fields towards her, wading through the rough, wet, winter grass. He jumped the railing a few yards in front of her, and stood waiting until she came up.

" Well," he began, " I thought I should meet you, How is Mrs. Maitland ? "

His voice dropped suddenly, and he walked slowly beside her, his hands clasped behind him, his eyes looking on the ground.

" She was much the same when I left home this after-noon—no better," said Alex.

" Ah ! They think she's going to die then ? "

" Well, she is still in great danger."

" Poor Maitland ! " said Van, but there was something so curious in the way he said it that Alex glanced at him in surprise.

" What is the matter with you, Van ? "

" With me ? Why should anything be the matter with me ? *My* wife isn't dying."

" Van, how can you speak like that ? You must not," began Alex, indignantly, but Van went on with an ugly sneering sound in his voice—

" No, of course, we must all pull long faces and try to look broken-hearted whatever we may feel, as you and Maitland do."

Alex stopped short, and looked at him in silence. She wondered for one minute if he was drunk, or going mad. Indeed, a sort of insane jealousy seemed to have possessed the young man. His face was white, his fine eyebrows drawn into a deep frown, as he looked at her, and went on in a low, hard voice—

" Well, it's better to speak the truth, to my mind. When she is dead everything will go well with both of you, I suppose. You can have him then—you've loved him long enough, at any rate." He laughed brutally at the look of cold terror creeping over Alex's face. " Do you think I don't know that, Sandy ? I'm young and stupid, not like Maitland, but you couldn't hide that, for all your cleverness. But he was married—married and supremely virtuous. Now the kind Fates are intervening on his behalf, and he'll be rewarded like the good hero in a play—the sort of character he is, I suppose."

Alex was standing still, gazing at him with a look of such terrible reproach that nothing but the insane fit of jealousy with which the young man was possessed could

have resisted its eloquence. All a woman's wounded
pride was in that look, a world of surprise and disgust
at the coarseness of the words he had uttered—a sort of
bewildered, outraged dismay that he, Van, her own
friend, should have insulted her so. She looked at him
without saying a single word, for she could not speak.
But jealousy is the most cruel passion among the many
that prey upon our poor nature: it rejoices to see its victim
suffer. After a minute, Alex turned slowly away. Van
sprang after her, laying his hand almost roughly on her
arm.

" Stop, Sandy," he began. " You've got to listen to
me now ; you've kept me from it again and again, and do
you suppose I didn't know the reason why ? But you
shall hear me now in spite of yourself."

Alex was no coward. Her colour had come back again ;
her fighting spirit was roused. She wheeled round and
spoke at last—

" I won't listen to you, Van, nor answer you, nor look
at you—nor speak to you again. What you said just
now is what no woman can ever forget or forgive. I've
had my last speech with you and I never wish to see you
again as long as we live."

Then suddenly, along with her blinding anger, a wave
of regret swept over her. Was this the end of such a
pleasant friendship as had been between him and her ?
O frail humanity ! O poor human nature !

" There ! " she cried, flinging out her hand to him,
" I'll shake hands with you ' for auld lang syne '—but
it's the end of our acquaintance, Van, and you have
yourself to thank for it."

He took her hand for a moment, and then drew her
quickly to his arms and kissed her with hasty, defiant
kisses that seemed to scorch her cheeks.

" There ! " he said, as Alex had done a minute before ;
" there, Sandy, you may never forgive me, but I've had
this, even if we never shake hands again."

Then all in a moment his fury seemed to leave him, his face softened ; he stood before her abashed, ashamed of his words and his actions.

" You will forgive me ? " he began, in a breaking voice, but Alex was already walking away, her head held down to hide her burning cheeks, her hands clenched.

" Don't speak to me again, don't dare to speak to me," she answered, and without another glance at him she hurried on.

Van did not attempt to follow her. He stood watching her retreating figure, then, heedless of the gathering winter twilight, he jumped the low railing, and flung himself down amongst the wet grass, under one of the great trees. He lay face downwards, one arm thrown up across his head in the despairing attitude of weary vagabonds when they huddle asleep on the ground. There for a long time he lay, without stirring a muscle, only the quick hard breathing and the pounding of his heart seemed to shake his whole body.

Great cold drops fell from the branches now and then, upon his hot head and neck. The chill of the winter night closed down upon the damp ground, but he never moved. A crow settled on the branch above him, and gave a harsh cry : he never looked up. At last he rose to his feet, rubbed his hands across his strained face, stretched his arms, and then, with a long shiver, shook himself like a man that awakens from a horrible dream, and went slowly back to the house.

Van lay on the grass in the dusk, and Alex walked home, hurrying at first until she was out of breath, then pausing for a minute to press her hands against her burning cheeks and try to regain a little composure, before she had to face the eyes of her family. She was still trembling all over from a passion of anger such as she had never believed herself capable of feeling.

" I will write to the Admiral to-morrow," she said to

herself—"the very first thing in the morning, and tell him that I cannot read to him any more. I must make up some kind of excuse, I suppose. Anyway, it must be done, for it would be impossible for me ever to enter the house as long as Van is there. I'll never see him again, if I can help it."

She hurried along, still hot with anger and yet cold at heart, too. For what would this mean to them all at home? Less comfort for the children, more anxiety for Matilda, new work to be sought for, and probably none to be found. As she came near the village Alex drew herself together, and fought a strenuous mental fight.

She resolved to say nothing to Matilda that night. "I'm too angry," she told herself. Next morning she would be cooled down—more able to take a reasonable view of things. Then the letter would be written, and Matilda would help her to consider about other employment.

"You're late, dear, and you look so tired," Matilda said, meeting her at the door. But Alex would not even confess to much fatigue.

"Still, I mean to go to bed early. I've a lot to do to-morrow," she said.

The evening seemed as if it would never end. The children had to be played with and put to bed, then Matilda had to tell Alex all about the Maitlands. She had gone to see Miss Elizabeth in the afternoon, and reported that Laura was a little better.

"Thank Heaven!" said Alex, when she heard the news; and again Matilda wondered at the fervour of her sister's feeling. At last the evening was over, Alex went to bed and cried herself to sleep. And in her sleep she dreamed a dream.

She thought that she sat beside Maitland and his wife. Laura, though still alive, seemed no longer to be of this world. Some indescribable change had passed over her; such a change as only dreams make real. They all three

sat there in a curious, unnatural silence, and then Laura,
with one of her graceful languid movements, took Alex's
hand and laid it gently in that of her husband.   "Take
it, Robert," she said, as if she therewith renounced all
earthly claim upon him.   A fraction of a second's ecstasy
flashed across Alex before the dream vanished, and she
woke in the chill dawn to find her pillow wet with tears.
The thrill and awe of the dream was strong upon her ;
the unearthly look on Mrs. Maitland's face, the sense of
her aloofness from the things that mortals hold most
precious.   Alex rose and drew up the blind to let in a little
more light.   She looked out across the sleeping orchard in
the dead, shadowless light of dawn.

"Oh, happy kingdom of Heaven, where they neither
marry, nor are given in marriage !" she sighed ; then
crept back to her bed and lay long awake, gazing out into
the coming day.

CHAPTER XXXV

MANY times before she rose that morning Alex had composed her letter to the Admiral. Yet each version, as she mentally reviewed it, seemed to involve some further explanation, and that was what she could not give. She found herself in a peculiarly difficult position when she came to consider how her quarrel with Van was to be explained to the little Crossriggs world, for that it must sooner or later be explained she did not doubt. Even Matilda, she felt, could never be told the real story of the quarrel. She tried once or twice to fancy herself describing the whole scene to her sister, but always when she came to Van's words they refused to utter themselves. She knew that she could never repeat them to any one.

" To one person only," she thought, " and he must never know !"

As Alex came to this conclusion she had very nearly finished dressing. She stood before the looking-glass twisting up her long hair without, it must be said, much thought of how it was going to look. As she stuck in the first hairpin she heard the door bell ring loudly.

Now the sound of the door bell at Orchard House was, Alex used to say, as startling as the trump of doom, because there was always an element of unpreparedness in the household—an uncertainty as to who was to open the door in response to the summoning bell. At that moment Alex knew that Katharine was very busy

cooking breakfast and grumbling—the two things always
went together. Matilda would be half dressed, and the
children in various stages of the toilet.

The bell rang again, more loudly. Alex crossed the
passage and leaned over the stair-rail.

" Katharine ! " she called. " Don't you hear the door
bell ? "

Distant grumbles from the kitchen followed the appeal,
then Katharine hurried along the hall, tying on a clean
apron, flung open the door, and confronted the intruder.
Alex could not see who it was, but leaning still farther
over the railing she caught the tones of Van's voice.

" Is Miss Alex up yet, Katharine ? "

" Oh, surely, sir, yes, sir, but not to say ready to come
downstairs yet, sir."

Katharine was always very profuse in her civilities to
those whom she considered " the real gentry," or, as she
once happily phrased it, " none of these halfs."

" Couldn't she come and speak to me for a minute ; go
and ask, there's a good woman," Van pursued in a wheed-
ling tone.

Alex tip-toed back to her room and softly closed the
door. She heard Katharine coming upstairs, grumbling
as she came.

" Miss Alex, that's Mr. Cassilis wantin' to see you very
special," she said, standing at the door, much out of
breath.

" Sorry, Katharine, I can't see him," Alex answered.
" I'm not dressed, and won't be for some time."

" And it close on nine i " Katharine ejaculated *sotto
voce*, while aloud she asked suspiciously, " Shall I tell the
young gentleman *that ?* "

Katharine had great ideas of decorum, which were
rather offended by this allusion to the toilet.

" Yes ; say I can't—*won't* see him," said Alex,
shortly.

Katharine turned away with this message, but only to

return a few minutes later, red in the face between anger and exertion. She held a letter in her hand.

" Here, Miss Alex, and I'm sure I wonder what yon Mr. Cassilis thinks I'm made of—at his age stairs is easier, no doubt—and the breakfast burnin' black on the stove by this time."

Alex received the note in silence ; she was too much disturbed to pay any attention to Katharine's grumbles. The old woman descended to the kitchen again, and Alex sat down by the window to read the letter.

" DEAR SANDY," it ran, " I am going to London by the first train, and shall stay there for some weeks, perhaps months. I know you will wish to break with Gran, too, but I want you not to yet. If I am not there it can't hurt you to go on reading to him. By the time I come back you may invent an excuse for giving it up. Oh, Sandy, *forgive me*—do, do—just this once—write and tell me you do.—VAN."

Alex's eyes filled up with tears as she read the hastily scrawled letter, it seemed just like Van speaking to her, and yet her heart hardened against him the next moment —what he had said was unpardonable. Let him be never so delightful, she could not forget how he had insulted her. She flung the letter into a drawer and went down to breakfast.

The meal was not a success, for Katharine's culinary efforts having been interrupted at a critical moment the result was a failure.

" What did Van mean by coming here so early ? " Matilda said, mildly annoyed by the fact that the children had all to eat singed porridge.

" He's going off to London suddenly, he wanted to let us know," said Alex.

" London ! what takes young people to London ? " Old Hopeful exclaimed, beaming down the table at Alex

through his round spectacles, as if she could answer this
perplexing question. " A restless age this, and London
is a restless, money-getting, money-spending place ; our
young friend had better far have stayed in the healthful
country :

' Getting and spending we lay waste our powers '

—you remember Wordsworth's noble sonnet, Alex ? "
If his daughter's reply was rather absent, the old man
did not observe it, but chatted away in his gentle mono-
logue—with London for text—till the meal was over.
Matilda, however, was not so unobservant as her father,
and under the pretext of helping Alex to make the beds,
she followed her upstairs. This was generally Sally's
business, but Matilda sent the child downstairs that
morning.
" There's something wrong, Alex," she said. " Do tell
me what it is."
They sat down on the edge of the unmade bed in Alex's
room to discuss the situation.
" I've quarrelled with Van—badly. We can never
make it up, that's all," said Alex.
" Oh, Alex ! It isn't possible. Why, we all love Van.
You couldn't quarrel seriously with him, not really."
" Yes, out and out."
" Why ? What was it ? " Matilda asked curiously ;
but Alex shook her head.
" He said something to me that I could never forgive
—that I *should* never forgive. I can't even tell you
what it was, Matilda, so you may know that it was bad
enough."
Matilda would not have been human had she not tried
to find out what Van had said, but nothing would make
Alex tell a word that had passed between herself and Van.
" I can't, Matilda ; you needn't ask me. I'm going to
stop reading to the Admiral as soon as I can do it without
rousing his suspicions. I don't wish him to find out about

this, so I won't break off all at once, but I must try to get
something else to do that will need all my time, then he
won't suspect anything just at first.   Later, I suppose, he
must find out that we are not friends with Van as we have
been."

"You won't refuse to speak to him surely ? " Matilda
asked, in amazement.

" I won't speak to him more than I can help certainly ;
but he won't come to the house as he has done."

There was a moment's silence.   Matilda sat looking
down at the floor, her face puckered into an expression of
great perplexity.

"Do you know, Alex," she said at last, " I had begun
to think that Van was in love with you ? "

" Did you ?   Perhaps he was."

"Was—is, you mean.   I think he wishes to marry
you."

" That he will never do," Alex said, with sudden
decision.

To escape from the questioning in Matilda's eyes she
rose and walked across to the window.   Matilda did not
follow her, but could not resist a further inquiry into this
interesting subject.

" He's so nice," she said tentatively.   " Do you think
it would be quite impossible for you to think of it, Alex ?
After all, your circumstances are not very brilliant, and
a really delightful young man like Van, with plenty of
money, is *not* to be met with every day, and he is devoted
to you and——"

" Matilda ! " Alex cried.   " I am ashamed of you when
you say things like that.   Marriage isn't an affair of
expediency, of so much money, and getting into ' comfortable circumstances ' ; at least it isn't to *me*. and never
will be."

The implication in Alex's words would have enraged
some women, but Matilda was too good-natured to take
offence at it.   She sighed, and shook her head.

" Well, Alex, you have already refused James Reid, one of the best men I know; and if you haven't refused Van, you seem to have come very near to doing it. You must allow that in our circumstances it seems rather silly."

" Silly to refuse a man years and years younger than I am ? Oh, Matilda ! "

" Don't interrupt me, Alex. What does a few years' difference of age matter ? "

" It's the difference of outlook, not the years," Alex interpolated.

Matilda went on: " I know all you feel, dear, but do believe me, these ideas are foolish. I've seen more of life than you have—I've been married. I know what the probabilities of life are——"

" Oh, don't be so prosaic ! " Alex cried, almost fiercely.

But Matilda went calmly on, as if she had not heard her—

" I know that young girls expect to have all manner of interesting and romantic lovers—they always do— but *they don't have them.* The men they have to choose between are just ordinary unromantic men who want wives. Now, Alex, you are not a young girl any longer, and you should have got past all that sort of nonsense. Don't suppose you will have better or more interesting men than James Reid and Van Cassilis to choose from, *for you won't.* Do, like a dear, be sensible, and make up your mind to take Van."

" He has never asked me to marry him," said Alex, shortly.

" Then *let* him ask you," Matilda urged.

Alex smiled a little tense smile. " I can assure you, Matilda, that he will never do so now," she answered.

At this Matilda rose and crossed over to where her sister stood. In the pitiless morning light all manner of tell-tale lines showed round Alex's mouth and eyes. She was no longer young, though, as years went, she might still have claimed to be so.

"Alex," Matilda cried, half angrily, half pityingly, "what do you want, what do you expect from life?"

"All or nothing. All is what I want, and nothing is what I expect. Come, Matilda, we've put off enough time over this. Let us begin to tidy things up. The house is like a pigsty, and Heaven knows what the children are about!"

Matilda looked at her in silence. Something in Alex's manner showed her that this was no ordinary matter. She dared not ask another question, and they separated and went about their morning work in silence. Miss Maitland came across the Square shortly afterwards to say that Laura's slight improvement continued. Alex, standing in the dining-room, heard her voice in the hall, and listened, holding her breath until she heard the words "decidedly better this morning," then she drew a long breath of relief and went back to her work, with the colour returning to her face.

CHAPTER XXXVI

" WENT off like a sky-rocket, without a word," grum-
bled the Admiral. "He was gone before I was out of
bed this morning. I'm sure I don't know why he did not
mention his plans to me—young men nowadays take
matters so into their own hands. I have spent a most
uncomfortable day, Miss Hope, between one thing and
another. I have been a good deal annoyed. It is astonishing when one has not, h'm "—he coughed—" the full
use of one's eyesight, how trifles upset one."

He was fidgetting about in his chair, and would not
settle down and let Alex begin to read. She was not
an unsympathetic person in general, but that afternoon
somehow the poor old man's vexations seemed to her so
imaginary, compared to her own troubles, that she had
no real sympathy to give him. With the obtuseness of
self-absorption she forgot at the moment his blindness,
the weariness of his old age, and fretted nerves. Blake's
phrase, "The wren, with sorrows small " came into her
mind. She tried to console him with a few half-hearted,
rather impatient comments, as he went slowly through
the category of his little worries. When at last there
was a pause, she turned to lift the book they were going to
read from the table. As she did so, she saw lying on the
top of it a pair of Van's gloves. Alex lifted them, and
laid them aside, feeling a curious thrilling sensation up
her arm as she touched them, partly pain, partly nervous
remembrance of her last sight of Van. Her cheeks

burned again and she hastily bent down, forgetting that
the old man could not see her face. She read very badly,
and the time seemed long. When the hour was up she
left rather abruptly, though her heart smote her as she
thought of the old man settling down to his long, dark
evening alone.

" I just *had* to harden my heart," she thought. " I
should have been such poor company to him, if I had
stayed to-night."

She did not go down the avenue on her way home; she
could not—but returned as she had come, by a path across
the fields. The murky November twilight hung over the
dead-looking land. There was no wind, no sound, for her
footsteps fell almost noiseless on the soft earth. As she
came near the gate at the end of the field a tiny stoat
creature ran across her path: it had such a vicious face,
looking round at her with its intent little cruel expression for an instant before it wriggled out of sight. It
seemed to add the last touch to Alex's depression.

" That a thing so small, not as big as my hand, should
look like the origin of evil!" she thought. "And oh! all
the way up, people's hearts full of jealousy and cruelty
and evil passions. Where does it stop? If there is a
higher race of beings than men, have they, too, only
greater capacities for ill ? "

It was not a lively vein of thought, and the draggled
grass, limp with moisture, the sodden brakes and leaves
by the road edges, were not cheering to look upon. The
gate, when she came to it, was surrounded by a number of
bullocks, which had plashed the ground into mud, and
were now standing shoulder to shoulder breathing a
kind of surly patience, till the herd should appear to open
the gate.

Now, Alex was afraid of cattle. She wondered if she
could go up and slap them and shove them aside and get
the gate open. Then one of them turned and blew out
his nostrils and puffed at her, and she retreated a few

paces. How tired she would be if she had to go all the way back—she couldn't. The fence was high and of barbed wire, impossible to climb, but she could not face the bullocks at the gate. Just then a piercing whistle sounded behind her, and, looking across the palings which divided the field from the road, she saw a young woman, whom she recognized as Miss Orranmore, sauntering along with a dog whip in her hand. Alex knew that she was staying in the neighbourhood, at a house some two or three miles away.

She nodded to Alex, and asked if she had seen her dog in there.

" No, I wish I had," said Alex ; " it would have moved those beasts from the gate, and I want to get out."

Miss Orranmore stared. " Lord ! You don't mean to say that you're afraid of them ? " She advanced to the gate.

" Of course I am," Alex acknowledged, disgusted by her own timidity.

Dolly opened the gate with one tug of her small strong hands. She pushed herself right in amongst the bullocks, slapping one on the nose, thumping at the flanks of another, scattering them far and wide with the butt end of her whip, and laughing at the immoderate, clumsy bounds they made to get out of her way.

" Come now," she cried, " will that do ? "

Alex, feeling her humiliation a good deal, came somewhat limply through the gate, and Dolly shut it again, and began once more to whistle for her dog.

" Thank you very much," Alex said, " are you going this way ? "

" Yes. I must find that wretched dog."

She whistled long and loud once more, and then walked along beside Alex with her hands in the pockets of her coat.

" You've been up at Foxe Hall, I suppose ? " she began.

" Yes. I go every day to read to the Admiral," said Alex.

" Oh ! " said Miss Orranmore, then added, " what is Van about ? "

" I don't know. He's just gone to London."

" Gone to London ? Isn't that sudden ? "

" Yes, I think it is. He went this morning."

" Oh ! " said Miss Orranmore again, thoughtfully flicking her knee with her whip.

The dog came bounding out of a thicket, and she turned to scold him, Alex meanwhile taking the opportunity of bidding her good night and hurrying on.

" To think that I allowed that woman to help me—even about a trifle," she said to herself. " It seems just the crowning touch to this horrible day."

She was very tired and longing to rest and read quietly for an hour, but when she reached home she heard that there was some one in the sitting-room talking to Matilda. Something about the umbrella that lay on the table in the hall seemed familiar to Alex, and she glanced at it, wondering who the visitor was. It had a handle formed in the likeness of a bird's head, with bead eyes, and a little spring at the throat of the bird opened and shut a vivid scarlet beak—this Alex remembered in a flash.

" It's Bessie Reid," she thought. " Oh, I must go in and see her."

How much rather she would have stayed in her own room, but she felt it would be unkind. Bessie Reid, Mrs. Ferdinand Massie, it was—brighter, more arch than ever now, dressed more richly, but quite as confusedly as before, with tinkling ornaments, and a diadem of beads upon her brow.

" Ah ! " she exclaimed, jumping up to greet Alex, and kissing her warmly. " I'm so glad to see you again, but thin, Alex Thin and pale ! Naughty ! I'm just come down for two days to have a peep at Auntie. She's wonderfully bright, poor dear, and so overjoyed with

Ferdie's new photograph, at first she thought it was
James. 'And who's the lady beside him?' she asked
(it was me!) 'James isn't married.'" She looked meaningly at Alex. "Poor dear Auntie, she thinks the whole
world is marrying in these days. She even asked Miss
Binns if *she* was going to be married. Miss Binns is
quite a treasure, she has so many resources, keenly
interested in poker work—the new burnt velvet, I mean—
and imitation marqueterie, every minute she can spare from
Auntie, she fills in with that. She's made me a lovely
table-centre of emerald green velvet, with a deep border
of *edelweiss*, all collected on our wedding trip, just stitched
on with gold thread, and *just* a touch of salmon pink
here and there to keep it from being too cold. It has
a beautiful effect! 'I see an Alpine meadow!' Ferdie
exclaimed, when he looked at it. It's such a sweet
souvenir, and you know Ferdie's sisters gave us a sugar-
basin made like a silver châlet, so we've quite an Alpine
table."

She talked on, describing with friendly minuteness
every detail of her new home, in reply to Matilda's interested questions. In general, Alex would have been the
first to ask and to listen and rejoice in the kindliness of
it all but that evening she said very little, sitting with
her back to the light, and making no effort to be sympathetic.

"You're tired, poor dear! You should take more
care of yourself, or you should have some one to take care
of you, which is better," said Mrs. Massie, with an enthusiastic squeeze of the hand, as she bid Alex good-bye.
Matilda was going to walk back with her, and had left
the room to get on her walking things. "Good-bye,
dear Alex." She held her at arm's length for a minute,
looking into her face, and adding, "How I wish that
Love would come to you, too! Perhaps he's at the door
now!" she exclaimed, nodding coyly, as she took her
departure.

Alex sat down on the fender stool and covered her face with her hand, half laughing, half crying to herself. The clock ticked audibly in the silent, half-dark room.

" What a horrible day it has been ! " she thought. " How hard and bitter I am ! " She rocked herself gently to and fro, like a woman with an ailing child in her arms. " It hurts so much—so much—so much," she said to herself. " And how life is passing, and what is the good of it all ? None to-night."

There was a sound of voices, and the children came tumbling in a sort of stampede into the room.

" Oh, you're *here*, Aunt Alex ! " they screamed joyously. " You're not too tired, are you, to play for us ? We've got Cissy Scott and Tom, and want to have musical chairs."

It was not quite the nerve tonic she would have chosen, but there might have been worse, and when the last breathless child had flung itself upon the struggling, squealing heap that covered the last vacant chair, and she stopped the pounding little jig that had set them going, Alex rose refreshed, and was able to talk quite cheerfully to Matilda and her father in the evening.

She added the note to her journal: " A most horrible day, everything all wrong ; my own heart most of all." And under that the line from Dr. Johnson's diary: " ' Surely I shall not spend my whole life to my own total disapprobation.' "

CHAPTER XXXVII

FOR two or three weeks Mrs. Maitland continued very ill ; sometimes she seemed better and then sank back again to the state she had been in before. The neighbours were now, with the kindness of small communities, all sympathetic, and contrived to forget that she had never been a great favourite—every one spoke well of her now. After Christmas she began to get better steadily, and great was the satisfaction of Crossriggs when she was finally pronounced to be out of danger. Alex felt as if a weight rolled off her. Maitland, who had gone about looking very grave and pale, seemed almost gay. He came in to tell the Hopes that the doctors who had come for consultation, said there was no longer any immediate danger. Old Hopeful beamed upon him and wrung his hand, unable to express his friendly emotion.

Alex, who had been sitting by the window, rose and came across the room with one of her quick, stately movements, and held out her hand too.

" I am more glad than I can tell you," she said. " Please tell Mrs. Maitland how glad we all are."

Their eyes met : in a moment of understanding they were each aware of the other's truth. Alex looked straight at him, and the gladness in their faces was unfeigned.

" We have got through this, at any rate," she thought. " Nothing else could be as bad ; he knows I spoke the truth."

Twice since that angry parting of theirs, Alex had received a letter from Van. When she saw the handwriting the first time she hesitated for a moment, and then she sealed it up in a fresh envelope and readdressed it to his London club. Two days afterwards came another letter. Matilda brought it to her this time, when Alex was baking a cake in the kitchen.

" Here is a letter from Van, I think, Alex ; it seems a long time since we have heard from him," she said.

Now Alex had nearly finished making the cake, but she plunged her spoon deep into the dough again.

" All right, Matilda ; thank you," she said, in as careless a tone as she could muster. " I can't touch it just now."

When Matilda had gone she carried the letter away. It seemed to burn her fingers, as if something hot had been really enclosed in it. She stood for a minute looking at it, and then put it, too, into another envelope, and hurried out to the post-office with it herself, before she had time to repent. No more letters came from Van. Matilda asked Alex in the evening what he had written about.

" I really don't remember—nothing much," said Alex.

But Matilda was disquieted, and wondered all the more to herself what was passing between them.

" Haven't you made up your quarrel yet ? " she ventured to ask.

" No, we have not," said Alex, and turned abruptly away.

She couldn't help hearing a good deal about Van from the Admiral, who kept always talking of him, and Alex learnt that the young man had been in Paris for a while.

"The Orranmores have gone there, and he has seen something of them," he said. " I never can make out how people, always at the end of their resources, move about nowadays. When I was young, if a man with a family found himself hard up for a time, he stayed at home on his own property and cut down some timber—

of course . . . gamblers . . . fashion . . . nowadays."
He became disconnected and coughed, adding in rather
a tentative way, " The girl is lively, lively and bright
enough, not pretty, I understand from what my grandson says."

" Very lively, certainly ; and some people would think
her very handsome," said Alex.

" It's a strange thing," began the Admiral, peevishly,
" how contradictory—*contradictory* the young are now. A
word from an older person seems enough to send them
off at a tangent in the opposite direction. To take an
instance. There is a Miss Pym—Ah, you've met her, I
remember, a charming girl, could hear it from her very
voice, well connected, even "—he hummed and hawed
as if uncertain whether to treat the matter as jest or
earnest, and decided to make it a delicate pleasantry—
" even the most important of all things, Miss Hope "—
sinking his voice—" very well off, and with expectations
—expectations. Charmingly pretty, too, I've been assured. You thought so ? Ah, yes, exactly. Well, I
was unfortunate enough to say something to my grandson about her one day, and it has been sufficient, apparently, to keep him from ever looking at the girl again,
whereas——" He said no more, but Alex knew very
well that he was feeling uneasy about Miss Orranmore.

In the beginning of February Van returned. The
Admiral told Alex the day before his arrival, and as she
walked home that afternoon she began once more to try
to invent some reasonable excuse for breaking off her
reading for a time.

" I will never enter the house again whilst Van is there,"
she vowed.

That week she had two long days in town before her,
so that is was not difficult to send a note and tell the
Admiral she would not be able to read to him for some
days.

" When you have Van back you will not want me,"

she added, saying to herself, " I shall invent a new excuse by Monday."

Van called at Orchard House the day after his arrival. Alex had gone to town. Matilda reported that he was not looking " like himself "—that vague and most expressive phrase. Alex did not go to church that Sunday, and by the time that Monday afternoon came she was provided with a truthful excuse, for she had such a violent sick headache that she could scarcely see.

Matilda went off into town instead of her, promising to do all the messages, and return by the late train. Alex scrawled her note to the Admiral and sent George up with it to Foxe Hall, and then crept off to her own room and went to bed.

The day passed somehow. Sally would come in: " Sorry to disturb you, Aunt Alex, but Mrs. Scott is at the door, and she would like to know the address of the woman mother told her about, who will do up mattresses, and may we have figs after dinner, please, for Katharine says the ' water has got into the pudding ' ? " Or Katharine would come in with a letter, which proved to be from the school-mistress in Edinburgh, asking if Alex could come to give her lesson the next morning instead of on Wednesday. Mr. Maitland is here, Aunt Alex," said George, at the door, " and he's very sorry he can't see you, and he and Mrs Maitland are going into Edinburgh, and may we use the old bath as a cart ? "—and so on.

As the evening wore on Alex felt slightly better, and got a book and tried to read a little in order to divert her thoughts. Bedroom fires were a luxury that the Hopes could ill afford, so the only light came from a single candle placed beside the bed.

Alex went on reading until her hands got very cold, and her head ached so that she could scarcely see. Then she laid down her book and lay staring at the circle of light thrown on the roof by the candle. It was so cold that she could see her breath in the air like steam. Downstairs, the children were racing about, and every now and then came a thump or a crash of some kind that made her head throb. Two or three times a boy burst open her bedroom door, and hustled into the room with some question or complaint. Sally brought up her tea, and was followed by a kitten playing with a reel. It got under the bed, and skirmished madly about, and then had to be chased by Sally with much noise and laughter. Alex sat up in bed and drank the tea. As Matilda was away it had been made with unboiling water, and Sally had heaped sugar into the cup. The bit of bread-and-butter, too, was all splashed with tea. The girl stood watching her aunt, sorry enough for her, but anxious to get away back to her romp with the boys.

" Will you have another cup, Aunt Alex ? " she asked, and evidently relieved when Alex declined to have any more, caught up the kitten, shut the door with a bang, and raced off down the long, narrow passage with thundering steps. Alex sank back, and tried to find a cold spot on her pillow for her hot throbbing head. She was weak and ill, and an access of self-pity surged over her.

" If they could only be quiet for half an hour," she thought. " How cold and dismal this room is ; and how my head is burning." She began to think what it would be like to have money and the luxuries of life, and that somehow led her on to think about Van. " I wonder," she thought, " if I should be miserable if I married him ? Why after all, whose business is it but my own, even if I am older than he ? Would it—at the worst— be more dreary than toiling on like this for other people's children ? Matilda, after all, *had* her day—such a dull one it would have seemed to me! but it was what she fancied, and she has her children, and I have nothing, nothing, nothing. Shall I drop the bone to snap at the shadow ? " Her eyes filled with bitter tears for a moment, and then the image of Van—as she used to think of him before they quarrelled—handsome and comforting, young and prosperous and strong, stole into her mind, and seemed to warm the coldness of the dreary room. " How could he do it ! Oh, I wish I had never seen him," she thought, remembering that dreadful day.

Then she heard the hall door open, and the chorus of voices from the children, and presently one of them came racing along the passage, throwing himself against the door handle.

" May I come in, Aunt Alex ? Mother's come back, and she's brought us each a present, and she's not got half her messages done, and she's awfully tired, and she said to tell you she would come up whenever she had had tea ; and if you're not using the candle may we have it, for we're having an illumination downstairs ? "

Breathing deep and loud, clattering his boots upon the uncarpeted floor as he spoke, he stood working away at the candle with a match until the wax streamed down upon the table, then, nodding at Alex, seized the candlestick, and started off again, returning to bang the door, which he had left swinging open.

Alex lay in the darkness for half an hour, then Matilda came in, and brought a light with her. She was still in her outdoor things, and looked very tired. She stood beside the bed, unfastening her jacket, and telling Alex all about her day in town.

" I met Van in Princes Street," she began, playing a little nervously with the fringe of the bed-curtains as she spoke. " He was looking very cheerful, and when I stopped to speak to him, told me that he had meant to write to you himself, only was too busy, so he sent a message instead that he is going to marry Miss Orranmore."

" Oh ! " said Alex. She half sat up in bed, her face suddenly flushed. " Is it true ? Really, Matilda ? "

" Yes, of course, it is true, because he told me himself. He looked very happy, I must say. He asked me to tell you that he knew you would understand he hadn't time to write. I will go and take off my things," said Matilda.

" No, stay for a moment," said Alex. " Do tell me where you met him and all that he said."

" I can't just now really, dear ; my feet are as cold as ice, and I'm so tired." She paused, and turned in the doorway. " And oh, Alex, I've done such a dreadfully stupid thing—lost half a sovereign. I must have given it by mistake to some carman for a sixpence. I went back halfway along Princes Street in the rain, to see if I had given it to the girl at Clarke's. But if so, she knew nothing about it. It's gone anyway, and it's no good worrying about it now."

" Oh no, no good. But if you sometimes worried a little other people might have less to worry them ! " retorted Alex.

Matilda looked at her for one moment with a grieved expression, then left the room. Alex could hear her saying to Sally at the door—

" No, don't go in again. Your Aunt Alex has such a headache I'm sure she'd rather be left quiet."

" Mayn't I take her these ? " said Sally.

" Very well, but go in just for a moment."

The door creaked, and Sally ponderously tip-toed into the room. In her hand she carried a bunch—a huge bunch of fresh violets. Their inimitable perfume seemed to fill the cold room as she laid them beside Alex.

Alex's heart gave a great leap. " He hasn't forgotten after all ! " she thought. " Where did these come from, Sally ? " she asked, stretching out her hand for the flowers, and burying her face into the cold, scented bunch that seemed to kiss her with a hundred tiny delicate lips.

" Miss Maitland brought them, wasn't it nice of her ? " (Here the door creaked loud and long.) " Are you better, Aunt Alex ? Can I do anything for you ? " the girl inquired, bending down and beginning to play with the candle just as Peter had done.

"No, dear. Go away, please."

(Here the door groaned and creaked again, and the window blind flapped in the draught.)

"Wouldn't you like to put these in water?"

"No, no. Please go away and shut the door," called Alex crossly, and Sally departed, aggrieved, shutting the door with much fumbling three times over to make sure that it was shut.

Alex turned her face to the wall, and cried. Her tears seemed to scald her cheeks.

"Oh, what a fool I am! Oh, what a fool I *was!* Oh, what a fool I will always be, I suppose. Going to be married, of course, of course—and too busy to tell me—and looking so happy—*of course*, he is. Oh, how could I ever, ever, ever be so foolish? Why did I ever suppose he would care for any length of time? I'm not the sort of woman people care about like that. No doubt he's forgotten all about that miserable day. Perhaps Miss Orranmore is all he wants—they may be quite happy. I haven't broken his heart. How could I allow myself to imagine he had sent those flowers! And it was only Aunt E. V. after all—who else would it be? I needn't fancy myself a heroine of romance. I'm only the aunt of Matilda's children, and just going to become like Miss Bessie Reid." She laughed aloud, even as she cried, at this last thought; then dried her eyes, and in another minute turned round, and buried her face in the bunch of violets again.

"Whoever sent them they are just as sweet!" she said to herself. "The beauty of them speaks like a song. The world isn't such a bad place where things like this can grow."

By the time Matilda brought her supper, Alex was sitting up in bed quite cheerful again, and able to hear all her news. How long she lay awake that night no

one knew but herself.   She heard the clock chime from
the church tower through the frosty silence at midnight,
and saw the keen stars amongst the bare branches of the
trees about her window.

Something at her heart, more intimate than the voice
of reason, seemed to tell her that the young man, too,
was lying awake upon his bed, thinking. . . . But here
she stopped and spoke aloud to herself again.

" Happy, of course, as he ought to be, and very much
in love, and I am fool to think anything else."

CHAPTER XXXVIII

VAN was married to Dolly Orranmore in the middle of April. He and Alex never met after the announcement of his engagement, for she broke off her reading with the Admiral for a few weeks under the pretext of several odd bits of work that she had to do in town. Then the old man went away to England for the wedding.

Alex saw him for the first time on his return, a week or two later. He greeted her with something like affection.

" I have missed our quiet hours of reading more than I can say," he said. " All this bustle, somehow . . . when one is . . . at my age . . . when one has not the use of one's eyes . . . is rather fatiguing. I stayed with my old friend, Sir Bingham Peele—kindness itself—but I am too old now for going about."

" I hope the wedding was a success ? " Alex inquired, resolutely keeping her voice to its usual tone, for she knew how blindness quickens even the least sensitive hearer.

" Quite, quite," the Admiral answered. He moved in his chair, and Alex thought he flushed. " A great deal of talk and laughter, of course—so many young people. The Orranmore's friends are, perhaps, not quite the set I would have chosen for Van ; but you can't keep a young man of his age in cotton-wool, Miss Hope."

" Certainly not," said Alex, thinking to herself that the husband of Dolly Orranmore would certainly not be " kept in cotton-wool " in any sense.

The Admiral talked on, giving her such details as his limited opportunities had allowed him to gather. When at last he paused, and sat drumming with his fingers on the arm of his chair, Alex took up the newspaper, and was beginning to look over the article he wished her to read, when he observed suddenly—

"Had you ever had an idea, Miss Hope, that my grandson had fallen in love with any one else—all young men of his age do so ? "

Alex was utterly taken aback. She sat staring at the blind face in front of her. Her own grew pale, then she answered slowly—

"Yes, I did think so ; but these things are just youth and foolishness. They pass off and leave no trace as a man gets older."

"Quite, quite so," said the Admiral again, drumming on the arm of his chair. He was silent for a minute or two, but he asked Alex no other question, and presently she began to read.

"It's a wise old person after all, in a shallow worldly-wise old way," she said to herself. It seemed to her all that afternoon that at any moment the door might open and Van come in, as he had so often done—as he had done the first day she ever saw him—and stand on the hearthrug looking at her with his expressive eyes. She felt glad when the time came for her to leave.

"I must go a little early," she explained to the Admiral, "for I have promised to take my niece Sally to a party at Mrs. Bowman's this afternoon. It is the first time she has ever been to such a thing. and she's quite as excited as some girls are over a first ball, so I must not be late."

"Mrs. Bowman, ah ! " said the Admiral. " Worthy people, I suppose—their connection with trade is thread —isn't it thread, Miss Hope ? The distance makes it impossible for me to have much to do with them, but they are hospitable, I hear, in their own way, and give great entertainments—of a kind."

"Very nice people. They make excellent thread. I got a monster reel at a bazaar, sent by Mrs. Bowman, three years ago, and I haven't sewn it all up yet."

She went away smiling, and trying to speak as cheerfully as she could, but her heart was heavy and she felt as if something sad had happened in the house.

"I must try now to be lively for Sally's sake," she thought—"after all, how silly it is to suppose that there is much wrong. Van made a free choice. The woman mayn't be what I think nice, but if he likes her it's all right." Thus arguing with herself she got home, rather heated, for she had hurried a little in order to get back in good time.

She found, as she expected, the excited Sally all ready, and looking remarkably pretty, in spite of her freckles, in a very simple summer frock worn for the first time.

"Oh, Aunt Alex, this hook won't stay in, and the little bones in the collar do rub my neck so—but I think I look all right," she exclaimed, turning round to let Alex inspect her, and rubbing the angry little red mark on her white throat, where the whalebone had scratched it.

"Oh, these cheap dressmakers! I wonder their own bones aren't poking out of their skin, they seem to have such a power of doing it in whalebones! There, Sally, I've squeezed the top back, does that still hurt you?"

"That's much better; now the hook, please? Oh, Aunt Alex, I hope I'll meet somebody who'll talk to me," she said wistfully. Alex, who in the meanwhile, had been hurriedly making her own toilet, pinned on her veil, and took her gloves, and they went out together, followed by derisive hoots about "Grand grown-up young ladies going out to tea," from George, and the frank remark from Peter, "If any one thinks you're grown up, Sally, just tell them you were on the top of the pigeon-house roof for an hour this morning."

Mrs. Bowman's was one of the larger country houses in the neighbourhood, about two miles from Crossriggs. Miss Maitland had offered to drive Alex and Sally, so they had only to walk across the Square. Maitland and his wife had been away in town, ever since Mrs. Maitland's recovery, and they had not yet returned ; so Aunt E. V. alone, very upright and severe, was waiting by the door. She, too, was something of the Admiral's opinion, and "thread" was never far from her mind in connection with Mrs. Bowman. Alex was imprudent that afternoon, and when, as they were nearing the house, Miss Maitland said something about "thread," she broke out with—

"And what could be nicer—so clean and useful! How thankful I'd be if *my* father had ever been anything as practical as Mr. Bowman! And why on earth shouldn't a kind, clever young woman like that occupy Grimshaws? I'm sure she's much pleasanter and more wholesome than old Lady Ann ever was, with that horrible face, and her hands like sausages."

"I never liked her," said Aunt E. V. "But thread is thread, and villas are the place for it to my mind, not the houses of other people's ancestors. Your hat is on one side, Alex. Sally, do you *mean* that white string to show ? "

She sailed on in front of them across the lawn to where Mrs. Bowman ("In string colour, Sally!" Alex whispered) was receiving her guests.

"Oh, Aunt Alex, do let me keep near you—nobody will speak to me I'm sure," pleaded Sally, now red as a rose with excitement and shyness. "Perhaps when she asked you to bring me, she didn't know how little I was."

"You're not *little*, darling, whatever you are, and she

knew quite well, and particularly asked you. Try not
to think *all* the time about your gloves."

" It's not my gloves, it's my *hands*, Aunt Alex,"
whispered Sally, piteously. " I *don't* know what to do
with them."

" Put them behind your back, clasp them tight—hold
them at your waist, as you've seen Mrs. Scott do ; do
anything except think about them."

" If no one speaks to me what shall I do ? "

" Sit still, smile a little, and don't mind."

" Oh dear ! " sighed Sally, desperately, as they drew
near their hostess, who bestowed a very kind glance
upon her, as she shook hands. Alex, who was always
popular, was quickly surrounded by people, the hot
pink Sally clinging closely in her rear. In a few
minutes Alex saw her disposed of at a little distance,
grateful for the incessant conversation of a maiden
lady of slightly weak intellect, and cooling down
visibly.

" I can leave her now, for a quarter of an hour, with
an easy mind," thought Alex, " she'll be asked to play
tennis immediately, no doubt."

Half an hour later, she had forgotten all about Sally,
and then looking round to see what had become of her,
found that she had disappeared altogether. Alex concluded that she had gone away with the Bowman girls,
who were much about her own age. She sighted Sally
next at tea-time, standing by a table along with several
other young people, so smiling and radiant that there
was no doubt about her enjoyment. When, a little later,
Alex went to find her, as it was time for them to go
home, Sally was sauntering under the lilac trees with a
young man, and looking remarkably pretty and well
pleased.

" Come, Sally. I'm going home now," called Alex, as
they came up. The young man advanced to greet her,
smiling rather shyly. For a minute she could not re-

member who he was, yet the almond eye seemed familiar.
Then Sally said—

"Don't you remember Mr. Morse, Aunt Alex? He
came to see us last summer."

"Oh, of course, I remember now," said Alex, shaking
hands with him kindly, and noticing with amusement
that Mr. Morse seemed to look at Sally with evident
admiration.

"He was so kind," said Sally, afterwards, "and
behaved as if I were entirely grown up. He said he
supposed I was 'out' now, and I didn't know whether
I was or not. I said we had never been in, for we were
out of doors nearly all the time."

"Then you enjoyed yourself, dear?"

"Oh yes, very much. Miss Crosbie talked to me for
an age, Aunt Alex; she's so kind, and she took me into
the garden. It was there we met Mr. Morse. Then I
played tennis, and after that he and I went into the
orchard together, and the bone of my collar had rubbed
my neck quite raw, look "—pulling the collar at her
throat to show a red mark under one ear—" and I
began to tug at it; I felt I must get it off, I was so hot,
and he asked what was wrong, and when I explained he
cut it off so neatly with a penknife—it was all right to
let him, wasn't it, Aunt Alex?"

Sally raised a pink, freckled, pretty face; looking at
her aunt a little anxiously.

"Well, Sally, it wasn't very conventional, but it was
most obliging of Mr. Morse. I hope he didn't cut your
new collar."

"Oh no; and he gave me back the bone." She
produced the scrap of whalebone from her pocket and
looked at it.

Alex remembered the passage in "Emma" about the
pencil shavings, and her mouth twitched for a moment,
but with a resolute effort she kept her gravity and
answered—

" We'll sew it in better covered to-morrow, and it will be all right."

" *His* sisters," Sally continued, in a musing voice, flattening the little bone against her knee, " *his* sisters have gold things with coral tips, like those in the advertisements, to support their collars. He says they never poke into the neck."

" I'm sure your mother wouldn't like *you* to wear gold supports with coral tips, even if we could afford them, Sally—a little Jewish." She stopped.

Sally flushed. " Why are Jews so nasty, Aunt Alex ? "

" They're not, dear ; far from it. An ancient race, the cleverest and noblest in the world in many ways."

" Then why did you say that ? " the girl asked.

" Their taste in dress differs from ours, Sally. They are an Eastern people, and have a love of colour."

" Oh ! " said Sally. She thought for a minute, then said quietly, " Mr. Morse's Christian name is ' Charles Benjamin.' "

" We'll agree to call him Charlie, if we ever know him well," said Alex, escaping hurriedly from the room lest Sally should see her amusement.

" I wouldn't have her think it amused me for the world, Matilda ! I'd sooner rub the bloom off a butterfly's wings than throw cold water on the first moments of interest to a girl of Sally's age. Don't you remember what you felt when we were that age? Why——"

She stopped, and sat looking out of the window at the house on the other side of the Square.

" Yes," said Matilda. " I remember quite well how you used to adore Mr. Maitland in those days ; you always kept the envelopes of the notes he sent to father." Matilda mused for a little and then went on, " I remember, too, how you laughed at Peter because you said he looked like a young turkey, but I don't think I minded at all."

" Not a bit ! Dear creature—she never did see any

faults in other people, so much the better for her," sighed Alex to herself when Matilda had left the room.

Two days later, when she came down to breakfast, she found a little box addressed to Sally on the table.

"See, dear, some one is sending you a present," she called, as the girl came in, fresh and hungry.

Sally grabbed the parcel from George, who was examining it. Alex was reading her own letters, when a faint squeal of rapture made her look up.

"Oh, Aunt Alex! How beautiful! Are they real?" panted Sally, holding out on her blistered school-girlish palm a little jeweller's case containing two gold collar supports, each ending in a pink coral ball.

There was a slip of paper attached, on which was written in a tiny, stiff hand, "*From Charles B. Morse.*"

Sally, flushed, breathless, almost trembling with agitation, dived at her mother, who entered the room at the moment. As she hurriedly explained, Matilda and Alex looked at one another.

"Oh, please, mother, let me keep them; they're so lovely."

"Well, Sally, you must write a very nice little note to Mr. Morse, and say that your mother thinks you are rather too young to wear such ornaments as yet, but you will keep them till you are a little older, and thank him very much."

"Too young, miss! Oh, *far* too young! Where's the grand grown-up young lady now?" cried George and Peter.

Sally, blushing with pride and pleasure, ignored their remarks, and ate her porridge with a glance at the little ornaments between each mouthful.

"Bless it! Bless it! And I was once as young as that!" said Alex to herself. "But Mr. Morse was not *my* first hero."

CHAPTER XXXIX

TOWARDS the end of May it was rumoured that Van
Cassilis was coming home to Foxe Hall with his wife.
The news caused Alex extraordinary uneasiness. It
would be quite impossible to avoid meeting them, yet
it seemed to her equally impossible to face such a
meeting.

"How are you going to encounter Van?" Matilda
asked, but quite lightly, for to that hour she had no
idea how serious the quarrel between Van and her sister
had been.

"I'll leave it to Fate. Don't you remember the
Scriptural injunction not to take thought beforehand
what you are going to speak," said Alex, with a flippancy
that she did not feel.

One evening the boys came home from school in a
state of great excitement.

"Oh, Aunt Alex, who do you think we saw at the
station? No, you can't guess. It was Van and his
new wife," Peter cried, bursting into the drawing-room,
quite breathless in his desire to tell the tale.

"His *wife*, Peter, not his *new* wife," Matilda corrected. "Van had not a wife before."

"Well, his *wife* then," Peter went on. "But, mother,
she does look new, like the things in the shop windows.
I wish you and Aunt Alex looked new like that." He
stopped with a rueful glance at his mother's rusty black
dress, and then, filled with compunction, tried to atone

for the speech. "Not that you don't look heaps nicer really, mother, and Van looks quite different somehow. I expect he's got new clothes, too, and he was carrying the loveliest dressing-bag of hers, made of bright green kid——"

"Leather, dear, probably," Matilda said.

"Well, leather then, mother, and when he saw me he laid it down on the station seat and ran after me, because he always used to speak to us, you know, and Mrs. Cassilis was *wild* at him. You should just have heard how she scolded him! Golly, Aunt Alex, I wish you'd heard her——"

"Peter, how often am I to tell you not to say 'Golly'?"

"I'm sorry, mother. And Van didn't pay the least attention to her, but just went on asking me about you —*you*, Aunt Alex, not mother—and all about us, and I said was he coming soon, for it has been horrid his being away both at Christmas and Easter when we had holidays, and he might have taken us in the boat? And he said, 'Yes,' and I said, 'When?' and he said, 'Probably to-morrow,' and he said he's got a mechanical boat for George and a clasp knife for me; and d'you know, mother, *I'd* have liked the boat best, but I didn't say so, but don't you think perhaps, as I'm the eldest, I might have it, and George the knife for——"

Under cover of this lengthy and artless narrative Matilda and Alex exchanged glances of significance.

"I'm sure I hope poor Van hasn't made a life-long mistake," Matilda said, when the boys had left the room.

"He probably has," said Alex, drily, with a sharpness that was quite unlike herself.

Matilda turned upon Alex. "I don't understand you," she said. "You have a hard tone about poor Van that no little indiscretion of his can justify. It's not nice of you to forget how fond you once were of him."

But Alex's face only hardened more at this reproof, and she took up her work and stitched away in resolute silence.

The next morning was brilliant and delightful. Matilda took the children out for an early walk, and Alex went to the kitchen to help Katharine with the preparation of dinner. This done she took up the grocer's book, which had just come in, and began to scan its contents. These as usual were not pleasant reading. Alex came slowly into the drawing-room, reading, as she walked, the prosaic items of the family expenditure.

" Six pounds sugar—ahem !—one jar treacle, twelve pounds flour——"

Then suddenly she stopped in the middle of the floor, and the book fell from her hand, for Van Cassilis stood there waiting for her. He came forward to pick up the fallen account-book and lay it on the table, but he did not attempt to shake hands with her.

" As you have never sent me your forgiveness, I came to ask it once again, Sandy—this will be the last time," he said.

Alex looked at him, and it seemed to her that she could read him as easily as a printed page, and just as she would have closed a book the contents of which shocked her, so Alex turned away from her study of poor Van's face. The impression that forced itself upon her notice was that not a trace of boyishness or innocence was left in him, the lad she had known was gone, changed almost beyond recognition. So marked was this impression that Alex felt herself begin to colour slowly up to her very eyes, and a suggestion of the terrible unacknowledged forces of evil swept over her. In the few months since she had seen Van Cassilis, his young plastic features had hardened and coarsened unbelievably. Some deteriorating influence had been at work ; yet, looking at the young man, Alex had a sudden conviction that

this havoc had not been wrought by any evil inherent
in his own nature.

"Something from *outside* has done it," she thought.
"'Can one touch pitch and not be defiled?' It's that
woman."

All at once an overmastering tide of pity and affection
for "the lad that was gone" rushed over her. Where
were all his aspirations vanished to? Mazzini . . .
The life that was to be worth living . . . the upward
road, the ideals—all the beautiful unattainable dreams
of generous youth? Surely, surely, they were not all
perished! In pity and grief Alex caught hold of his
hands and held them in hers, and tears rose to her eyes.

"Oh, Van, I'll forget every miserable word that ever
passed between us," she cried. "Only don't look like
that; come back, come back."

"Like what?" he asked, but a vague, curious, and
quite comprehending smile flickered across his face,
and he added, "No, no, Sandy, he's gone too far away
to be called back."

With a tremendous effort Alex pulled herself together.
"As you see, Van, I am silly and unbalanced, and imaginative, as usual—saying all manner of nonsense to you
—and I had intended to be dignified and never speak
to you again, except on terms of distant civility, and
here I am"—she threw out her hands with one of her
expressive gestures, and rattled on to relieve the pain-
fulness of the interview—"and here you are, an old
married man, and these, I suppose, are the celebrated
clasp knife and mechanical boat that have been disturbing the peace of a decent family since you unwisely
mentioned them to Peter last night." She took up the
toys in her embarrassment and scrutinized them, and
laughed at the ingenuity of the boat, and chided him
because of their costliness. "It's spoiling the boys
altogether, to give them such things," she said, and
then a moment of silence fell at last.

"Poor little chaps, let them have their toys now, they'll find soon enough that they can't get the ones they set their hearts on in later life," said Van, bitterly.

She did not dare to look at him, and searched in vain for a prudent parry for this thrust; it was not to be found.

A whistle sounded outside in the Square, and, grateful for the interruption, Alex moved to the window.

"Who is that whistling?" she asked.

Van pointed across the Square. "That's for me," he said.

Lounging in the sunshine near the Maitlands' door, Alex saw Dolly Cassilis. She was dressed as usual in rather showy but beautifully made clothes. Two or three dogs were leaping about her knees; she would flick at one and another with the whip she carried, and then evidently becoming more impatient, she put the whip handle to her lips and whistled again long and loudly.

"*To heel*," said Van, in an undertone. "Well, good-bye, Sandy. You'll shake hands with me this time, eh?"

She shook hands with him in silence, and he turned away without another word. She heard him cross the hall and stand for a moment at the door, then he came back again.

"Have you left anything?" she asked.

"No," he said shortly.

He stood in the doorway then, looking round and round the room with a long, strange, indescribable look.

"Why, Van, what is it?" Alex cried, startled by his behaviour.

"I've had happy days here," he said, then turned away and closed the door.

This time he did not come back. Alex saw him join his wife on the other side of the Square. She watched them till they were out of sight, then sat down in the armchair and covered her face with her hands.

" I never saw anything so horrible," she said. " It's like the old torture of the live, clean man chained to the rotting corpse."

CHAPTER XL

THE next day was one of fresh unclouded heat. " ' Earth and sun and sky combine to promise all that's kind and fair,' " Alex quoted to herself, looking out at the brilliant world of early summer. Van had been much in her thoughts all the morning. On just such a day, two years before, they had gone together in his boat to the Island ; there she first saw Dolly Orranmore, and there she had witnessed the little scene she could never forget in her estimate of the woman who was now Van's wife.

" I think we ought both to go up to Foxe Hall and call on Mrs. Cassilis this afternoon, Alex," said Matilda.

" Well, I suppose we *ought*, in fact, I suppose we *must*," Alex unwillingly admitted. " We don't want to go, and certainly she doesn't want to see us, and she'll probably be very rude ; but I suppose it must be done."

" Why should she be rude ? " Matilda inquired.

" We're not people of the slightest importance, and we're not rich, and we're friends of Van's, and you're a goose, darling."

" Well, really, Alex, she ought to be pleased to see us. We are near neighbours, and she knows how fond Van was——" Matilda paused for a moment, adding firmly, " How fond Van *is* of all of us, and we of him."

" I'll explain no more. It must be done. It is an odious duty, like so many others. Put on your grey dress, Matilda—you, at least, will look nice."

" Alex, you mustn't go in that old gown."

" Must I not ? Well, perhaps it's foolish. I'll put on my other to please you."

She was woman enough to dress herself with more care than usual.

" All in vain," she remarked, laying down her hand glass, " I'm a haggard object ; but at any rate I'm tidy, and Matilda looks perfectly sweet."

It was a hot walk, in spite of the delicious freshness of the air. They sauntered very slowly up the avenue when they got into the shade. As they came to a spot where a gap had been left by a fallen tree, Alex unconsciously quickened her steps.

" Don't hurry, Alex. Why are you going so fast ? " called Matilda.

Alex walked on ahead. Her cheeks were flaming. " It's so hot," she answered, " I can't go at that snail's pace any longer."

(" Oh Van, do you remember, when you walk down here with your wife ? " she thought to herself, thankful when they had passed the accursed spot.)

Under the great low oak tree in the field where Van had lain so long after their angry parting, the cattle were now standing, taking shelter from the summer heat. The long grass in the park was shimmering like silk, the air was full of dancing insects and the smell of flowering shrubs. As they came up to the door, Alex said hurriedly to Matilda—

" If she's rude, don't stay more than ten minutes."

They were shown into the drawing-room, not into the library, the room that Alex was accustomed to, and there they sat for a long time, yet Mrs. Cassilis did not appear.

" It's just as if we had gone to call on one of the farmers' wives, who was changing her dress upstairs, whilst we waited in the parlour," said Alex, impatiently.

Then Mrs. Cassilis came sauntering past the open windows, her head bare, her hands behind her. She nodded coolly in at the window, saying—

"How d'you do? I'm just coming." And then proceeded to call a dog, and unfasten his collar.

At last she entered by the drawing-room door, shook hands coldly with Matilda and Alex, and sat down still bestowing most of her attention on the dog. Her small round-cheeked face was flushed with health, and her brief skirt very well cut : her shoes exquisitely fitted, and there was the same look of almost animal strength and agility about her that Alex had noticed at first. If there was any difference in her aspect, it showed itself in a sulky expression about the mouth. Alex looked at her hand, saw on it the pearls Van must have given her, and checked her own thoughts with a positive jerk from going any farther. Conversation had been proceeding in a very halting manner between Matilda and the bride, for Mrs. Cassilis interrupted Matilda's remarks every minute with some command or endearment to the dog, and never once looked at either of her visitors as she spoke. Alex did not mind in the least what she did or did not do, but Matilda was getting rather pink and indignant, and was just looking at her sister as a signal that the ten minutes were up, when other visitors appeared. Mrs. Cassilis received them with no better grace. Alex recognized the Misses Brinley and their pretty niece, the Miss Pym upon whom the Admiral's hopes for Van had once been set. Those ladies, who formerly had seemed scarcely aware of Alex or Matilda's existence, were now all graciousness.

They inquired for Mr. Hope. They asked about Matilda's children ; formerly ignorant of their very names, they seemed now, by some occult power, to have become acquainted with all the main facts about the Hope family.

"I expected them to ask if Baby had quite recovered

from mumps, and whether we still had the same cat ! "
Alex said afterwards.

This agreeability was chiefly from the eldest Miss
Brinley. She sat beside Matilda. Young Mrs. Cassilis
was staring at them all in turn, and being very rude to
the younger one, who was gradually but surely ruffling
under the process. Meanwhile, Alex found herself beside
Miss Pym, once more dressed in pink, with a wide hat
trimmed with roses. How the girl had changed though!
The softness was all gone from her face, in spite of her
long eyelashes and her pretty mouth : a little sorrowful
droop of the corners of it seemed to tell a whole story.
Alex noticed how the pretty colour fluttered on her face
and neck, and how she turned her head involuntarily
as some one banged a door in the hall.

" It is Van," thought Alex ; and she looked from one
of the young women to the other. " Oh, Van ! What
a fool you have been ! " she said to herself. She was
glad that Van did not come in, only the Admiral, supported by William, and decidedly nervous and unlike
himself. Mrs. Cassilis paid not the slightest attention
to him. She stared at Alex, who jumped forward to
take his hand, and lead him to a chair. But Alex was
entirely indifferent to her staring. She seated herself
beside the old man, and tried to interest him.

" Have you seen Van since he came home ? " he asked
presently.

" Yes, he came to see us on Monday."

" Ah ! He's gone off to bathe this afternoon, and to
sail in that cockle-shell of his."

" A lovely day. I wish I could go and bathe," said
Alex.

" Yes, yes, a fine day, but rather hot in the sun. I
was out of doors, and feel quite stupid now. I fell asleep
in the sun, and wakened with a start, hearing a carriage
arrive. You're not going away yet, surely ? " he said,
as Alex rose.

Matilda was determined to wait no longer, and said firmly that they must go home. Alex felt quite sad as she took the old man's hot, tremulous hand in hers, to bid him goodbye.

" You can't come at all this week ? " he said pleadingly.

" I'm sorry that it won't be possible this week," Alex replied, hardening her heart again, for she had decided that nothing would make her go on with her reading as long as Van and his wife were there.

" Well, well, of course you have many claims upon your time besides me. You will let me know whenever you are able to come again ? "

Alex hurriedly promised to do so. She looked into Miss Pym's grey eyes as she bid her goodbye, and a quick glance of sympathy passed between them without a spoken word. Then, leaving her and the Misses Brinley, Mrs. Cassilis and the Admiral, an uncongenial group as ever was, Alex and Matilda gladly escaped from the house. As they went down the familiar steps and across the wide space in front of the door Alex heaved a sigh.

" Here endeth a pleasant part of life," she said.

" Oh, I hope not quite *that*," said Matilda. " After all, *Van* is the same, but certainly that woman is disagreeable."

" Bravo, Matilda! It refreshes me to hear you say something severe about some one at last. Yes; isn't she—and hard and coarse and healthy and handsome— and bad ! "

" Oh, Alex, don't. You shouldn't judge people all of a heap like that ! "

" Of course I shouldn't ; but I feel it down to the tips of my fingers. I'm glad Van didn't come in, poor boy. I wonder if he's trying to wash it off this afternoon in that glittering sea——"

" What ? What absurd things you do say, Alex. I don't understand what you mean," said Matilda.

" Don't you, dear ? Very well, I won't explain, but

I think you do. Oh, Matilda, it was a day exactly like this, do you remember, when we went in Van's boat to the Island. I was thinking of it as I came along. How lovely it was, and how long ago it seems now ! "

" It does seem a long time. That was the first day we saw her, too," said Matilda.

" I wonder how often she's kissed that man since."

" Alex," said Matilda, " I can't have you saying such things. It isn't right even to think them. There must have been some explanation of that scene that we don't know. Perhaps she was engaged to that man. Anyway now she is married to Van, we must never speak about it any more, and just forget it." Matilda was very much in earnest, and greatly vexed by her sister's speech.

" Well, dear, I won't mention it again. There *was* an explanation, as you suggest, but a very, very simple one, just one of the elementary natural kind, that good and married people like you decide to ignore, and she was as much engaged to the man in the moon, but she's Van's wife now, as you say. So we'll allude to it no more, only you don't suppose, do you, at your age, that the things one doesn't speak about are the things one forgets ? "

" Sometimes, in time," began Matilda.

Alex laughed. She looked down the avenue before them. At one side was a gap where a tree had fallen, beyond, in the meadow, a great oak with spreading branches, and under it the cattle stood grouped in the shade.

" If there is anything that you have never been able to say to *any one*, Matilda, don't you know that you'll never forget it as long as you live ? Why, the bits of memory that have never even been put into words to one's self are those we'll carry with us into another life, they are the deepest of all experience. Oh, Matilda, surely you know *that*—think ? " Matilda walked on in silence. " Is she ruminating over her vows of love with Peter Chalmers, the dear creature ? " thought Alex. " The moon they saw—or the dawn—or the nightingale they heard—or something—well, I won't try to understand her feelings, for I never can, or could."

Presently Matilda remarked in her quiet way, " I was just wondering, Alex, why Van didn't marry that pretty Miss Pym, instead of that woman ? "

" Those are questions now that will be asked to the end of time. Why don't we all marry the right person at once, and be done with it ? "

" It would be so simple if we only would," said Matilda.

" *Could*, dearest, you have such a confusing way of putting those two words upside down. I've mentioned it to you before," said Alex.

They found the children in high glee on their return over a brood of young ducklings, just hatched by a hen in the back orchard. Even after supper, as the long bright day was drawing to its close, in the evening air laden with the spice of blossoming orchards, the scent of green leaves, and the last cries of the birds, Alex had to take Mike and Baby out to have a cautious peep at the yellow things nearly covered by the hen's outstretched wings.

" Is she just as fond of them as if they were her own ? " they asked, having offered their gifts of crumbs and milk, and withdrawn on tip-toe.

" Fonder, probably, as I am of you though you're not my own ; you're ducks, too, all of you," said Alex, hugging them. She stopped for a minute to look up at the beautiful sky. " Oh, Van, are you just coming back to that woman after a whole day on that magical sea," she said to herself with a sigh, as she followed the children into the house.

CHAPTER XLI

ALEX was not sleepy that night. She sat up late reading beside her father after the children and Matilda had gone to bed. In the quiet house there was not a sound. The scents from the orchard floated in through the open windows. Old Hopeful read, and from time to time nodded over his book. Alex was reading something that interested her deeply. She lifted her head as the clock struck twelve, and half rose from her chair, thinking that she had heard some one walk up to the front door.

" It can't be anything at this hour," she thought, and then laid down her book, for unmistakably some one was now ringing at the door bell. " Father," she said, and Old Hopeful roused himself with a start ; " there's some one at the door. Who can it be so late ? I hope there is nothing wrong."

" Why anticipate evil ? It may be a messenger of joy," said Mr. Hope, laying down his Homer with a smile. No visitor was ever too belated to claim a welcome from him. " I will open the door," he said, so Alex waited, listening as he went along to answer the summons.

She could hear a man's voice asking some questions, and in a minute Old Hopeful returned, looking a little perturbed.

" This is a messenger from Foxe Hall," he said. " It seems, Alex, that our friend Van has not come home to-night. He went off early in the day to sail and bathe from the boat. The Admiral is anxious—young men are rash in boats at times. The Admiral sent to ask if by any chance he was here."

Without a word, only with one expressive gesture of her hand, Alex went to the door to speak to the man.

" When did Mr. Cassilis leave home ? " she asked.

" Just after luncheon, miss ; he had no word of being late—told the Admiral he was going for a sail."

" Mr. Cassilis was not here to-day. I have not even seen him pass, but have you asked at Mr. Maitland's ? He often goes there. Suppose you go and ask if he is there."

" Why, miss, it's a bit late to be knocking people up, isn't it ? " the man asked.

But Alex pointed to the light in Maitland's study window.

" Mr. Maitland always sits up late, he will think nothing of it," she assured him.

The man went off across the Square, and Alex returned to the drawing-room.

" I trust nothing has happened to Van, Father," she said.

Dear Old Hopeful made instant reply. " Never anticipate evil, Alex ; in my long life I have come to see not only how vain it is to do so, but how harmful. It weakens our vital forces when the evil day really comes, which, when all is said and done, is seldom—very seldom."

" Oh, but accidents do happen sometimes," Alex said ; " and it does look strange that he should be so late."

" Hark ! another step on the path ; probably Van himself this time, let us come and welcome him ! " the old man cried, hurrying to the door, his face beaming with delight, and even as he went he read Alex a lesson against idle fears. " See how foolish your terrors were, dear Alex—— " he began, but before the homily had got any further Robert Maitland met them in the hall.

"Alex," he said, "I'm afraid something is wrong. I'm going down to Crossport myself."

"Oh, you don't think——" Alex began.

Her face was suddenly whitened. A thought that seemed too horrible to entertain had leapt into her mind.

"I don't think anything; but fear somehow—that boat of his was a very risky one," said Maitland.

"Ah, my dear Robert," said Old Hopeful, laying a detaining hand on Maitland's arm, "I have just been telling Alex not to anticipate evil, and now I think you need the same lesson."

"I hope you may be right, sir, most earnestly I hope it," said Maitland, listening, as he always did, with the greatest respect to the old man's words. "But you should not stand at the door so late at night, should you?" he suggested.

"Well, well, perhaps with this tiresome tendency to bronchial trouble——" Old Hopeful admitted, and at the word "bronchial" Alex drove him back into the drawing-room laughing.

She stood holding the door, so that he might be securely imprisoned.

"Alex," Maitland said, standing close beside her in the dark passage, and speaking in a very low voice, "did you see Van the other morning?"

"Yes."

"What did you think?"

"Oh, changed—changed horribly and utterly," she said.

"Yes. That is what makes me anxious about him. Look here, Alex, if there should be anything wrong—if there has been an accident, I'll send Purves up from the inn at Crossport with a message to you—better than sending it straight to the Admiral—you understand?"

"Yes; but oh, surely——"

"I may be altogether mistaken, but I can't rest here.

I'll drive down now, as soon as I can. Goodbye, just now."

He turned away, and Alex closed the door after him and returned to her father.

" I can't go to bed, Father," she said. " I know you'll say I'm absurdly anxious, but I'd rather sit up, or lie down on the sofa at least, and then if any one did come, I'd be ready in a moment. You go to bed like a dear and sleep, and perhaps in the cheerful morning we'll laugh together over these fears."

" I feel sure that we shall, Alex. And I am somewhat fatigued now, so will take your advice and go to bed. See that you do not take a chill—the old railway rug, my friend in a hundred journeys, lies on the study sofa; wrap yourself in it my dear, and forget your gloomy fears in sleep."

" Bless his cheerful heart ! " Alex ejaculated, as the door closed after him a few minutes later.

Tired as he was, he had trailed away to the study for the friend of a hundred journeys, and was not content till he had himself wrapped its almost tattered folds round Alex as she lay on the sofa.

For hours Alex could not sleep. She imagined all manner of sounds, footsteps, knocks, sighs, and once—but she must have been asleep for a minute—could have sworn that Dolly Orranmore's whistle blew out in the Square again.

She jumped up and drew the blinds to look out. No, not a soul was there. The dim light was beginning to break now. How strange the Square looked in the unearthly stillness of early morning. The only sign of life was a rabbit that had strayed in, and was moving with little bumping jumps across the cobble stones, stopping here and there to nibble a dandelion leaf, or a blade of grass that had struggled up between the stones. Alex stood by the window and watched its slow progress across the Square, and said to herself, that she wouldn't have believed a rabbit could look ghostly if she had been told so.

Then through the stillness she heard a horse come galloping up the street. It emerged in the dim light and turned sharply at the corner, and came towards Orchard House—a great gaunt old horse, that Alex knew well by sight. Long ago she had christened it the Death Horse from some fancied resemblance to the Pale Horse in the Book of Revelation. It belonged to the innkeeper at Crossport and had been almost jobbed to death, but could still break into a sort of desperate gallop, as if it would say, " I may die, but I'll gallop to the last."

Alex knew its loping paces well. How its hoofs clattered on the cobbles as the rider brought it across the Square now! Alex ran to the door and the man dismounted and handed her a note. But he could not forego the joy which lies so near the heart of every Scotchman, the joy of announcing a calamity. Nor did he in aught extenuate—

" Maister Cassilis is drooned," he announced. " They got the boat keel up in the bay, the tide was comin' in ye ken, an' he jist driftit in as ye micht say."

Alex stood holding on to the door post. Everything seemed to whirl round and round.

" How terrible ! " she repeated dully over and over again, and the man agreed in the matter-of-fact manner of his kind.

" It is that, miss," he said.

Then Alex opened Maitland's letter and read his instructions.

" It is as I feared and poor Van is gone. They have found his body, and it is lying now in one of the cottages. It will be nearly morning when you get this, send Purves to the inn for a carriage and drive up yourself to Foxe Hall, and tell the poor old man. It is kinder not to keep him in suspense any longer than is necessary. He will wish to come here. I will have everything done that is possible before he comes.

> " Bless you, Alex,
> " ROBERT."

Alex did not shrink for a moment from the task. She sent Purves for the carriage and went upstairs to waken Matilda, and tell her the terrible news. She told it calmly, and wondered at the easy tears that gushed from Matilda's eyes.

" I don't feel as if I could cry about it Matilda," she said, " d'you know I feel almost thankful. He made a ghastly mistake, and he knew it—he knew more than any of us will ever know."

" Oh, Alex, what do you mean ? "

" Don't ask me, Matilda. I've all manner of suspicions in my mind about that woman. She had her own ends in view in marrying Van."

" Perhaps she loved him," Matilda suggested, anxious always to take the bright side.

" Loved him ! Oh, my dear, *that* wasn't the reason she married him ; but whatever it was *he found it out*—that I'm tolerably certain of."

Alex got up from her seat on the edge of Matilda's bed, and began to tidy her hair and arrange her dress.

" The carriage will be here immediately," she said.

Long shafts of light were pouring across the land now, and the soft dusk of the spring night was nearly gone ; but an intense quiet brooded over the sleeping village still.

At last a rumble of wheels came along the street, and the old gig from the inn drew up before the door. Alex ran downstairs and climbed into the vehicle with a word or two to the driver. He would have liked to speak of the tragedy that was taking them both out at such an unwonted hour, but Alex had no heart for speech. Every turn of the road had some memory to her of the man who was gone.

How many and many a time they had walked down
these roads together in rain or shine! The familiar ways
seemed curiously different at this hour. The morning dew
lay white along the roadsides and revealed hundreds of
tiny dew-spangled spiders' webs, unseen by day. Whole
families of rabbits were squatting on the roads or feeding
by their edges, all the shadows were turned the wrong way,
and the light came from low down instead of high up.
Yes, everything was strange and unusual and unfamiliar,
and, strangest of all, this knowledge that Van, so lately
a part of the little Crossriggs world, had left it for ever.
The gig lumbered up the avenue. They passed a spot
where there was a gap between the trees. Alex leant
forward, pressing her hand against her heart, looking
at the place. Under the great low oak tree the grass
was heavy with the morning dew.

" Just here we quarrelled," Alex thought. It seemed
as if she should see Van standing there.

Then they came in sight of the house. All the blinds
were down except those in the library, but the household
apparently was not asleep, for the door was opened before
the gig had quite drawn up at the steps, and the man-
servant came out to help Alex to alight as if he had
expected her.

" I'm afraid there's bad news, Miss Hope," he said.

" Yes, David ; can I see the Admiral ? Mr. Maitland
has sent me up to tell him—Mr. Cassilis was drowned last
night."

" Eh, dear, dear ! "

The man stood holding the door open for Alex, and
poured out a stream of questions, the half of which she
could not answer. She glanced round the well-known
hall, where poor Van's coats and caps were lying, and the
sight of these everyday things brought the tears rushing to
her eyes. Then the library door opened, and the Admiral
came out, feeling his way through the hall. He had heard
the sound of wheels outside and could wait no longer.

" Is that you, Van, at last ?   You have alarmed me
by your absence," he said, as he came slowly forward to
where Alex stood.   She could not speak for a moment,
and the butler turned away with a muttered exclamation
of " Eh, poor man ! " that would have sorely grated on
the Admiral's dignity if he had heard it, but he did not.
Then Alex gulped down her tears, and spoke at last.

" It is not Van," she said.   " I have come up to tell
you about him.   Let me give you my arm back into the
library."

The old man caught the sound of tears in her voice.
" Ah, Miss Hope ! " he exclaimed.   " Why are you
here ?   There's something wrong, what have you come
to tell me ? "

She led him gently back to his chair and, closing the
door, knelt down beside him and took his hand in hers.
The tears she could not shed before came running down
now on the poor old hand she held, and she scarcely
needed to speak.

" He is gone, that's what you've come to tell me ? "
the Admiral said.   " Oh, Miss Hope, and I did not always
get on with him ! "

" Forget that now," she said.

" Tell me how it happened ?   How did you hear ? "

" I had a note from Mr. Maitland.   He went down to
Crossport late.   Van must have taken cramp when he was
bathing.   The water is cold still."

" Yes, the water is cold," said the old man.   He
drummed nervously with his fingers on the arm of his
chair, then faced round again towards Alex, making a
great effort to control the pitiful working of his face.
" Have they found—him ? "

" Yes."

There was silence for a moment.   " I must go down—
I must go down myself and see——" he began.   Then he
suddenly asked, " Did the boat capsize ? "

" I don't know.   Mr. Maitland didn't say—I will read

you all he says about it." She took Maitland's hurried
note and read it aloud, the Admiral listening in silence.

Then he turned again to Alex.   " It sometimes happens
to the strongest swimmers—he shouldn't have gone into
the water after a long walk on a hot day—it often happens——"   There was in his expression something that
seemed to say, " Do you know what I mean ?   What I
would say if I had the heart to say it ? "   Alex knew.
She laid her hand on his in silence.   The Admiral gave
a great sob, then straightened himself, half-rising in his
chair : " I am old and blind and deaf, but I am a man of
the world still, Miss Hope," he said, with a shadow of his
old pride that almost made Alex smile.   " I know life—
and I know—I know—this marriage——"   He paused.

" I know, I saw it.   I saw him once—the other morning," Alex cried.

" Was he changed ?   Did he look different in any
way ? " the Admiral asked.   " For every word he said to
me I felt an intangible change had come over him.   How
did he look yesterday when you saw him ? "

" Older," said Alex.   She would not say more.

" Aye, older, but that was not it——"   The Admiral
seemed to grope about in search of some impression which
eluded his not over subtle perceptions.   Alex could have
enlightened him, but she held her peace.

Then, being very far from " himself again," as he had
thought, the poor old man broke down suddenly into
womanish sobs which he could not restrain, and Alex sat
and wept beside him.   At last he pulled himself together
and tried to explain his weakness.

" I am an old man now, and I have been sitting up all
night.   Time was when I had nerves of steel—but those
days are gone, gone with many another thing—my youth
and my strength, and my sight—and now my poor boy,
the last link I had with life.   What is left to me ? "   It was,
indeed, one of those questions—those staggering questions
—that it seems cruel to answer truthfully.   Life surely

could have little value left for the poor man now.   Even
Alex's ready tongue was silent, she found nothing to reply.

"Where is Mrs. Cassilis?" she asked, to change the
subject, and the Admiral groaned.

"Asleep, I fancy. She laughed at my anxiety last
night, and went to bed as usual."

"Oh!"

"Miss Hope, will you go and tell her?" the Admiral
asked.   "Perhaps I should not require such a painful
task from you—you have been kind enough already—
but I shrink from it myself."

Alex hesitated for a moment. The intense repulsion
she felt from Dolly Cassilis made it difficult to face such
a scene with her.   But, after all, it was easier for her to
do it than the Admiral.

"Yes, certainly.   Shall I ring for David?"   Alex rose
and went out into the hall as she spoke, and David, after
some delay, produced a sulky looking French maid to take
her up to Mrs. Cassilis' room.   She followed the woman
up the broad staircase through the morning silence of the
house.   Even as the maid opened the door and went in,
Alex, standing on the threshold, smelt a waft of the scent
of carnations that she had always associated with Dolly
Cassilis.   It swept into the fresh air of the dawning day,
that filled the corridors from the open door downstairs.
Alex bit her lips as she stood in the doorway.

"Madame is still asleep," said the maid in a whisper,
returning on tip-toe.

"Well, she must be wakened," said Alex, pausing no
longer, but stepping into the room.

"Madame will not be pleased," began the woman, but
Alex pushed her aside with an imperative gesture, and
advanced towards the bed.

The light, or perhaps the unusual sounds downstairs,
seemed, however, to have awakened Mrs. Cassilis already.
There was no sound of sleep in her voice.

"Is that you at last, Van?   What on earth have you

been doing?   We all thought you were drowned!" she
said, from behind the bed-curtains.   Alex closed the
door, came forward into the room, and held back the
curtain.

"It is not your husband, Mrs. Cassilis," she said.

Dolly was lying high up on her pillows, all her long hair
falling across them.   The nightdress she wore was un-
fastened at the throat, and fell open across her breast;
she made no attempt to cover herself from the eye of
a stranger.

"Why, what has brought you here at this hour, Miss
Hope?" she demanded, sitting up in bed and rubbing
her eyes with her knuckles to make sure that Alex was
not a dream.

"I have brought very sad news to you," Alex said,
as gently as she could.   "There has been an accident,
Mrs. Cassilis."

"An accident?   What?   Where?" said the young
woman, now opening her round eyes wide, but her colour
did not flutter, and there was no agitation in her voice.

Alex advanced and laid her hand on Dolly's arm, round,
firm-fleshed, and bare, where the sleeve of her nightdress had fallen back.

"It is your husband—Van—who has been——"   She
paused one moment before adding the word "drowned."

Then Mrs. Cassilis did grow pale, grew quite white for
a moment, and uttered a sort of cry that she choked with
her hand.

"Drowned!" she gasped, sitting forward and clutching at Alex convulsively.   "Van drowned?   Did he
upset the boat?   What happened?   Oh, perhaps it's
not true!" she cried, suddenly flinging herself back on
the pillows, and turning on one side, crammed the sheets
about her head like a child who hides from something
that affrights it.   Alex knelt down and put her arm
about her.

"Yes, my poor girl, I'm afraid it's true—they have

found him—he must have taken cramp when he was bathing. I'm afraid there is no hope at all——" She paused, for she did not know what to say or do. Somehow the words of sympathy and comfort were dried upon her lips. She looked at the woman, who lay still, with her face buried in the pillows, and she wondered at herself because her heart was not rent with pity, but she had nothing to say.

After a few minutes Mrs. Cassilis raised her head: her eyes were dry, but there was an expression in them of mingled terror and defiance. She pushed the heavy hair impatiently away from her face with her little, thick, strong hands. Then she began to pour out a string of questions and comments. How had it happened? How had Alex heard it? Who had found Van's body? Where? Had the boat been upset? Had the Admiral been told? To all of which Alex answered briefly; she had very little to tell, and marvelled at the extraordinary callousness of the nature that could receive such news in such a manner.

"And do you know I believe the worst of it is——" Mrs. Cassilis began, after a short silence, turning her face, now feverishly flushed, towards Alex, and twisting her wedding-ring round on her finger as she spoke. "I believe that I'm going to have a child—it's most unfortunate——" She paused, arrested by the expression on her listener's face. Alex had caught hold of the rail of the bed and gripped it hard, holding herself so straight that she seemed to tower up above Dolly, and for the moment her eyes positively blazed with anger.

"The worst of it—most unfortunate," she said, repeating the words very slowly, with such a world of scorn in her voice that the other woman quailed before it. "Oh, Mrs. Cassilis! You make me ashamed that I am a woman too; indeed, if you feel like that, it *is* most unfortunate for yourself, and ten times more unfortunate for the child." She turned away and walked to the open window, and stood staring out, tears of anger in her eyes; and in her heart an echo of the final words which she had checked whilst they were on her lips : " Fortunate indeed for my poor Van, who has got away from it all now." Out of doors the light had broadened fully—light of an early summer morning, fair and full of joy. The windows of the room looked into the garden, and as she stood gazing out Alex saw, with a quick pang at her heart, the straight path between two borders all gay with flowers that led up to the great yew tree. The black bulk of it rose up in the distance, sombre even in the humming, flower-scented, early dawn, like some great sad fact unalterable in the midst of life. She remembered how she had stood under its branches that day with Van, how his face had seemed to her to look so pale and strange,—" As if under water," she remembered. Drying the tears from her eyes, she turned round again to Van's wife, who was lying now with her face flung against the pillow, as she had done before. " I must be patient; how awful it all is," thought Alex, and she bent down and touched her.

Dolly lifted up her face. " I say," she began, in a hurried whisper, " don't, please, say anything to any one about what I told you just now; it's perhaps not going to happen, I may be mistaken."

Alex stood still, and they looked at each other steadily. Then Dolly's eyelids fell, her lips quivered, and tears began to drop upon her hands. Alex drew a long breath.

" I will tell no one what you have said. I hope, on all accounts, that it is not true." She paused and then said, " I am going now. Is there anything I can do for you ? "

Dolly shook her head.

" The Admiral wished to go down to Crossport at once," said Alex. " I am going with him. You,"— she looked at Dolly and added—" you would rather not go just now ? "

" I can do nothing," Mrs. Cassilis said.

" You could do nothing ? " Alex repeated. She gave one more glance about the room, and shuddered with sudden cold, as if a chill had struck her.

"Will you send my maid? I must get up," said Dolly.

Alex went to the door, and found the maid lingering in the passage, talking in whispers with the house-maids.

" Mrs. Cassilis wishes you to go to her at once," she said, and she thought she could hear a sudden torrent of talk from Dolly, as the woman slipped in at the half-open door.

" Van, Van, my poor boy !" said Alex, to herself, as she crossed the empty hall and went back to the library. She was angry no longer with the woman she had left ; a fierce unreasonable resentment at the universal plan was burning at her heart.

" That the very badness and rottenness of her should give her the privilege of creating a new creature ! Where's the sense, or the justice, or the order of that ? Oh, my poor Van is happy—did he know this ? I don't be-lieve——" She stopped herself suddenly, saying, " Per-haps I do her injustice."

The Admiral was sitting as she had left him. He did not hear her come in, and she had to speak to him twice before he realized what she was saying. Then he started up, holding out a groping hand.

" I must go. Will you order the carriage ? I must go at once. You said you would come, too, Miss Hope —I—my blindness makes it difficult for me to arrange things."

" Yes, yes," said Alex, holding his hand, " I will come with you, of course ; but I have asked David to bring you a cup of tea first, before you go out. You must eat something before you start. May I ring now ? "

The old man protested that he was quite fit to go at

once, but Alex coaxed him to drink the tea and eat a morsel of bread before they set out.

"Well, you have told her?" he asked, when the servants had withdrawn.

Alex briefly told him of her interview with Dolly. "She was much excited, of course," she said, "but after a time she grew more composed, and I left her."

The Admiral listened in perfect silence. Then he got up saying—

"I am able to go now—let us go."

He leant on Alex's arm as they went down the steps, and he sat holding her hand in silence as they drove away out into the broad sunshine of the morning.

CHAPTER XLII

It was nearly six o'clock when they drove through Crossport. The early housewives were already busy in the little houses, and a group of people, attracted by news of the accident, stood about the harbour as the Admiral and Alex alighted.

Maitland met them and gave his arm to the old man. "Are you able to come now?" he asked.

The Admiral straightened himself. "Yes, yes—which way?"

"They carried him in here," said Maitland, turning towards a shed close to the harbour wall. "Alex, you had better wait outside."

The Admiral put out his hand. "Where are you, Miss Hope?" he said, "you will come too?"

"Oh, yes, yes," said Alex. She did not know quite what she was prepared to see, and did not pay any attention to Maitland's glance of warning, but stepped after them into the shed.

The Admiral was trembling, but held his head erect, only he could not walk as straight as usual, and kept blundering from side to side, first against the wall of the passage, then against the doorpost. He stopped for a moment, and disengaged his hand from Maitland's arm.

"Where is he? Where is he?" he muttered.

The room was small and whitewashed, dazzlingly bright for the window was a skylight, and the sun streamed down upon the rough table where the drowned man had been laid.

One of the men who had carried up the body stood beside it, and as the Admiral spoke he came forward, saying—

"Here, sir, step this way; mind the corner of the table."

Maitland guided him forward, Alex following a step behind. The Admiral stretched out his hand and felt the sheet that covered the body.

"We laid him here, sir," said the fisherman, "just as we found him."

He threw back the sheet, leaving the young man's body half uncovered, and guided the Admiral's trembling hands towards the face. Then they were all silent.

Van lay on one side, with his head slightly thrown back. The water had washed the lock of hair away from his forehead: there was no mark or stain upon it; a half smile played upon his parted lips, the smile of a sleeper in a happy dream.

Slowly, very slowly, the old man felt over face and head, shoulders and breast, passing his hand down the long limbs, and laying it for a moment against the motionless heart.

"Van, yes—yes—my boy," he muttered.

Maitland looked at Alex, noticing the quick shiver she had given at first, and how she had averted her head, with a moment's embarrassment, before the uncovered body, as if she could not look again.

"What's that in his hand?" asked the Admiral, suddenly, and Alex raised her face, darting one glance of entreaty at Maitland that he could not understand.

The drowned man's right arm lay out along the edge of the table, the rigid muscles tense, the strong hand still clasping a little leathern case.

"It's a little pocket-book or something, sir," said Maitland. "Shall we leave it there?"

" No, no. I want to see it."

Alex bent towards the Admiral. She had a lovely voice, even half choked with tears.

" He holds it very closely," she said. " Let us leave it in his hand, it will hurt him to take it away."

" Well, leave it—leave it—what does it matter now ! " said the old man. He straightened himself suddenly and, signing with an imperious little gesture that was habitual to him, he said sharply, " Cover the body again." He turned and held out his hand to Maitland, " Now take me back to the carriage, and tell the man to speak to me at the door."

Maitland and the other man went out along with him, and Alex, while they spoke together, was left in the shed for a few minutes alone. When Maitland came back to fetch her, she was not crying, only standing looking down at Van's face with her hands clasped in an attitude of piteous, almost childish, distress.

Maitland came and stood beside her, then repeated slowly—

" ' Many prophets and righteous men have desired to see the things which ye see and have not seen them, and to hear those things which ye hear and have not heard them,' " and he looked half enviously at the still face.

Suddenly Alex broke out with a sharp, sobbing cry, and caught hold of his arm.

" Oh, what can I do ? I cannot bear it, I don't know what to do. See here——" She turned the sheet down and pointed to the little case. " It's mine," she sobbed. " He got it once, long ago."

" Let him keep it then," said Maitland, almost sternly. He looked at her, and made no movement.

" Oh, but I cannot—I cannot." Alex raised her face, looking at him wildly. " Think of what—his wife would say, if she knew—if she opened it. I persuaded the Admiral to leave it there. What shall I do ? "

Maitland hesitated for an instant, then took her by the

shoulders, and gently turned her away. He knelt down beside the table, and a minute afterwards came up to her holding the little case.

"Take the picture out yourself, Alex. Then put this back again, and no one will ever know."

Alex tore the picture from its setting, and thrust it into the bosom of her dress. All stained with water it was now, a shabby little photograph at the best. She remembered how Van got possession of it against her will, and had laughed at her annoyance. She took the empty case, and kneeling down, with some difficulty forced it back again between the stiffened fingers.

"Forgive me, Van; forgive me, please," she sobbed, half aloud, and then she rose.

All her passionate heart was visible in her face, as she stood between the dead man that had loved her, and the man she loved. Then a sudden reeling faintness overcame her, and before Maitland could catch her, she sank upon the ground. When she came to herself again, she was lying in a cottage with Maitland and some woman bending over her. Through the open doorway, she saw a strip of sandy road, and the twinkling, dancing sea. She drank a mouthful of water and sat up.

"I'm better now—I'm all right," she said; then, remembering what had happened, she tried to rise to her feet. "Where is the Admiral? We ought to go now."

"No, no, you are not able to move yet; sit still for a little while, and I will come back. Mrs. Wilson will look after you," said Maitland, and Alex, feeling the faintness swim over her again, leant back her head, and closed her eyes once more.

The woman, seeing that she was better, moved away to attend to the fire. Maitland had gone out. Alex lay still with closed eyes for some time, then feeling her head clear again, she sat up, looking vaguely out at the square of sunlight made by the open door. Suddenly, the space of roadway was filled by a group of figures. At first, she scarcely realized what it was—four men, walking very steadily, carrying something between them, Maitland walking alongside, directing them where to go. It was all past in a moment; the solemn little procession had marched across the yard of sunshine that she saw through the open doorway, then had disappeared as if it had passed across a stage.

Alex sprang to her feet with a cry, hiding her face in her hands: the woman ran to the door to look out, and then Alex heard the pattering feet of children running to see what was going on. It seemed a very long time until Maitland came in and touched her arm.

"We are ready to go now," he said. "Will you drive up with me? The Admiral wished to go alone."

Alex followed him out into the blinding sunshine, scarcely seeing the ground before her. A knot of the villagers moved aside to let them enter the carriage. As they drove away she looked back once more at the little harbour, so blithe with its boats and glistening water. An old man in a blue jacket, who was propped upon two sticks, stood by the harbour wall, and watched them pass. She remembered in an instant how he had stood there that bright day two years ago, when Van had sailed with her; how the young man had sprung past him up the steps, and how she had winced at the contrast between them. Here he was, still alive, dragging through the last months of his disease, and they had carried Van's body past him in the morning sunshine half an hour before.

"May I get out and walk home?" said Alex to Maitland, before they came in sight of Crossriggs. "I think it would do me good to walk for a little."

He stopped the carriage, and they both got out and walked slowly together, side by side, in silence, until it was out of sight. Above them the hot sun poured down upon the green world. There seemed an exuberance of summer joy in the air that morning. The road was long and slighty up-hill, and Alex began to feel strangely tired.

"You go on," she said. "I will rest a little here before climbing the hill."

There was an open gate in one of the hedges, and she went in and sat down on the bank in the shade. It was a high, sloping bank, and all along the top grew a row of tall red foxgloves. Maitland would not go on alone, and sat down beside her, making no attempt at consolation, though Alex had hidden her face in her hands, and was sobbing aloud. The foxgloves were surrounded with bees, that buzzed into the red hoods, and then tumbled out again and flew humming away. He sat watching them, now and then looking at Alex, sitting there, still he did not speak a word. At last she raised her head and caught an expression in his face—a look that made her rise in sudden terror.

He started up, but before he took her in his arms, Alex pressed her hands against his breast.

"Don't—oh, don't," she said, looking at him now with a white face and trembling as she spoke. "You'll never forgive yourself, nor will I; won't you help me, dearest?"

He gazed at her for a moment; his hands were on her shoulders, and her face was very near his lips. Then he drew himself away, and turned from her without a word.

"Go, go now. Tell Matilda I will come presently," said Alex; and Maitland walked away.

She watched him till he was out of sight. Then she sat down again, and looked vaguely about the green field, at the shining woods in the distance, at the long row of foxgloves with their secretive red hoods, haunted by the bees. What a fair world! And everything made beautiful there by the fulfilling of its own nature. She looked beyond the fields northwards towards the sea in the direction of Crossport. A bank of wood hid the village from her sight, a wood sloping curiously at its outer edges, where the trees were dense. Those outer trees—Alex had seen them so often—were shaped almost flat on the top by the searing gales. They were twisted, and stunted, and bent out of the shape of beauty, contending always with their winds. Trees in more sheltered places grew and threw themselves out into lovely forms.

Would bitter experience, denial of all that her impulses craved, her constant struggle, so thwart and impoverish her in time ? Ah ! why were not easier places hers, a less high moral attitude, on a lower level ? She thought of Maitland's face. She felt again his hands upon her shoulders . . . might they not have had just a moment of forgetfulness of everything except one another ? Was it at all worth while ? The excitement of last night and the morning had strung her nerves to the cracking point, and she felt as if she did not want to have a hold upon herself any longer. Her head swam, as she rose up in the hot sunshine and vaguely heard the bees humming in the foxgloves, busy, so busy, on their little errands, never noticing the mortal who stood there, looking at them from her other world of consciousness.

" Why did I send him away ? *Why did he go ?* " she thought passionately. " Van kissed me once—— " Then she paused, and stood still, looking down at the green grass, a sudden blinding misery beating all about her, as if the whole world were growing dark. " *He doesn't care enough.*" After all, he was wise who said—

" Oaths are straw to fire i' the blood."

" He doesn't care, he doesn't really care," she said half aloud.

Yet even as she said the words she denied them in her heart. No one has tried, even feebly, to keep the right way, and in a moment has been lost. She moved forward mechanically, taking the road home, walking slowly, scarcely conscious where she was going—life, as she looked into the future, seemed to stretch like that before her—a long, empty, and up-hill road.

Matilda was quite frightened when she saw how Alex looked as she came in.

"Oh, dear, this has all been too much for you, Alex," she cried. "You should never have gone."

It was still early in the forenoon, and the familiar household life seemed all strange to Alex, as she entered the house. Dinner being cooked, letters written, children playing in the garden, her sister moving about as usual. Why on earth should people concern themselves about trifles of living? All, for the moment—with the shock of death and passion still upon her—struck her as being minute, and far, far away from herself, like the industry of the bees, as she had watched them busy in the foxglove hoods. She stood looking vaguely about the room.

"Nothing seems quite real again yet, Matty," she said. "I'll go upstairs, and rest for a little now."

She lay still for a long time, listening to the absurd far-away sounds in the house, and, after a while, she fell into a deep sleep. Twice Matilda looked into the room and found her still asleep : when she awoke, the sun was in the west.

Alex made a note in her diary, as she sat up late that night—

". . . Then I went down with the Admiral, and we saw Van—the water had washed the lock of hair back from his forehead. There was no mark or stain upon it, and *when I saw his face I was ' in love with Death ! '* "

But she wrote no word about her morning in the sunny field !

CHAPTER XLIII

THEY buried Van on the little knoll where three pine trees stood, in the new part of the churchyard. Young Mrs. Cassilis, at first reported to be overcome with grief, left Foxe Hall soon after the funeral, and went to her own people. So, in a few days almost, it was all over—the brief life and sudden death: the whole house changed and silent; only the empty rooms with their boyish pictures and trophies (that the blind man could not see), Van's dogs wondering where their master was, and the grave on the side of the hill.

Alex went up to Foxe Hall one day, meaning to read as usual. But she only sat and listened to the Admiral's broken talk about Van. She made a few inquiries about Mrs. Cassilis, half afraid to trust her own voice to do so, then, heavy at heart, she bid the old man goodbye.

" I won't see you again for some time," she said, " for I am going away from home."

" Ah, I'm sorry to hear that, you are the only comfort that is left to me, Miss Hope," he said, rising formally to bid her goodbye. " Are you to be away for long ? "

" I'm not quite sure how long as yet, but I will write to you, and I will very often think of you," she answered.

Van's dogs came snuffing about her as she left the house, eager to follow her down to the gate. She could not bear to look at them, and her voice choked as she tried to call their names. It seemed cruel to leave the old man, sitting uncomforted in his long darkness, and it wrung her heart to tell him that she was not coming back. But Alex had decided that she must leave Crossriggs.

" I must get away—I must, I must, or I do not know what will happen," she said to herself the day after Van's funeral.

There comes a time in a monotonous life led in a small place when it simply can be borne no longer, when a break of some kind must be made unless the heart fails altogether. The quiet Square, the round of her home duties, had become to Alex like the walls of a dungeon, from which she must escape or die.

" Go, I must," she had thought, " but where to go and what reason to assign for going is more than I can conceive."

Matilda, for all her sweetness, was not an understanding person. She always needed to have things " explained " before she took them up. " Whereas," Alex used to say to herself, " it almost spoils my grasp of any situation to have it explained. The instinctive, blind plunge I make towards apprehension serves me much better than any amount of words." No, shocked and saddened as she too had been by Van's death, Matilda could not be expected to understand why Crossriggs had suddenly become unendurable to her sister.

" I might say mildly that I felt in need of a change, and Heaven knows that would be true ! " Alex pursued, looking at her thin cheeks reflected in the dim little glass in her bedroom. " I might say that, but then that's just the last reason I'd ever give *naturally*, and she would know that—and then, if I went away, it would mean giving up all my school work, and my readings, and how in all the world should we get on without the money ? " She sighed in perplexity, there seemed no doorway of escape.

But, as occasionally happens, help came to Alex in a most natural and prosaic way.

" A letter from Liverpool to you," Matilda said that same morning of Alex's perplexities, handing the letter across the table to her sister.

" Doesn't it smell of money? That sort of thick writing-paper made of linen rags because cotton ones aren't expensive enough," said Alex, as she broke the seal. She read the letter once, then turned back to the beginning and read it over again before she spoke.

" The Aunt has been ill, it appears," she said, after a minute's silence, " ' not seriously, but gravely ' (a fine distinction), feels ' her social duties a burden,' and is ' unable for the busy life of Liverpool,' in short, she wants one of us to come and be ' companion ' for a little, and she bribes us, she offers us money."

" Alex ! "

" Well, it's a straight deal enough ; she knows I earn money for the family, and that you run the house-keeping, and so she has to bribe either of us to make it worth our while to leave home. She thinks us worth paying for, that's all."

Matilda was almost offended by the suggestion that she might care to accept the Auntly offer.

" The poor woman has never had children of her own, so she, perhaps, can't be expected to know, but how *could* she think that I would leave my family and go to look after her ! " she said.

" Quite true, O indignant matron ! but perhaps I'm not so important. I almost think I'll go. Seriously, Matilda, I've been feeling rather played out of late— these lessons and readings have been too much for me. I've been feeling—oh, may you never know the feeling, my dear !—' all to pieces ' expresses tolerably what I mean."

And Alex suddenly began to cry—a sight so unusual that Matilda ran to her and flung her arms round her.

" Oh, Alex dearest, you never told me ! You've been working yourself to death for me and the children, and

I never guessed it. Oh, how could I be so horrible and so blind ! "

But Alex mopped up her tears and smiled. " D'you remember the bit in the Psalms where ' he said Tush ' comes in ? That's what must be said to you, Matilda— Tush, tush ! Don't be alarmed by a few tears. I'm all right, only a bit ' run down ' (that mysteriously easy process), and Van's death gave me such a shock. I want a change to help me to get over it. I'll accept the Auntly offer and go to Liverpool."

" What *would* you do with yourself ?　Remember what I suffered there long ago, and you're much more impatient than I am," Matilda said.

" Oh, I'll roll about in the Auntly carriage, and munch up the Auntly foods for a month or two without even a random thought turned in the direction of the butcher's book ; perhaps I'll come back to you as fat as the Aunt herself."

" It will be horribly dull for you, Alex," Matilda objected.

" I believe dulness will be beneficial to me just now ; vegetating, soulless nutrition, with no thought of ways and means, that's the sort of rest I need."

She jested on, but Matilda, watching her with newly awakened anxiety, could not join in these jokes. The instinctive selfishness of maternity had been too strong for Matilda ; in her intense desire that her children should have everything they needed, she had sacrificed Alex without realizing that she was doing anything unkind. Now that her eyes were opened she was overwhelmed with self-reproach and dismay.

" Oh, Alex, mothers are the most selfish creatures in the world ! " she exclaimed.

" Dear Matilda, how can you say anything so unorthodox ? I wonder how many sermons we have all heard about the unselfishness of maternity ! " said Alex, with an irrepressible smile at the corners of her mouth.

Matilda looked up quickly, and Alex added the next minute, "And so you are, dearest, you never think of yourself from one year's end to another."

Matilda crumpled her smooth white brow with a moment of intense thought, which made her at last arrive at the truth.

"That may be so, Alex, but then I haven't thought about *you* either, and that was only another form of selfishness, whatever you say to justify me."

This was incontrovertible, and Alex, feeling that it was, closed the discussion by sitting down there and then to accept the Auntly offer, with as good a grace as she could muster.

They had many consultations after this upon the grave question of Alex's wardrobe. For dresses that were good enough for Crossriggs were by no means good enough for Liverpool. It is ill work worrying about clothes when sick at heart, and with little money to spend, and Matilda was several times grieved and surprised by Alex taking a paroxysm of nervous crossness that was very unlike her usual temper.

"She really does need a change," she thought; "and even going to Aunt Clara's will be better than nothing."

"It's like my unromantic lot," sighed Alex, "that Providence should send me the chance I wanted, in such a singularly uninteresting form : a fat, heavy, and familiar hand opens *my* door of escape—no angel's hand there. But it *is* opened, though only on the road to Liverpool, and I'm glad to go."

She found it increasingly difficult to maintain outwardly her ordinary relations with the Maitlands. People who know each other very well are so terribly apt to notice a change in one's manner, a change in one's voice even, and when she and Robert met now, they averted their eyes from one another, rather like acquaintances who disagreed than like old friends.

"I'm afraid Alex is fickle about some things," thought

Matilda. " There was that quarrel she had with poor Van, and now she and Mr. Maitland seem so cold to one another, almost as if she had quarrelled with him, too."

" I told you I would go. I am going, you see," said Alex in a low voice, when she found herself alone with Maitland the day before she left home. They were standing by the Manse door. Alex had bidden good-bye to Laura and Aunt E. V., and Maitland had come with her to the door. " It's easier for me to go," she went on, not looking at him as she spoke. " I want to—I must—I should die, if I lived on here much longer just now."

" Dying is not the difficulty, it's living sometimes," Maitland answered.

Alex held out her hand. " Good-bye then, I'll hear from Matilda about you all. Good-bye."

She hurried off, without looking again, and he turned away silently into the house.

The children were disposed to be tearful at the loss of Alex, and she had to cheer them up with many promises of letters to each in turn. Now that her boxes were all packed, and everything ready, even Liverpool seemed less distasteful to her. She was going to sail from Glasgow, just for the pleasure of the thing, for all her life she had had a passion for the sea that was seldom gratified.

" Father and I would like to go round the world," she used to say, " and then begin and go round it again, I think."

" I have a questing soul," said Old Hopeful, " I would fain see more of this world, our goodly heritage ; of late years life has been more restricted in its area ; but ' whatever is, is best.' We learn our lessons, if our hearts are earnest, just as well in the little school of a village like Crossriggs."

" Well, I'm about to learn some lessons in the little school of Aunt Clara's sick room that will make me thankful for Crossriggs, I expect," said Alex. " I wonder how ill she is ? Can you imagine Aunt Clara looking thin or

pale or anything but what she always does ? Oh, Matty,
I don't know how I shall live without you and the children ; you must write to me every day at first."

When the morning came, and Alex was about to start,
neither of them could laugh at anything. It was ridiculous, of course, that they should think of such a short
journey in the light of a separation at all, but anxiety and
poverty are curiously uniting in their influences. Together they had faced so much, it seemed hard to leave
one another, even for a time.

"What shall I do without you, Alex ? The house will
feel horribly empty."

"And I'll always be thinking how things are getting
on, Matty ! "

"Good-bye, Alex ; bless you a thousand times."
Matilda turned away when the train was out of sight,
Baby dragging at her hand, Mike running in front of
them. "What would the house be like without Alex
even for a few months ? " she thought sadly, as she
walked homewards. "I wonder what it was that
changed Alex so much, if she *didn't* care about Van,
as I once thought possible, even though it has been all so
sad and dreadful."

Her thoughts were interrupted by a kindly greeting
from James Reid, who had just arrived at Crossriggs
station as Alex's train left. Matilda was always glad to
see him, and they walked back to the village together.

CHAPTER XLIV

THE summer rounded into autumn, and Alex was still in Liverpool. One Sunday when Mr. Scott happened to be away from home a " stranger " was preaching at Crossriggs.

As Matilda came out of church, holding Mike by the hand, she paused in the porch to exchange a few words with Mrs. Scott. Robert Maitland joined them, and they walked down to the gate together, making some of the usual banalities on the weather.

" This east wind," said Mrs. Scott, " is very trying. Mr. Scott was quite upset by it, he could digest nothing. I said to him, 'Dear, I think a week in Edinburgh would do you good,' and I'm sure I hope it has, for he was far from well."

" I am afraid Mr. Scott will not escape from the east wind in Edinburgh," said Matilda, smiling.

" No more he will, but then he'll be out of Crossriggs, at least," said Mrs. Scott. She had an ungracious habit of carping at Crossriggs, which grated sadly on her neighbours the older residents, and did not add to her popularity with them.

Matilda made no response to this speech, and Mrs. Scott turned to Maitland for sympathy.

" Surely you agree with me, Mr. Maitland ? Crossriggs is a dull hole of a place ? "

" Do you really think so ? " he asked, smiling.

" Yes, indeed ! " she answered, not noticing that he

had not answered her question. " And when Mr. Scott is from home it's duller than ever."

Maitland walked along, looking on the ground. Half to himself, or it might have been to Mrs. Scott, he quoted—

> " ' The village seems asleep or dead
> Now Lubin is away,' "

and then he hummed over the florid little tune to himself, with its curtseying movement.

Mrs. Scott probably did not recognize the quotation, but Matilda did.

" Oh, that's what I feel just now," she cried. " ' *Now Alex is away* ' nothing is right, and everything is ' *asleep or dead*.' "

" A sweet old song. Yes, she wakes us up, doesn't she ? " Maitland said.

" I had a letter from her last night," Matilda pursued, after Mrs. Scott had left them. " Come in and let me read it to you, Mr. Maitland. It's almost worth while to have her go away for the joy of getting her letters."

" I'm sure it must be," he assented.

They walked down the sunny old street together, under the shade of the lime trees, and Matilda led Maitland into Orchard House and asked him to sit down in the drawing-room while she went upstairs to fetch the letters. The room was tidy and quiet for once, as all the children were out. He looked round it, " The body without the soul," he said to himself. Matilda came down then, a little out of breath, holding quite a bundle of letters.

" I'm so fond of them, I never burn even the shortest note from Alex," she explained. " I'll read them all to you, but perhaps I'm taking it too much for granted that you wish to hear them. I forget she isn't *your* sister."

" I think I've tasted their flavour before, and thought it would be worth while to edit a volume of Alex's letters," he said, settling back in his chair to listen.

Matilda took out one at random.

" Oh, my dear," it began, " something dreadful has happened, or rather is happening daily—the Aunt is becoming dangerously fond of me. I mustn't stay very much longer, or it will be impossible for me ever to get away again. She takes me like a tonic—' an hour ' (instead of a dessert-spoonful) ' thrice daily after meals.' Have you noticed how difficult it is to invent a sound excuse for getting away from any place you want to leave, just as there are always a dozen different and imperative reasons for at once quitting the places where you are anxious to remain ? You'd have thought it the easiest thing in the world to say, ' Dear Matilda needs me, and Father is missing me '; but dear M. happens not to need me in the least. and though I hope Father misses me, I sadly fear he is too occupied with the new ' Booke of Symple Livinge ' to spend many thoughts on me.

" Well, there isn't much ' symple livinge ' here. Aunt has an interview every morning with the cook, and I'm quite sure they consult together as to what ingredients can be added to the sauces and puddings to make them a little richer : it's astonishing the consistency they get into them ! Uncle James has a way of eating his food with his eyes before he begins upon it that makes me feel ill ; he kind of gloats over it for a moment. turning the dish ever so slightly from one side to the other, and the butler aids and abets him, saying in a fat, gravy-fed voice. ' This will be the best cut, sir,' and indicating the precise spot to him. By the time dinner is over he is flushed and his eyes stand out from his head with sheer stuffing and enjoyment of all the over-good things he has been eating. It's horrid of me to notice all this, for they *are* kind to me in their own way, and want to stuff me, too. What the Aunt is needing is solely and entirely a course of anxiety, and less food. I think I'll go in for specializing as a healer of the rich only, by means of an *anxiety cure*—the difficulty (insurmountable) being to create genuine anxieties for the poor dears.

" Ye gods ! How they would thin down—*pounds* every day. I'd have them lean and healthy, and with the appetites of wolves before the month was over, if only I could guarantee that there would be a real question of where their next meals were to come from ! The Aunt looks at me daily, and says, ' Alex, you need nourishment,' but I'm afraid I need more than that—to ' be made over again, and made new is more what I want. When I remember the immense fund of vitality I started life with, the buoyancy of heart and incredible faith in life and my own powers, I often wonder if I am the same woman now——"

Matilda stopped and looked across at Maitland. " I hate Alex to write in this sad way," she commented.

" She has been working too hard," he said.

" This is more like herself, though," Matilda went on.

" I haven't described the drawing-room to you yet. Well, I believe there is enough of brilliant pink Wilton pile carpet on the floor to cover our orchard handsomely from end to end ! It really spreads into acres, not only yards. The imagination fails before the sums Uncle James must have paid for this floor covering—all bright burning pink, with great, brighter, burnier, pinker leaves curving over it in a sort of reeling pattern. Then it is ' kept ' in such a way that it feels profane to tread upon it, never a speck or a crumb. I have such a desire at tea-time to put a splash of melted butter on to it, or to squash a currant ' accidental like ' into its august surface with my foot. It would make it more lovable—a carpet should, like one's friends, have a few faults.

" We sit above this obsessing carpet on great fat caressing armchairs, that seem to embrace one with their padded arms, but there's no rest in them all the same—the old springless sofa at home is worth a dozen of 'em. Then the pictures! Uncle James at one time decided to be a patron of art. Many a thousand pounds he has spent, and the result makes me cry out ' Oh, for an hour of Nelson,' *i.e.* a cutlass with which to slash the atrocities from their frames. The tables have never a book laid upon their shining surfaces, and I'm afraid to lay any of mine upon them. When I observe the sort of fatted, unintelligent life the Aunt and Uncle have lived now these thirty years in this Liverpool, I say to myself that any poverty and struggle—*anything* is better than this. We've had our anxieties and troubles, but oh, we've been alive—struggle is, after all, a proof of life. This death in life induced by too much meat and drink and over ease of mind, is just going into one's grave before the time. Beloved, complain not of these our afflictions, they have kept our souls alive. It seems desperately easy to let the soul die of ease—drowned, as it were, in its butt of Malmsey.

" When you compare Uncle James with Father—Father with all his faults—you see what I mean. Who would go for sympathy to Uncle James, and *who wouldn't* go to Father ? The Uncle, no doubt the more prudent of the two, but prudence isn't everything. Uncle J. has got so case hardened by prosperity and ease that he fails to understand the great, solid, sordid troubles of the majority of the world. But I'm getting prolix. Adieu, dear, for to-day, and more anon.

" Yours,
" ALEX.

Matilda folded up the letter. There was a moment of silence.

" Mr. Maitland," she said, in her simple, almost childish way, " what is the matter with dear Alex just now ? "

He looked into her candid eyes and smiled. " The soul has times of stress that no one can explain, Matilda," he said.

" It puzzles me," she said. " I feel as if I *should* understand and I don't."

CHAPTER XLV

FOR a while Alex's letters grew more serious. The Aunt, instead of getting better, had become gravely ill.

" It's wonderful how we get on now that she is really suffering," Alex wrote. " But oh ! my dear, it's terrible how fond she is becoming of me ; I don't want to be heartless, but I cannot stand this too long."

Then the Autumn came on, and Alex was still in Liverpool.

One day Matilda opened an envelope and, instead of any letter, there fell out of it a cutting from a newspaper.

" At——, on the 3rd, Mrs. Van Cassilis (prematurely) of a son, who survived only a few hours."

Matilda had already heard this information from the Admiral, and something in the old man's tone as he told her checked the condolence even upon her unsuspicious lips.

In reply to what she wrote to Alex on the subject, Alex wrote back—

" Sad ? Dear Matilda, try to look at things sensibly, and to realize the relief all round that the death of this poor child is likely to be."

It was only September then, yet Matilda felt as if Alex had been away for a year. As the winter darkened down she only missed her more. Mrs. Maïtland was stronger that winter than she had been since her illness. Robert worked very hard, and the Hopes only saw him occasionally. At Christmas-time Alex reported the Aunt to be getting better.

" They are speaking of going abroad in spring," she wrote, " and in that case, as they take a trained nurse with them, I will come home then. Coming back yesterday afternoon through these dark, clanging streets filled with hurrying men, I seemed to *feel* the quiet of the home roads, on such a winter's day when the wind is still and the soft greyness everywhere wraps you about in soothing thoughts. I seemed to see the long bit of road just before you come into the village, with the children advancing to meet me with whoops of joy, and it was all I could do not just to pack a box then and there, leave the Aunt to her drugs and doctors, and hie away home. Instead of that, however, I came back to the fatted house (Uncle James was having two business friends to dinner) and I put on my new and most magnificent silk gown, which Aunt Clara herself has selected (not the colour, don't mistake me, only the superior richness of the fabric), and went downstairs to sit at the head of the table—Aunt Clara was not able to be there—and passed, I regret to say, a remarkably pleasant evening. You may well be astonished at this, but of the two business friends, one was the most usual sort of person—the other, who came straight from some outlandish place, was delightful, with such a nice, dark, heavy face, that all lightened up in a moment when he smiled. After I had discovered this he smiled frequently, I need hardly say. It made me feel quite queer to see how nice I had been looking, when I saw myself in the glass afterwards. Mirth is a good thing. ' Yes, if you can catch it,' as Socrates retorted.

" Adieu, dear. I'm sending Father a new banana, just imported to the shops here. It is too big for one meal, but can be shared with some of the poorer neighbours ! "

In April, Alex wrote that the Aunt and Uncle were going abroad, and as soon as she had seen them off she was coming home.

After all, she thought to herself, the time had passed wonderfully. The change—repugnant as her Liverpool life had been to her in many ways—had done her good ; a current of different, even if not very inspiring thought had filled her mind ; the old grief was more bearable, some of the terrible impressions were less vivid, she felt better able to face life again, and the prospect of getting back to her sister and the children once more made her heart glow. She knew that the Maitlands were still at home. She did not allow herself to think about that.

" They always go away in the summer, anyhow : it won't be for long, and we needn't meet so often."

It was a bright fickle day of alternate sun and shower when she came home. She arrived early in the afternoon, tired enough from her journey—the last half-hour in the train had seemed particularly long. Many times Alex had looked out, expecting to see the blue hills in the distance, and the group of tall trees by Crossriggs station. At last the train stopped. Yes, there was Sally, dear Sally, conscious of a new hat, very much grown up, very pink in the cheeks, looking up and down to see where she was ; and George,—so big, too—running up the platform, waving to her. But Matilda was not there. She must be staying to welcome her at home. Oh, how good it was to be back to them all. She jumped down from the carriage, pushing up her veil to kiss Sally and the boys, and trying to hug them all at the same time.

Home ! How delightful to come home again, away from the annihilating dulness and stiffness of the Liverpool household—the fat death in life that it all meant—back to poverty and struggle, to stir and wholesome activity, and freedom of thought and speech. Her eyes were shining, her thin cheeks glowing, as she walked up the platform, inhaling the good country air.

"We'll walk, of course; I'd much rather walk. Johnson will bring down the luggage. Children, I've got such nice things for you all. Sally, you're too big altogether; you might be eighteen."

"I *am* half-past seventeen now, you know," said the proud Sally.

She walked on one side, and the boys on the other, all talking at once, as they took their way home.

"What a lovely coat!" Sally exclaimed, stroking the sleeve of Alex's very ordinary jacket.

"You look much older, Aunt Alex," says the candid George.

"Yes, I think you do," says Sally.

"Well, darlings, I've been away for nearly a year, you know, and one can't grow much younger in one year," laughed Alex.

It was a warm afternoon, with sudden heavy showers; there had been a plump of rain just before she arrived. Now the birds were shaking the drops off their wings, and fluting in every tree, the soft roads had almost sucked up the wet already, the fresh orchards were glowing behind the old walls, and a burst of sunshine, as sudden as the rain, had followed the shower.

"Here is Mr. Maitland!" said George, and Sally hurriedly straightened her new hat.

Alex smiled at the involuntary little gesture. She knew that Maitland would never notice Sally's hat. "Nor mine either," she thought, for she had suddenly remembered how tired and dusty she must be looking.

"Well, Alex!" he said, as he came up. "How glad we are to see you back again. We've all missed you— even the very dogs and cats in the village, I think."

Alex looked at him gratefully. The dreaded momen of their first meeting was over then, on the public road with the children beside them. She was conscious of the relief, and replied quite gaily—

" If you only, only knew how heavenly it is to get back to everything at home. It's worth while being away in a sort of mental Black Hole, like my uncle's house, to get back to freedom of speech, and children and life again."

He had turned to walk beside her, Sally and the boys going on ahead, lugging Alex's bundle of wraps, and quarrelling as to which boy was to carry it.

" Alex, I have something to tell you," Maitland began sharply. " I came to meet you on purpose, because Matilda wanted you to hear it before you got home."

" What ? Who ? Is anything wrong ? Oh, is it Mike ? " Alex exclaimed, turning quite pale, and standing still.

" No, no ; nothing wrong—absolutely nothing wrong," he answered, horrified at the effect of his speech. " It's only something that will surprise you, I think."

" Oh, then it's only somebody going to be married," said Alex, drawing a breath of relief.

Maitland answered quickly. " Yes, you are quite right, Alex. It's your sister Matilda."

" Matilda ! " The surprise of this announcement brought her colour flooding back again in a moment.

" Oh, is it true ? Is it possible ? But who in the world is she going to marry ? "

" She is going to marry James Reid, Alex, and she asked me to tell you."

" *She—Matilda is going to marry James Reid !* " Alex repeated the words slowly, with a fulness of intonation that made them sound quite awful.

The sky for the last few minutes had been overcast. Now suddenly, as if with a laugh, the sun burst out again from behind the thick cloud that had hidden it for a while, and a whole chorus of birds shouted from the trees.

"*Matilda is going to marry James Reid!*" said Alex again. "Oh! What a foolish, absurd, most entirely ridiculous lie all that has been said and sung about romance in this world is! Don't you think so? Don't you really now, deep down in your heart of hearts, believe that more and more, as every year goes on, the light of *common* day is the truth! Yes, of course, she's quite right to do it. I've often heard her say that James Reid was an excellent man, so he is—good as gold. Peter Chalmers was an excellent man, too. Poor Peter Chalmers, now underground! And she married him when she was eighteen, and now she's going to marry James Reid!"

"Well, Alex, you must remember that *you* are not going to marry James Reid, though I understood that was once what the poor fellow wanted," Maitland added, in a lower tone.

Alex took no notice of the last remark. "But Matilda is a dear," she went on, "a darling, a hundred times better than me, and so pretty too, still, which I have never been; and she's done that, and now she's going to do *this!* Oh, my heart!" She looked up laughing now, and rubbed away the tears that had gathered in her eyes. Suddenly she began: "But what about the children? Will they—oh, oh! It's not possible—they couldn't—he wouldn't want them *all!*" A sudden passion thrilled her voice. She looked up at Maitland, her great, grey eyes full of such quick misery, that he turned away his face.

"Well, remember," he began, "James Reid is a man with a comfortable income, he naturally looks forward to making a home for Matilda's children. You wouldn't wish to separate them from their own mother?"

"And what about me?" cried Alex, her voice thin and high. "She bore them and nursed them, I suppose, but I—why, I starved and worried about them night and day. I've given them everything—my time, all the poor little talents I had, all the money I've made, my health, too—I'm never well now. The spring of life has gone out of me, and now they are all going to be taken away."

In the bitterness of her heart she turned and leant on the edge of the wall, and covered her face with her hands, and wept. Maitland stood beside her. Far ahead Sally and her brothers were racing on and had disappeared round the corner. She could not see the pity in Maitland's face, nor how his hand was clenched as he looked at her.

" Now, Alex," he said, after a minute, " you must pull yourself together. It's not like you to need to be told to think about other people, but I must say so. Are you going to cast a gloom over the whole house by the way you receive what is, after all, a piece of very good news ? " Still Alex would not look up. " Your sister is perfectly right," he went on. " She is doing what she thinks is best for herself and her children, and is making a good man happy." Here Alex gave a smothered laugh, and raised her face. He continued, smiling now, " You won't lose the children, how could you ? Oh, Alex, do you think we give love like money to get something in return ? "

" Yes—love," said Alex. She had dried her eyes and looked more like herself again.

" You've had enough of that, surely," he answered.

" Yes," said Alex again, " but I want to keep the children." They were in sight of the village now. " Do they know ? " she asked anxiously.

" The children ? Of course not, no one knows except me. Matilda thought you would tell your father, the thing was only settled yesterday."

Matilda was standing on the doorstep in a blue gown, and the sight of the colour made Alex realize all at once, quicker than words could have done, that her sister was happy. Matilda looked as well pleased and pretty and contented as any woman could look, and when she had given one anxious glance at Alex, she threw her arms about her, and Alex whispered—

" I know, dear; it's all right—bless you, bless you ! "

It was difficult for Alex to listen without a smile as Matilda developed her little history to her that evening, when they were alone together.

" James feels he made a mistake at first, dearest," said Matilda. " You and he could never have been happy together."

" Indeed, we could not," began Alex, perhaps too fervently, and she added, " you and he will suit each other perfectly, and I am sure he will be an ideal *brother-in-law*."

CHAPTER XLVI

MATILDA was married in the beginning of June, and went off to Switzerland, leaving the children at Orchard House.

The time between Alex's return from Liverpool and the marriage had passed like a confused dream : there was so much to be thought of and arranged, everything was going to be so different. In the bustle Alex was only too thankful to have no time to think.

Crosstown, where James Reid lived, was the county town of Eastshire, a pleasant, clean, habitable, and thriving place, with wide quiet streets, wearing the usual atmosphere of cheerful dulness common to its kind. There, about the middle of July, to a roomy, comfortable, remarkably ugly villa, with huge plate-glass windows that looked out on the neatest of lawns spotted with beds of lobelias and red geraniums, Matilda returned, a very happy and contented woman.

Two days after her arrival the children were to go to the new home. Matilda had engaged a nice elderly servant to look after them. Alex did not dare to call her " nurse," as even Baby resented the name, and Katharine regarded her with extreme disfavour.

" It is much better that they should have some one to look after them, Katharine," Alex argued. " Mrs. Reid won't have time now to dress and undress Baby, and keep all their clothes in order as she has done."

" Maybe," returned Katharine, with a doleful sniff.

" But many's the bath I've given them, Miss Alex, and them bairns has been as well washed as if all the nurses in Paris or creation had been in the house. We've darned them, and sewed them, and done for them as well as any of them."

" I know it, Katharine, I know it ; but everything is different now," said Alex, her own heart very heavy as she went to see about the packing, for the children were going to Crosstown the next day.

Alex had pleaded hard that Mike might remain with her, and Matilda had given her consent. But when Mike saw all the others getting ready, in glorious excitement, for their start to the new house (which to the eyes of childhood will always seem a far finer place than any old one) he broke into tears.

" Want to go with Peter and George and Sally," he cried, sobbing.

" Won't you stay with *me*, Mike ? " Alex said. There was an almost wild intonation in her voice that she could not repress.

" No !—want George and Peter," Mike persisted, though even as he spoke he turned and clutched Alex's skirt, adding, " You too, Aunt Alex—want you too."

" You can't have me too, Mike," she explained. " If you go with the boys and Sally you've got to leave me behind."

Mike could not grasp the situation at all. There was Alex, his undisputed slave for the last four years, saying that he was going to leave her. He did not like this, but he wanted his brothers dreadfully. A child, if given a free choice, will always choose the immediate delight without any thought of the future.

That day Mike happened to be tremendously in love with two magnificent sailing-boats, which the elder boys had got from James Reid. The brothers had been sailing them in the pond all Saturday afternoon, and Mike had been allowed to join in the sport. By his childish calculations George and Peter would go on sailing boats into all Eternity with himself, Mike, looking on in rapture. This, then, was the only consideration that came within the scope of his tiny horizon—he must stay with George and Peter and the boats. How could he be expected to heed or to understand the hard note in Alex's voice as she asked him again—

"Then you want to leave me and go with the boys?"

"Yes, please, Aunt Alex, want mother and Sally, *and* you come too, please," the child persisted.

Seeing that it was impossible to make.Mike understand, Alex went upstairs to speak to Janet Grant, the new maid.

"Janet," she said, coming into the room where the woman was packing the clothes of the elder boys. "Janet, I believe I shall have to send Mike with the others, he is very unhappy."

"Unhappy, Miss Hope? Oh, the child will do very well once the others are gone; it's unsettling for him, all the talk about their going."

Alex sat down and looked round the room, and Janet picked up some of Peter's frayed schoolboy collars and examined them critically, shaking her head. Alex watched her in silence: it was curious to see this stranger doing her work. After a moment, Janet pursued—

"Children are like that, Miss Hope. He'll fret for a day or two for the others, and then be quite pleased again. Don't you be disturbing yourself!"

Alex sat forward with a sudden fierce movement. "No, indeed, Janet, I won't disturb myself. I've done it too often, he's not *my* child; he wants to leave me, and he shall leave me. I won't keep him against his will, he'll go to-morrow with the others to their fine new home, where everything is to be so much more comfortable than here."

Then, unable to watch the packing any more, Alex

sprang up and ran out of the room. Janet let the collars fall on the floor and made a step or two as if she would follow Alex, then closed the door softly and shook her head.

" Dear, dear ! It's an ill thing to mind other people's children," she mused. " It's queer if she's to be an old maid ; she, with such a taking way with her—they say Mr. Reid wanted her first. I wonder was it true ? I misdoubt me there's some story behind it all."

In her own room Alex was tasting moments of poignant sadness. To what purpose had all her struggles been if the children did not care enough for even one of them to stay with her ? All the life and brightness were leaving the house with them. There rose in her mind the remembrance of a nest she used to visit in spring, when it was full of little eager, gaping birds ; and then how she had passed the hedge in winter and seen the nest empty and sodden with the rain. So the old home, with all its poverty, would soon be forgotten like the poor discarded nest—good for nothing ; not even re-membered by the careless brood that had been sheltered in it. And she—she who had put her whole life into the task of providing for the children—was going to be forgotten too ; for had not Mike, her well-beloved, turned from her without a thought ?

Alex sat up and brushed the tears angrily from her eyes. " It's true—ever so true. What one has to do in this terrible world is to *look out for one's self*, not for other people. The children would have grown up some-how without me. Perhaps God would have helped them more if I hadn't tried to take such a lift of them. There's no doubt He does aid entirely helpless creatures. They're *thrown* upon Him, as it were. Yes, I believe the children would have got on better without me. And most certainly I would have got on better without them. I'd have had some youth left in me still. The works wouldn't have been all worn out as they are. I might by this time have had some life and prosperity of my own!"

She sat there and reviewed the time past of her life, and a sad enough review it was. Her misdirected, ill-regulated childhood, her anxious and poverty-stricken youth, always shadowed by some care more or less pressing, her womanhood filled with the ceaseless effort to keep things going at all. In this mood of bitterness Alex did not admit the many joys that had lightened for her the uphill road of life; she chose to paint everything quite black, even though aware that the picture was untrue. Well, Mike must go! That was quite certain. She would not have him now at any price. She would compose herself and go back to the nursery and tell Janet to pack his clothes. She got up and brushed her hair, smiling a smile that was very much assumed as she opened the nursery door.

"I was silly and upset, Janet," she said carefully, "but I've decided all the same that Mike is to go with the others to-morrow. I have thought it over, and it will be better. We must get his little garments ready, bless him! Come, I'll go through them with you."

"Perhaps you're right, Miss Hope. You look tired a bit; the children have been a deal on your hands all the years since they came here."

"Oh, they have been a great joy, but it's different now somehow. Changes must come in families," Alex replied evasively, and plunged into the discussion of Mike's rather deplorable little wardrobe.

"He *must* have a new suit immediately, Janet. This is the best he has—not much, as you see. He wears these little holland overalls to cover deficiencies; but I had meant to make him a new suit. Oh, yes, I made all his clothes. But he will soon be too old for that, and Mrs. Reid can get him smart new suits from a tailor now. Dear me, Janet! I think it is so generous of Mr. Reid to be nice about another man's children, don't you ? See, these collars are getting too small for Mike now, and all his little shoes are worn at the toes. Don't tell Mrs. Reid of *all* these wants just at once though, for to fit out five young creatures suddenly from head to heel would be a big pull on even the good nature of Mr. Reid."

Alex seemed quite herself again before the packing was done, but as she sat beside her father in the evening, the old man looked at her uneasily.

"Why, Alex, you look weary," he said. "Is there anything wrong ?"

"Nothing special, father; I'm vexed about Mike, of course, and I do feel weary—very weary." Her voice seemed to die away in her throat for a minute, and then she asked, "Have you ever known what it was to feel that you had come to the end of effort, Father ?"

Old Hopeful was shocked by the suggestion. "The end of effort, Alex !" he cried, sitting forward in his chair, and grasping the arms with his knobby old hands. "The end of effort ! Never ! As well be at the end of life, for what *is* life but effort—effort and energy ? These are our life, to push on and up, attempting, pursuing, always with some great, even if unattainable, goal ahead of us." His fine old eyes gleamed with the courage that a lifetime of failures had never quenched.

Alex felt her heart stir with admiration. She rose and kissed him, bidding him good night.

"Finite to fail, but infinite to venture !"

she repeated to herself as she went slowly upstairs.

Somehow a warmth had been kindled round her heart by his words. Futile, Quixotic, absurd and unsuccessful, as she knew her father to be, she recognized that he had the right of the argument of life.

"It's the sane view of things, after all," she said. "What does defeat matter ? If I've come to the end

of effort and energy it's because they're *worn* out, not
because they've been wrapped up in a napkin and never
used at all. That would have been the shameful thing.
Well, they were lovely and pleasant in their lives. I
wonder if I shall ever see their happy faces again."

The next morning you would scarcely have guessed
that Alex had held such sad communings with herself.
The household was all a-bustle, humming like a hive
of bees. Peter and George, Mike and the baby, each
vied with the other as to which should make the most
noise. Sally affected very grown-up ways now, and
tried to seem shocked by the uproar at the breakfast-
table, but in reality she rather longed to join in it. Alex
had not the heart to repress the boys' wildness on this
last morning, and Old Hopeful, blandly consuming cereal
at the end of the table, would only exclaim, " Youth !
Youth ! " occasionally, and smile at the young people.

But when Alex returned from the station and entered
the now terribly silent house, then was the time for her
to realize what a change had come over her life.

" Why, Father, it's unbearable ! " she cried. " Did
you ever hear anything like the silence ? We'll have to
adopt some children to keep ourselves alive ! " '

Old Hopeful, as was to be expected, took the suggestion seriously.

" I have always held with the theory of adoption,
dear Alex," he exclaimed, his face brightening as he
spoke. " The solitary should be ' set in families,'—
now is the time indeed ; we may not have as much of
what is falsely called this world's goods as some, but I
always have maintained that there being enough and to
spare in the *Universe*, the Individual who trustingly
throws himself on the Universal Bounty will not fail to
be provided for. There are little ones needing our care
and our training, we should not shrink from undertaking
their maintenance——"

" Stop, stop, father ; please, not yet ! " Alex cried,

putting her fingers in her ears in mock despair. Even as they stood there together, a boy from the post-office came running up to the door, with a telegram in his hand.

"What has Matilda forgotten, I wonder?" said Alex, as she tore open the envelope.

"Nothing of importance, I hope?" her father asked.

Alex looked very grave. "Father," she said, "this is from Liverpool; poor Aunt Clara died suddenly this morning—isn't it dreadful?"

But Death like Life had no terrors for Old Hopeful. "Our last and best friend!" he was wont to name it. So he gazed at Alex in surprise.

"Why dreadful, dear Alex?" he asked. "Sudden, perhaps, but for that very reason less worthy to be named dreadful—a swift translation—what more would one ask?" And then he seemed to fall into a musing mood, sitting there and from time to time muttering a few words that showed the drift of his thoughts: "Clara a spirit . . . very strange . . . compassed by the dust of the world . . . free of it? . . . shall all hereafter taste of the same joys—or shall we have separate spheres? Secondary Elysiums—Clara's Elysium . . . the Elysium of Milton, of Shakespeare . . . Luther's heaven, the Martyr's reward . . . 'to every man a penny'——"

Alex broke in upon his musings, laying her hand on his shoulder.

"I wonder if Uncle James will want you to go to him," she asked.

"Ah, Alex, James and I are so curiously at variance on many great subjects! Even, alas! on the very question of burial. You know my views on cremation, the views of the most advanced among us. James could never take in a new idea. I fear my presence might only annoy him; yet, Alex, should he want me, I am more than willing to go. How would it do to telegraph our sympathy and ask if I, or both of us, should come to him?"

"All right, Father, but oh, how I *hope* he won't want me. People of his pompous kind are so terribly difficult in grief, they can't even be natural about that!"

She put on her hat and walked down to the post-office to send off the message, musing as she went.

"What shall I do if Uncle James wants me? I feel so unfit for it somehow, utterly unfit. I want some great big, happy change in life to make me young again. A new world with new people in it—no vestige of the old troubles or worries left; new hopes, new joys—yes, even new loves, and I believe I'd almost welcome some brand-new hates. I'm played out, oh, so played out—all the spirit gone out of me now that dear Matilda and the children have left."

Till a year ago, before Van's death, Alex's buoyant nature had carried her through every trouble; but where was this buoyancy gone? And she had realized how she had lost it.

"How shall I ever get on without it?" she asked herself, with a thrill that was almost fear.

Like a willing horse that has run on beyond its strength, she had kept up in the race of life. Now that the whipping and spurring of want were relaxed, she stumbled and fell where she stood. There were not five hungry children to provide for now.

"How did I keep going so long?" she asked herself wearily.

It was indeed an inopportune time to be called to Liverpool; she wanted only to rest, and instead would probably have to minister to her Uncle James.

"Well, Heaven knows it's the last thing I wish to do," she said, as she wrote out the message, and turned her steps homewards to the quiet house.

CHAPTER XLVII

No reply came to the telegram that day, but by next morning a thick black-edged letter lay upon the breakfast-table. It was a very long letter apparently, and Alex opened it with some anxiety: she could not imagine her Uncle James giving such lengthy expression to his grief.

"But perhaps he was fonder of her than I knew, perhaps I misjudged them both; I go on misjudging all the time," she told herself.

Mr. Hope indeed entered upon the details of his wife's latter end at considerable length. We have all read such letters, harrowing in their own bald unimaginative way: how at six-thirty, so and so complained of a feeling of faintness; at seven was worse, and the doctor was summoned, who did everything it was possible to do, yet, at eight-thirty, unconsciousness set in, and ere midnight "all was over." Such was the style of James Hope's letter, but Alex gave it the reverent attention that details of the kind will always command from right-hearted people, even while they wonder at the strange taste which prompts the writer to give them. But as she read on, Alex suddenly laid down the letter and stared blankly at it.

"Why, Father—*Father!*" she cried. "This can't possibly be true. I must be dreaming."

Old Hopeful was sorting out his usual heterogeneous collection of letters and pamphlets before beginning his breakfast. He looked up at Alex in surprise.

" Why, what is it, dear Alex ? " he asked.

" Uncle James says that Aunt Clara has left me money, lots of money—*me*—Father, I must be mistaken." She came round to where he sat, and laid the letter on the table before him. " Look—read," she said, pointing to the page, and Old Hopeful slowly read aloud the contents of the letter :

" Some months ago, your Aunt Clara went into the subject of her money matters with me. She had, as you are probably aware, a considerable fortune of her own, apart from mine. Her own blood relations are few and distant, and she was never on good terms with them. During your stay with us last year, Clara became much attached to you, and repeatedly expressed the desire that you should have a comfortable income in your middle life. Finally, and with my entire approval, she decided to leave most of her fortune to you. When making this will, we little thought how near the end was. I cannot enter into particulars to-day, but you will shortly have these from our lawyers."

There was no doubt about it. Alex would soon be a rich woman. She sat down and tried to realize all that it meant to her. When she looked up a minute later, she saw that her father had taken off his spectacles, and that tears were running down his ruddy old face.

" Why, Father ! What is it ? Why do you weep over my good fortune ? " Alex asked, kneeling down beside his chair.

The old man wiped his eyes. " I scarcely know, dear Alex," he replied. " I scarcely know, but the smile of Fortune will sometimes unnerve those whom grief cannot shake. I have had a long life and many troubles, and the sudden sense of relief I felt just now—of foolish, quite foolish, material relief—gave me a strange feeling of weakness that unmanned me altogether. . . . ' All the beasts of the forest are His, and the cattle on a thousand hills,' so why, fully realizing this, I should have of late felt the strain of slight pecuniary embarrassment, I cannot say. ' In His hand is our poverty or our abundance '—I know this, yet age makes cowards of us all. I have somehow, just of late, had sinkings of heart when I looked into the future—faithless, faithless! for out of the inexhaustible riches of the Universe our bite and sup would surely have come unfailingly——" His old voice quavered again, and another furtive tear stole down his wrinkled cheek.

Alex herself could scarcely speak. She knelt there in silence, and tides of feeling passed over her. Had the wished-for come too late ? This was the first thought that assailed her, but she thrust it away, and then, like her father, experienced an extraordinary relief. She had spoken to him the night before of the end of effort ; well, here it was in quite another sense, the end of struggle for the bread that perisheth ! With a sudden delicious throb of returning hopefulness, Alex felt her heart leap up at the thought of all the possibilities that now lay within her grasp. Why, it was a wonderful, glorious, unexplored world, and she was young still. She need worry and work no longer—the time had come to see and do a thousand splendid things. After a few moments, Old Hopeful broke the silence—

" There is another side to this, too, Alex. I am afraid of this money, the root of all evil. Ah, what if our hearts become set on riches ? What if it proves a snare to us ? We must hasten to dispense of our abundance to others." In his simple way the old man spoke as if the money was quite as truly his own as Alex's.

" We'll find all manner of ways of spending it," she assured him. " And you mustn't worry one bit about being too rich, Father."

" It eateth like a canker, Alex. Oh, the terrible corruption of wealth ! And I am not clear on the question of private property : all should be dispensed for the common weal."

" Well, it won't be, dear ; mine won't be, for some time at least," Alex said almost gaily. She sprang up and began to pour out tea, but it had stood so long that it was now quite cold. Alex rang the bell, and told Katharine to make more tea.

" Very strong and very hot, please ;" and as Old Hopeful expressed some surprise at the order, she explained, " It's my first dash into extravagance, Father, and it won't be my last."

They sat long over the plain little meal, discussing this strangely unlooked-for event which might change their whole life. When at last breakfast was over, Alex had a sudden inspiration.

" I'm going to begin to spend my money right away, Father. Can you guess how ? No, you can't, for I've never done such a thing before in all the years of my pilgrimage." She came and stood beside him, laying her hands on his shoulders, and looked down laughingly into his bewildered old face while she explained her scheme. " Well, I am going to send to the inn for a carriage, with two horses, and we'll drive down to Crosstown to tell Matilda."

" A carriage, with two horses ! " her father cried in dismay.

" Yes, and if I could get a coach and four, I'd have it instead," said Alex, gaily. " I *want* this to be an expensive expedition. We'll drive down to lunch with Matilda, and keep the carriage and drive back in the afternoon, and it will cost quite a lot of money ! "

This simple yet, to their minds, audacious programme was soon put into execution. A telegram was very quickly despatched to Matilda, and by twelve o'clock they had started off in as comfortable a carriage as Crossriggs possessed.

" Luxury, Alex, luxury, the sin of the age," said the

old man, as he leant back against the not over springy cushions of the hired landau.

Alex laid her hand quickly on his knee. " There's a wonderful saying in the Bible, Father, that is quite as wonderful when it's reversed : ' Have we received evil from the hand of the Lord, and shall we not receive good ? ' "

" Ah, Alex, not much evil ! Mine has been a happy, a blessed lot ; a life filled with good things, with the *best* things—friends, health, books, a thousand interests and joys, far outweighing the trials which are an inevitable part of life."

" Well, you have to receive more good things now," she told him, laughing.

They began to talk then in the eager, impulsive way that was so characteristic of them both, about what was to be done with their money ; and on this point, for once, the father and daughter were entirely unanimous.

" It has been the dream of a lifetime with me, dear Alex, to see more of foreign lands. I am not yet too old for travel. What do you think ? "

" Think ? Father, I don't think that I can stay another week in Crossriggs after I have the money to start off to see the world ! "

The old man sat up in the carriage, his face lit with animation.

" The very names of other lands sound in my ear like a clarion ! " he exclaimed. " It was a brave spirit, surely, that christened New Zeal-land—*New Zeal*, Alex, dwell upon the significance of the name. And the Cape of Good Hope—another splendid idea lies there ; and Endeavour Straits—yet another in that name ! They flock to my memory, Alex ; why, even ' Doubtful Island ' has in its name a suggestion of mystery and interest—a suggestion too, of the terminology of our Bunyan——"

He chanted on, and Alex listened and smiled, shaking

her head a little now and then at his more daring propositions.

" Remember your age, Father dear," she told him.

Then Alex began to speculate on how they would find Matilda. She was filled with curiosity about her sister's new home, for though she knew the outside of James Reid's house well, Alex had, for obvious reasons, never entered it. How often, in former days, she had told Matilda that the house was exactly like James Reid, so solid, so comfortable, so plain, leaving nothing to the imagination.

" Oh, dear me, how many thoughtless words I'll have to eat ! " she thought. " But happily, Matilda is of that blessedly good-natured temperament that *forgets* easily, she will somehow manage to forget all these things."

Just as you entered Crosstown, there, full in the eye of the sun, the house stood : large, square, uninteresting; its big, wholesome plate-glass windows giving full entrance to the wind and sunshine. Commonplace, tidily kept lawns in front, a comfortable kitchen garden at the back.

" My Matilda will not want for vegetables ! " Old Hopeful cried, rising in his seat as they passed the wall of the garden. " I can note the graceful leafage of the artichoke at this distance, and surely that is an asparagus bed I spy in the corner."

Matilda, looking extraordinarily happy, met them at the gate. She took kindly to prosperity, dear woman, just as she had taken uncomplainingly to poverty.

" James will be in to lunch," she said, leading them into the dining-room.

It was the usual room—so usual; and there was the usual luncheon table, spread with the usual viands, and decorated with red geraniums arranged in accordance with Matilda's quite ordinary taste in a very ordinary flower glass.

They sat down on a plump Chesterfield sofa in the window, and Alex began to explain to the rather mystified Matilda the reason of their unexpected appearance. In the first place she told them of Aunt Clara's death, and Matilda, who had a great faculty for making obvious remarks, exclaimed—

" Ah, Alex, if you only had been there with her, how sad that they were alone ! "

Alex agreed. " Yes, but then I just wasn't there, and when we telegraphed to Uncle James asking if we should go to him, he wrote to say he didn't want us, quite kindly, it's true, but also quite firmly—poor man, he hasn't the genius for affection."

There was a perceptible pause. Alex felt it difficult to let the tidings of her fortune follow so hard upon the news of her aunt's death, yet the words were almost saying themselves. Matilda noticed her embarrassment.

" Dear me, Alex, what's the matter ? " she asked in surprise.

For reply, Alex turned round suddenly, and buried her head against her sister's shoulder, crying out in a stifled voice—

" Oh, Matty dear ! It's so strange, so impossible to believe. Aunt Clara has left me most of her money."

" Alex ! " There was another silence, and looking up, Alex saw that Matilda was crying. " It makes me almost too happy," she explained, " for I did feel as if all the good things had come to me who didn't deserve them, instead of to you who did."

(" She means James Reid and his house—ye gods ! " was Alex's mental ejaculation.) " Well, you see that hasn't been the case, Matilda, and really, if every one is going to weep over my fortune it will be a little difficult for me to go on telling people about it. Father has been weeping—do you think James will weep ? and what about Sally and the boys ? "

Matilda began to laugh, and dried her eyes. " You

understand, dearest, it's just that we are *so* glad," she said, adding, " That's the meaning of the carriage ! I couldn't think how you came that way. Oh, yes, Father, I don't think it was in the least foolish ; you had to come and tell me at once, you couldn't have gone on knowing all this even for a day without letting me know, too."

Matilda sat close beside Alex on the sofa, holding her hand, and began to question her as eagerly as Sally might have done.

" What will you buy first ? " she asked.

" Buy, Matilda ? Have you known me these thirty years and more, and think I'll buy anything ? If you asked me what I meant to do and see that would be more to the point."

" But, Alex, you don't know how nice it is to have all one's things pretty again," said Matilda, the joys of her modest trousseau still in her thoughts.

" Pooh ! " Alex cried. " Clothes ! Why, Matilda, *there's the world*—the great round, interesting world to see ! "

" Oh, is that what you are thinking of ? Well, James and I did enjoy Lucerne very much; the steamer trips up the lake were just lovely," said the simple Matilda.

Alex and Old Hopeful kept silence ; but they exchanged glances like conspirators, and when Matilda a minute later was called out of the room, Alex stole up to her father, and putting her mouth close to his ear, whispered—

" Lucerne ! " and they both laughed darkly.

" Now come upstairs, Alex, and wash your hands, and see my room," said Matilda.

She led the way upstairs, and Alex found herself repressing a smile, as they entered the light, large room. Deep and soft was the carpet that covered the floor, rosy and shiny the wall-paper. All the light that could glare in at an immense window fell upon rows of silver toilet appurtenances—every one bulbous with bad taste —on glittering modern " Sheraton " furniture, and wardrobes with bevelled mirror doors. As she glanced out at the cheerful lawn with its brooch-like beds of geraniums, and then looked round at the perfect maze of true love knots, and roses, and " Empire wreaths " upon cretonnes, and carpet, Alex thought involuntarily of an old story that their mother used to tell them about the rapture of a school friend of hers, who exclaimed on returning from her wedding journey, " All this—and Heaven besides ! "

" James Reid, too," she added, and then she sat down and laughed so heartily that Matilda, who had gone into the next room, came hurrying back, saying—

" What is it, Alex ? How delightful to hear you laugh again like that."

" Oh, it's just that I'm so well pleased to see you looking so happy, Matilda, and that this news about Aunt Clara's money has made me feel quite hysterical."

" But I had another bit of news to tell you, Alex," said Matilda. " I waited till we were alone. Do you know that I had a letter, when we were in Switzerland, from Mr. Morse, and he came to see me at the hotel in London. He was really so nice, and spoke, James said, in the most sensible and gentlemanly way, saying that he knew that Sally was too young——"

" Oh, oh, don't, Matilda, or I shall begin to cry now. I can't laugh any more—Sally—dear thing, it seems only yesterday that she was in the nursery. Well, did you give him leave to pay his addresses to her ? "

" He's coming here immediately. I said of course that there was to be no engagement, no formal engagement for some time yet, but I spoke to Sally yesterday, and she seems——"

" Just a thoroughly sensible girl, with a happy dis-

position like your own, Matilda. It will all go as well
as a fairy tale, I believe."

"And he's really not so——" Matilda paused.

Alex, who was fastening her shoe, and bending down
her head at the moment, remarked gently—

"Semitic, dear, is the word you want."

"Well, if you like. His mother's name was Mac-
Alister. There can be nothing Jewish about *that*."

"One would certainly think not."

"And his Christian name was Charles."

"B," Alex interpolated, remembering the "Benjamin."
"What does it matter, Matilda, though he traced his
descent from Abraham? If he's a good man, and Sally
cares for him, so much the better."

"Oh, but there can be nothing settled for a long
time," said Matilda, with a lurking smile, and then they
went down to luncheon, and Alex found time to press her
niece's hand and whisper—

"You must wear your coral collar supports every
day now, Sally darling."

"But they're both broken," said the artless Sally.
"George bit the top off one of them trying to see if it
was hollow, and I stood upon the other one day by
mistake."

"You're really too young to have ornaments at all,
Sally—certainly rings," said Alex, holding the hard,
sunburnt hand fondly in her own.

It was a very happy afternoon, and the evening was far
advanced before Old Hopeful and Alex started on their
long drive home. A delicious recklessness possessed her
as she leant back in the fragrant twilight and watched the
last rose colour fade out of the sky. Part of their road
lay by the sea. In the warm summer dusk, she heard
the long, soft wash of the gentle waves breaking one
after one upon the shore; a smell of wood smoke arose
from some gipsy encampment near by. She could see
the twinkle of their fire, and the forms of the men lying

out at full length upon the still warm turf. In the far distance a ship in full sail was moving out with the tide.

"Oh, Father," Alex exclaimed suddenly, "I'd like to go round the world, and do you know that I *could* now?"

"Why should we not then, Alex?" he replied. "It seems to me that this curious windfall of yours"— so he alluded to Alex's new prospects—"could not be better employed. I have longed to travel more than I could ever do in my youth. The data of the work I had always hoped to accomplish, but which of late years I have been obliged to lay aside, requires accurate knowledge and at first hand. I should like, personally, to investigate *all* the sources of diet—fruit-eaters, fish-eaters, meat-eaters—from the frugal Hindoo, with his bowl of rice, to the blubber of the Eskimo, before I could sit down to begin the book in earnest——"

"But, my dear Father, consider your age."

"My age," said Old Hopeful, "will just be my appointed time; let us work while it is called to-day."

"But, Father, you are not fit for long voyages, even if you could ever write your great book," said Alex, half touched, half inspired by his perennial eagerness, "you are seventy-five nearly, and your health is not what it was."

"Health of body, Alex, is a blessing—the greatest of merely outward blessings, but I would amend Jeremy Taylor's saying, and remind you : ' Let him never despair of Mercy or Success who hath Life and *Health of Soul.*' "

He spoke no more for some time, and Alex was silent too, lost in the thought of all the new possibilities that opened before her.

"It can't be that money makes so much possible," she said at last. "How wrong and sordid, but, after all it's not the money, it's the energy and power to do something interesting with it, isn't it, Father?"

"If a fish were to swallow my favourite old volume of Homer, Alex—they have large capacities—what good would the written word do him?" said Mr. Hope. "Mere money—a symbol of much, though not of some of the best things—is just as useless to a self-indulgent and inert soul: it means food and drink, and mundane enjoyment merely. All the poetry of life that may be extracted fron it is lost to them."

Alex thought of her Aunt Clara and the household she had lived in the winter before, and mentally agreed. But all the same she was half ashamed to feel how new ideas and plans came thronging into her head.

"It's the effect of all the excitement I've had to-day; I'll feel as flat as a pancake to-morrow," she thought.

They drove on through the deepening summer twilight, and passed Crossport a little to the right. Alex could see the light at the pier head, like a jewel against the pale greenish sky, and again she felt the stab that had gone through her heart as she entered the shed where Van's body was lying. Up the long road they went driving slowly, where she and Van had so often walked together; past the very field where she had said good-bye to love in her own mind, as Maitland turned away from her.

"Oh, Life is over for me," she thought, "the best of it—the zest of it, and nothing—not all the money in the world, not anything, could ever bring it back again!"

It was almost dark when they reached and re-entered the strangely quiet, empty house.

CHAPTER XLVIII

OLD HOPEFUL, heedless of the gloomy prognostications of some of his neighbours, entered radiantly into the idea of a year or two of travel.

"The programme I have before me," he explained, "is a very wide one, its completion would be the dream of a lifetime realized, but that I cannot confidently expect. My years are already more than the threescore and ten, but though so many of them—and happy, happy years, too—have been passed at Crossriggs, I confess that the climate has of late, at times, become somewhat trying to me. As for Death"—he glanced at Aunt E. V., whom he was addressing at the moment—"our last and best friend, whenever he comes, welcome! But I must say I should like the idea of translation from a shining strand and by a bluer sea."

"Tastes differ; let me die the death of my fathers, and be laid beside them, Mr. Hope," said the lady.

When Alex had satisfied herself about her father's wishes, she felt that she need hesitate no longer. Matilda, of course, would be sorry to think of her going. But Matilda had many new interests now—Sally's engagement and marriage probably coming on, the boys going to College, *and* James Reid. This, somehow, had always a way of coming last to Alex's mind in thinking of her sister's blessings. Matilda could not lawfully object. It was undoubtedly better for Mr. Hope to escape the chills of another Scottish winter, and Alex arranged finally that she and her father were to leave Crossriggs early in September, and after spending two days with Bessie Reid in her London home, were to set sail for Japan, Old Hopeful having fixed his affections on that country as a beginning of his travels.

Laura and Robert Maitland were away at the time, only Aunt E. V. remained in the Manse. The Admiral, too, had gone off on his annual excursion to Homburg. But when Alex set out to pay some last farewells the day before their departure, her heart misgave her. The fatigues of packing and final arrangement had nearly worn her out. A hundred reasons against going away at all leapt into her mind, and in her depression she only wished they had never thought of leaving home.

"An old man like Father, and a worn out creature like myself, it seems *so* foolish," she thought, in a disheartened way, as she stepped out into the village street.

She went first to the Scotts' " to get it over." That only took a few minutes; then she sat for some time with old Miss Reid, still propped up in the corner of her stuffy parlour, mumbling over Bessie's letters. Miss Reid's mind could take in no long voyages then (her longest journey, poor soul, was not far off, for she left her little parlour before many months had gone), but she grasped the idea that Alex was going to see Bessie, and mumbled out a message for her.

"And it's so curious that you and James never come *together*," she whispered, as the companion came in to signify that the visit had been long enough. She never had, and now never would, understand that Matilda and not Alex was her nephew's wife.

Alex hurried across the Square. The lime trees were just beginning to turn a pale and glorious yellow, but they had not lost a leaf in the quiet early autumn weather. She stopped for an instant to gather up her courage, then

knocked lightly at the Manse door and went in. Aunt
E. V. was disposed to be severe. She couldn't approve
of the projected voyage. However, she mollified a little,
and bid Alex an affectionate good-bye.

"Might I just look into the study for a moment,
Miss Elizabeth," said Alex, as they walked together
to the door. She added, "Somehow I've the feeling
that I won't return to Crossriggs, and I'd like to see it
again."

"Go in? Of course, why not?" said Miss Maitland,
who thought farewells sentimental. Alex opened the door
of the study and went in alone. She drew the door close
behind her, and stood for a moment looking round and
round the room. She stepped to the writing-table, and
bent down and laid her hand on the desk. Lines of the
handwriting that she had known so long, since the days
when, as a girl, she treasured the envelopes that Maitland
addressed to her father, were on the blotting-paper. The
pen that Maitland always used was lying there on the
tray. She smiled a bitter, half-tender smile.

"I'm as bad as Sally, I'd like to take a pencil or something," she said, to herself. Then she saw in the lid of
the desk, a little grey feather, and remembering how he
had asked her for it, her face grew red for a moment, and
she turned quickly and silently away, without filching
even a pencil from the desk.

Miss Elizabeth walked across with her to their own
door to bid Old Hopeful good-bye, and Alex stood and
watched her walk across the Square again, and re-enter
the Manse, before she closed the door for the night.

As the train left the station next morning, Alex looked
out of the window. She caught a last glimpse of the
blue hills, the woods, the village, and the old church.
Saw once more the pine trees that marked the new mound
in the churchyard, where Van was lying now, and she
sighed for the passing of much that had been sweet, as
she looked her last at Crossriggs.

It is needless to say that their welcome was warm in Bessie Reid's suburban home. All that old friendship and kindness could suggest was done for their comfort. Mr. Massie, chinless though he was, had the kindest of hearts, and at a table, rendered curious rather than beautiful, by the emerald green table-centre with the border of edelweiss, they made a cheerful party that evening. Bessie and her husband came down to the docks with them the next day. When they were all going up the gangway of the vessel Bessie suddenly laid her hand on Alex's arm.

"Here is another friend come to see you off. Well, Mr. Maitland, this *is* kind."

"Ah, Robert, is this you? But what else could I expect? Why, thinking of the friendship of a lifetime, should I be surprised at another token?" cried Old Hopeful, as he seized Maitland by both hands, and greeted him almost with tears of joy.

"We knew you were in London, but we never thought of your being able to come here," Alex managed to exclaim.

A sudden pulsing at her heart sent the blood rushing into her cheeks. She leant against the railing of the ship, and for a minute the pushing, chattering crowd of strangers faded away, and she saw nothing but one face—heard nothing but one voice. They stood together for a moment after the last bell had rung.

"Come, Robert, you must go, I fear. We'll not say ' Good-bye,' but ' Au revoir,' " said Old Hopeful, hurrying up to them with outstretched hands.

Alex opened her lips to speak, but no words came.

In silence they shook hands and Maitland turned away. The gangway was just going up as he sprang down to it. He stood in the crowd on the pier, and as the vessel moved slowly out of the harbour he watched Alex standing amongst the line of people along the railings, until he could distinguish her figure no longer. Then, passing through the crowd, he turned slowly away, uttering a little sigh, that was not of sorrow. 'Twas the breath of a spent swimmer that had but just reached the shore.

" You look better, to-day, Alex, less tired; better, I think, than you have looked for long," said Old Hopeful, the next morning. " There is life in this breeze."

It was still very early, and as yet they were the only passengers on deck. He was pacing slowly, his face beaming with contentment and anticipations.

Alex turned away from him, and stood by herself leaning on the rail of the ship.

" Better, better—am I? Oh, perhaps I may begin to live again after all," she thought.

She felt as if she had no tears left to shed, no power left to hope as she stood there and looked out to the limitless distance, where a faint steady wind was blowing from the south.

> " Leagues and leagues onward though the last league be,
>   Still leagues beyond these leagues there is more sea."

She thought—was there no future left for her? the end of one part of life had come ; for a while it seemed to be the end of all.

But the roots of the tree of life, in a healthy nature, strike very deep. Again, and yet again may come a spring-time to the soul, and as she stood there Alex knew suddenly a sort of delicate encouragement, hardly of the senses, a reviving of the mind. The world was wide and life—all real life—was rich in beauty and in new experience, and the very saying that she had smiled at so bitterly when Old Hopeful repeated it to her before they left Crossriggs came back into her memory, the gentle, steady wind that blew against her face seemed to whisper it in her ear.

Let no man despair of Mercy or Success, so long as he hath Life and Health of Soul."

She turned quickly to look once more at the land they had left behind, but already it had vanished out of sight.

THE END.